IN THE SILENCE LONG-FORGOTTEN, ALMOND TREES BLOSSOM

IN THE SILENCE LONG-FORGOTTEN, ALMOND TREES BLOSSOM

A NOVEL

DAVID B P MAYNE

First published in Great Britain in 2021 by
The Book Guild Ltd
9 Priory Business Park
Wistow Road, Kibworth
Leicestershire, LE8 0RX
Freephone: 0800 999 2982
www.bookguild.co.uk
Email: info@bookguild.co.uk
Twitter: @bookguild

Typeset in 11pt Adobe Garamond Pro

Printed and bound in the UK by TJ Books LTD, Padstow, Cornwall

ISBN 978 1913551 995

British Library Cataloguing in Publication Data.
A catalogue record for this book is available from the British Library.

To Lynne, Nicola and Lisa.

PART ONE

THE EARLY YEARS

1

Benghazi, July 1985

Jack Meredith examined his naked body in the cracked mirror, surprised at how thin and emaciated he'd become in the last few months.

'Come back to bed, Jack,' drawled a woman's drugged voice from the room next door. 'It's not light yet.'

He winced. Ignoring her, he pulled on shorts and an old T-shirt over his sweat-drenched body, grabbed his wallet and moved silently through the chaos of her living room. Gingerly unlocking the steel door, he eased back the bolts, hoping she wouldn't hear, and slipped out.

Without warning, the loudspeaker hanging by its cable from the local minaret crackled into life; the muezzin was calling the faithful to Fajr, the prayer before sunrise. Single-storey whitewashed terraced houses opened directly onto a dimly lit sand-strewn street, devoid of all life save for scavenging dogs fighting over rotting garbage.

When he'd arrived back on local leave four days earlier, Eli had complained that she no longer felt safe in this shadowy part of town. The last of the few foreign nationals had recently moved away, their homes quickly appropriated by members of the murderous Green Brigade, the regime's henchmen. She was right of course, but this small unkempt place was all she could afford.

He had been in Libya for several months before they'd met. It was during a period when his early optimism had been crushed by the drunken aimlessness of his time spent away from the desert. He'd been living in a small airless apartment in a shared compound just back from the seafront. What might have sounded exotic when writing to his mates back in London was in fact more like an army base – four badly maintained low-rise blocks around a threadbare earthen square.

Being the latest and youngest recruit, he was the only company employee in the compound. He'd befriended several neighbours including a couple of older Greeks and an Armenian, all of whom were drillers. When they could, they spent their leave together in the incestuous rundown overseas club and a couple of illegal bars and brothels masquerading as restaurants. All this had taken its toll on his physical and mental wellbeing. Meeting Eli by chance one morning in the market had been a godsend, dragging him back from certain self-destruction.

A long-legged blond South African in her early thirties, she had recently been deserted by her husband, a cantankerous and abusive Afrikaner. Her residency status was perilous, her future uncertain. She was totally dependent on an unreliable employer for part-time work who was reluctant to get her a work permit. She survived on the scant rewards of a demeaning job, the generosity of a few friends and the unlikely patronage of an old Benghazi family.

Eli was tough, a hard-living woman who displayed no outward vulnerability except to a few intimate friends. She and Jack had a companionable but non-binding friendship which suited them both. Neither sought a long-term relationship, nor could they commit to one. Their exhaustive lovemaking during his week's leave seemed to satisfy them. They shared books, food and the odd trip to the beach; outside these interests, their time was largely spent in bed. They needed no other human comfort during their time apart.

She had no work for a couple of days, so he was happy to leave her to catch up on her sleep. He set off for the early market and was soon joined by chattering locals, some carrying baskets of bread and couscous, others pushing bicycles loaded with fresh vegetables, oranges and lemons, slabs of fly-infested meat and dried fish, all headed in the same direction.

*

In '82, at the tender age of twenty-one, Jack qualified in London as a petroleum geologist; he had everything he could have wished for. Tall and athletic, he was a man who enjoyed the attention of young women. Somewhat enigmatic, he appeared confident yet distant, as if he lived in a parallel universe, destined for a life quite different from his peers. With an interesting job, a decent salary and the hedonistic freedom of the city, he wanted for nothing.

A couple of years on, however, it started to unravel. The daughter of a senior partner in the consultancy where he worked had been promoted ahead of him and he'd lost his driving licence to drink. However, it was his striking but increasingly staid girlfriend, Charlotte, who had put the fear of God in him. He sensed she was angling for an engagement ring; the thought of marriage had terrified him.

Just before Christmas the previous year, he planned his escape. Without telling a soul, he had applied for a job as a field geologist with a multinational energy company in Libya. He managed to convince them that he had the ability to spend weeks on his own in the Sahara, prospecting for oil. It happened quickly; within three months, he was working in the Sirte Basin, 500 kilometres south of Benghazi.

Charlotte was horrified, her plans thwarted. She was ambitious. Coming from a wealthy middle-class family living in London, she was expected to be 'somebody' in the City by the age of thirty. In hindsight, he should have ended their relationship before he left. He hadn't the heart and took the cowardly way out. He promised her he would return within twelve months, implying that they'd get married.

In early March, he found himself on a bumpy flight over the Mediterranean heading for Benghazi, a once colourful port in eastern Libya now being casually destroyed by an unpredictable and cruel dictatorship.

He relished the dangers and difficulties of living in the country. He would spend three weeks of each month absorbed in his work in the desert, away from the filthy bustling city. Towards the end of his week's leave in Benghazi, he longed for the ethereal peace of the Sahara, the intensely bountiful life of small oasis villages, isolated against a backdrop of limitless empty horizons; multi-coloured landscapes of flat stony plains, dry wadi beds and the great rolling dunes of the sand seas.

*

'Where the hell have you been?' she cried.

She was standing in the middle of the living room, a towel wrapped around her naked body, as he pushed through the steel door.

'The market,' he said, dropping a heavy plastic bag on the floor.

'They were here again, a few minutes ago, shouting, threatening, banging on the door,' she rushed on. 'I saw five, maybe six of them, through the shutters. Some with green armbands, rifles. I hadn't a clue what…'

'Stop, Eli, stop,' he said, taking her shaking body in his arms.

'You've got to get me out of here, Jack. I'd live anywhere but this bloody place,' she sobbed. 'This used to be a great area, but it's gone to hell. It's just too bloody dangerous now.'

Gradually her fear subsided.

'When did it all go wrong?' he asked eventually, trying to distract her.

'May last year,' she whispered.

'After the failed coup?'

'The backlash was terrifying. Individuals, whole families disappeared overnight. The leaders, including anybody not closely associated with the regime, were considered foreigners.' She shivered in his arms. 'Given that the leaders are from the west – Misrata, Sirte, wherever – most people are now considered their enemies.' She paused. 'Especially local Benghazi people, people from Jebel Akhdar.'

'I can imagine.' He hesitated. 'So what do you want to do?'

'I could stay in your place while you're in the desert, make the place a bit more homely.'

Homely, he wondered, casually eyeing the wreckage that was her home. He realised he had little choice. He'd have to ask Shultz, who wouldn't have a problem, but the authorities… well, he'd worry about them later.

'We've a couple of days before you go back, it could be done.'

'I'll see Shultz this evening, see what he says.'

She reached up and pulled him down in a languid kiss. Suddenly he was tired, not physically tired, just tired of this constant, cloying intimacy.

'Let's eat,' he said, pulling away, 'I'm famished.'

'I'll get dressed, prepare something,' she said, examining the shopping bag on the floor. 'There's a jug of fresh orange juice in the fridge. You could add a little flash to pep it up.'

'God, Eli, I couldn't face any more of that stuff. It's brutal, pure alcohol.'

'No worse than the Ghanaian flash you bought,' she laughed.

'They don't make it like they used to,' he admitted. 'What the hell, I'll add a tumblerful. We can sit in the yard in the shade, pretend we're drinking rum and Coke at some fancy Italian beach hotel.'

'Now you're talking.'

He took the spiced-up jug and his book into the back yard, while she prepared a meal.

Encouraged by Eli, he'd started to read up on the ancient history of North Africa, more specifically on the part-Greek, part-Roman cities of Tolmeta and Cyrene. She had visited these historic sites, several hundred kilometres along the coast to the east, and knew them well.

Ten minutes later she returned and after placing a heavily laden tray on the plastic table, she poured herself a generous glass from the jug.

'More?'

'Slow down, Eli, slow down.' He grinned. 'I haven't recovered from last night's fill.'

They ate in silence, the shade slowly circling the yard, the only clue to passing time.

'I've been thinking,' he said, indicating the book, 'why don't we spend a few days in Cyrene and Tolmeta on my next leave?'

She was dozing, leaning back precariously on her chair, head propped against the wall. An eye opened, regarding him quizzically. He sensed her nervousness, not wanting to leave the comparative safety of the city; it would be a tough call for her, he thought.

'It'll be my birthday. I could book us into the old hotel just outside Cyrene for a couple of nights. You could be our tour guide,' he laughed, adding as an afterthought, 'More time sightseeing, less time in bed might be good for us both,' immediately regretting what he'd just said. 'Sorry, Eli, just a joke,' he muttered, trying to laugh it off.

'It's OK, Jack, it's OK,' she said, pulling herself upright.

She picked up the book and flicked casually through its well-thumbed pages.

'I haven't been there for ages, not since Pete left. He didn't give a shit for the place, ignorant bastard,' she said, bitterly. 'Going with you, yes that would be fun.' She seemed distracted.

'Well?' he asked, sensing her hesitation.

'I don't know, it's just…' again the uncertainty in her voice. 'It's not you, it's just that I wouldn't feel safe being out of Benghazi. Out there, on the road, anybody might stop us for whatever reason. My residency status crap would give those thugs a massive opportunity, could cost me hundreds, maybe thousands in bribes to buy their silence. And still no guarantee that I wouldn't be deported anyway.'

He didn't press her and let the subject drop. They became absorbed in their reading as the afternoon morphed into evening.

'Are you hungry yet?' she asked, as the back yard finally succumbed to the failing sunlight.

'What's the time?'

'Must be around six.'

'I think I'll go and see Shultz. I might catch him in the office before he heads home.' He got up to leave. 'He's probably wondering why I haven't been yet. I have to meet him at least once while I'm in town.'

'How will you get there?'

He'd had to leave the jeep in his compound; it would have been stolen within the hour had he parked it on her street.

'I'll get a taxi from the market. There's always a couple hanging around.'

'Maybe he'll give you a lift back.'

'Maybe.' He grinned. 'Depends on his sobriety. He always insists we have a whisky or two.'

'On top of the flash, you'd better be careful,' she laughed. 'We've plenty to do this evening.'

Yes, he mused, knowing that 'plenty' meant several hours of riotous lovemaking, the thought of which left him unusually deflated. He could see that her earlier despondency had lifted; the flash perhaps or maybe she was just hopeful that she'd be moving away soon.

'Don't wait to eat,' he said. 'I might have something with Shultz.'

*

'Down, Jack, get down, you bloody fool,' shouted Shultz, from somewhere beneath a huge wooden table. 'They can easily see you, pick you off, standing there.'

What the hell's going on? Jack wondered as he crawled under the table where Shultz was poring over an old field report; what a bloody odd place for their meeting. He could smell whisky on his boss's breath or was it his own, he couldn't tell.

He could hear a faint 'rat-tat-tat-tat' coming from God knows where.

'They're getting closer,' cried Shultz. 'I need to read this stuff before they get here.'

RAT-TAT-TAT-TAT followed by a large bang brought Jack to his senses.

He was sitting on the floor next to his bed; it quickly dawned on him that he'd been dreaming. Not unusually, the air-conditioning had cut out; it was deathly quiet. He got to his feet and in the dim light was startled to see Eli standing naked on the far side of the room.

'You fell off the bed,' she whispered. 'You're drunk.'

He stood staring at her, unsure what to say or do next.

'You couldn't have heard it then.'

'What?' he said, his brain trying to connect with the present.

'The tapping, it's been going on since the AC went off and then there was this…' She froze. 'There it is again. I think somebody's knocking on the back door.'

'I'll check it out,' he said quietly, pulling the sheet from the bed and wrapping it around his shivering body.

'Just be careful,' she whispered.

He went through to the darkened kitchen, which opened onto the back yard and peered through the shutters. Hazy moonlight revealed nothing, so he turned on the yard light; the place was empty. Breathing a sigh of relief, he unlocked the back door and stepped outside.

'God almighty,' he cried, staring at the carnage at his feet.

Eli came rushing to his side, stopped and screamed. A dismembered mongrel, its head and each limb torn from its body, lay bleeding in the dust. The stench was gut churning; she promptly threw up. He could see the blade of a deeply embedded knife pinning a white sheet of paper to the carcass.

'There's a note,' he gasped, as he pulled the bloody sheet clear. Gingerly he held it up to the light.

'What does it say?' she asked, tearfully.

'"Mr Jack,"' he read, '"get your South African whore out of this house by dusk tomorrow and don't come back... we have a way of dealing with these bitches."'

'Holy shit,' she cried.

Suddenly it dawned on Jack: whoever did this had to have come over the wall from one of their three neighbours backing onto the yard; their predicament was serious.

'We'll leave straight away, as soon as you're ready.'

'Now?' alarm in her voice.

'Now.'

'What about all my stuff?'

'Just pack personal things, anything you value, but be quick,' he said abruptly. 'I'll replace the stuff you leave when you're settled in my place. Let's get the hell out of here.'

'How?'

'We'll bloody walk and get a taxi in the market. The bastards won't bother us if they see we're running away.'

2

Cyrene, August 1985

When Jack had asked Shultz a few weeks earlier if he could borrow a jeep and take off for a few days to explore Cyrene and Tolmeta, his boss had initially been reluctant to give his approval knowing the dangers that Jack might face. His instinct, however, told him that his young geologist was desperate to go and could be trusted. In the end, he'd consented.

Full of optimism, Jack left the modest hotel after an early breakfast on a beautifully still and sunny morning. He was alone. Eli had opted to stay in Benghazi, where she was now happily ensconced in his small bachelor flat, making it habitable. In truth, he was relieved to be away from the place and out of the city, which had become increasingly edgy over the last few months. He found peace only in the remoteness of the desert, a feeling he hoped to replicate here over the next couple of days.

Cyrene was completely deserted. He had read that the ruins here were more spectacular than any ancient Greek or Roman city you'd see in Europe. Walking there was a bizarre experience given its historic significance – no tourists, no vendors, no fencing, no security, no information boards, no means of selling tickets or collecting money; virtually nothing ahead of him other than ancient ruins.

He found an old Bedouin outside a dilapidated building on the edge of the archaeological site, whom he assumed to be the caretaker. He didn't speak English and Jack had little Arabic, so he showed him Eli's book with its maps and plans. The old man quickly appreciated Jack's interest and enthusiastically beckoned him into the building, which appeared to be the site museum. It consisted of an office and several large rooms containing numerous artefacts, a few catalogued, all scattered haphazardly throughout, on wooden tables, benches, on the floor.

Somehow, the two men bonded. Perhaps, thought Jack, he'd been the curator before the revolution when many people would have visited the site and sought his knowledge. After a lengthy and largely incomprehensible tour of the two main rooms, the old man handed Jack a faded brochure, written in English, and indicated the best route around the site.

After an exhausting morning wandering through the ruined city without meeting another soul, he found a shady corner in the amphitheatre, located at the edge of a rugged north-facing escarpment. In the shimmering air he could make out the vivid blueness of the Mediterranean fringing a coastal plain of varying shades of green and brown. The heat was stifling; he could barely keep his eyes open. He had a long drink from his flask and promptly dozed off. An hour or so later, he awoke and, feeling marginally more refreshed, pulled a pad from his backpack and started sketching.

Soon he realised he had company; a young woman and an elderly man, whom for some unknown reason he took to be a relative or an old retainer, appeared on the far side of the amphitheatre. They moved silently, looking closely at some of the detailed carvings, which she appeared to be photographing. She was modestly dressed and wore a floppy khaki sunhat. Apart from her expensive-looking camera, there was nothing unusual about her, although he had an uncomfortable feeling that she'd taken a picture of him.

Just at that moment, he was distracted by a car which arrived in a cloud of dust outside the museum building. Three young men, dressed casually in Western clothes, disappeared inside. He thought no more of them and turned back to his sketching.

Minutes later, he noticed the three men leave the museum building and stride towards him. To his horror, he saw they were wearing green armbands – members of the murderous Green Brigade. Two were armed. He looked in vain for the couple who might witness what was unfolding; they'd vanished. To his dismay he was alone. The men were soon on him, whipping him around, locking his hands tightly behind his back, shouting incomprehensively at him. It happened so quickly he barely had time to register any fear.

He was roughly searched. They snatched his sketchbook and threw it away, removed his ID card and pulled dollar bills from his shirt pocket. They examined his ID before throwing it on the ground in disgust; like most Green Brigade thugs, they were illiterate.

One of the three pulled a small fossil from Jack's trouser pocket that he'd picked up earlier. The man waved it around in the air for the others to see, screaming and spitting in his face. Then without warning Jack was struck from behind. He fell, cracking his skull on a rock and lost consciousness.

*

Sometime later he came to, completely disorientated, to find himself lying awkwardly on a rough plank in a filthy, stinking, windowless room. The space, hot and deathly quiet, was barely three metres across and lit by a single fifty-watt bulb hanging from the ceiling. His heart stopped when he saw dried blood and excrement smeared on the walls and floor. It dawned on him that this might be some sort of torture chamber. The pain in his head was excruciating. His jaw seemed locked and he could hardly open his mouth. Even the cicadas had been driven from this hellhole.

He was there for two days and two nights; for the first twenty-four hours he was barely conscious, his body contorted in agony. Three times during daylight hours he was fed. A filthy plastic box containing a cup of boiled rice, a chunk of stale bread and a bottle of foul-tasting water was pushed wordlessly through a small opening in the heavy metal door before dropping on the floor.

There were times when he thought he would suffocate to death. On the second afternoon, he managed to stand and lean against the door, pushing his face to the opening, his sole source of air. From there, he could just make out a row of similar doors directly opposite, disappearing in each direction.

It was about that time that he started to take in his surroundings, hear noises: from time to time, boots pounding up and down the corridor, rough voices shouting incomprehensibly in Arabic, sudden and prolonged screams. They were the worst, usually followed by minutes of muffled sobbing. Twice he heard gunshots. Nothing else appeared to happen. He spoke to no one, saw no one. He soon realised that absolutely nobody, save for his captors, knew he was there. For the first time, he was truly scared for his life.

Before dawn on the third day, they came for him, the same three thugs. It was still dark when they burst in, shouting and cursing. The next fifteen minutes were the most terrifying of his life. He was kicked and punched repeatedly, brutally. He pissed his pants, crapped himself with fear. Blood drained into his eyes, drenched his torn shirt. He felt ribs snap after several mighty kicks while on the floor. He slipped in and out of consciousness, became disembodied. His screaming seemed to come from somebody else. He saw a stranger being beaten; it wasn't him.

About midday, he regained consciousness. He was lying on his side on the floor, his face stranded in a pool of congealed blood.

Filthy and reeking of shit and vomit, he was completely broken, unable to move. Slowly he became aware of people hovering overhead, heatedly talking. To his surprise, he heard a woman's voice speaking in Arabic. She appeared to be giving orders. He had no idea what was being said, what was going on.

Without warning, he was rolled onto his back and lifted roughly onto a battered aluminium stretcher. He screamed in pain as if every bone in his body was broken, every muscle torn. He was carried down a corridor and out into the blinding sun; everything was blurred, confused. Somebody, the same woman, he thought, grasped his arm tightly to prevent him from falling off.

It became imperative for him to concentrate on this woman; his very survival seemed to depend on her. He vaguely noticed that she was wearing Western clothes: jeans and a man's loose cotton shirt. From the little of her that he could see, she seemed young, possibly his age. She was an alien in the presence of the others.

He was lifted into the back of an old jeep, laid out between the seats like a corpse, his battered frame shrouded in a coarse, foul-smelling blanket. After much cursing and shouting, the doors slammed, the vehicle driving off at breakneck speed.

He had little idea how long the drive was but guessed it must have been minutes rather than hours. He was feverishly hot, suffocating and unable to move. His tortured body registered every single rut and stone they bounced over; the pain was unrelenting.

Eventually they came to a sudden stop; despite being in agony, his mind was alert. As he was lifted out into the swirling dust, he saw two battered green crescent ambulances parked outside a dishevelled whitewashed two-storey building. It occurred to him they'd arrived at a local hospital.

The place was crawling with people – staff, patients and visitors, hardly distinguishable one from the other. He was admitted with much fanfare and excitement. A young woman appeared at his side. Quietly and confidently, she gave instructions. Several orderlies lifted him onto an iron bed in what appeared to be a ground floor ward.

The large airless room was crammed. He noticed men of all ages, many of whom were bandaged and dressed in old torn gowns, wandering about aimlessly. Shapeless cloaked women squatted on the floor around closely packed beds. He became aware of many voices, frequently interspersed with anguished cries, cries of the bereaved and the dying. He gagged at the putrid smell, a cocktail of rotting food and flesh, sweat and faeces.

A middle-aged woman, dressed in a grubby white hospital coat with a stethoscope protruding from one of its pockets, stepped into the dazzling sunlight and administered an injection. He quickly passed out.

3

Tolmeta, August 1985

Jack woke in the night, bathed in sweat, lying on his back on a stinking mattress, naked except for a pair of shorts. He struggled to remember where he was before vaguely recalling arriving earlier at the hospital. It was uncomfortably hot. A couple of moth-infested low-watt bulbs threw out yellowy pools of light at each end of the ward. All he could hear, apart from the cacophony of night-time insects, was the gentle swishing of an overhead fan and the persistent hacking coughs and rumbling snores of his fellow patients. As he stirred, he became aware of a figure leaning over him staring into his face. With a start, he recognised Shultz.

'How are you feeling, Jack?' his boss whispered.

For no apparent reason he was speechless. He couldn't get a word out, he just grunted.

'A drink?'

It was a woman's voice. He could just make her out at the end of the bed. She moved into his line of sight. He vaguely recognised her as somebody he'd seen before, but where, he had no idea.

'Jack, this is Bushra, Bushra Benamer,' said Shultz, quietly.

He acknowledged her, nodding.

'If it hadn't been for her courage, we wouldn't have found you. I doubt very much whether you'd still be alive.'

'Found me', 'still be alive'? What the hell was he talking about? He had no recollection of what had happened, why he was in so much pain. Clumsily, he propped himself up on his elbows, indicating to the woman that he was thirsty. After a long drink, he settled back and slipped into a dreamless sleep. Despite the relentless pain, his last waking thought was one of relief.

He had no concept of time passing. When not asleep, he gradually took in his surroundings. The staff, who genuinely seemed to care for him, followed a simple but effective routine, which he later realised had only been made possible by the generosity of Bushra and her family. Every morning before dawn, she would be at his bedside, assisting the orderlies who washed and fed him. Quietly and without fuss, she took control of his recovery.

Beneath her calm efficiency, he sensed a restless and sensual woman. She was strikingly beautiful. Of medium build, she had toned olive skin and short dark hair stylishly cropped, framing an open and engaging expression. It was her penetrating blue-black eyes, though, that transfixed him.

From the beginning, he thought of her as a professional, perhaps a junior doctor or paramedic. As time passed and the fogginess cleared from his throbbing head, he became increasingly aware of her presence. He could see that she was different from the others in the ward. She wore smart Western-style clothes and spoke with a quiet authority to everybody no matter what rank. Her time seemed to be devoted entirely to him.

She would meet the middle-aged female doctor on her early ward rounds. They spoke earnestly, incomprehensively in Arabic at the end of his bed. Sometimes she would leave well-thumbed out-of-date English language newspapers or magazines, which he never had the energy to read. She would return at midday to help him with his lunch and then later in the evening at suppertime.

On the fourth day, the doctor and resident surgeon gave him a thorough medical check-up and sent him for an X-ray. Although the equipment appeared outdated, it gave clear pictures of his damaged body. Later, he discovered that technicians had cannibalised parts stolen from other hospitals in the region to keep it going.

Initially he was heavily sedated and in too much pain to converse with Bushra, who in turn kept silent. They communicated using hand signals and facial expressions, their own private language. It was on the sixth day, when he first managed to mumble some words, that he discovered the extent of his injuries: three cracked ribs, a fractured arm and multiple bruises on his back and thighs.

His left arm had been encased in plaster, but they had decided not to treat his ribs. The surgeon believed that given time, nature would take its course and repair the broken bones. Despite the limited availability of drugs, they were able to supply him with painkillers, keeping him semi-conscious for hours.

Very slowly, he started to recall the beatings. Gradually the trauma, which he reckoned had caused his amnesia, started to subside. He vaguely remembered the attack in the amphitheatre. Hazy memories of three men marching towards him from the museum building floated around his head. One thing he did recall clearly: his sense of isolation after realising that the couple he'd seen moments earlier had vanished.

As his memory improved, the full horror of what he'd experienced returned. Every night Bushra stayed by his bedside until the small hours, holding his hands as he shouted and screamed in the trapped hellishness of his nightmares. He would come to, confused and delirious, drenched in sweat. She would gently mop his saturated body, give him water and settle him down again. On bad nights this was repeated several times. He was only vaguely aware of their increasingly physical intimacy. Exhaustion would eventually sweep him away into an agitated sleep.

*

On the eighth night he woke shortly after midnight. Something was amiss, but he couldn't be sure what. Then it dawned on him: this was the first time he hadn't come to, seething and shouting, fleeing the claustrophobic grip of his dreams. Although hot and sweaty, his fever seemed to have eased. He heaved himself gingerly into an upright position and surveyed the slumbering ward.

She was sitting on the edge of a chair beside him, slumped over with her head on the bed. He was mesmerised. Just as he was leaning forward to brush back her hair plastered in sweat, she stirred and sat up.

'Have you been awake long?' she whispered.

'No,' he replied, hoarsely, surprised at how clear her English was.

'Drink this,' she said, handing him a glass of water.

They sat in awkward silence, unable to break the spell. He realised that they'd never conversed properly other than his brief requests and her equally brief instructions. He wanted desperately to say something to her, anything that would convey his gratitude. She was in shadow, her body silhouetted by the single light bulb at their end of the ward. He felt vulnerable speaking to her unseen face.

After several minutes, he summoned up his courage.

'Where are we?' he whispered.

'Tolmeta hospital, it's on the outskirts of town,' she answered quietly.

'Tolmeta?'

'We're twenty minutes from the jail where we found you.'

His heart missed a beat at the mention of the word jail.

'I was in Tolmeta jail?'

'It's a disused colonial-era building on the south side.' She paused. 'A perfect clearing house for the Green Brigade.'

It took him a moment to digest what she'd said.

'Is it safe here?' he asked, fearfully.

'Yes, your jailors have been dealt with,' she grinned, 'until the next time.'

'Until the next time,' he repeated, trying to grasp its significance.

'Don't think about it,' she whispered.

Without warning the lights went out, all was in total darkness. He struggled to contain his anxiety. After a minute or so, the hospital's standby generator came to life and the lights reluctantly flickered back on. He was at a loss for words, before suddenly remembering her name.

'Bushra,' he whispered, her name on his lips sounding strange. 'Can I call you Bushra?'

'Of course.'

'I'm very much in your debt, you've…'

'Don't, don't say anything,' she interrupted softly.

He fell silent.

'You'd have done the same,' she said after a few moments, 'if the roles had been reversed. Anyway, you're our guest.'

'Guest?'

'Shultz and my father have been close friends for years. He's helped the family on many occasions.'

The mention of Shultz brought an unwelcome dose of reality: fleeting thoughts of work, of how much time he must have had off already, of Eli in his cramped flat unaware of his predicament; all this he quickly suppressed.

'Helped?'

'It's good that we've had an opportunity to repay his generosity,' she said, ignoring his curiosity. 'Anyway, I've enjoyed looking after you. It's made a pleasant change from normal life.'

At the far end of the ward, a man suddenly shouted out, caught in the terror of a nightmare. Others, disturbed, groaned and shifted restlessly on metal beds. As everybody settled down again, he tried to process what she'd said.

'What's "normal"?' was all he managed.

'In truth, nothing's been normal in this country for years.'

Her frankness intrigued him.

'Maybe before the revolution it was,' he ventured.

She hesitated, perhaps gauging how much she should tell him.

'For the extended family, yes. It was different for my parents though.'

'Your parents?'

'My father's Libyan, my mother's Greek. They've lived most of their married life in Athens.'

'And you?'

'My brother, Alexis, and I were born there but spent most of our early childhood in Benghazi. We went back to Greece for secondary school, university.'

He was silent, unsure where this openness was leading.

'I've always loved this country,' she continued, 'and feel close to my father's family here.'

'That's understandable.'

'I'm half Libyan after all,' she laughed, quietly.

Things were slowly starting to make sense, why she was so different from the others in the way she spoke, dressed, behaved.

'Are you living here now?'

'No, actually I am or was,' she corrected herself, 'on a week's holiday.'

'Which you've spent looking after me.'

'A pleasant change from photographing old carvings lying around ancient Greek cities.'

'Cyrene,' he gasped, suddenly recalling where he'd seen her before.

'Keep your voice down,' she whispered urgently.

His neighbour, a young Bedouin, who'd had all his fingers on his right hand hacked off for some trifle offence, sat up suddenly on his bed and stared at Jack. Nobody moved. Silently the young man lay down and within seconds was asleep, snoring erratically.

'It was you I saw taking photographs,' he whispered. 'You were with an old man.'

'Uncle Abdullah. I'd been staying with him. He has a smallholding where he goes to escape Benghazi. It's on the coast close to Apollonia. Most days we were up at Cyrene. I was photographing stone carvings for my dissertation.'

'And because of this, you've had to put everything on hold.'

She nodded.

'I'm very sorry,' he said, quietly. 'I've really wasted your time.'

'Don't apologise, I put my camera to good use.' She lowered her voice, looking around furtively to ensure nobody was listening. 'We saw members of the Green Brigade beating you, taking you away. I photographed the whole thing.'

'Good God, you're brave.'

'Hardly, foolish perhaps,' she said, lightly. 'After they'd driven you away, we found your ID card and sketchbook. From the ID, we got your contact details. Getting hold of Shultz was easy.'

'What happened then?'

'It took us two days to discover that you'd been taken to the jail.'

'Given what you saw, most people would have got away as quickly as possible.' It was his turn to laugh. 'They wouldn't have hung around taking photographs. Or bothered to find out where I'd been taken to. You must both be a little crazy,' he whispered.

'Perhaps,' she conceded. 'Abdullah insisted on checking the old museum curator. He'd known him for years. We found him slumped behind his table, barely conscious and too terrified to talk. He had a nasty head wound, which was bleeding profusely. Once he recognised us, he relaxed a bit.'

'Is he here in hospital?'

'No, he thought he'd be safer staying put. By coming here, he'd incriminate the thugs, putting his own life at risk.'

'God, the poor man.'

'Abdullah got his first aid box, cleaned and bandaged the wound, gave him painkillers.' She paused. 'Eventually after a little persuasion, the old man told us what had happened. The thugs claimed you stole a valuable clay statuette. A national treasure, they said. They told him you'd be fined, possibly imprisoned.'

'It was nothing, only a fossil.'

'Which explains why the old man wasn't shown any evidence. He suspected the whole thing was fabricated. He recognised the men, however. They'd been several times before, beaten and taken people away on similar false charges.'

He hesitated, momentarily fearful again.

'Are they local?'

'No, he thinks they're from Sirte,' she said, lowering her voice. 'He never hears what happens after people are arrested, suspects that once the victims have been beaten and sufficient cash has changed hands, everything's quietly forgotten.'

'Green Brigade?' he asked, knowing full well the answer.

'Yes.'

Jack knew these same people were responsible for driving Eli from her home. They were everywhere, invariably at odds with the regular police, and beyond the reach of law. They had the regime's unyielding support, both politically and financially. In return the regime could rely on them to deal with any threat to its leadership, real or imaginary, with brutal efficiency.

His neighbour suddenly sat up again and slowly raising his fingerless hand, pointed it at Jack as if it were a gun.

'Don't move,' she whispered fiercely.

For a few moments, Jack was motionless, staring down the imaginary barrel of his neighbour's gun. Suddenly, the effort was too much; an overwhelming drowsiness swept over him. As he fell back on the mattress, he heard his neighbour whooping with delight, believing he'd killed Jack.

*

During daylight hours, he started to take an interest in his fellow patients. They were mostly heavily bandaged men, who lay on their filthy bug-infested mattresses, suffering from appalling injuries. These men, he discovered, were casualties of the regime's brutality. Sufficiently important in Tolmeta to have been terrorised and brought into line, they weren't a threat so were spared execution.

The ward was constantly overrun during the day – men and women of all ages, mostly destitute, bustling, chattering, laughing and crying out. There was absolutely no privacy, the closely packed iron beds reminding him of his school dormitories. Most appeared to be the patients' relatives, augmenting meagre hospital resources by providing water, food and care or simply comfort for the dying. The whole place seemed tired, rundown, reflecting the dispirited attitude of well-meaning but overworked staff.

Throughout all this, Bushra remained steadfast. He came to rely on her more and more, marvelling at her spirit and unswerving attention to his care. Her lithe body moved through the ward with the grace and sensuality of a dancer. She was so different from other women he encountered – shapeless bodies defined by poor diet, indoor living and frequent child bearing, chattels of dominant menfolk, virtual prisoners within their own communities.

She rarely spoke to him during the day, other than to ask him how he was and whether he needed anything. However, late at night, after the other patients had settled down, she would sit with him, whispering earnestly until sleep overtook him.

Her faintly discernible accent intrigued him – the alluring voice of the well-educated, widely travelled, cosmopolitan European. He could see that she was used to exercising authority. Her tone suggested privilege, private education, cultured living. This had led him to speculate about her family, perhaps one of old wealth and influence, commodities certainly in short supply in Libya since the revolution. As time passed, he found her enigmatic smile increasingly unsettling, inducing in him both alarm and longing.

She was keen to hear about his life before he came to Benghazi. He was surprised to find himself telling her about his unhappy childhood – lonely days spent in boarding schools in Ireland, his parents' acrimonious divorce – carefree days in university in London and his long-term girlfriend, Charlotte.

She spoke at length about her family. Her father, Sheik Ali Benamer, was head of one of the leading Senussi clans under the late King Idris and a well-respected member of the king's *majlis* or inner court. He was a polygamist with three wives, the youngest of whom was Bushra's mother, Elena.

Elena was the only child of a wealthy Greek shipping family, whose fortunes had peaked in the '70s. Ali and Elena's marriage had been a union of dynastic families both now in terminal decline, precipitated by the dictatorship in Tripoli on the one hand and the fall of the Junta in Athens on the other. They had two children, Bushra and her elder brother, Alexis, whom she adored. He was destined to take over his mother's family's shipping business, based in Athens.

For generations, the Benamers had been successful traders, travelling across the once borderless deserts of North Africa, gaining trading partners and influence in equal measure, accumulating wealth and property in Libya, Egypt and Greece. The family had always played a part in the affairs of state, as ministers, diplomats and senior army officers.

After the revolution in '69, the family's fortune had almost been wiped out. But because of their practical experience in government, a commodity in short supply among the regime's illiterate Bedouin followers, they were one of the few families who had been spared annihilation or death. As such they were tolerated, even respected by the regime, to the point of being able to challenge the daily terror inflicted by the Green Brigade. Other well-connected families had failed and disappeared.

Jack got the impression that her family was a fearless clan, non-partisan and untainted by favour or corruption, moving around with relative impunity. Despite the great difficulties of living under the dictatorship, they all dreamed of the day when their country would embrace a dignified and tolerant civilisation, free of fear and violence.

Bushra told him that before the revolution in '69, Ali's younger brother, Abdullah, had been a popular mayor of Tolmeta. The regime's people understood the respect the local population had for him and so left him in peace. Jack therefore wasn't surprised to learn from her that the day before he was released, Abdullah had challenged the local Green Brigade leader, demanding that he produce evidence of Jack's alleged crime. She told Jack that she showed the leader her photographs, all of which were identified by time and date. They clearly demonstrated that the attack had been unprovoked. The man reluctantly agreed to free Jack early the following morning.

Jack learnt that Bushra and Abdullah, having obtained his release, knew that this would not be the end of his troubles. They suspected that the thugs would extract their revenge before he was set free. And of course they were proved right; having been caught out and unable to extract cash, the thugs vented their frustration by beating and leaving him for dead, just hours before they were charged to let him go.

*

For ten days, Bushra and the hospital staff nursed him to the point where he was able to leave hospital. She told him that they wanted him to be sufficiently fit to withstand the uncomfortable drive back to Benghazi. On the tenth day, although still in pain and his arm in a sling, he was deemed well enough to travel.

The following morning, propped up on the back seat of Abdullah's old truck, they left before dawn and the searing heat of the day and took to the coastal road.

'Where are we going?' Jack shouted above the noise of the engine.

'To Benghazi, to the family compound.'

'Does Shultz know?'

Sitting in the front, she turned to face him.

'You're not strong enough to live on your own yet, you need to convalesce. Shultz agrees.'

'What about your family? Won't I be in the way?'

'No, there are plenty of rooms. It's our custom to accommodate family and friends in need, for days, even weeks if necessary,' she said, before turning away. He knew this was entirely in keeping with the deep-seated hospitality of desert people over the centuries.

A couple of days after he settled in and his pain had eased she took him to meet her father, Ali. Dressed casually in Western clothes, he rose to greet Jack. He was a tall striking man with a shock of white hair who could have been mistaken for a wealthy Greek businessman. He held a priceless *misbaha* in his right hand, noiselessly thumbing the ivory beads, suggesting to Jack that he was a religious man. Every day after that, the two men would meet, happy to be in each other's company, whiling away the time in the older man's study, discussing common interests including the history of the Greeks and Romans in North Africa.

*

One evening, a week after Jack had taken up residence, Abdullah announced that he was going into town the following morning, on the pretext of looking for second-hand parts for an ageing well pump located at his smallholding near Apollonia.

'Why don't you come with me?' he asked Jack. 'You haven't left the compound since you got here.'

Although still physically fragile and with his arm in a sling, Jack had begun to feel restless and uncomfortable in the Benamer household. He wanted to leave as soon as his health would allow, keen to get back to work, to escape the confining comfort and good nature of his generous hosts.

He had become increasingly infatuated with Bushra. He was terrified that he could so easily abuse the family's unlimited hospitality, destroy their trust in him and dispel the magic in which they had cocooned him. He owed Bushra and Abdullah an enormous debt of gratitude because of the selfless way in which they'd rescued him from a probable painful and anonymous death. He was fearful of repaying this debt with ignominy.

'I'd love to,' said Jack, seizing the opportunity.

'You'll have a great day,' beamed Bushra, clearly happy for him to go.

After a fruitless search the following morning in Benghazi's main souk, Abdullah took him to a local coffee shop on the waterfront.

'You know, Jack, it's time for you to leave,' said the old man, after they'd settled down.

'Leave?' he asked, taken by surprise.

'Back to your apartment. You're quite well enough to be on your own now.'

'Of course, of course,' he said, unsure what had triggered this.

'How old are you?'

'Twenty-four, just gone twenty-four.'

'Ah, to be young again,' laughed Abdullah. 'You know we're all very fond of you, especially my brother, Ali,' he hesitated, 'but he loves his daughter.'

Jack went crimson with embarrassment.

'She's only nineteen and still in university in Athens. Like her brother, the family have great plans for her.'

Suddenly, Jack could see where this was going.

'God, I'm sorry if I've…'

'No,' Abdullah interrupted abruptly, 'you've nothing to apologise for. It's just that she's young and impressionable.' He laughed. 'And I think she's fallen under your spell.'

'I'll call Shultz this afternoon,' he stumbled on, shocked at this turn of events. 'I'll be away by the evening.'

'I've spoken to him already. He's picking you up here in thirty minutes. I'll get your stuff over to you later this afternoon.' Abdullah paused, placing his hand on Jack's arm. 'Don't take this badly, Jack, you've done nothing wrong.'

Sixty minutes later, a wordless Shultz dropped him back to his squalid, empty apartment, handing him an envelope as he got out of the jeep.

A folded sheet of lined paper had been left inside the front door. Jack instantly recognised the spidery handwriting.

Where the hell are you, Jack? You've been gone for weeks and Shultz won't tell me anything. So, I'm off. Eli.

This had not been a threat; she'd packed and left. He tore Shultz's envelope open.

See you in the office at seven tomorrow morning. You've a busy schedule for the next few weeks. I need you to rerun the Al Waha seismic survey. You'll be going straight from here so be prepared, bring your desert kitbag with you. Shultz.

Holy shit, he thought, *a few weeks in the desert. I'm not sure I'm ready for this. And when I get back, no Eli.* He poured himself a large glass of flash and slumped into his chair. He was back to reality with a bang.

4

Athens, March 1986

Getting through Benghazi airport had been a nightmare. It wasn't so much the heightened levels of security, but the sheer ineffectiveness of its staff that Jack found frustrating. Ever since the PLO had hijacked a Cairo-bound aircraft from Athens the previous November, airports in the region had introduced lengthy searches to ensure nobody could smuggle weapons on board a flight again.

Athens airport was no less chaotic when he disembarked ninety minutes later. In the pouring rain, a taxi drove him at breakneck speed to Omonia Square in the city centre, where he was to meet Bushra in the St George Hotel. Since November, he had spent his local leave with her in Greece.

He'd been haunted by her from the moment he'd been unceremoniously removed from the Benamer household the previous August but had given up any hope of seeing her again. Then in the middle of October, on the day he'd arrived back in town from the desert for his week's leave, Shultz handed him his mail. The bundle consisted mostly of letters from Charlotte, either demanding or begging him to return to London.

He'd been surprised to find a handwritten letter, posted in Athens two weeks earlier. It was from Bushra – short and to the point. She wrote how embarrassed she was about the way the family had treated him, making it impossible for her to see him in Benghazi; however, she'd love to meet him if he happened to be passing through Athens. She hadn't included an address, just a local telephone number.

Theirs had become a passionate affair, known only to Shultz, who had to arrange for his exit visa each month, and a few of her close friends. In the beginning, they'd stayed in her apartment in Glyfada, but in February, she'd driven him through the night to a deserted family holiday villa in the coastal village of Stoupa in the Peloponnese.

'Jack,' she shouted with delight, as he dropped his soggy kitbag at the front desk of the small family-run hotel. She threw her arms around him and buried her face in his soaking jacket before reaching up and kissing him. Eventually she stood back, her penetrating blue-black eyes fixed on his, exciting and frightening him in equal measure.

'You're late,' she grinned. Before he had time to say anything, she continued, 'Bloody Benghazi airport, it's hellish now, I hate the place.'

'You were there? Perhaps we could have…' he stammered.

'Another time, another time,' she said brusquely, turning to a middle-aged man behind the desk. 'Jack, this is Yannis, he owns the George.'

Jack smiled and nodded, rendered speechless under her spell.

'Yannis' family, our family, together we go back a long time.'

With a broad smile, Yannis came from behind the desk and retrieved Jack's bag, indicating that Jack should follow him.

'We're meeting a few of my university friends in Plaka as soon as you're ready,' she called after him. 'I'll wait for you here.'

His room was at the back of the hotel, thankfully away from the noise and pollution of the street. Without warning, and clearly unable to speak English, Yannis gave Jack a big hug as if to say, 'You're family, you're welcome', and promptly left.

He was in an emotional tailspin: seeing Bushra again, her off-hand reference to being in Benghazi and Yannis' unquestioning acceptance of their relationship. He showered, changed and in a few minutes was back at the front desk where she was talking animatedly with the old hotelier as if they were related.

'You look better,' she said, taking his hand and rushing out. *'Don't wait up, Yannis, I have a key,'* she shouted back over her shoulder. 'My car's around the corner. We'll be at the taverna in ten minutes.'

The rain had eased; light from the full moon reflected from the shining cobbles as she gunned her small car through Plaka's narrow streets. The intensity of their love for each other, her energy and enthusiasm for living life to the full left him breathless. She pulled over in a dark, narrow alleyway and turned to him.

'Oh, how I've missed you, Jack,' she laughed, throwing her arms around him in a passionate embrace.

*

He came to from a deep sleep, utterly disorientated. He kept his eyes squeezed tight, afraid of what he might encounter. He was lying on his back, naked, his head pounding, a high-pitched ringing noise in his ears as if he'd been sitting near an aircraft engine for too long. Slowly other senses stirred: an acrid aniseed taste welled up in his throat; a strong smell of Turkish tobacco tinged with marijuana invaded his nostrils.

A single finger lightly traced across his chest as if checking his ribs, working ever closer to his groin; a faint breath caressed his cheek.

'I want you, Jack,' whispered Bushra. 'Now.'

He opened his eyes. In the dim light, he could make out the curves of her nakedness, lying beside him. She had propped herself up on her elbow and was looking down at him, smiling longingly; his erection grew. Seamlessly, she mounted him, pushing him deep inside her. With her hands on his shoulders, she moved slowly and rhythmically. Suddenly throwing back her head and with a final thrust, she cried out, a terrifying primeval sound, as they both climaxed. Whimpering, she fell back on his chest, tears of relief wetting his face.

'Bushra, Bushra,' he whispered. 'I love you.'

'I love you, Jack,' she said, as she rolled off his sweating torso. 'I love you too.'

Their bodies entwined, they quickly succumbed to sleep.

Sometime later, he woke with a start; it was still dark, but he could make her out sitting on the edge of the bed.

'What time is it?'

'Four-fifteen,' she whispered. 'You've been asleep for an hour or so.'

'Where are we?'

'The George, your room in the George,' she said, switching on the bedside light. 'We got back at one. We'd both had too much ouzo. Too drunk to fuck,' she laughed. 'A couple of hours' sleep did wonders though.'

He staggered to the bathroom and dunked his head under the tap, the cold water anesthetising his overwrought brain.

'Are you OK?'

'Fine, just sorting out the old head.'

They climbed back into bed and lay down facing each other. He was mesmerised by her, completely besotted, all other thoughts banished.

'You look so serious, Jack,' she whispered. 'For heaven's sake, smile.'

'Sorry, I can't really believe I'm here with you,' he grinned. 'That was a hell of a party last night. A few friends, you said. That must have been your entire class.'

'Most of them are members of the university's Socialist Society, everybody from respected PASOK student members to Marxists and anarchists on the extreme left.'

'They're an interesting bunch. The older men and women, the ones in their mid-thirties, they'd be old for undergraduates in England.'

'Those guys are perpetual students, they're our heroes. They barricaded themselves in the university in November '73, the time the Junta sent a tank crashing through the main entrance.'

'I vaguely remember reading about it.'

'Some of their friends were killed, many were injured, many went into hiding. A few became politicians after the military government was overthrown the following year.'

'I spoke to a couple, can't remember their names.' He laughed. 'They weren't impressed with my working for an American drilling company in Libya.'

'The society is a broad church, but we're all conflicted one way or another. I am an activist but my parents are seen as wealthy capitalists, owning tankers that carry Libyan crude across the Med.' She paused. 'I'm still part of the group though, still accepted.'

He was reminded of her parents' shipping interests but surprised when she described herself as an activist, realising that there was so much he didn't know about her.

'An activist, what does that mean?'

'It's nothing really,' she said, offhandedly. 'I help out in one of the poorer districts of the city, you know, helping tenants deal with rogue landlords, ensuring people get their entitlements from corrupt local government officials, running food banks, that sort of thing.'

'You never cease to amaze me,' he said, quietly, 'and you still find time to go back to Benghazi.'

'You were certainly a big hit with my girlfriends last night,' she said, abruptly changing the subject.

'Hardly,' he laughed. 'I was telling them how much I enjoy

working in the Sahara. I said nothing about what happened in Cyrene of course, or how we met.'

'They've been pestering me too, although they've stopped now, thankfully.' She paused. 'You're still fair game though.'

'What do you mean, "fair game"?' he asked, a little worried.

'Any one of them would screw you if they'd half a chance.'

'Come on,' he laughed.

'It's true. They're good friends and I love them dearly but they'll do anything to bed you,' she said, grinning. 'Spike your drink, slip you their telephone numbers, even a pack of condoms. You should always check your pockets after a party like last night.'

He got out of bed and rummaged in his trouser pockets, pulling out a crumpled sheet of paper.

'This is new,' he said, handing it to her.

She flattened out the sheet, which was covered in dense Greek text, with several words and phrases heavily underlined.

'Notice anything here?' she asked, quietly.

'Good God, I can't read, never mind understand, Greek,' he said. 'Give me a clue.'

She pointed to the number 1117 underlined clearly in the text.

'So what?' he mumbled, baffled by its significance.

'A revolutionary group. The number refers to the final day of the '73 uprising against the Junta. It's a far-left militant group aimed at bringing down the government, getting Greece out of NATO and the US out of Greece.'

'What's it got to do with me?' asked Jack, alarmed at his innocence in the midst of so much intrigue.

'Possibly you're being put on notice because you work for a US company,' she said. 'But that's too obvious and misses the point. Whoever put this note in your pocket – and I think I know who it was – is sending you a message: "Don't trust Bushra, she's a member and could hurt you".'

'Bullshit, absolute rubbish,' he said, vehemently. 'But the group…'

37

'No, Jack,' she interjected, 'I'm not a member, I'm not a left-wing militant.'

'And the Americans, do you want them out of Greece, or Libya for that matter?' he asked, quietly.

'Jack, Jack,' she laughed, 'whatever my thoughts are on Libya, Greece, the US, they're irrelevant, they have no bearing on my love for you.'

*

Sunlight was beaming through the shutters when he woke again around eight. She had gone, leaving not a trace, as if her nocturnal presence had been a figment of his overwrought imagination. He had a long shower before going down for breakfast. The dining room was empty except for a young girl, maybe nine or ten years old, who was clearing the tables, suggesting that most of the guests were working people, up and away early.

The menu in Greek was incomprehensible so he decided to try his luck in a local coffee shop. Just as he was leaving, Bushra rushed out from the kitchen, surprising him.

'Jack, where are you going? You must have breakfast, here's an English menu,' she said, grabbing one from the sideboard.

'You work here?' he asked, incredulously.

'With Chara,' she said, indicating the girl, 'Yannis' daughter. At nine she goes off to school, I'm free at ten. I don't have any lectures today so we have the time to ourselves,' she said, happily. 'Don't worry, I'm not deserting you.'

He failed to see why she would want to work in this small, rather insignificant hotel, or work at all for that matter. She was a nineteen-year-old university student, daughter of wealthy parents, with her own apartment. This was not the time and place, however, to get to the bottom of this latest twist in her multi-layered existence.

Ten minutes later she returned with a large tray: freshly made coffee, warm croissants, apricot jam, a bowl of natural yogurt and a plate of fruit – peaches, figs, dates.

'I suspect you're hungry,' she grinned. 'We need to keep your stamina up.'

'What time did you leave?'

'Five, we start work at five.' Before he had time to say anything, she continued, gaily, 'I'm afraid I can't stay to keep you company, you know, no fraternising with the guests.' Then, dropping her voice conspiratorially, 'Of course there's no rule about sharing your bed provided we're discrete.'

And with that she left. Alone in the dining room, his brain unpicked every minute of their time together since he'd arrived at the hotel. He was completely smitten by her – a loving, feisty, enigmatic young woman, full of surprises which constantly threw him off balance.

Last night he had crossed a threshold; he had never declared his love for anybody, not even Charlotte, to whom he was unofficially engaged. He was very fond of Charlotte but she'd morphed into an old mate with whom one occasionally has sex. His few days with her in London over Christmas hadn't been great, but they hadn't been all bad either.

Throughout his leave, Charlotte had maintained the dialogue of their relationship, talking about where they might live, what sort of jobs they would have, how many kids – the whole scope of middle-class angst. He had listened dutifully, careful to conceal his rising anxiety. He promised to take her on a decent European holiday in the spring, suspecting that she inferred from this that he might formally propose to her then.

'I'll meet you out the front at ten,' Bushra called from the half-open kitchen door. 'Bring a waterproof, something warm, we're going to Glyfada, to walk the beach. It'll be wet and windy.' The door banged shut.

*

She drove furiously along the seafront as the wind and rain buffeted the car.

'There's your apartment,' he said, as they flew past an elegant 1960s building.

'Was my apartment.'

'Was your apartment?'

'My parents decided I needed to experience how ordinary people live.'

'So that's why you're working in the hotel?'

'No, that was my idea,' she said. 'I moved there the day they sold the place. They think I'm staying in university accommodation; give me a small monthly allowance, a lot less than it used to be, to cover the costs.'

'Have you fallen out with them?' he asked, suddenly realising that perhaps he might have had a part in all this.

'This has nothing to do with you, with us,' she said, reading his thoughts. 'It suits the life I lead, is more in tune with the people I meet.' She paused. 'I can come and go as I please, am accountable to nobody except Yannis.'

Without warning, she pulled the car over into a vacant space facing the beach, gritty sand streaking down the windscreen. She turned to face him. He was startled to see her eyes welling up.

'Bushra, Bushra,' he said, putting his arm around her, pulling her to his chest. She slumped against him, the tension in her body slowly easing. 'What's the matter?' he asked eventually.

She sat back and looked steadily at him.

'Last summer while I was in Benghazi on holiday from university, Abdullah asked me if I could help him.'

'On his farm?'

'Oh, Jack, I love your innocence,' she laughed gently, wiping a single tear away with the back of her hand. 'Abdullah, unknown to my parents, helps many of his old acquaintances and their families in the Tolmeta area, you know, people who are suffering under the regime.'

Suddenly things started to fall into place: why Abdullah wanted him out of the Benamer compound, why she apparently visited Benghazi yet they couldn't meet there.

'Back in August my parents were worried that I might fall for you. They were too late as it happened,' she said, her old spark never far from the surface. 'However, Abdullah was the real reason you had to leave my father's house. He was concerned that you might get caught up in our work. In his own way, he was protecting you.'

'Bushra, this is crazy, you're a student,' he protested. 'Your whole life's ahead of you. When you're not working or studying, you're helping the poor and destitute in Athens. How much can you give of yourself?'

'Life's not so simple for people like us.' She paused. 'I love you, Jack. I have never met anybody before who I can completely open up to, somebody who I can trust with my life.'

He was flattered and terrified in equal measure.

'How can you be sure?'

'I am, Jack, I am.'

'So, your visits to Benghazi are to see…'

'Yes,' she cut in. 'Initially, Abdullah asked me to act as a courier, you know, conveying messages, carrying cash and small parcels between Athens and Benghazi. Coming from a family still regarded by the regime, I can travel in and out with relative ease.'

'But your thesis you were working on when we met…'

'I'm still working on it, but it's also a useful cover now, allowing me to come and go without drawing attention,' she admitted. 'Soon Abdullah had me organise clandestine shipments of books, computers, radios, medical supplies and other essential items, items only available in Libya to the regime's leaders. All this stuff arrives in containers marked as equipment for the oil industry.'

'I knew the pair of you were slightly mad,' he said, grimly, 'but this, this is lunacy. What if you get caught?'

'Things have got more difficult, more dangerous, recently,' she continued, ignoring his question. 'The country has become

41

increasingly unstable since last year's failed coup. The leaders have turned their vitriol on the outside world to distract the population.'

'A classic ploy,' said Jack.

'Exactly,' she continued. 'Relationships with the West, especially with the Americans, are deteriorating rapidly. Everybody is waiting for something really bad, really catastrophic to happen.'

'I'm aware of this. It's starting to affect how we operate there. It's not good.'

'The latest shipment I organised included light arms, munitions, that sort of thing. I had to meet a couple of very unpleasant men here in town, international arms dealers.'

'God almighty,' he exclaimed. 'I just wish there was some way I could help. I feel so bloody useless. My life's so pathetic compared to yours.'

'Don't go there, Jack.' She paused. 'There's one way you can help though.'

'Yes?'

'Just be there for me, Jack. Trust me, love me,' she said, quietly.

He leaned across and gently kissed her. In the silence that followed, the wind intensified, rocking the car, while the rain drummed relentlessly on the roof.

'I don't think a walk is a great idea,' she said brightly, changing the subject. 'I'm getting cold. Let's get a coffee and warm up.'

'Excellent,' he said, relieved that they could move onto something more mundane.

'I'll take you back to the café near my old apartment. I've good friends there. It's noisy but discrete.'

Ten minutes later they ran through gale force winds to the smoky steamed-up café, full of soaked walkers sheltering from the storm. Bushra was greeted by the owner, an ageless, elegant woman, with much laughter and gesticulation.

'I was out of order earlier, you know, questioning you about the Americans,' he said, after they'd settled down with their coffees. 'I'm sorry, it just came out all wrong.'

'This is difficult for you,' Bushra said, quietly. 'You must understand, I am proud to be Libyan, I love Greece, but I am not a nationalist, if that makes any sense.'

'Sort of,' he said, struggling to understand her.

'What really motivates me, what I'm constantly struggling to do, is to help the downtrodden, the oppressed – the destitute in the slums of Athens, those suffering in Libya, whomever, wherever.'

'I think what you do is incredible.'

She reached across the table and took his hands.

'Who knows what the future holds. Today's tyrants, corrupt Greek governments, Libya's dictatorship, the Americans; all these players one day will be swept away and we'll be faced with another bloody lot of dishonest leaders and nothing will change.'

'What a depressing thought,' he said, 'but who'll follow this lot?'

'I'm convinced it'll be the Russians.'

'Russia,' he exclaimed.

'Consider Syria, through which much of Iraq's crude is pumped to the Med,' she continued. 'It's been under the thumb of Moscow for decades. It's only a matter of time before Russia will start to squeeze Turkey, put more pressure on neighbouring countries.'

'I hadn't really thought about it.'

'And we'll all get dragged in. It's all part of a long-term plan to control the eastern Med, the ports and pipelines exporting Iraqi crude and ultimately the reserves themselves.'

'Not in our lifetime,' laughed Jack uneasily, not fully convinced by what he'd said.

'Maybe, but whoever'll govern these countries in the future, whether by popular mandate or dictatorship, there'll always be people at the bottom of society, suffering, needing help.'

*

The next five days, every minute of which they spent together outside her early morning shift and occasional lecture, passed quickly. As much as they could, they turned their backs on the outside world, as the belligerent rhetoric between Libya and the US intensified, casting a shadow over their relationship.

At the end of his leave, Jack had great difficulty getting back through Benghazi airport, where he was treated with the utmost suspicion. Like many expatriates, he had had some good and some bad experiences with the border police; now suddenly they all seemed to despise him.

After a short evening meeting with Shultz, he returned to his bleak, featureless apartment and went through his mail. He was surprised to see a letter from Bushra, a rare event in itself given the postal system, and given that he had only left her that morning. She had written it the day they'd been in Glyfada, reiterating her love for him and urging him to have courage in their relationship.

There were two letters from Charlotte, the most recent of which was postmarked five days earlier; he chose to read this first. Her opening line was so shocking, he screamed with anger and frustration, ripping up the paper and letting the pieces fall to the floor like confetti. Eventually he calmed down and reassembled the letter on the kitchen table.

Dear Jack,

I have wonderful news; I am nearly three months pregnant!! The other day, our family doctor, Dr Grace, told me that our baby is due at the end of September.

Mummy and Daddy were a little shocked at first but they are thrilled now at the prospect of being grandparents. Of course they said we need to get married as soon as possible. We agreed that shotgun weddings are quite fashionable in London these days, not the terrible stigma they used to be!

They will help with all the arrangements including paying for everything… they know you are permanently broke, ha, ha.

The letter went on in her usual self-absorbed manner: setting a provisional date for the wedding, her parents' venue suggestions, who would be her bridesmaids, who she should confide in. After several more paragraphs of indulgent rubbish, she finally wrote:

I am sorry you're not here with me in London to share our exciting news. Your boss will no doubt give you the extra leave you'll need for the wedding, our honeymoon etc.

Wherever you are in that wretched country, I hope you are well. I know you are missing me and will be in touch, one way or another, as soon as you read my letter.
Lots of love,
Charlotte.

PS I see in the papers the Americans are getting very angry with Libya, so they should be!!

Jack slumped to the floor, crying like a child.

5

London, December 1986

The flight from London to Athens had been delayed by nearly four hours. Atrocious weather over the Alps had closed many airports in central Europe, leading to widespread delays in the UK. Jack was booked on the return flight to London which was not due to depart now until nearly nine. He'd be lucky to get to Primrose Hill by three the following morning.

Unknown to Charlotte, he had spent several days in Athens before heading home for an extended break over Christmas and the New Year. Bushra had dropped him out to the airport earlier in the afternoon; seeing her driving off into the gloomy smog had left him devastated.

He retired to the bar, ordered a large whisky and downed it in one. With another one to hand, he retreated to a quiet corner. Without any doubt, his life had become an unmitigated disaster. He was flying home to a loveless marriage to meet his three-month-old son for the first time, and for whom he hadn't the remotest sentiment. His complete lack of feelings for Charlotte and Tom appalled and frightened him.

From an early age, Jack had craved a conventional, comfortable middle-class existence; a loving wife and kids that he could bond with, given that his own childhood had lacked so much warmth and stability.

Since working in North Africa and meeting Bushra, he'd had some of the happiest and most stimulating times of his life; the life he'd once sought was now an anathema. But because of his earlier cowardice and inertia, he'd become trapped in a cobweb of deceit and conventionality, now powerless to change the course of events. Twelve months earlier, while he was on leave in London, Charlotte had become pregnant. Determined that they should get married, she had outwitted him by coming off the pill without his consent – the oldest trick in the book.

After a bitter exchange of letters in the spring, he agreed that they'd get married during his next leave at the beginning of August, seven or eight weeks before the baby was due. The wedding was a nightmare. Within hours of arriving, he'd been unceremoniously rushed off to a brief ceremony in a London registry office. The reception, in an overrated hotel in Wimbledon, was a riotous and drink-fuelled affair, reminiscent of a Hogarth painting. And there, centre stage, was an obviously pregnant Charlotte, radiant in her defiance. While she and her parents had gathered a large group of relatives and friends, Jack had invited his only sibling, Peter, an eccentric Church of Ireland vicar from a remote parish in the west of Ireland. To his credit, Peter did Jack proud, making up for friends that he was too ashamed to ask.

Claiming that if he didn't return immediately to Benghazi his job was at risk, Jack had excused himself from the planned weeklong celebrations and left London the following day. Nobody, least of all his new wife, seemed unduly concerned by his departure. He hadn't been back to London since, promising Charlotte that he'd take an extended leave over Christmas to be with her and Tom.

All this had taken place against an unfolding political crisis engulfing Libya, just as Bushra had predicted on a cold, wet day in Glyfada back in March, when everybody had been anxiously waiting for some catastrophic event to overtake the country. In the middle of April, days after several US servicemen were killed by a bomb in a Berlin nightclub, the US Air Force retaliated, bombing key targets in Tripoli. The country went into lockdown.

*

The public address system came to life, bringing Jack to his senses. British Airways was pleased to inform its long-suffering passengers, who were waiting to travel back to the UK on the return flight, that its aircraft had finally left London and was now due in Athens at nine-fifteen.

I must call Charlotte, he thought, *she still thinks I'll be getting home around ten.* He got a handful of change from the barman, who pointed out the phone booths at the end of the departure hall.

'Charlotte, hello, this is me, Jack,' he shouted down the crackling line, as if shouting would make any difference.

'Jack, darling, the line's dreadful,' came the distant reply. 'I can hardly hear you. Where are you? I thought you'd be in the air by now. We're all expecting you later this evening.'

Who the hell's 'all'? he wondered, vainly hoping she wasn't throwing one of her infamous drink's party; there wouldn't be a man or woman left standing by the time he got there.

'I've been delayed in Athens, the weather's…'

'Athens? What are you doing in Athens?'

'The few direct flights from Benghazi for the week before Christmas were booked up ages ago,' he lied, inwardly cursing himself. 'Athens is one of the better connections.'

'What time will you get here?'

'Could be three, three-thirty tomorrow morning, maybe later.'

'Three-thirty,' she shouted down the line. 'Three-thirty, Jack, everyone will have left by then.'

'Everyone?'

'A small group of our friends, just to welcome you home for Christmas.'

'I'm really sorry. It was difficult enough getting to…'

'It's Jack,' she shouted to somebody at her end. 'He's stuck in Athens, mightn't be back till after three.' There was a pause. He strained to hear her muffled voice, guessing she had her hand over the mouthpiece. 'Yes, that's what I asked him, something about full flights.' Another pause. 'Of course you must all stay, the night's young yet.'

'Charlotte.'

'Sorry, darling,' she said clearly now. 'I was just telling everyone that you'll be late and not to worry. We'll be here waiting for you. Have a safe flight, bye for now.' The line went dead.

*

The taxi dropped him outside Charlotte's parents' vast Victorian terraced house in Primrose Hill, North London at three-fifty in the morning. He and Charlotte lived in the large garden flat, where all the lights appeared to be on. The rest of the house was in darkness. Her parents had both taken early retirement from well-paid jobs in the City and now spent most of their time in their villa in the hills above Nice. It wouldn't be long, he thought, before his wife took possession of the entire house, something she'd been pressing for since the day they were married.

He found the key in the usual place and noiselessly entered the flat to be confronted by a large note, scribbled in garish red lipstick on the hall mirror.

Welcome home, darling, you're in the spare room, I'm in our room with the cot… DON'T disturb us! I suggest you DON'T go into the living room… a few friends are staying the night. See you at breakfast xx

He tiptoed to his room, a cacophony of snoring and grunting emanating from the living room; the smell like a pub at closing time, laced with a hint of marijuana. *God*, he thought, *what a bloody nightmare this Christmas is going to be*. Numb with exhaustion and too much whisky, he sprawled out on the bed fully clothed and instantly fell asleep.

He awoke to the sound of shouting and laughter. His head was pounding, his throat parched. The thought of having to stand around over endless cups of coffee trying to be sociable with Charlotte's bunch of boisterous friends was too much. He undressed, got into bed and pulled the covers over his head, feigning sleep. Minutes later, he heard the bedroom door open.

'He's here, Lotte,' a man's voice whispered, none too quietly.

'Leave him be,' said another. 'He must be knackered after all that travelling.'

'And whisky,' said Charlotte, her voice clearly recognisable. 'It's like a distillery in there.'

And with that, he heard the door close.

The next time he woke, the flat was deathly quiet. He checked his watch, surprised to see that it was one-thirty in the afternoon. He guessed that he'd slept for over four hours, that they'd given up on him and gone out for lunch.

His thoughts turned to Bushra and the last few hours he'd been with her in Athens. Despite his woeful predicament, he took heart from what she'd said to him on the way to the airport. She told him she didn't care 'whether you're somebody else's husband, somebody else's father, all I know is that I love you and trust you with my life'. What an extraordinary thing to say, he remembered thinking at the time. And finally, just as he was getting out of the car, she declared, 'Remember we'll always be there for each other. You must do what you have to do in London, that's your business. Go now. Take courage from our love.'

*

Their relationship had barely survived after the country had gone into lockdown following the US bombing of Tripoli in April. Shultz had insisted at the time that Jack extend his three-week work schedule in the desert by at least two weeks until things got back to normal, whatever that meant in Libya. Eventually he took his week's local leave at the beginning of May and, with great difficulty, got a return flight to Athens.

When they'd met in the George, Bushra had shown little surprise when he told her that Charlotte was pregnant and that a wedding date had been set for August.

'I knew one day this would happen,' she'd said without any bitterness. 'You told me about Charlotte in the hospital in Tolmeta shortly after we met. There's never been any question in my mind that she was to be your wife,' she said, before adding with a grin, 'although I didn't think it would happen this way.'

He acknowledged that he hadn't expected this either, admitting that the thought of marriage to anybody, least of all Charlotte, had been way down on his list of priorities back in March.

Arriving back in Athens in early August after his wedding, he'd felt even less well disposed towards Charlotte, their unborn child and her plans for their future together than he had ever been. The whole charade had happened so quickly, he'd almost convinced himself that it was simply a bad dream. It certainly didn't change the way he felt about Bushra or her feelings for him.

Tom was born nearly four weeks early, at the beginning of September. Charlotte, who had the undivided attention of her doting parents, was quite happy for Jack to wait until Christmas before he got home again, on the understanding that he would be on extended leave.

Throughout the autumn, Jack had more pressing worries. At the start of each local leave, Bushra would drive him straight to the family villa in Stoupa in the Peloponnese where they'd stay until he was due to fly back to Benghazi. At first Jack felt she was avoiding her parents, hardly surprising given that they'd fallen out months ago. It was only in November that she'd admitted she had been warned that Libyan agents had been asking about her in Athens.

She told him that she'd stopped visiting Benghazi for the time being and was only safe now on the university campus or working in the George. Outside these two sanctuaries, she felt vulnerable. Jack had been shocked by the news, realising just how involved she'd become in helping Abdullah with his clandestine operation in Libya. She wanted nothing from Jack, just his love and support.

*

He pulled on his trousers and left the bedroom. Another message had been scrawled on the mirror.

Have booked a table for one-thirty in the Engineer, the party continues without you! xx

He had no choice; it was now time to face everybody. Having showered and dressed in fresh clothes, he drank a large black coffee and set off for the pub, a fifteen-minute walk along the canal. What a bizarre place to meet his son, Tom, for the first time, he thought– in a noisy pub with a bunch of his mother's fancy friends. What chance of a normal, healthy life did the poor little sod have?

His worst fears were realised as soon as he pushed his way into the crowded bar. In a smoky haze, he could make out Charlotte's party, a group of ten or twelve gathered around a couple of tables. He recognised a few faces from their wedding in August, mostly her friends from university and her cousin Sally and her husband, but nobody that he had been close to. There was no sign of a pram.

'Jack,' shouted Sally, the first to see him, 'you've made it.'

Charlotte got to her feet, rushed over and threw her arms around him, smothering him in the process. He noticed that she had put on weight since the wedding, her once clear complexion now puffy, perhaps a sign of unhealthy living, he guessed. She was only slightly shorter than him and had been a good athlete in university; they'd been well suited, or so he'd thought when they first met.

'Jack, darling, how are you? How was your flight? How's the head? We've missed you.' Her words poured out as she hung onto him. She was barely sober. He quickly realised she wasn't alone.

They all staggered to their feet in a great shuffling mass, full of merriment, and greeted Jack, knocking over several glasses in the process.

'Where's Tom? Who's got him?' shouted Charlotte to nobody in particular, as she released Jack. 'He must meet his dad.'

Jack's heart sank.

Sally emerged from the crowd, cradling his son, whom she passed to him rather formally.

'Your son and heir, Jack,' she said. 'He's utterly adorable, just like his dad,' she added with a wink. Of all Charlotte's friends, he'd always had a soft spot for Sally and she for him. He gazed down at Tom, two frightened eyes silently peering up at him. Without warning, his little body stiffened and he let out a piercing shriek, the likes of which Jack hadn't heard before; he froze, unsure what to do.

'Let me have him,' Sally said quietly, reaching out for the bundle that was his son. Fortunately, she didn't drink and had always been there to pick up the pieces when Charlotte had gone off on one of her prolonged benders.

'Sally's terrific with him,' laughed Charlotte. 'He loves her, more than his mother, I suspect.' Turning to the others, she shouted, 'Somebody, get Jack a drink, a pint of Guinness in case you'd forgotten.' Then to Jack, 'We're all having burgers and chips. We've ordered the same for you. It'll be a nice change from your rotten desert rations.'

She grasped his hand and pulled him into the middle of the group, forcing a space for them on a wooden bench.

'How are you managing in the desert?'

'Is it worth leaving London for?'

'Is it worth the money?'

'What the hell's Libya up to?'

The questions rolled over him, too quickly for him to reply, from people not in the least bit interested in what he had to say. Soon the conversation reverted to the latest rugby and football results, distant race meetings, what certain jobs were worth in the City – their usual Sunday lunch pub banter.

'Bet you can't get one of these out there,' said a gaunt man with deeply etched dark eyes, as he pushed a pint of Guinness across the table.

'Sadly, no,' said Jack. 'Thanks…'

'It's Harry. We knew each other at uni. I studied business and commercial law with Charlotte,' he said, before adding, 'I was at your wedding.'

'Of course, I thought I recognised you,' Jack said awkwardly, realising with a start how drastically this man Harry had aged. 'The wedding went by in a bit of a haze,' he laughed. 'I've lost touch with so many old university friends since I left, the real downside of working abroad.'

'Why not work in London?' asked the woman on his right. 'You were quite the party man in your day.'

He looked at her blankly.

'It's Jenny,' Harry said. 'She was with Charlotte and me. We all studied together.'

'God, I'm sorry, Jenny,' Jack said, colour rising in his cheeks. 'You got a First I seem to remember.'

'We don't discuss that crap anymore,' she said brightly, unexpectedly squeezing his thigh. 'Life's moved on, it's more fun now.'

An intelligent but unsettling woman, a natural blonde who turned heads. As a student, she'd been relentlessly on the prowl for a wealthy husband; judging by the rings on her very white fingers, she'd succeeded.

With a great flourish, lunch arrived, waitresses coming in from all sides with plates of burgers and enormous bowls of chips. Jack breathed a sigh of relief as everyone's attention turned to their food. As another Guinness magically appeared in front of him, he quietly resigned himself to a drunken afternoon of infinite weariness.

*

'Pete, it's Jack.'

'Jack, good heavens, man, you must be in the UK,' exclaimed Peter. 'We – George and I – were only talking about you the other day. How the hell are you?'

'Well, thank God and you?'

'Can't complain. Still have a decent job at the old firm and holding my place on the squash ladder at Lord's. Are you still prospecting in the Sahara? You're a tough old bugger if you are.'

'Yes,' said Jack, laughing, 'although I'm hardly a tough old bugger. I'm just not ready for an office job, maybe I'll never be.'

'You're in London?'

'For another week.'

'Listen, Jack, I can't talk now, I've got to go, got a meeting in Fitzroy Square at ten. Let's have a drink some evening before the New Year,' Peter said. 'I'll see if George can join us. We play squash every week. I'll try Freddy as well, although we don't see much of him these days.'

'It would be great to catch up with you all.'

'We'd love to hear about your adventures in Libya,' said Peter. 'What about the Crown on Cromwell Road at eight on Wednesday evening? It's usually where George and I meet.'

'Great, I'll see you there.'

Just as the line went dead, he heard Charlotte at the front door.

'Who was that?' she said, breezing into the hall, pushing the pram ahead of her.

'Peter, you might remember him, we studied geology together. I'm meeting him, George, possibly Freddy, another geologist, in the Crown on Wednesday evening.'

'I vaguely remember Freddy, nothing of the others though,' she said. 'I hardly knew your faculty lot, they were all a bit nerdy,' she laughed.

'Bright, I'd say,' he said, ignoring her gibe.

In one sense she was right though. While he'd made an effort to get to know her friends in university, she'd never ceased reminding him that economics or commercial law were the way to riches and success. She only really wanted to be surrounded by like-minded people, those seeking glamorous and highly paid jobs in the City.

*

It was a cold clear evening as he left Cromwell Road tube station. He was suddenly reminded of his time at Imperial, happy carefree days, surrounded by like-minded people in one of the best cities in the world.

Charlotte had encouraged him to go out for a drink with his friends – a tacit recognition that they'd been constantly in each other's company since the day he'd got back. Christmas had been horrendous, just as he had predicted. Her family, whom he had never really got on with for pretty obvious reasons, took over, organising every waking minute of the holiday period.

He and Charlotte were on amicable terms, with little pretence that they were wildly in love. While he could rationalise his barely modest feelings for her, he was uneasy about her apparent lack of interest in him. He stayed on in the spare room; to his relief, there was never the slightest suggestion that she wanted to sleep with him. In a strange way, their passionless relationship suited him.

As he approached the Crown, he still had no idea how he was going to tell his friends that he had a wife and a young baby; he certainly didn't feel married. Given that it was the week between Christmas and New Year, the bar was quiet and he soon made out Peter and George.

'Well, look who's here, it's great to see you, Jack,' said Peter, jumping to his feet and giving him a bear hug.

'Look at the pair of you, you've hardly aged,' Jack laughed.

'It's my call,' said George, getting to his feet. 'A Guinness, I presume, Jack.'

'Thanks, you've a good memory.'

'You're the only one I've ever known who drinks the stuff,' said George, with a big smile. 'How could I forget?'

'So, you're still with the old firm?' Jack turned to Peter, as George wandered off to the bar.

'I'm leading an investment team specialising in Russia, a modest promotion from my post-grad training days.'

'Good for you. You were always going places, clever sod,' laughed Jack. 'And George, what about him?'

'He works for me, happiest when he's away off in Siberia poking around in the field. He's a bloody good geologist, fanatical about his job, always straining to get away from Fitzroy Square.'

They chatted of this and that in the easy familiarity that's only possible between old friends, giving Jack the weird feeling he'd only been away on a week's holiday.

'Do you think we were a nerdy lot, you know, when we were in college?' he asked, remembering what Charlotte had said a few days earlier.

'Nerdy, no, reasonably bright, yes,' said Peter. 'I mean, we had a life outside lectures, especially you, as I recall,' he said, a twinkle in his eye. 'Why do you ask?'

'It's nothing really,' said Jack. 'But you're right, we did have a life, a great life, in college.'

Soon George appeared with the drinks.

'Guinness for our man from the desert, best bitter for us mortals,' he said, setting the tray down on the table.

'To us, who are still alive, still making a living as geologists,' said Peter, raising his glass.

'To us,' from the other two in unison.

And so they talked on, of what it was like working with the old firm, living in London, trying to balance work and raising a young family.

'Enough of us,' said Peter, abruptly. 'And what about you? Are you married yet? What's it like working in Libya?'

'Let me get a round in first,' said Jack, playing for time. 'Same again?'

He returned a few minutes later, drinks on a tray.

'Good luck,' he said, raising his glass. 'I think the last time we met was just before Christmas, two years ago. I'd been working with an oil and gas consultancy.'

'I remember,' said George. 'You took off in a hell of a hurry.'

'My boss's daughter was given the job I'd been promised, so I thought, sod you lot. The following March I started with an American company in Libya, prospecting in the Sirte Basin.'

'Which is where exactly?'

'South of Benghazi, nearly 500 kilometres from the coast,' said Jack. 'I've been working there, three weeks on, one week off, for quite a while now.'

'My God, man, you're a glutton for punishment,' said Peter.

'Actually, I really enjoy it.'

And so he regaled them with his stories, avoiding any mention of Bushra, Charlotte and his unhappy marriage.

'Jack!' a voice boomed from across the bar.

'About bloody time, Freddy,' said Peter. 'Jack's been telling us harrowing tales of working in the desert.'

Unlike the other two, who had kept fit and trim, Freddy, once a fine squash player, had turned decidedly rotund, reflecting his high-paying City job, one which no doubt Charlotte would have approved of.

Peter ordered another round and then George again, followed

by Freddy, then Jack once more, their stories becoming more colourful as the evening wore on. *God*, thought Jack, his head spinning, *I'm completely out of practice for these sessions*, suddenly realising how their lives had diverged from their time together in university.

'Talking of dropouts, I bumped into that old bastard Harry a few months ago, drunk as a lord,' said Freddy. 'The man's a shadow of his former self.'

Jack shivered involuntarily, the mention of Harry making him feel slightly nauseous.

'We hardly knew the man,' George said, 'too fancy for the likes of us.'

'I'd heard recently on the grapevine that his family had thrown him out, disinherited him,' Peter said, 'something to do with his heroin addiction.'

'You're right, not that it stopped him from getting some bird pregnant, boasting that they'd recently had a son,' Freddy laughed. 'He admitted she wouldn't marry him, which hardly bothered him. He's still screwing her though, she paying for their habit. A contract made in heaven, he said.'

Jack felt his throat constrict, his insides heave.

'Fortunately for Harry she comes from a wealthy family. I think her name's Charlotte.' Freddy paused. 'Didn't you go out with a Charlotte once, Jack? Hardly your type, this one, by the sound of it,' he added with a grin.

Jack dropped his half-finished pint, which smashed on the floor, and rushed to the gents, hand over mouth. He managed to get to the nearest cubicle before falling on his knees and vomiting breathlessly into the bowl. He wretched till his gut was empty; salty tears streamed down his face. He could hardly breathe, his nostrils blocked with vomit.

As his head cleared, all he could think of was Charlotte, how the bitch had used him, deceived him. *There's no way Tom had been born four weeks early. He'd arrived right on time, conceived while he himself was still in the desert.* Slowly he regained his composure, his anger like cold steel cutting through his soul. After what seemed like many minutes, he felt a hand on his shoulder.

'Jack,' Peter said, quietly. 'Jack, are you OK?'

'I'll be fine,' grunted Jack, 'just give me a minute. I need to clean up. I'm in a bit of a mess.'

'Take your time. I'll wait here for you, there's no hurry.'

Ten minutes later, the two men returned to the bar. The broken glass had been swept up. Four large tumblers of whisky had replaced the standing army of empty pint glasses.

'God, I'm sorry, Jack,' Freddy said, as he stood to welcome him back to his seat. 'I'd no idea.'

'Forget it, you couldn't possibly have known, none of you,' Jack said awkwardly. 'What's truly shocking is that she'd written to me in March telling me she was pregnant, insisting that I was responsible and to man up.'

'You married her,' exclaimed Peter.

'In August, it was an awful day, the worst of my life. I was too embarrassed to ask you guys. Only my brother came.' He paused. 'Tom was born in September. We're complete strangers.'

The others stared at him in disbelief.

'You poor bastard, Jack,' whispered Peter, 'you poor old bastard.'

6

Stoupa, February 1987

J ack woke to the sound of muffled voices. The room was in near total darkness and bitterly cold. He reached out under the heavy quilt; the bed was empty. Just then, the door opened and he briefly caught sight of Bushra's silhouette in the hallway light.

'It was Hera,' she said quietly. 'She's gone now.'

'What time is it?'

'Six-thirty.'

'God, it's early,' he exclaimed.

'Her mother sends her every morning with fresh bread. Sometimes she brings honey, maybe olives, occasionally a bowl of home-made yogurt.'

'The poor kid, she was here till after ten last night. Does she get any sleep?'

'Her mother's been my parents' housekeeper for years. Hera will take her place someday.'

'The kid's only, what, nine, ten? How can you be so sure?' he laughed. 'She needs to live the life of a child.'

'Jack, Jack,' Bushra whispered, as she dropped her robe and got into bed. 'This is how many families live in these parts, don't knock it.'

'It's the mid-'80s, for heaven's sake.'

'So what?'

'I'm sorry,' he said quietly, reaching out to her naked body, all other thoughts erased.

'You're insatiable, Jack Meredith,' she mumbled, as he drew her to him.

'And you're adorable, Bushra Benamer.'

*

'We've run out of diesel oil,' Bushra said, as she was swept through the kitchen door by a cold easterly wind howling across the sea. 'No wonder the heating wasn't on when we got here last night.'

'Can we arrange for a delivery?' asked Jack.

'Hera will drop by shortly on her way to school. She'll ask her dad, who delivers oil. We should have it before it gets dark.'

'God, it's cold,' he grimaced. 'How do your parents survive in the winter here?'

'They stop coming down in October and only open the place up again in March or April, depending on how early spring is. You must be hungry.'

'Starving.'

'I'll make porridge, it's great with honey and yogurt,' she said, busying herself in the spotlessly clean kitchen. 'We need warming up.'

Soon they were huddled at one end of a vast scrubbed oak table, coarse Berber blankets pulled over their shoulders, feasting on porridge, warm bread, cheese and olives.

'The sky's due to clear shortly,' said Bushra. 'I bet there's snow on the mountains above the village.'

'Snow in the Peloponnese?'

'We get snow in southern Greece every six or eight years. My mother told me she once skied into Syntagma Square in the centre of Athens,' she grinned. 'Even high ground in Cyrenaica gets snow. The Jebel Akhdar has been covered a couple of times in the last five years.'

'I've so much to learn.'

'Indeed you do, Jack,' she laughed, 'indeed you do.'

After they cleared everything away, they retreated with a pot of fresh coffee to the large spacious living room. The place was simply but tastefully furnished, with comfortable soft leather chairs, beautiful Berber rugs scattered on the tiled floor, books stacked precariously in long low bookcases, and several seriously valuable Impressionist originals hanging on the white walls.

Jack was drawn to the patio doors, running the full width of the room, from where there were panoramic views over well-manicured winter gardens to the bay beyond. As the last remnants of cloud whipped across the sky, the sun picked out waves crashing onto the village beach.

'God this place is beautiful. How can your parents leave it even in the depths of winter?'

'Work, they work, Jack. Perhaps when they retire, they'll spend more time here, but they'll also want to be in Athens and, from time to time, Benghazi.'

She poured the coffee and settled back on one of the settees, legs tucked under her body, cocooned in the Berber blanket.

'Come and sit down,' she said quietly. 'I need to talk to you. There are things we should discuss.'

His heart skipped a beat as he took his coffee and sat beside her.

'Is there a problem?' he asked, nervously.

'Two days after you left for Benghazi at the end of January, I followed you. I only got back to Athens the day before yesterday.'

'Bushra, Bushra,' he exclaimed, turning to face her, 'I thought you'd decided against going back, to stay here, lie low until you were sure Libyan agents had stopped looking for you.'

'To hell with them,' she said, abruptly, 'life's too short to hide away and not get on with what has to be done. Abdullah needs me, his people need him, I had to get started again. Besides, I miss Cyrenaica, the winter light on the jebel, the early promise of spring, exploring ancient Cyrene and Tolmeta with Abdullah, trying to put some form on my dissertation.' She paused, looking directly at him. 'It would have been so much more fun with you there.'

'You know I worry about you, am constantly thinking of you,' he said quietly. 'I couldn't bear it if anything happened to you.'

'Jack, you must understand,' she continued, gently, 'I am part Senussi, a child of the desert. I am, and always will be, drawn back to Cyrenaica, to my father's family, my people.'

'I'm beginning to see that now.'

'The regime's leaders, their tribes,' she continued, 'they're Bedouin from Tripolitania, from the barren coastal flatlands to the west, from Sirte, Misrata. They don't represent us. We Senussi in Cyrenaica are a proud people with a long tradition of independence,' she said with passion. 'We fought the French, the British in Egypt and Sudan in World War I and then the Italian colonialists in Cyrenaica. You will have heard of Omar Mukhtar. We fought the Nazis and Italian Fascists on behalf of the British.'

They sat in silence gazing out over the wild sun-flecked sea. It slowly dawned on Jack that this was only a preamble to what she really wanted to say, what was really on her mind.

'After you left the last time, you set me thinking about what you told me when we were here together,' she said, after a lengthy pause.

With great clarity, he remembered the moment when he'd had to admit to her that he was not Tom's father, that he'd been cuckolded; a feeling of abject inadequacy descended on him again. At the time, she was vehemently angry, not with him, but with Charlotte, describing her as a thief in the night, somebody who'd stolen his identity.

'Which was what exactly?'

'I kept going over and over in my head that you had a son, not of your own choosing, not of your own making.' She paused. 'I believed, and still do, that something had been stolen from you, something very special, something unique to you.'

'Unique?'

'Your identity.'

Of course she's right, he thought, *but why raise this whole woeful episode again and why now?* He got to his feet and wandered to the window, looking out over the bay. He suddenly felt profoundly depressed, the idea that the one and only person he had ever truly loved was now reopening fresh wounds. He turned to face her, unsure what to say.

'Jack, dearest Jack,' she whispered, 'please hear me out, try to understand. I love and will always love you, like no other person in my life.' She got up and went to him. Taking his hands in hers, she continued, 'I want you and I to create a future together, not in a conventional marriage sense, but in a bond that represents hope for the future, for Cyrenaica and especially for its people.'

'A bond?'

'I want us to have a child.'

'A child,' he exclaimed.

'A new soul that will bring out the best that we have to offer humanity, somebody that, with love and good luck, will shape a peaceful and prosperous destiny for that wretched land.'

Jack was speechless, completely thrown off balance.

7

Athens, January 1988

Jack spread the crumpled paper on the table. How strange, he thought, that this single sheet containing a simple handwritten note might be the key to the rest of his life. He ordered another coffee and reread the message for the umpteenth time.

Jack, I suggest you return to Athens as soon as possible… B in labour since yesterday evening in private clinic on Agrafon opposite Church of St Nicolas in Koukaki. She needs help. Your friend Abdullah.

So much had happened since Shultz had taken the envelope from a messenger in his Benghazi office early the previous morning. He knew about Bushra's pregnancy and had arranged for Jack, fresh from his leave in London over the New Year, to spend time in the office finalising a long overdue field report. This would give him the opportunity to get to Athens quickly when the need arose; the baby had been due in ten days' time.

Things were changing for both men; their American boss had been approached by the National Oil Company to extend their exploration work in the Sirte Basin for at least eighteen months. Shultz, who needed a break from Libya, was considering a posting in Oman. However, Jack now saw his own future bound up with that of Bushra, made infinitely more complicated by the arrival of their child.

There was much about the note that was worrying. Was her life or maybe the baby's life in jeopardy? What possible help could he provide other than being at her side? Why had she confided in Abdullah about her pregnancy, something she had resolutely withheld from her parents? And now Abdullah considered himself his friend, strange indeed.

Jack had flown into Athens at ten that morning and taken a taxi directly to the clinic. After a lengthy and incomprehensible consultation with people unknown, the receptionist had advised him to return at five in the evening. It was noon. With time on his hands, he'd taken a cab to the St George Hotel and booked a room for three nights. Yannis, as always, was delighted to see him, but because of his very poor English, had little to say except to ask generally after Bushra. Jack was thankful for this, given that he had no idea who was supposed to know what and how much about her situation.

It was now close to four and getting dark. The café he was sitting in was directly opposite the clinic, so he had a grandstand view of people arriving and leaving. Just as the streetlights came on, a large white chauffeur-driven saloon pulled up and an imposing middle-aged man got out before the car tore off into the evening traffic. For an instance, Jack thought he recognised Ali, Bushra's father, entering the building.

Whoever it was, Jack was getting paranoid, hugely frustrated at being so near to Bushra and yet so helpless. He tried to calm down, realising that he had no choice but to return to the clinic at the allotted time. He ordered another coffee, his fourth, hoping that the next hour would pass quickly.

His thoughts were disturbed by the same white saloon,

which drew up again outside the clinic. It was four-twenty. Nothing happened for several minutes, his curiosity rising. Then without warning, he saw the man he thought might have been Ali and two smartly dressed women of indeterminate age leave the clinic and get into the car. He noticed that the driver took what appeared to be a Moses basket from one of the women and placed it gently on the back seat. The whole episode took less than thirty seconds.

As time crawled agonisingly towards the hour, Jack convinced himself that it couldn't have been Ali; perhaps the group were grandparents taking their daughter and baby grandchild home.

Punctually at five, he entered the clinic and asked the receptionist if he could visit Bushra. After further lengthy consultations, she asked him to take a seat, that somebody would be with him in a few minutes. Nearly an hour later, a young nurse breezed in.

'Mr Meredith, please come with me.'

Dressed in a sombre grey uniform, she was the first person he'd seen who gave him any indication that he was in some sort of medical facility. After trekking up four floors and along a maze of corridors, the nurse stopped abruptly.

'Your friend has had a very difficult couple of days,' she said, quietly. 'She is on medication and may be sleepy. Don't be frightened if she doesn't recognise you.' She reached out and touched his arm. 'Ring reception on 010 if you need help.'

With that, Jack was shown into a dimly lit private suite. The door closed noiselessly behind him.

*

The previous June, he'd spent his week's leave in London, where he hadn't been since the New Year. Then in July, when on leave with Bushra in Stoupa, she'd told him that she was pregnant. Although she had known for some time, she'd kept the news to herself; with post to Benghazi haphazard at best, she'd decided to wait and tell him face to face.

He remembered when she told him, the numbing thought of parenthood, something he had never experienced on hearing about Tom. They discussed endlessly how they would bring up their child, the potential pitfalls they faced. He suggested that he should look for a job in Athens; she would have none of it.

As soon as she discovered that she was pregnant, she stopped going to Benghazi, stopped running clandestine errands for her uncle. Although initially she hadn't said a word to Abdullah about her pregnancy, she suspected that he knew. She had kept the news from her parents and her brother. Even Yannis had not been informed, although she said at the time that he would be the first to know if she was going to be able to keep a roof over her head.

Since August, the week they had together every month had been spent away from the family villa in Stoupa. One of her university friends let them stay in his small holiday apartment in Nafplio overlooking the Argolic Gulf on the north-east coast of the Peloponnese. She hadn't seen her parents for months; the only contact they had was the odd phone call she made to check that they were keeping well. The calls were friendly but short. With the possible exception of Hera, Jack suspected that nobody connected with the family in Greece would have known of her pregnancy.

Even as recently as their last time together in November, they hadn't decided on a plan for their future and that of their unborn child. The only thing they were certain of was that the baby was due in mid-January; the only thing they could agree on was the child's name: Stavros if he were a boy, Emma if she were a girl. Despite, or maybe because of, the precariousness of their situation, their days together were filled with magic. He never ceased to be amazed by her courage and pragmatism; nothing was going to stop her living life to the full.

This was all in stark contrast to his situation in London, where he'd spent a wretched Christmas and New Year with Charlotte and Tom. She barely acknowledged his presence, high on drugs or alcohol from morning to night. Her frequent mood swings between sullenness, hysteria, even suicidal at times, had slowly driven him mad. The only time he spent in the flat during the second week was to sleep. He saw virtually nothing of Tom, whose upbringing had been delegated to her parents. They clearly blamed him for their daughter's very obvious deterioration. Tom's reaction on seeing Jack was always the same; he simply screamed until Jack was out of sight.

It was only on his last evening that Jack fully understood what was going on when he met his old friend Peter for a drink. Apparently Freddy had heard that Harry, Charlotte's lover, had died quite recently under mysterious circumstances. Although word was put about that he'd had an overdose, Freddy believed it was suicide.

In his heart, he knew that in the not-too-distant future, there would have to be a day of reckoning. He would have to confront Charlotte about Harry, if for no other reason than to help her come to terms with his death.

As his eyesight became accustomed to the dimly lit room where he was about to meet Bushra and their baby, nothing in his life from now on, he realised, was going to be straightforward.

*

From a low light on the bedside table, he could make her out. She was lying back on a pillow, a thin cotton sheet pulled up under her chin, lacklustre eyes silently staring at him. He was unnerved, shocked at her appearance; it was as if he'd been confronted by a ghost.

'Bushra,' he whispered, 'my dearest Bushra. It's me, Jack.'

He went to her slowly, not wishing to alarm her, thinking that she might not have recognised him.

'They've taken him, Jack,' she said, so quietly he could barely hear. 'I don't know where they've taken him, but they've taken him. He's gone.'

He stood beside the bed. As he reached down to stroke her hair, she closed her eyes and turned away. He remained transfixed by her motionless body for several minutes, at a total loss, not knowing what to do. He dialled reception.

'Mr Meredith, can I help?' A woman's voice, which he recognised, answered immediately. Before he had time to collect his thoughts, she continued, 'Please don't leave her room. I'll be up straight away.'

Two minutes later, the same young nurse who had brought him to Bushra's room appeared at the door.

'She was awake when I arrived, think she recognised me,' he whispered. 'She kept repeating that he'd been taken away and then turned over and hasn't moved since. She looks,' his voice trailed off, 'she looks as if she's ill, very ill.'

'No, she's not ill,' the nurse said, gently. 'Tired and traumatised, yes, but not physically ill.'

'Where's her baby?'

'Come, Mr Meredith, come with me.'

She took him into a small windowless room next to Bushra's. The place was full of medical equipment, including several incubators. She pointed to the nearest one. He peered in and saw a tiny hooded baby lying on its back with arms outstretched, a face half turned to him, blissfully asleep.

'He's beautiful,' he whispered in awe.

'There's nothing to worry about,' she said, quietly, 'it's just that the doctor wanted to keep Emma under observation for a day or two.'

'Emma?' he asked, turning to her. 'I thought Bushra said that *he'd* been taken away.'

The young nurse hesitated.

'You didn't know then?'

'Know what?'

'Bushra had twins, beautiful twins, a boy and a girl.'

'Twins,' he exclaimed.

'Emma and Stavros,' she said quietly, her earlier confidence ebbing away.

It occurred to him that she had no idea who he was.

'Where's Stavros?' he asked, trying to stay calm.

'He's stronger than his sister,' she said obliquely. 'He didn't need to be kept under observation.'

'Yes, but where is he?'

She hesitated again.

'They came for him earlier this afternoon.'

'They?'

'It was her parents and an aunt, I think,' she whispered nervously. 'They spoke Arabic.'

Jack stared at her in disbelief.

PART TWO

2031

8

Southern England, April 2031

It was a cool windy evening. Isabel walked up from the station into the centre of the old market town, cradled in the Downs, south of London. She arrived at the Royal Oak fifteen minutes before the others. They were meeting for supper. Once a regular and happy event, they hadn't done this for at least twelve months. She was trying to remain calm. She knew this wasn't going to be easy for her, for her mother, Emma, and most certainly for her grandfather, Jack.

Isabel, who had just turned twenty, was completing her final year at university. She was an attractive woman, shapely but not as tall or as slim as her mother. She once told Emma that she had childbearing hips which she hoped to put to good use one day; her mother was horrified. She had a healthy tanned complexion, a hint of freckles around sparkling blue eyes. Her shoulder-length, naturally curly, blond hair was roughly combed out giving her an untamed appearance which caught people's attention.

Although he knew virtually nothing about it, Jack had become increasingly negative about her recent job offer. The more he went on about it, the more determined she was to pursue it.

Over the past few months, she'd started to see him in a new light, so different from the man she had adored when she was a teenager before going off to university. The change had dismayed her.

She knew that her final interview had gone well and wasn't surprised when the offer came through. She had tried to project herself as somebody who was open-minded, flexible and realistic. The two interviewing staff officers, on special leave from Tripoli, had been impressed by her thesis.

'Tell me about your job,' Jack asked, as they settled down in the pub twenty minutes later. She noticed the weariness in his voice, so unlike the old optimism.

'I'll be working for the European Defence Alliance, based in Tripoli,' she replied. 'They're responsible for governing the UN mandate of Tripolitania and Fezzan.'

'What a bloody mouthful. I presume you'll be seconded from the UK Government, qualifying for a UK pension.'

'If I survive that long,' Isabel said, trying to lighten the atmosphere.

'Bel,' cried Emma, 'don't say such a thing, it could be self-fulfilling.'

'Sorry, Mum.'

'And the work?' he said, ignoring her quip.

'Well, it's challenging, more interesting than I first thought,' she said, trying not to sound too enthusiastic.

'Interesting?'

She felt as if she were being interrogated, which made her uncomfortable. Her mother just looked on in silence.

'The military governor's anxious…'

'"Military governor"?'

'EDA is a military government,' she replied, knowing full well that he was aware of this. 'He's German, ex-army and has a good reputation for resolving local issues. FRSS operates a similar military administration in the UN mandate of Cyrenaica to the east. They're based in Benghazi. We're neighbours.'

'FRSS?'

Still the persistent, unnecessary questioning.

'Come on, Dad,' Emma said, clearly frustrated by his attitude. 'Everybody knows of the Federation of Russian Slavic States.'

'You could be working in a war zone before...'

'For heaven's sake, Dad, give Isabel a break,' Emma broke in. Her intervention brought an apology.

'I'm sorry,' he mumbled, just as the waitress arrived with their drinks.

After she'd gone, Isabel continued, determined at least to inform him even if she couldn't win him over.

'Officially both governments work together on UDP issues, principally trying to stem mass migration northwards from the Sahel and other areas of north and central Africa.' She paused. 'Universally Displaced People have been much in the news in the last few years.'

Jack remained silent for a moment, taking a long draught of beer.

'And how can you help in all this?' he asked.

'I'll come to that,' she said, noticing a slight change in his attitude. 'After Syria and Iraq totally disintegrated in the '20s, international agencies saw how the militias were trying to distance themselves from Islamic fundamentalism as their *raison d'être*.'

'I remember.'

'Likewise, national identity began to disappear with the collapse of so many sovereign states,' she continued, trying not to appear too smart. 'Borders were meaningless, non-existent in many cases. People naturally started to identify themselves either by their ethnic or tribal origins.' She paused. 'But you know all this.'

'Go on, Bel,' Emma encouraged her. 'There's always more to learn.'

'The issue of identity became even more complex as refugees and displaced people moved constantly throughout the region. At the same time, many observers began to see Islamic fundamentalism not so much as a unifying but a controlling force.'

'Remote warlords, far from the horrors of war and refugee camps, imposing their will on intimidated followers,' Jack said, starting to take an interest.

'By the end of the '20s, agencies started seeing yet another shift. Ethnic, religious or tribal identities no longer gave displaced people the protection and stability they craved. In fact, being labelled anything came to be a distinct liability.'

'Fascinating,' said Emma, clearly surprised. 'So are UDPs people who have shunned their original identities?'

'Yes, in a nutshell.'

It occurred to Isabel that the three of them had never had this sort of conversation all the time she was in university, despite the fact this was what she'd been studying. She realised sadly how, in a few short years, they'd all drifted so far apart.

'But more than that,' she continued, determined to press on now that she had their attention, 'they've lost everything. In fact, the UN has recently started to use the word "dispossessed" rather than "displaced", UDP now being Universally Dispossessed People.'

'I've heard both terms used and found it confusing,' Emma admitted. 'Dispossessed though does seem a more accurate way to describe their plight.'

'They've been subsumed by a common cause,' continued Isabel, 'a cause based entirely on survival. In many regions, they've formed their own militias based only on the principle of survival, survival at all costs,' she added, emphatically. 'They've totally rejected all forms of ethnic, religious or tribal ideology. This makes them very powerful and beyond the reach of most civil and religious authorities. They're utterly ruthless. Many see similarities with past secular warlords in Iraq and Syria.'

'In the early twenties,' commented Jack.

'Yes.'

The young waitress returned with their food, which she placed unceremoniously on the table.

They ate in silence. Isabel could see that her mother was struggling, her daughter's future apparently inextricably linked to murderous warlords.

'I still can't see how you can be involved,' said Jack, his scepticism never far below the surface.

'One of the innovations the governor is looking at,' said Isabel, ignoring him, 'is the possibility of integrating the various Bedouin and Berber tribes.'

'That sounds pretty radical,' said her mother.

'He believes it's one way of creating a more homogenous population, a way of bringing stability to the country.'

'God, he's ambitious,' said Jack, sounding less than convinced.

'And this is where you come in,' said Emma, trying to close out her father. 'Your thesis on the Berbers in North Africa would certainly have been of interest to them.'

'As an anthropologist, my role will be to develop a better understanding of the various ethnic and tribal groups and hopefully work on integration initiatives.'

'Good for you,' said Emma, as if her daughter had just won the reading prize at primary school.

Not for the first time in recent weeks, Isabel felt an unspoken rift between them all as her departure date approached. She felt that she was to blame, seeking out a career that she knew would cause them both great anxiety. She sensed that their relationship would inevitably change once she was abroad and this saddened her.

'What else occupies your military governor?' Jack asked.

'They're overseeing the construction of massive solar farms in the desert. I think it's one of EDA's top priorities,' Isabel said, ignoring his sleight. 'Solar is one of Europe's most important and stable sources of energy and will be for years to come. Expanding into North Africa is a logical extension.'

'North Africa, stable,' Jack laughed. 'How bloody ironic is that. I presume the Russians see the same potential.'

'I don't know about elsewhere within the federation, but the Russians in the mandate are still focused on extracting every last barrel of crude, every last cubic metre of gas from the remaining reserves in the desert,' she said, before adding, 'they're still in climate change denial.'

The waitress arrived again, wondering how they were getting on, if they needed more drinks. Her constant interruptions frustrated Isabel.

'Well, from my experience of the area, this will all end in...' Jack started, as the girl left.

'Forget your experiences, Dad,' said Emma, abruptly. 'That was forty, fifty years ago. People, politics, attitudes change, move on. This is Bel's time now, her generation's opportunity.'

He looked at her, somewhat taken aback.

'They must have their chance to bring about change there. They'll have their own ideas – how to eradicate prejudice, poverty and injustice and tackle climate change,' she said, adding emphatically, 'give her a break.'

'Well said,' Isabel said quietly, reaching across the table for her mother's hand.

'The historian speaks. You're right,' Jack said, chastened.

'Come on, Dad, remember why we're here,' Emma said cheerfully, raising her glass. 'Here's to your new job, Bel, to a bright future with EDA.'

'To your future, Bel,' said Jack, at last breaking into a smile.

*

Emma marvelled at how her daughter had changed over the last year. A more confident, focused and assertive character had emerged, somebody on a mission, bent on making something of her life. She was surprised and a little frightened to admit to herself that her daughter appeared to be following in her father's footsteps.

As she'd watched Jack over supper, Emma was reminded of the younger man, seeing him as he was back in the late '90s. Tall, erect, with craggy weather-beaten features, he'd been a good-looking man who would turn heads as soon as he walked into a room. He had a reputation for being tough, driven on by his work, at ease in harsh environments and dealing with difficult and dangerous people.

Emma was still hoping that he would come to terms with Isabel's job. She recalled his initial reaction after the first interview. At the time, he appeared to turn in on himself, tortured features betraying ancient fears, long-dormant demons swamping his innermost thoughts. She loved her father dearly. However, for years now, she recognised that there was a side to him that she would never know, a personal odyssey buried forever in a past he seemed anxious to forget.

Behind his gentleness and generosity, she'd always feared that there was a worryingly darker and less predictable side to his character that might at any moment, without warning, manifest itself. She sensed that he had carefully concealed all this from her and Isabel, struggling to protect them from his past. She worried now, that whatever memories had so afflicted him on first hearing of Isabel's job, they were still very real.

To her, throughout her early childhood, he often appeared angry. A courageous man, he seemed to be constantly fighting unexplained and very personal battles in wildly exotic places with unpronounceable names, to which he would disappear for months at a time. His anger would add to the misery of an already dysfunctional household, a place which absorbed his temporary insanity and purged his soul until his next home leave. His long absences, his emotional returns, his general inattentiveness to all family matters and his abrupt departures ultimately shattered any remaining mutual affection he shared with her mother, Charlotte, and her only sibling, Tom.

But his love and consideration for her, she'd long recognised, had survived those traumatic homecomings. She recalled how his behaviour towards her differed appreciably from his treatment of Charlotte and Tom. After her parents' divorce following nearly twenty years of unhappy marriage, she and Jack became inseparable, yet she never understood how this complex relationship had come about.

*

'I'm far too wide awake to go to bed,' Isabel said as her mother led her into the small front room of her cottage. 'I think I'll get a glass of water, sit in the garden and stargaze. I never see anything in south London, there's too much light pollution.'

'Go on out, Bel, I'll get your water.'

She settled into one of her mother's old wickerwork chairs and looked out over the darkened garden to the black featureless woodlands beyond, feebly bathed in the light of a crescent moon. An owl shrieked without warning, emphasising the night-time wilderness of the surrounding countryside.

'Was Granddad sober enough to walk home?' she asked, as Emma came out a few minutes later.

'It's only fifteen minutes up to his apartment. It'll have done him good.'

Isabel took the glass and sank back in her chair.

'Is he OK, Mum?'

'Fine,' she hesitated. 'Why do you ask?'

'I don't know.' Isabel paused. 'He seems so distracted these days. Is it something to do with my job?'

'Perhaps,' said Emma, 'partly that, I suppose.'

'Or that I split up with Andrew?'

'You know, we're both very fond of him, always have been, ever since we met him in your first year in university.'

'Oh, Mum, it wasn't working out. I didn't want either of us to be tied down after I go.'

'Maybe when you…'

'Mum,' Isabel interrupted her, 'please don't go there.'

Emma suspected that the real reason for Jack's behaviour had nothing to do with Andrew but Isabel's imminent departure for North Africa.

'I expect his golf has taken a nosedive recently. His mood swings generally reflect his performances on the course,' said Emma, rather lamely.

They both laughed.

Emma glanced at her daughter. In the yellowy kitchen light filtering through the back door, she could make out the girl's striking profile, staring out over the cottage garden.

She reflected that her father and daughter had much in common: the same restless curiosity, the same contempt for the ordinary, the mundane, the simple pleasures of life. She felt instinctively that Isabel's life was about to become as eventful, uncertain and dangerous as his had been.

She and Jack had anticipated a turbulent future for Isabel but reacted differently. Emma knew that he lived vicariously through his granddaughter, which made him excitable one minute, depressed the next, trying to guess what lay ahead. Emma saw her only child embarking on a life-threatening venture and could only see trouble, tragedy and perhaps loss.

'North Africa is so different now than it was when he worked there,' Isabel said, tacitly acknowledging that she was responsible, in some way, for Jack's present grumpiness.

'I'm sure you're right,' Emma agreed, not wishing to argue.

'Things have changed, Mum, perhaps for the better.'

Not enough, Emma thought, *to make any difference to the problems you're going to face.*

'I mean working for EDA should be like working for any large government department,' continued Isabel.

Emma shuddered.

'I'll be working with like-minded Europeans,' she said, clearly trying to appease her mother. 'We're all focused on rebuilding the country.'

'You know for years Jack prospected there for oil, living in constant fear under a dictatorship,' Emma said after a few moments. 'From the beginning, he worked against the grain of international politics, public sentiment and outside most people's comfort zones.'

'Comfort zones?'

'Libya had become a pariah state, the regime cruel and unpredictable. Few were prepared to risk their careers there and Jack took a beating from the start, his college mates getting the better jobs in the UK.'

'Mum, I know much of this from his stories. He had rough times wherever he went, which I understand he'll never talk about. It's just that when I was a kid, he used to speak to me so enthusiastically about his work, especially in Libya.'

'You're right, he was always enthusiastic.' Emma paused. 'My earliest recollections, however, were of his anger and frustration when he was home on leave. To this day, I've never really understood why he behaved as he did.'

'Can you remember a time as a child when he was happy?'

'Only really when he was with his brother, Peter,' said Emma. 'He'd visit us several times a year for a few days. The pair of them would walk around central London, the museums, galleries, the Royal Parks, any and everywhere, endlessly talking, laughing. They'd invariably retire to a bar, regaling each other over glasses of whisky.'

'I'd forgotten about Peter. I remember you telling me he died in a fishing accident just before I was born.'

'From about the age of twelve, they'd take me with them. Peter would always make a huge fuss of me, which made me feel very important. He brought out the best in Jack.'

'But what about when he was at home with the family?'

'Life wasn't easy. My parents were constantly at each other, arguing, fighting, driving each other to the point of exhaustion. They couldn't seem to agree on anything.'

'You never mentioned any of this before, Mum,' said Isabel, quietly. 'It must have been very difficult for you and Tom.'

'When I was about ten or eleven, Dad and I became really close, much closer than I'd ever been to my mother and brother,' said Emma changing the subject, not wishing to reveal her unhappy childhood, the root of which she was still at a loss to explain. 'We'd spend a lot of time together when he was on leave. He'd tell me about his work, people he met, places he visited, things he'd seen, done. His life fascinated me. I was a good listener, the only one in the family who showed any interest.'

'Strange that Tom wasn't interested. Jack's work was much more a man thing.'

'Tom and he never got on,' she said, immediately regretting it.

Emma was twelve when she realised that Tom was born only weeks after her parents got married. She often wondered whether this had any bearing on Jack's relationship with his son.

'Never got on?'

'Jack had a real thirst for life, was full of fantastic ideas, theories on everything,' said Emma, ignoring her question. 'How, for example, a country should exploit its natural resources for every citizen's benefit, how to tackle corruption in the Third World, the list was endless. He was obsessed.' She paused for a moment. 'He always wanted to do more, you know, more than simply prospect for oil.'

'Such as?'

'It was nothing definitive, it was the way he approached his work. I think he saw himself as an agent for change, somebody who could really make a difference to the lives of ordinary people.'

Apart from the shrieking of a restless owl, nothing stirred beneath the still night sky.

'I can relate to that,' Isabel said, finally.

'I know you can.'

Neither spoke for several minutes.

'When I was in my early teens, he mentioned that something significant had happened to him early on in Libya,' Emma continued quietly, 'something really unpleasant, which I believe traumatised him, affecting him for years.'

'Neither of you've ever said anything about this,' Isabel said, clearly surprised.

'From my perspective, there seemed little point, especially as he never gave any details. But it did go some way to explain his mood swings when I was a child – one minute somebody very positive, excited about life, the next, shouting and cursing like a man possessed.'

'Did you ever find out what it was?'

'No, although I think it occurred about the time I was born. Over the years he vaguely alluded to some life-changing event, but he never said more than that. I've always felt that whatever it was, it had a profound effect on his life.' She paused. 'I'm sure it still bothers him today.'

In the stillness of the night, Emma looked out over her muted shadowy garden, thoughts of her father swirling around her head. She reflected that Jack would never have wanted such a beautiful retreat; the same would inevitably go for Isabel. It was, she realised, because of the way they chose to live. In his case, life was episodic, each phase a complete story. He'd never been interested in creating a conventional working or family life, becoming an integral part of society, of the local establishment.

To create and nurture a garden like hers required patience and a personal commitment over many years. She knew instinctively that he would never have been willing to devote time and energy to such a project, to commit so far into the future; likewise Isabel. Neither would compromise their thirst for life, a life lived on the edge.

From a young age, Emma recognised that her father was living the life he'd always craved – the freedom to explore the world and face down every challenge that came his way. As soon as he was bored or satiated, he'd move on. Given this predilection, she often wondered why he got married.

She also knew that this haphazard existence was one of the many reasons why their marriage imploded. Charlotte, who had had problems with alcohol when Emma was very young, had gone back to work part-time in the City. Her own parents had stepped in to look after the two children.

Her mother loathed Jack's emotionally draining comings and goings, which upset her carefully choreographed lifestyle. His apparent total disinterest in all family matters, especially in her career, clearly angered Charlotte, whose unspoken ambition was to work up through the establishment to which she'd felt so entitled. She failed to see that their marriage was to him just another phase in his life. At its *dénouement*, he was bored, and she was desperate, the result of which led to acrimonious divorce.

Emma looked at Isabel in the steely moonlight and sensed that history was about to repeat itself. Despite her strong protective instincts, Emma was resigned to the fact that there was nothing she could do to influence her daughter's future. She knew that Isabel was predisposed to mimic Jack's existence. Perhaps like him, with his good fortune, she would survive to tell her own stories.

'Mum, are you awake?' Isabel whispered, minutes later. 'I think it's time to turn in. We've got to be up in a few hours if I'm to catch the early train.'

They shuffled stiffly inside from the chill of the night and climbed the creaking stairs to tiny bedrooms under the eaves.

'I'll set my alarm,' said Emma, kissing her daughter on the cheek. 'I'll make coffee while you're in the shower.'

'Thanks, Mum,' she laughed. 'Despite Granddad's grumpiness, I really enjoyed the evening.'

There was so much more Emma wanted to say to her that was left unsaid: how she had started to appreciate where her daughter might be going with her life; how although not fully understanding or necessarily agreeing with the way Isabel did things, she loved her dearly, unconditionally.

Unbeknownst to Emma, she had missed the last opportunity to say what she desperately wished to say before her daughter left the country.

9

Northern England, May 2031

It was only after Isabel had showered following a hard game of tennis that she noticed an envelope addressed to her on the bedside table. Inside, there were several closely typed sheets entitled 'Current Issues relating to Demarcation 1822', under which was written 'Important information for all personnel working in the border areas, May 2031'. *Damn it*, she thought, *they'll expect me to read this tonight.*

She was staying in an old country house hotel to the north of York at the invitation of the Ministry of Defence; but this was hardly a holiday. Along with fifteen new EDA recruits, she was nearing the end of a week's indoctrination course – fascinating but exhausting.

At the start of the week, an Andrei Tupolov had lectured to them on recent Russian history. A former professor of political science at St Petersburg University, he had moved to Paris in the early '20s. He was a small, balding, unimpressive middle-aged man, who had the furtive look of somebody on the run.

She found his lectures absorbing and was soon convinced that EDA was justifiably obsessed with its North African neighbour.

She quickly discovered that recruits were obliged to share this obsession if they valued their jobs. Tupolov analysed the events that led to the creation of a new super-state in the mid-'20s. The Federation of Russian Slavic States was a union of countries under Moscow's autocratic rule, embodying a nationalist Slavic identity, Christian Orthodoxy and imperial leanings within a limited democratic framework. He described how it had come about after Russia had rapidly occupied the Baltic States, Ukraine, the Balkans, Greece and Turkey.

At the time, Europe was embroiled in a regional political crisis, caused principally by millions of refugees from the Middle East and North Africa. A subsequent dramatic rise in unemployment and urban terrorist attacks, and mounting national debt across the European Union, had left it vulnerable to Russian expansion. Without the support of an inward-looking US, NATO collapsed, leaving Europe to fend for itself; EU forces were no match for the Russians.

Having lived through these years as a teenager, nothing of what she'd heard had been truly revealing. Although not directly affected since leaving the EU, the British had watched the unfolding horrors of European anarchy. What was new for her, though, was seeing recent European history from a Russian perspective, a perspective with which, somewhat surprisingly, she was not entirely unsympathetic.

On Tuesday evening, the rather dour Tupolov was replaced by a former Egyptian ambassador to the UN. Anwar El Sahla was a corpulent *bon viveur* in his mid-fifties; he dressed carelessly in expensive Armani suits, finding life constantly amusing. His buffoonery masked the towering intellect of a man who had been professor of mathematics in Cairo University, spoke six languages fluently and in other circumstances might have been an international concert pianist.

Given her knowledge of North Africa, Isabel greatly appreciated El Sahla's talks. She found his description of life in Libya prior to UN intervention in '25, harrowing. The country had become increasingly fractured and ungovernable since the dictatorship's ultimate collapse in October 2011. El Sahla spoke knowledgeably of the intervening years in which the country had been torn apart, rendering it ungovernable.

He took a shine to Isabel, noting her obvious enthusiasm in everything he had to say. More importantly, they both enjoyed tennis and formed a doubles partnership, playing in the evenings before supper.

Over the next couple of days, he outlined how the situation in North Africa had become more fraught, caused by the ever-increasing hordes of refugees moving north from the Sahel to seek asylum in Europe. For years, international agencies had been unable to staunch this northward flow – refugees fleeing Islamic fundamentalism, the ravages of an increasingly hostile climate and the scourge of overpopulation. The problems for these blighted and stateless people had been compounded by aggressive Chinese expansion, whose plans for most of Africa were based on pure mercantilism, without regard for the people they effectively colonised.

Libya's downward spiral was further compounded by the EU and FRSS, a situation which El Sahla described as 'two scrawny old vultures, scavenging over the remnants of this once beautiful, rich but devastated country'.

He described how the UN had to intervene to prevent confrontation between the two super-states. With Syria and Egypt effectively under Russian control, the UN had been forced to recognise FRSS's powerful influence in the region. As a result, in '25, it was agreed at the UN that Libya should be divided into two UN mandated territories: Tripolitania and Fezzan in the west, and known as UNMTF, was to be governed by the European Defence Alliance on behalf of the UN, while Cyrenaica in the east, and known as UNMC, was likewise to be governed by FRSS.

Again, Isabel had known most of what she was hearing. What she learnt, though, was how differently European and

Russian authorities governed their mandates. The EU delegated its responsibilities to EDA, which was made up of all EU members and those closely aligned such as the UK, Norway and Sweden. EDA administered UNMTF relatively efficiently under a military governor.

FRSS on the other hand didn't have the resources to govern the mandate effectively, so it 'contracted out' its authority in UNMC to a semi-autonomous Russian militia, with disastrous consequences for the local people.

*

As usual before supper, the bar was busy. Isabel noticed that after nearly a week together, everybody, especially the British, Dutch and French, were at ease in each other's company – progress indeed.

'What will it be, Isabel?' shouted El Sahla, holding forth to a noisy group at the bar.

'Glass of house white, thanks,' she replied, joining them.

'I hear you two beat the Dutch at last,' laughed a tall skinny Frenchman.

'It was Isabel's net play that clinched the match,' said El Sahla, handing her a drink.

'Hardly,' she grimaced, 'but thank you, Anwar.'

'Anwar was asking if anybody had received a note on Demarcation 1822 this evening. What about you?' asked Gert, an over-anxious Dutchman, turning to Isabel.

'I did,' she admitted.

'Ah, one of the chosen few,' exclaimed El Sahla. 'Tomorrow morning, you and Gert will have the pleasure of Signor Scarletti, EDA's refugee co-ordinator and expert on UDPs.'

'Why just us?' Isabel asked, self-consciously.

'There's a number of possibilities, but you'll have a better idea after hearing Scarletti tomorrow.'

'Do you know the man?' Gert asked.

'By reputation. Scarletti was the one who promoted the construction of sustainable, semi-permanent refugee camps along the Mediterranean coast in '25. His initial idea was to prevent UDPs from leaving the shores of North Africa.'

'Of course, I remember the name now,' said Isabel. 'It was controversial at the time,' she added, thinking back to her studies.

'Scarletti was demonised in the world press for shifting the refugee problem to the camps of North Africa, but he persisted,' continued El Sahla.

'I know he had a rough time,' said Isabel, 'especially from African ambassadors at the UN.'

'He had no choice, he had to come up with a radical plan,' said El Sahla. 'Despite thousands of kilometres of razor wire fencing and numerous off-shore patrol vessels, millions of UDPs were getting through to Europe, circumventing its southern borders.'

'Fences never work, not then, not now,' Gert said.

'Scarletti's proposals were only taken seriously at the UN after UDP groups started to fight their way ashore in Sicily using modern Russian weapons.'

'I'd always understood the Russians had specifically armed them to extend their occupation of southern Europe,' said Isabel.

'You're right, that was their original plan,' said El Sahla. 'European intelligence services were aware of this for at least six months before the first attack but didn't think it would ever happen.'

'Why, for heaven's sake?'

'Because they reckoned that the Russians had had a change of heart during that time. Rather than using UDPs as a vanguard force in southern Europe, the Russians had suddenly found themselves potentially competing with UDPs in the international drugs trade in the region and had to rein them in.'

'God, the whole UDP business is so bloody complicated,' added Gert, grimly.

'Don't worry yourselves,' El Sahla assured him. 'Scarletti will explain everything: how some UDPs in the desert still have their own militias; how they terrorise each other, local Bedouin and EDA, competing for diminishing resources, driven by desperation to survive.'

Isabel was familiar with the UDPs and their survival instincts, driving them to commit barbaric acts throughout the Sahara. However, she thought that these had all but stopped in the last few months.

'EDA's been completely silent on UDPs,' she said. 'I thought they'd been finally subdued.'

'Sadly, this isn't entirely the case. The facts have been withheld from the public, don't make good press for the administration,' continued El Sahla. 'UDPs are still active, although much less so than they once were. As a force to be dealt with, they're rapidly on the wane.'

'But this Demarcation 1822 business, what is it? What's it got to do with all this?' Gert asked.

'It's our common border with the Russians,' said El Sahla. 'EDA forces operate from fortified bases in the Sahara. From there they patrol D1822, keeping a close eye on the Russians and clearing swathes of the desert of the remaining militias. Unfortunately, they manage to destroy much of the Bedouin's traditional nomadic way of life in the process.'

'And Isabel and I are expected to work there?' said Gert, clearly alarmed.

'So it appears.'

What the hell have I signed up for? thought Isabel, suddenly confronted by the reality of her new job. The warmth and camaraderie of the bar evaporated, leaving her in a cold sweat.

10

Southern England,
Early September 2031

There was a terrifying, blood-curdling scream. In the silence that followed, he could hear someone breathing steadily, as if asleep. He tensed, waiting, eyes wide open, yet he couldn't see anything in the impenetrable darkness. The sound was hypnotic. Gradually the tension eased, drowsiness invading his weary body. Suddenly another scream, so close, he thought that he himself had cried out. This gave way to uncontrollable sobbing which gradually abated.

Then the pain started. The throbbing in his head was intense; he became breathless. He pressed broken hands to his temples, desperately trying to numb the agony. He yelled out but heard no sound. A warm viscous fluid seeped through his fingers. He licked the palms of his hands tasting the saltiness of his own blood. Just as he started to lose consciousness, he became aware of the breathing again, closer now. He strained to see who was there; there was nothing. He felt a cloth, cold and damp, being pressed to his forehead. Icy water washed his brow, trickling into his eyes, coursing down his cheeks.

In an instant he saw large blue-black eyes hovering just above his face, staring impassively into his. Not flinching, he returned the stare. Two pairs of disembodied eyes locked together in a passionless embrace. It seemed to him that his life depended on these unknown eyes. His concentration was resolute. The pain eased. Nothing else impinged on his senses except for a sweet aromatic smell, which he couldn't name. Then, very slowly, the blue-black eyes started to recede. Panic rose, restricting his chest. Like a man succumbing to the deep, he knew he was drowning. The eyes grew steadily smaller, fainter until they disappeared. At that moment, another scream rent the air.

This time there was no doubt; it had to be him. He sat bolt upright on the bed. He had a severe hangover, the searing pain behind his eyes dulling his senses. The room was in near darkness. He remained motionless, shaken, unable to recall the slightest detail of why he'd screamed. Clearly something had freaked him out. As other thoughts crowded in, the shock of his violent awakening faded.

He called out, 'Daylight', as if instructing some unseen valet. Gradually light filtered through the previously opaque glass wall, permeating every hidden corner of the room, bringing into focus familiar surroundings. He noted the time on the bedside panel: six-fifteen. Hauling himself off the bed, he wrapped a towel around his naked body and walked unsteadily to the glass wall.

In response to a whispered 'Open', a discrete panel within the glass wall slid silently to one side. He stepped out onto a wide rooftop terrace. The coolness of the marble slab underfoot drained the heat from his body. He winced when he saw the empty whisky bottle lying on its side under the steamer chair. Leaning on the metal rail, he surveyed the view, still shaking involuntarily. Below him lay the town, partially hidden by trees, indistinct in the pre-dawn light, bracing itself for another day of near tropical heat.

A word floated aimlessly into his head: 'jasmine'. In a flash, he recalled the smell and the terrifying detail of his dream. *Good God,*

he thought, *Bushra, she's still there, eerily present after all these years.*
He was overwhelmed. Feelings of fear, frustration, guilt and a deep-seated longing tumbled awkwardly around his head. Although he'd lost touch with her decades ago, she still sought him out in his sleep, reminding him of her presence. Dumbstruck, he gazed out over the horizon, early sunlight crowning the trees below.

In his early years, Jack had always seen himself as a simple being, unperturbed by superstition and religion. A trained scientist absorbed by the physical nature of things, he was, by his own definition, a pragmatic man. If something wasn't logically provable, it didn't exist.

Over his long and fractious life, however, experience had taught him that this simple philosophical outlook was increasingly inadequate. It was Bushra who had derailed his early certainties and undermined his dogmatism. It was she who demanded that he share her thirst for life, and ultimately it was she who taught him how to love and be loved.

During the ten years or so that they were lovers, circumstances forced them to live apart for most of that time. Their relationship was as much spiritual as it was physical, a relationship that he could never have previously imagined. When the end inevitably came, he was suicidal, completely distraught at the thought of never seeing her or holding her in his arms again. Yet as time moved on, he began to realise that she was still there, unseen, still demanding his attention, his love.

And when the nightmares started years after they'd physically parted, he knew instinctively that their relationship had entered a very diffcrent, more demanding phase. She would come to him usually in the darkest hours of the night, presaging some significant event in their intertwined lives. Her sudden and unexpected presence always shocked him. The nightmare would invariably take him back to the place of their first encounter, Tolmeta jail. From that earliest moment, she had cared for him unconditionally, whether she was physically present or not.

The nightmare never varied significantly: screams followed by excruciating pain, her unexpected presence which brought him relief, her gradual disappearance, his sense of impending death by drowning. Sometimes, before she faded away, he could feel the brush of her lips on his, her fingers caressing his cheek. In these brief final moments, his longing for her would overwhelm him, leaving him shaking uncontrollably as if in a near-death fever. Of her, all he ever saw were those blue-black eyes, uniquely and unmistakably hers, watching over him, forewarning an uncertain future.

The first nightmare, perhaps the most harrowing, occurred in the spring of '95, ten years after they'd first met. Over the previous twelve months, their relationship had become increasingly fraught and unsustainable on so many levels. Several days after she had appeared to him in his dreams, he received her letter. It was short and to the point. Although she loved him with all the strength and passion she possessed, she could not go on. She was finished with him. She did not want to see him again, ever. She gave no reason; he knew there was no point. He was devastated, unable to function sensibly for months afterwards.

Years passed. His complex lifestyle, spent mostly working abroad away from his London home, started to unravel. Finally, in 2005, his estranged wife, Charlotte, announced she was leaving him and wanted a divorce. Several days before she left, the nightmare reoccurred. In her own way, Bushra had anticipated the end of his marriage and foresaw the anguish and bitterness that lay ahead. The divorce was acrimonious, so much hatred on both sides.

And then one night five years later, just when he thought he was safe from the vicissitudes of life, the nightmare returned. A few days later he received Bushra's brief letter in which she recounted Stavros' fate. There was no date, no address, nothing. Her news devastated him, leaving him in a state of emotional paralysis which he couldn't shake off. He made no effort to find her, completely unable to provide the love and support she so desperately needed. In the end he lost all contact with her.

There were other nocturnal encounters over the years, many of which he had forgotten. They always reminded him that despite turning his back on her, she was still there in his life, looking out for him, caring for him, loving him.

One night, six months after the start of the Arab Spring in 2011, she returned to him in his sleep, the nightmare as intense and terrifying as the first. A week later, the dying flame of the dictatorship was finally and unceremoniously snuffed out. 'Look,' she'd predicted, 'you and I survived this brutal regime, we lived, we must be thankful.'

The most recent occasion she appeared to him was in the summer of '25. Ten days later, the FRSS flag was hoisted over the Greek parliament in Syntagma Square. In the preceding months, the Russian Fifth Army, complete with thousands of troops and hundreds of tanks supported by warplanes, had ruthlessly fought and bombed its way south from Ukraine through the Balkans and finally into Greece, annihilating great numbers of people and laying the countryside to waste.

He frequently wondered how Bushra and her family could possibly have survived this latest misfortune and yet to his undying shame, he had made no effort to find her.

Despite the reality of her presence in his dreams, he often questioned if they were just that, dreams, or was she indeed communicating with him in the only way she could, well beyond his reasoning and understanding.

*

The lift door opened. Jack lurched into his private lobby scattering the contents of his pockets over the wooden floor. Eventually, after scrabbling around on his knees, he found the key card; he was drunker than he realised.

Since Isabel had left for Tripoli nearly three months earlier, he had started to drink heavily, something he hadn't done for years. He'd avoided Emma as much as he could, ashamed that he'd capitulated again to the demons of his past, unable to articulate what was driving him so demented. And then, two nights ago, Bushra had returned to him in his sleep. The tension was unbearable, because he knew from experience that her nocturnal visit was a precursor to some life-changing event.

Standing in the darkened room, he saw the last hints of daylight draining from the night sky to the west. At his feet, the town's lights flickered in detached silence. The only sound he registered was his laboured drunken breathing. Although it was still quite early, he resolved to drink plenty of water, take a cold shower and get to bed as soon as possible. As he staggered towards the kitchen, a message on the wallscreen lit up the living room. He'd forgotten to turn it off when he'd left hours earlier. *It'll wait till tomorrow*, he thought, pouring himself a glass of iced water.

Heading for his bedroom, he heard the ringing tone. Somebody was online, prompting him to respond. He glanced at the short message on the screen, reading and rereading it several times. He was dumbfounded as he sank into the settee.

'I've been trying to call you for hours. It's my birthday in case you'd forgotten, you old bastard. Remember? Of course, you remember! You're probably too drunk to operate the screen. Just press the damn red button so we can talk. I'm here all night. I don't sleep much these days.'

So, this was what Bushra had been planning when she hovered over him in his sleep the other night. How extraordinary; she was out there somewhere, real, alive. She had lived on the edge of his consciousness for years, had become an inescapable presence in his life. How could it have been otherwise? In a few crazy short-lived years, they had shared so much – dangerously, intensely, passionately. They hadn't spoken in decades, yet the words on the screen evoked an immediate helplessness in him, a feeling he only ever associated with her.

His tiredness evaporated. A false drunken clarity lifted his spirits, stirring deeply embedded memories. He would call her, but not just yet. He needed time to clear his head, to think. There was so much he wanted to say, to ask her. *Where to start?* he wondered.

Time passed. Folding himself deeper into the leathery comfort of the settee, he stared at the screen, his mind wandering back to the years they'd spent together.

*

The ringing tone brought him abruptly to his senses. He must have dozed off. He gazed at the screen, a new message illuminating the darkened room. He was shocked to see the time: two-thirty.

'Your local pub has been closed for hours. If you're not lying in a ditch somewhere, I assume you're at home reading this. You're probably thinking, what am I going to say to her after all these years? I guess you're astonished I'm still here. Take a chance, Jack, for old times' sake. Call me back, now, tonight. I can't stay awake much longer and God knows, I might be dead in the morning.'

Conflicting thoughts raced through his head, his heart pounding with anticipation. He wondered if he'd ever have the strength and courage to love her as passionately as he once did. He knew there'd be a real danger that he'd let her down again, screwing up their lives permanently this time. He'd hurt her enough already. Whatever, she clearly wanted to see him again. He knew that to remain silent was not an option; to ignore her call would be cowardly in the extreme. Besides, deep down, his old longing for her was rising like sap through parched limbs, a feeling he hadn't experienced for years.

She was right though, what to say? Their past together seemed long gone. Years ago, she had slipped irrevocably into history, circumstances having driven them apart forever. Suddenly, overwhelmingly, the thought of losing her again terrified him. Tonight, although totally unprepared, he knew he had to call her.

He went to the bathroom, splashed water over his face and straightened his hair. He needed a whisky before he called. After pouring a generous measure, he slumped into the settee and pressed the button.

He couldn't make anything out at first. A watery light nearby flickered on, dispelling the darkness. He could just make out a timber-decked veranda, a couple of ancient patio chairs and a variety of hanging baskets swaying gently in the night air. He heard faint noises, the wind or was it waves crashing on a shore somewhere, the metallic sound of cicadas. He imagined a tropical or maybe Mediterranean coastline. It occurred to him that she was probably in Greece.

She was sitting cross-legged on a large cushion on the deck, dressed in a white smock, looking straight at him. Even in the poor light, he recognised those eyes, eyes that had captivated him all those years ago.

'About bloody time, I was just dozing off.' Rich laughter echoed across the ether. 'So, you're alive, Jack, thank God for that,' she said in her quaintly exotic accent. 'I'd hate to think you'd passed on without me ever knowing.' She raised a glass from the floor. 'Cheers, to you, to us.'

Perhaps she was tipsy, he thought.

Abruptly the laughter stopped, the image froze, her glass hanging in mid-air. Wherever she was, the signal must be weak. After a second or two, she jerked back into life.

'How are you?' he bellowed at the flickering screen, as if to compensate for the poor link.

'There's no need to shout, Jack, I can hear you clearly.' Again the laughter. 'I'm well thank goodness, and you?'

'Sorry, Bee, the line's dreadful,' he said, surprised how easily and naturally he'd addressed her after all these years. 'Yes, I'm fit enough thankfully. You look radiant as ever,' he said, trying to bring his runaway emotions to heel. 'Where are you?'

'Stoupa, you remember the family villa overlooking the beach at the north end of the village. You and I hid down here many a time.'

'Of course I do,' he said, tears pricking his eyes. 'How could I ever forget?'

'We had so much fun here.'

'I loved the peace and solitude,' he added lamely.

'Stoupa's changed, you'd hardly recognise it.'

'In what way?' he asked, struggling, unsure what to talk about.

'It suffered badly in late '25 when the Russians occupied the Peloponnese.'

'It must have been hell for you,' he said, deeply ashamed that he hadn't made any attempt to contact her since the occupation. 'I'm so sorry I never…'

'Don't, Jack,' she interrupted. She paused, draining her glass and placing it on the deck. 'The village is the holiday retreat of senior Russian officials now. They treat us like animals.'

The image shocked him.

'And you, how do you manage?' he asked, realising how vulnerable she must have been, maybe still was.

'No, they don't bother me. I'm OK really,' she said a little unconvincingly. 'Fortunately, the place is remote. Most officials prefer the brasher island hotspots and mainland resorts closer to Athens.'

'And tourists?'

'There aren't any foreign tourists here now, not like old times.'

'The occupation must be terrifying,' he said, aware how trite he sounded.

He watched her as she rose unsteadily to her feet, holding the balustrade for support.

'Don't worry, I'm not an invalid,' she laughed. 'I've just been sitting cross-legged for too bloody long. My legs have locked up. And maybe I've had a…'

Her image froze again, silence. After a minute or so, the screen flickered into life.

'… render you speechless,' she was saying.

'Bee, you keep cutting out. You were just getting up when the system crashed again.'

'Damn it.'

'How on earth did you know how to contact me after all this time?' he asked hurriedly.

'You remember Sophie, the young Danish journalist who lived off Syntagma Square, the one who fancied you?' she laughed. 'Well, we've kept in touch over the years. She helped me to…'

Her image stalled for a moment then jumped into life.

'… through a colleague working in London.'

'I wish I was there with you,' he blurted out, ignoring her explanation, afraid that he wouldn't be able to say a fraction of what he wanted to before the signal was lost completely.

'Oh, so do I, Jack.' After a moment's hesitation, she rushed on as if reading his thoughts. 'Before it shuts down completely, promise me you'll come out to Stoupa someday, someday very soon. In my dotage I need you more than I care to admit.'

'You're not old, you're younger than me. You look at least ten…'

'Jack,' she reprimanded him, 'I need an answer. Will you come out to see me?'

'Of course,' he replied, without hesitation.

'I can't visit the UK,' she said, getting straight down to business. 'I'd need an international travel permit to leave Greece and then there's the UK entry visa, impossible without a sponsor. Anyway, I'm broke.'

He couldn't help smiling to himself, remembering her plain speaking.

'I'll try to get a visitor's visa from the Greek Embassy here in London.'

'You'll find it unbearably hot and dry here in the autumn, as bad as North Africa.'

'I've read about your droughts and forest fires. They sound terrifying.'

'In winter, they regularly ski in the mountains of the Peloponnese, our new reality.'

'The climate's going crazy,' he said. There were so many more important things that he desperately wanted to talk to her about, yet he felt strangely tongue-tied.

'How's Emma? Is she as stunningly beautiful as her mother was…?'

Her laughing image froze. He finished his whisky. If only he could have another couple of minutes to talk to her, pleading with some unseen deity for a little more time. He got to his feet and moved towards the screen, willing her back to life.

Suddenly she came alive again, talking to herself. She'd moved closer, as if to inspect his frozen image more closely. He saw her open generous smile, those mysterious blue-black eyes staring at him. Her smock, the only thing she appeared to be wearing, hung loosely, tantalisingly seductive. His whole body ached with longing, a feeling he'd quite forgotten; it frightened him.

'Jack,' she laughed, 'you're back.'

'I'll call the embassy in the morning,' he rushed on, breathlessly. 'Call me in a couple of days. I hope I'll have news for you.'

'Oh, Jack, that's wonderful. Seeing you so close, I feel I can almost…'

She froze, an arm stretched out as if to touch his face, like a supplicant in some ancient religious rite. The screen went blank. He staggered backwards and dropped heavily into the settee.

*

The following morning, he contacted the Greek Embassy, where he was confronted by mind-numbing officialdom. He soon realised that the visa process was far from simple and could take weeks. To distract himself, he spent several hours planning the trip, checking flights and bus timetables. Trying to arrange anything came as a shock. Athens now had the same appeal as flying to some remote East German city before the fall of the Berlin Wall back in the '80s. By lunchtime, he had made as much progress as he could.

He had given little thought to Greece after Bushra had left him.

He had only started to take an interest again when the country started to slip into a hell of its own making, more than twenty years ago now. From that time, he had followed with alarm the miserable fortunes of a proud people he once loved: consumed by poverty and bankruptcy, swamped by hordes of fleeing refugees, before being torn from the heart of Europe and brutally subjugated under a fierce new Russian imperialism.

He could no longer pretend that seeing Bushra again would put paid to the past. He knew he could not simply tell Emma of his plans and then disappear off to Greece for several weeks. Bushra's nocturnal call had left him raw and exposed. He had no idea what or how much he should tell his daughter, but he knew he had to start somewhere. 'Bushra' was a name that had caused so much havoc in the family, a name long-suppressed and airbrushed out of its history.

After lunch, he set off to walk over the Downs above the town, trying to put the last twenty-four hours into perspective. He needed time to reflect on what he was letting himself in for. He hoped a brisk walk would help him resolve what to say to Emma, and indeed Isabel, when the time came.

As he walked the woodland path, he vainly tried to square the past with the present, Bushra with Emma. It dawned on him that he had to tell his daughter everything about Bushra as soon as possible, preferably that evening. He knew he had no choice; his story was long overdue. There was so much to admit to her, so much that he knew would cause her anger and pain. He cringed at the thought of what she would think when she heard how he'd spent most of his leave from the desert with Bushra in Greece, instead of back with the family in London. And that was only the beginning.

He wondered how she would react to his infidelity, what she would make of the reasons for his marriage break-up and, most importantly, whether she could appreciate the Bushra he first met – a wild, courageous and intoxicating young woman with whom he had been insanely in love. He prayed that Emma would come to understand the tragedy that they all faced at the time and accept the consequences of his actions.

He strode steadily on up through the woods, completely lost in his thoughts. The exercise helped to clear his hangover. Trees gave way to open fields as he reached the crest of the Downs, walking directly into the startling sunlight of an autumnal afternoon. He could just make out the first wisps of storm clouds above the hills to the east, skies that reflected his gathering despair.

There was so much he had hidden from Emma throughout her life, partly out of not wanting to hurt her, partly out of shame, partly from pure cowardice and partly trying to put a failed marriage behind him. In the telling of his story, he would finally have to admit to her why her childhood had been spent in such an unhappy and dysfunctional household.

He sat on a fallen oak at the edge of the wood, gazing aimlessly into the distance at the darkening sky. The thought of unloading so much on his daughter in the next few hours terrified him. And yet he knew that if he was to see Bushra again and attempt to seek her forgiveness, he had to have Emma's first.

11

Southern England,
Early September 2031

In the early evening, just as Jack returned home, the long spell of fine weather broke. Within minutes, storm-force winds blew dense black clouds from the east over the Downs, battering rain hard against the glass walls of his penthouse. Sporadic flashes of fork lightning raked the darkening sky, briefly lighting up the town below as if it were under aerial bombardment. Rolls of ear-splitting thunder echoed from the surrounding hills.

The wind shrieked, tearing at trees and shrubs, filling the air with swirling leaves, twigs and dust. Light faded quickly, obliterating the landscape and lingering memories of recent golden sunsets. There were no half measures in this increasingly skewed climate, he thought. The weather was either hot and dry or cold and stormy, veering unpredictably in a matter of hours from one extreme to another.

His walk hadn't tamed his raging emotions. He still had no idea where to start and, even now, exactly what he was going to say to Emma. All he knew was, he had to speak to her, tonight.

'I was wondering if I could drop over later if you're not busy? We need to talk,' he said on the phone, more abruptly than he'd intended.

'Are you OK, Dad?' Before he could reply, she went on quickly, 'How about nine? I've a couple of chores to finish. Are you sure you want to drive over? The weather's atrocious.'

'No problem, see you at nine.'

Before he left, he dug out a dilapidated shoebox full of old letters. Postmarked in England and Greece, they were dated in the '80s and '90s. If his courage failed him, he would leave the box with her. From the letters, she might learn of Bushra's part in their lives.

The short drive out to Emma's cottage was a nightmare. Several trees had fallen across the flooded road which, while not blocked, was dangerous to navigate. This, combined with the torrential rain and wind buffeting his car, meant he took nearly twenty minutes, a journey that would normally take ten. He was late, and he could see that she was worried.

'I thought you'd never make it,' she laughed nervously, as he was bundled through the front door, followed by storm debris scattering over the living room floor.

'It's shocking out there, cold as well,' he admitted.

'I can't remember lighting a fire at this time of year,' she said, as he settled into his usual chair in front of the kitchen range. 'Whisky?'

Unnoticed, he placed the shoebox on the floor, out of sight.

'No thanks, tea would be great though.'

She joined him with two mugs. They talked of this and that, mostly of Isabel. Her departure for Tripoli was still raw in their minds. They considered the merits of her job, avoiding their unspoken worries.

The rhythm of the old wall clock countered the clamour of the raging storm beyond the door; time passed. He fell silent, suddenly weighed down with sadness. He felt uncertain, unsure of what he was to say or do next. But say something he must; he knew that he was the most important person in her life, somebody who had loved him unconditionally for as long as he could remember.

'What's on your mind, Dad?' she said, at last.

Mug clasped in both hands, elbows on knees and head bent down, he stared blankly at the range.

'When I got in last night, I had a message.' He hesitated. 'It was Bushra. Yesterday was her birthday.'

'Bushra, her birthday,' she whispered, very deliberately.

He couldn't begin to imagine the terrifying images from her early childhood flashing through her head; he shuddered involuntarily.

*

She was speechless, unable to get to grips with this unexpected and woeful intrusion into their lives. She must have been three when she first became aware of the enmity between Jack and her mother, Charlotte. On his infrequent visits home, a simmering mutual hatred would explode without warning, reducing herself and Tom to a terrorised silence. In many cases, it was the mention of Bushra that triggered the row.

She could still hear her mother's shrill set-piece phrase, a frequent precursor to a violent argument between her parents: 'That bloody harlot Bushra and her bastard children are the curse of this family.' This was invariably followed by the noise of smashing crockery, furniture overturning and doors slamming. She and Tom would scramble upstairs to their rooms, barricading themselves in for hours until silence returned.

As a child, Emma often wondered who these 'bastard children' were; who answered to this blasphemy. In later life, she found that the use of the word 'harlot' reflected her mother so aptly: biblical, prissy and detached. 'Whore' would have been too streetwise, not sufficiently derogatory.

Spiteful tales swept through the house when Jack was away. When she was older, her brother would accuse her of putting a curse on the family. He said she was a witch and taunted her with being adopted. She would relate all this to Jack when he returned, which invariably led to more arguments and, sometimes, beatings.

Weighed down by the storm, the silence stretched out before them, each unable to break through their own suffocating thoughts.

*

Finally, Jack stirred, taking a draught from his tepid tea.

'I never told you how and when we met,' he said quietly.

He felt awkward, on the point of revealing an intimacy long-forgotten. There was so much he wanted to tell her about Bushra. She waited for him to continue, clearly not wishing to disturb his thoughts.

Over the next twenty minutes, he painstakingly related his fateful trip to Cyrene back in August '85. From the moment he left Benghazi to exploring the ruined city on his birthday, being beaten up by Green Brigade thugs, his time in Tolmeta jail, his rescue by Bushra, the time spent in the hospital and recuperating in her father's house in Benghazi.

He felt compelled to tell his story in all its dreadful detail, praying that it would provide the catharsis that he'd longed for, for over forty years. Eventually he had to stop, his voice wearied by the weight of memory.

'Don't, Dad, don't go on. I can't bear to hear this,' she whispered, moving closer to him.

Several minutes passed in silence. He sensed that she was desperately trying to control her emotions, knowing he'd been talking about the woman whose unseen presence had long plagued her childhood.

'The day you first saw her must have been your birthday,' she whispered, clearly unable to think beyond the mundane. 'Your twenty-fourth birthday.'

'Yes.'

At last, after all these years, she'd been formerly introduced to Bushra.

'Why don't you rest for a minute, Dad, have a whisky?' she insisted quietly. She took his silence for a 'yes', went to the sideboard and took out two glass tumblers, which she filled generously. He nodded and, taking his glass, turned back to the range, a dwindling island of warmth. To keep herself occupied, she threw more logs on the fire, which quickly came to life again. Time slipped by unnoticed. The storm started to abate, the wind dropping away; it was eerily quiet. Their breathing filled a silent void.

*

She could see that he was shattered, emotionally done in. She was reluctant for him to continue, yet she desperately wanted him to reveal more of Bushra and their past lives together. She'd always known that, hidden deep within this man she loved so dearly, there lay tragic and uncomfortable truths, which he'd kept from her. She knew that one day he would tell her everything, although she could never have anticipated the when, where and how.

As a young teenager, she had long suspected that Jack and the unknown Bushra had been lovers, that their relationship had ultimately destroyed his marriage. What had really worried her and preoccupied her early years was that he and Bushra might have had a child or even children, Charlotte's infamous 'bastard children'. This evening that fear, long dormant, resurfaced with a vengeance. She was at a complete loss as to what to do next.

Should she confront him at the risk of shattering an illusion that had bound them together all her life?

Should she just let it go and be satisfied with what she already had accepted about him, seeking nothing more, nothing less?

Becoming ever more anxious, she instinctively played for time. 'Dad, why don't you stay here tonight?' He made no effort to answer, as if he hadn't heard. 'The bed's made up in the spare room,' she continued. 'I've nothing to rush for in the morning.'

He gently squeezed her arm by way of acceptance and lapsed again into a dark silence, staring vacantly at the range. She glanced at the clock; it was after eleven. She finished her drink and stood up, deciding that there was nothing more to be gained that evening and perhaps it was time they should go to their beds.

Seeing that she was about to leave, he reached down and pushed the shoebox into view.

'There are things that I should have told you years ago but failed to,' he whispered hoarsely. 'I bottled every opportunity I had. As time passed, I persuaded myself that the telling would destroy the one truly loving, lasting companion I had, namely you. I was an utter fool and tonight I'm paying for my deceit, my cowardice.'

She was suddenly speechless with terror, as she stared at the shoebox. It sat threateningly on the floor between them like a bomb which, if triggered, would surely shatter their relationship. Her mood darkened, fear giving way to resolve.

'This is all about Bushra, isn't it?'

'Yes.' He paused. 'The box contains her letters going back years.'

'Her letters,' she repeated needlessly, her blood rising.

'They tell of our relationship, a loving, compelling, complex and dangerous relationship. It's all there, uncensored. Take the bloody box,' he said, now barely audible. 'Read and learn about your wretched father, the sins of his past.'

Her response was to fetch the whisky bottle and pour them both another large measure. She was prevaricating, trying to control her frayed emotions, waiting for some godlike intervention to navigate her through the next few perilous minutes. She couldn't return to her seat but wandered away from him, from the warmth and security of the fire.

She couldn't take her eyes off the shoebox, squat, challenging. *Will we survive its revelations?* she kept asking herself, repeatedly, insanely. Her resolve turned to anger. *Why was he putting so much at risk?* In the deep recesses of her mind, she heard Charlotte's shrill voice down through the years screaming at him, '… bloody harlot Bushra and her bastard children are the curse of this family…'

Without warning, she heard her own hoarse, disembodied voice.

'I must know, you have to tell me: "the bloody harlot Bushra and her bastard children", what does it mean?'

'Charlotte hated her and probably with good reason,' he whispered flatly.

Emma felt she was about to explode, crossing a threshold from which there would be no return.

'Am I one of her "bastards"?' she rushed on, giving vent to years of frustrating silence. 'Was I adopted?' she said, raising her voice, and finally, 'Are you really my father?' she shouted accusingly from the other side of the room, terrifying herself now beyond belief.

Slowly he turned to her, tears streaming down his weathered features.

'I am your father, you are my daughter,' he whispered, 'Bushra is your mother.'

Emma groaned and slumped to the floor.

12

Sabha, Early October 2031

Isabel unpacked, showered and lay on the bed, rereading her briefing notes for the eight-day trip to the desert. The Desert Patrol Group was due to pick her up from her Sabha quarters before dawn the following morning, prior to setting off on the arduous journey. This was her fifth since her arrival in the mandate in early June. From the day she joined EDA, her life seemed to hurtle along at a pace she could barely control. The only constant had been the daily grind of lessons in basic Arabic, starting several weeks before she left England and now in Tripoli, for two hours every morning.

After reading for an hour, she turned out the light and settled down, but sleep eluded her; she felt agitated. Perhaps, she rationalised, it was because much was expected of her on this trip, given her boss's instructions for the meeting with her Russian counterpart. For no apparent reason, she wondered to what extent the DPG would be familiar with her quest. Her thoughts kept going back to the first time she'd become involved with the group and, more especially, its charismatic leader, Colonel Philippe Marin.

Three days after she'd arrived in Tripoli, she had her first full working day at EDA's HQ. Within hours, she'd been surprised to learn that as well as working on plans for possible Bedouin and Berber integration for which she'd been recruited, she'd also been given a second assignment; no details were forthcoming. She was subsequently asked to attend a briefing at the office of the chief administration officer, the thought of which had freaked her out at the time.

At the briefing, she'd learnt that EDA had started discussions with the Russians on border co-operation. Apparently, this was now possible because the once fraught relationship between the two mandates had improved over the previous twelve months. It had been agreed that liaison teams would have regular face-to-face meetings at prearranged locations on the border, which it was hoped would benefit both administrations and build mutual trust. The first one had been scheduled for the end of June. The teams were initially tasked to discuss wide-ranging and practical issues affecting the nomadic Bedouin on either side of the border.

Isabel had been astonished to be told that she would be the EDA representative at these meetings. Apparently, the person originally assigned to the role, an army doctor with many years' experience working in the Middle East, had been rushed back to England with a suspected brain tumour. There being no other suitable candidate at the time, she'd been chosen to replace her. It was only after the briefing that Isabel had begun to appreciate the significance of what she was being asked to do. Several days later, she'd attended a second meeting, a briefing for new recruits.

She tossed and turned restlessly on the bed. In her mind's eye, she was swept back to that meeting, reliving the scene, every word and nuance.

*

She was shown into an air-conditioned, windowless room promptly at nine in the morning, intrigued to find six men dressed in military fatigues, already seated at a metal table. They nodded vaguely as she took the one remaining place. The time passed aimlessly, nothing happened, nobody spoke. Suddenly, just before ten, an army officer entered. The six men jumped to attention and saluted. She remained seated.

The officer introduced himself as Colonel Philippe Marin, commander of EDA's Desert Patrol Group, a paratrooper division which had been based in the garrison town of Sabha in northern Fezzan since the formation of the mandate in '25.

She learned later that he was considered the most experienced EDA staff officer in the ways of the desert, with a deep understanding of the northern Sahara and its diverse peoples. Within a matter of weeks, he was to become her work colleague and knowledgeable travelling companion. His fluency in Arabic increased her own proficiency.

'Welcome to the Desert Patrol Group,' he said, with the trace of a French accent. 'You're here because each of you will need to have a good understanding of our border with the Russians,' he said, getting straight to the point.

She remembered Scarletti's talk in Yorkshire and wondered what more there was to learn about Demarcation 1822.

The lights dimmed. A large map of former Libya was projected onto a screen at one end of the room. Colonel Marin, using a laser pointer, traced a line on the map.

'The border is known as "Demarcation 1822" or "D1822" for short. It follows longitude eighteen degrees east, from the Mediterranean coast in the north to a point where it intersects latitude twenty-two degrees north in the south of the territory, effectively dividing former Libya in two. Can you make it out?' he said turning to his audience.

It was only when she heard several of the men reply 'Oui' that Isabel realised that the soldiers were probably newly arrived French paratroopers.

'Yes,' she replied clearly.

'D1822 represents the southern-most extension of our common border with the Russians. It runs from north of the Arctic Circle to the Sahara in the south.'

Another smaller-scale map flickered onto the screen replacing the first.

'Take a look.'

She joined the soldiers, examining the map more closely.

'I can't emphasise the importance of this border,' he continued. 'It separates two mutually hostile political ideologies: a democratic EU and a despotic FRSS. It has to be defended at all costs.'

She followed the long red line southwards over thousands of kilometres. Although she'd seen a similar map in Yorkshire, the sheer size of it projected onto the screen made her shiver involuntarily. It showed with startling clarity how Europe had been squeezed by an expanding Russia over the last few years.

The new Russia, morphing into FRSS, had overrun and reoccupied all the former Soviet republics and more. Many newly occupied countries, such as Finland and the Baltic States, all the Balkan republics south of Slovenia including Macedonia and Greece, were not uniquely Slav states, but simply FRSS vassals.

She felt exhilarated, keenly aware of D1822's significance. The fact that she'd been selected to represent EDA at meetings on the border greatly excited her. Without thinking, she turned to Marin, seeking his confirmation of what she already knew.

'I've heard there's no fence or anything running between the Mediterranean coast and the border with Chad. Is that true?'

They all turned to look at her; nobody spoke. Suddenly she felt foolish, like a kid at school asking a stupid question out of turn. She looked directly at the colonel, taking him in for the first time. In his mid-forties, he was lean and short, not much taller than her, his dark hair swept back revealing a tanned fine-featured face; his dark pitiless eyes caught her attention.

'Good question, Miss Meredith,' he said, his stare softening to a broad grin.

'Isabel, Isabel Meredith,' she said, regaining her composure.

'D1822 doesn't need fencing – electrified, razor wire or otherwise. There are no fortified watchtowers, search lights or the usual military hardware. It's featureless,' he said, as if to drive home the point. 'It's a virtual border controlled and operated by satellites, twenty-four seven. They pick up the smallest signal generated by anything crossing the eighteenth parallel, which in turn triggers an appropriate response.'

Somehow, hearing Marin's description here in Tripoli made it much more real than listening to Scarletti in England. She noticed the others simply nodded, as if they were familiar with this type of border. She wondered, however, if they were too frightened to speak. Perhaps they knew something she didn't.

'But how does it work?' she asked. 'I mean, how are people physically prevented from crossing it?'

'They're alerted when they come within fifty metres of the border. Essentially there's a hundred-metre-wide virtual security zone straddling it. Any unauthorised person entering the zone triggers a warning system. A flare as bright as the noon-day sun shoots up into the sky, followed by a series of terrifyingly high-pitched screeches.'

'Do people know what they have to do?'

'Everybody travelling across the desert is aware of the system now. They have three minutes to retrace their tracks, to get as far away as possible,' he replied, with mind-numbing certainty.

'And if the warning is ignored?'

'If, for example, a Bedouin group doesn't heed the warnings and continues to cross, they will be incinerated by a soundless guided missile. The whole operation takes less than a minute. They're launched from one of many sites hidden in the desert well inside our territory. Satellite imagery confirms the group's extermination.'

She saw the soldiers visibly relax; he was talking their language. They didn't have to pretend anymore that they understood how D1822 functioned. She realised that Marin had provided them with all they needed to know. For her, though, there were still many questions to be answered. She sensed that he was aware that he had failed to satisfy her.

'D1822 bears no physical resemblance to the border between North and South Korea or the US-Mexico border,' he continued. 'For all that it's unseen, it's effective.' He paused. 'Its purpose is to prevent the incursion of one super-state into another's territory. In this regard, it's fit for purpose.'

'How long has it been operating?' she asked, pressing on, realising that she might not get another opportunity to acquire this knowledge so easily.

'For years, both sides recognised the inherent dangers of not having a secure border. It also became important that they co-operated when dealing with UDP militias and smugglers as these threats from the Sahel increased, common problems faced by both administrations. It started operating in '29, after a year of intense negotiations.'

She knew from her studies that knowledge of desert routes was the stuff of Bedouin folklore, where survival depended on being able to navigate accurately across vast featureless landscapes. She realised that this border concept must have been meaningless to so many of these people, unhindered as they had been for millennia by Western-imposed borders: caravans trading their produce across the desert, nomadic herdsmen driving their goats and camels from oasis to oasis, pilgrims moving to and from Mecca to the east and, more recently, the myriad of refugees escaping the clutches of tribal warlords in the Sahel, running from famine, war and slavery. She wondered how knowledge of D1822 and its hidden viciousness had first entered desert mythology.

'What happened to the Bedouin and people like them while you were still developing, refining the system?' she asked.

'It was trial and error at first,' he admitted. 'Many innocent travellers died in the first few months before people became aware of D1822, its whereabouts and its effectiveness. To avoid loss of life and preserve traditional trading routes, border crossings are now prearranged,' he continued, clinically. 'The whole process is closely co-ordinated and managed by the two administrations.'

'Perhaps people don't die unnecessarily anymore,' she said, more to herself, shocked at his casual attitude.

'UDP militias were quick to learn and soon kept well clear after experiencing their first bloody encounters. Nowadays most Bedouin groups carry GPSs, which we provide. Those that don't are soon reminded by the charred remains of their kinsfolk strung along the border,' he added, pointedly.

She resisted asking further questions sensing that he was getting irritated. She knew that she'd pushed him as far as he was prepared to go. He handed out an official booklet, speaking in French to the others for the rest of the meeting. English was the official language of the mandate; she ignored his slight and pretended to read the text, wondering how she was going to work with these men.

*

As she yielded to sleep, her memory of the meeting morphed into a surreal dream. The colonel, standing in front of the new recruits, was replaced by a host of familiar faces – Emma, Jack, Andrew, university friends, colleagues in Tripoli, even El Sahla and Scarletti – all pressing in on her, gesticulating wildly, shouting, 'Why? Why? Why?', demanding answers to their incomprehensible questions. She felt emotionless, entirely detached; it was a weird sensation.

*

It was still dark when she dragged her kitbag onto the pavement outside her quarters. Philippe and his Desert Patrol Group were not due for another fifteen minutes. She was tired and on edge, last night's dream weighing heavily on her mind.

It was the thought of Jack that really bothered her. Before she went to university, they were inseparable; he'd been her mentor, always there to encourage and guide her through her childhood and teenage years. But during her three years away studying in Edinburgh, he seemed to withdraw into himself. By the time she qualified, she hardly recognised the man she once adored. It saddened her to think how they'd parted in June; her letters to him went unanswered, which she was at a loss to explain.

Emma was no help. Her infrequent letters to her daughter were vague and unsettling, with little mention of Jack, a state of affairs Isabel would have found unthinkable a few months ago.

She felt in some way that she was to blame for what had transpired at home and yet, surprisingly, felt no remorse. Her academic interest in the Berbers of North Africa, her acceptance of the EDA appointment, the break-up with her long-time fiancé, Andrew, and even her newsy messages home all seemed in some way to exacerbate their ill will.

*

'It's bloody hot, hotter than normal for this time of year,' said Philippe, sitting at her side, as the battered army truck pushed on into a blinding sandstorm. 'These days the Ghibli can occur anytime throughout the summer months. It must be at least forty-five out there.'

The radio crackled into life. He grabbed the handset. Isabel could hardly hear him above the engine noise.

'This is DPG Unit One, come in please, over.'

She could just make out the response, an incomprehensible chattering over the airwaves. He listened intently for a minute before replying clearly in French.

'*Yes, yes, I understand, we'll manage. This is Unit One, out.*'

She noticed the strain on his face as he absorbed the news.

'Is there a problem?'

'The damage to the axle is going to take at least a day to fix, maybe longer. They're waiting for parts from Sabha. Given the bloody sandstorm, there's no knowing how long the whole business will take.'

'Are we going on?'

He ignored her.

As EDA's senior military commander in Sabha and East Fezzan, he was responsible on the ground for the border liaison meetings, although he took no part in them. FRSS and EDA liaison teams travelled to the meetings under the protection of their own security convoys. For this one, he had arranged for two armoured trucks to support the EDA Border Liaison Team of which Isabel was, as usual, the sole representative.

She and Philippe always travelled in the lead vehicle followed by a second larger one, carrying an armed escort of twelve French paratroopers. In the early days of the mandates, UDP militias had caused havoc throughout the desert, randomly killing thousands of Bedouins and hundreds of EDA and FRSS personnel. The last significant UDP militias had been driven to the far south, the Tibesti massif, by early 2030. Although there'd been very few reports of UDP militias in either mandate for over a year now, Philippe took no risks and always brought an armed escort.

Despite the appalling weather, they'd left Sabha for the remote meeting location in good spirits, at dawn the previous day. Unfortunately, on the drive south, the larger vehicle had suffered a fractured rear axle close to Ramlit al Wigh, which forced the group to stop and camp there that evening. This poor, squalid oasis village was still 200 kilometres to the north-west of the meeting point. Unusually for him, Philippe decided to push on that morning, leaving his security detail behind to repair the axle, which he thought might delay them by a day. Isabel instinctively trusted his judgement.

*

Relationships between the two liaison teams were good. Isabel had got to know and trust her Russian counterpart, Ramil, who had trained in the University of St Petersburg. He had specialised in forensic anthropology which she found fascinating. He told her how his skills were useful in dealing with a multitude of ethnic and tribal issues, many of which she was becoming familiar with. He jokingly suggested that she would benefit from a year of study in St Petersburg.

As she got to know Ramil, she realised that EDA was not dealing with a straightforward politically and culturally homogeneous Russian community. She sensed that the administrations on either side of the border, for their own reasons, were anxious to portray that it was.

She learned much from Ramil. His people, of whom he was intensely proud, were Tartars originally from the Caucasus. They hailed from old Muslim communities which had been suppressed for centuries for their cultural and religious beliefs by marauding and semi-nomadic Cossacks. The Russian Tsars had used Cossacks, the 'Old Believers', to control the empire's restless southern borders, terrorising the largely Muslim populations of the Balkans and Asia Minor. A longstanding antipathy based on mutual ethnic and religious bigotry and hatred had been sustained by successive Russian rulers and the Tartars right through to the present day.

Ramil in turn was fascinated by Isabel's stories. She told him of Jack's experience of working in Libya under the dictatorship. It wasn't just the prospecting that interested him, but Jack's later efforts to initiate plans to build vast solar energy projects in the northern Sahara. The idea of supplying power to Southern Europe intrigued Ramil.

Isabel found his interest in Jack's work somewhat at odds with his specialist knowledge as a forensic anthropologist. She felt frustrated that she hadn't listened to Jack more closely, hadn't more detailed knowledge of his work to pass on. If only Jack were here to listen to such an enthusiast she thought, what fun he'd have had.

She always looked forward to their meetings and enjoyed Ramil's apparent independent thinking, in what she imagined was a tightly controlled political environment east of the border. She felt a bond between them based on their common interests and approach to solving problems.

However, at their last meeting in September, he'd appeared reticent, withdrawing into a moody sullenness. She'd noticed how he stood apart from his security detail but was always polite and firm when issuing instructions. She didn't understand Russian, a language which she found abrasive, so could not gauge their relationships. She'd found this change in him unsettling and wondered how he would behave on this trip.

Although he was not present at the meetings, she was acutely aware that Philippe was watching her closely. She was resigned to the fact that, very probably, he had been asked to report to the administration in Tripoli anything that she might do that would compromise EDA's mission.

*

The armoured truck veered, pitched and rolled in one seamless ride. Their driver, Omar, wrestled with the wheel, like a skipper steering a yacht through the relentless waves of an ocean storm. Much to their annoyance, the Ghibli had reduced visibility to less than fifty metres. The dense swirling sand shrouded the stunning ochre-coloured desert floor, a vast gravel plain scattered with dazzling white sand dunes sweeping down from the remote Tibesti massif to the south.

Isabel and Philippe sat hunched together on a bench seat behind Omar, weary and overheated. On a small scrolling screen, they tried to follow the route through the invisible landscape.

A day and a half's drive south-east from Sabha had brought them into the endless Sarir Tibesti, the southern extremity of an area once known as the Libyan Desert. Since the founding of the mandates nearly six years earlier, few Europeans had ventured this far south. They were travelling to a prearranged meeting point still over a hundred kilometres north of the mandates' southern boundary with Chad.

With the virtual border now dangerously close, Philippe and Omar had to be extremely vigilant. Following any track during the Ghibli was hazardous when visibility was poor and satellite communications distorted. A wrong turn out of a wadi so close to the border could bring the unwelcome attention of a missile and a guaranteed emollition by 'friendly fire'.

Isabel saw a vertical black line on the screen. She guessed that it was longitude eighteen degrees east, running due north-south, the virtual border about which she'd heard so much – the Europeans to the west, the Russians to the east.

'*Omar, what are our co-ordinates?*' Philippe shouted in Arabic, above the noise of the engine.

Omar reeled off information from the instrument panel on the dashboard. She had only a vague idea what they were discussing, her Arabic still basic.

A red line, which she assumed represented their vehicle, had converged snake-like southwards with the straight black line, and was now running parallel to it. The black and red lines were close, representing perhaps a hundred metres on the ground. She pointed out the red line to Philippe.

'That's our track. We're getting close to the border now.'

'How long to go?' she asked, suppressing her anxiety.

'Not long, maybe five minutes at this rate. We're nearly there but we're very late, it's already two-thirty. The Ghibli has really slowed us. We should have stayed at Ramlit al Wigh with the others and all driven down together.'

'But Ramil…'

'We should've rescheduled the meeting for another time,' he said, abruptly.

They watched Omar intently as he guided the truck through the sandstorm, his deeply lined Bedouin features now reflected in the darkened windscreen. Although it was only midday, it seemed like dusk.

'We'll only have an hour at most with Ramil if we're going to get back to Ramlit al Wigh before dark.'

'I'll need more than that.'

'Do you have much to discuss?'

'Yes,' she answered emphatically, barely suppressing her frustration; he was there to facilitate, not direct the meetings.

'*Omar, stop, stop the vehicle,*' he shouted in Arabic, without warning.

The engine shuddered violently and fell silent.

'Really?' he said, turning to her, barely hiding his scepticism. 'What exactly?'

'The Russian's views on recent UDP incursions into Cyrenaica from northern Sudan, lower Egypt; why UDPs are on the move in the far south again; what the FRSS military are doing to stop them.'

'News to me,' he said, clearly not believing what she'd told him.

She held her tongue, frustration turning to anger. She could see that he was irritated; perhaps, as she'd suspected, he wasn't up to speed on the latest developments.

'We've had no significant northerly migrations, especially from the south-east, for months now,' he continued. 'What do you expect to hear from Ramil?'

'I really don't know,' she said, vaguely, not wishing to involve him in her business. 'HQ is hoping for a detailed analysis of their current situation.'

An awkward silence followed; her anger lingered.

'Anyway, we'll need some time for the football match you've planned,' he said, bitterly. '*Drive on, Omar.*'

She'd heard recently through the grapevine that he'd been

making light of her work, especially with his military colleagues in Tripoli. Initially it had bothered her, but no longer; she simply ignored the gossip. In the last couple of months, she had developed her job into a wide-ranging brief, now seen as important by many in EDA High Command.

However, not all were convinced; how could a recently qualified social anthropologist add any value to EDA's mission in the desert areas along the border? Some older, more sceptical heads, especially in the military, were not persuaded to co-operate with UNMC, an exercise which they saw as futile and irrelevant. She knew that Philippe was one of those sceptics, which put her in a moral quandary; she was angry with him for undermining her, yet indebted to him for her progress in everything she had achieved since her arrival.

The previous month, Ramil had suggested that, after their next meeting, the two groups should play football. The protocol agreed by both administrations stipulated that their security details were each not to exceed twelve military personnel, a perfect number in his opinion from which to select a team. She warmed to the idea, believing it would be a small but significant step in building trust between the two administrations. Philippe had forewarned his squad that they would be expected to play a match against Ramil's men.

'*How far now?*' shouted Philippe.

'*Less than 300 metres,*' came Omar's muffled response.

Suddenly, without warning, the engine faltered. She felt Philippe brace. She glanced at him, his normally relaxed features now etched with uncertainty. For the first time since they left Sabha, a steely fear invaded her. His unquestioning instinct for the desert had always allayed any anxieties she may have had. After months of travelling together, she knew she had become totally reliant on him. Now, for the first time, she sensed his fallibility.

Endless scenarios began to stream through her throbbing head. What if the engine failed completely? How long could they survive in this heat before succumbing to death by dehydration? Could HQ's search and rescue helicopters find them in the Ghibli?

'*Sir, the engine's struggling,*' Omar shouted, hoarsely.

Right on cue, the spluttering engine gave one final lurching cough and stopped.

'*Bloody hell, what's the matter, Omar?*'

The noise of the sandstorm intensified, shrieking around them like a wailing banshee. Visibility through the front screen was down to just a few paces. With the air-conditioning off, the heat, already just tolerable, rose rapidly in the buffeted truck. The atmosphere was suffocating, claustrophobic.

'*The air filter's probably blocked. I've a mask. I may be able to fix it,*' shouted Omar. A moment later, he pushed the heavy armoured door against the wind. '*Sir, I'll be a couple of minutes.*' He slipped out and instantly disappeared in a haze of swirling sand, the door crashing shut behind him.

'Can we get Ramil on the VHF, let him know how close we are?'

'We still haven't any protocols for this type of communication,' Philippe said abruptly. 'It's never been necessary before.'

'That's unfortunate,' she said, unable to conceal her frustration.

'Anyway, all our radio frequencies are down,' he admitted. 'It's probably the storm.'

She was worried; his attitude was too casual.

'Poor Omar, what a thankless job.'

'No worse than working with camels in a Ghibli,' he said, reasserting himself. 'For men like him, sandstorms are there to be lived through. They aren't life-threatening,' he added, dismissively.

When they'd first worked together she'd found Philippe's attitude offensive, racist even. As she got to know him, she learnt of his *Pied-Noir* background, how it affected everything he thought and said. For decades, successive generations of his family had enjoyed the privileged life of the colonial French in Algeria, until they fled in the '60s.

Both his parents, born in Algiers in the '50s, had lived through the last days of French colonial rule. Like many ousted European colonialists, they found it difficult to live back in the mother country. Penniless and ostracised, they struggled to survive. The *Pieds-Noirs* who did, proudly asserted their colonial past. She was surprised that despite not having lived in Algeria, Philippe was *Pied-Noir* through and through.

'*Fixed*', shouted Omar, as he squeezed back into the cab minutes later, encased in sand and dust. The following heat rush was blistering.

'*Good work, Omar*,' shouted Philippe, evidently relieved.

Omar started the engine and the truck trundled slowly on into the screaming, engulfing sandstorm. Isabel's fear subsided.

'Still can't see our opening in the border,' Philippe said, as they stared at the screen.

Just then, two short green lines appeared, crossing the black line orthogonally. She assumed these demarked the prearranged temporary corridor crossing through the security zone and virtual border, through which it was safe to pass without being annihilated; they'd arrived.

She knew that the width of each corridor varied; for their meetings, one hundred metres sufficed. However, if a caravan of several hundred camels and its entire entourage needed to cross, the corridor might be a kilometre wide. Being millimetres outside the corridor and milliseconds outside the prescribed time limit would result in the same destiny meted out to the hapless Bedouin.

She understood that between the green lines, the border had been deactivated by satellite for a specific period, enabling the two teams to hold their meeting. It was here that they'd planned to meet Ramil. After a minute, a red light flashed on the dashboard; the truck stopped abruptly.

'*We're here, sir. The crossing point is 120 metres to our left*,' shouted Omar.

'Even if we could contact Ramil, there's no way we can meet

in these conditions,' he said, turning to Isabel. 'We'll have to agree a new opening schedule via HQ.'

'When?'

'I'll contact them when I can get a signal after the storm moves through,' he replied. 'I'll reschedule the meeting for tomorrow at dawn.'

'And in the meantime?'

'Just wait,' he replied, apparently resigned to their new situation. 'The Ghibli should blow itself out in the next few hours, hopefully by midnight. The skies will clear then.'

A meeting in the cool of the morning, that would be pleasant, she thought, relieved that nothing was expected of her until the storm eased.

'We might even get an opportunity to play our football match,' she laughed uncertainly, trying to lighten the grim atmosphere in the truck.

'Yes,' he said, with little conviction.

Her fear started to subside.

'We won't go hungry,' she said. 'I had the canteen prepare some food packs, enough to feed Ramil and his crew as well. They're always ravenous. I think they live on starvation rations in the desert.'

Philippe turned to Omar.

'*We'll wait here until the Ghibli blows through, hopefully in the next few hours, then I'll reschedule the meeting. We've food and water so it's just a case of sitting tight.*'

'*Sir,*' grunted Omar, by way of acknowledgment.

She glanced at Philippe. His usual bravado seemed to have evaporated; he looked strangely unsettled. Perhaps, she thought, he too was fearful, realising their vulnerability.

Her mind drifted in the stifling heat. Not for the first time in the last month or so, she wondered why she'd been so besotted with him within the first few weeks they'd worked together. Without little thought of the consequences, she had submitted to him early on and had slept with him. A feeling of disgust and self-loathing seeped through her now; she felt fragile, bewildered.

As the wind continued to rattle and shake the stifling truck, she moved to the bench seat behind where they were sitting and quickly fell into a troubled sleep. Within a few short hours, darkness crept up on the isolated truck. The sandstorm eased, the buffeting, howling wind ceased.

13

Athens, Greece, Early October 2031

Four weeks after Bushra had re-entered his life, Jack found himself in Athens airport, after a bumpy flight over the Alps. He walked across the tarmac, sweat encasing his weary body. The dated terminal building looked broken, uncared for. It was a far cry from its former pomp as gateway to the Athens Olympics for which it was built. Bushra had been right about the heat. The Russian pilot had warned his unsuspecting passengers that the morning would be a little hotter than normal; it was forty-two degrees.

He followed his fellow travellers through security to passport control. The fact that he was in Russian-occupied territory suddenly hit him. Experiencing twinges of fear and resignation in equal measure, he shuffled towards a kiosk in the dusty hallway. He recalled similar dawn arrivals at airports around the Middle East many years earlier, a sullen apathy masking underlying tensions between the border police and new arrivals.

The counter was above his head. All he could see was a disembodied hand, fingers drumming on the metal, waiting to take his passport. As a means of intimidation, the set-up was effective.

No sight of the official, no eye contact, just his stamped passport being slapped down impatiently before the fingers resumed their ritualistic dance. He'd experienced this many times. He could only guess what would have happened if there had been a problem with his visa.

He avoided the hordes of hovering taxi drivers and joined the queue for the city bus to Omonia Square. Standing in the crucifying heat, he saw his reflection in the unwashed windows of the terminal building. His ageing frame stood out above the jostling crowd. He felt decidedly out of place.

A sense of *déjà vu* cut through his aimless thoughts. Here he was again, travelling into an unknown future with stomach-churning apprehension. He was trapped between leaving a devastated Emma in England and seeing Bushra for the first time in decades. His old fatalism kicked in; he joined the crowd which surged forward to meet an ancient sandblasted bus, trundling up to the terminal.

He didn't recognise any of the areas they passed through. Gone were the scattered villas and their gloriously unruly orchards and vineyards; the colourful roadside tavernas doubling up as workshops, awash with rusty vehicle carcasses, discarded air-conditioning units and the endless detritus of modern-day living. Gone were the small stark-white orthodox churches imprisoned between garish advertising hoardings. Gone was the chaotic melee of dogs, goats, mopeds and battered cars furiously competing for every square metre of the road.

The bus, locked in horn-blaring traffic, crawled along a prematurely ageing six-lane highway between an endless cliff face of overbearing residential blocks. Thick smog added to the sensation of driving through a deep sunless canyon. All to a standard Soviet-era design, the buildings rose twenty storeys above the jumble of street-level shops, bars and restaurants, each advertising their trade in gaudy signs, painted incomprehensibly in Greek, Cyrillic and Arabic.

He was struck by the dilapidated appearance of the buildings, many of which had only been built in the last ten years; likewise, with the cars, buses, roads, bridges and factories. In fact, he saw neglect and decay in everything, even reflected in the faces of ordinary people in the street. Their lives clearly shortened by the appalling and unyielding conditions under which they lived; so much suffering by so many. The young had a weariness about them, an ageless maturity that he found unsettling.

How could people survive here and remain sane? he wondered idly, mesmerised by the sheer scale of what he was witnessing. Where was the work to sustain this huge faceless community? Acrid diesel fumes infiltrated the leaky bus windows adding weight to his pounding headache. The relentless streetscape challenged his memories. He was vaguely reminded of places like Moscow and Damascus, places he'd visited on business in the '90s, a motley mosaic of cityscapes challenging his senses.

Bushra had arranged for him to stay in the St George, the small hotel owned by her old family friend Yannis, the place where she had lived and worked when a student all those years ago; he remembered it well. It was conveniently located, within walking distance of the bus station in Omonia Square, and only minutes away from Syntagma Square and the city centre.

He was met in the foyer by Chara, Yannis' youngest daughter, who ran the place. He'd last seen her as a ten-year-old, when she helped out in the kitchen with Bushra, before going off to school. Now in her mid-fifties, she was an engaging and attractive woman, who had managed to keep her youthful figure. She was expecting him and had been well briefed. Fussing over him like an old family friend, she brought him to the quietest room at the back of the building, Bushra having warned her that he could never cope with the traffic noise in front of the hotel.

*

Late in the afternoon, Jack and Chara settled down in her cluttered office behind the reception desk, over a jug of retsina. They talked

135

of Bushra, whom she clearly regarded as a very close friend. Ten years her junior, Chara would have been an impressionable young girl when Bushra worked there.

She recounted Bushra's life as a student in Athens, her time as a political activist and her frequent visits to Benghazi, where, it was rumoured, she had a reputation as a critic of the regime. Although he was familiar with much of what Chara was telling him, he had no idea how much, if anything, she knew of his relationship with Bushra or the fact that they'd had the twins.

'I adored her, still do,' said Chara, getting up to refill the jug. 'I would have done anything for her, she was my hero. As a kid, I told her that when I was older, I wanted to help, I wanted to become a revolutionary as well.'

'Did she see herself as a revolutionary?'

'No, that's how I saw her. When I was fourteen, maybe fifteen, I told her I wanted to join the struggle, although I had no idea what that actually meant.'

'And that included going to Benghazi?'

'Whatever. Anyway she said that having me to confide in was all the help she needed. It went to my head,' Chara laughed. 'I felt giddy with importance, and of course I didn't say anything to anybody.'

'Did you see much of her after she left university?' Jack asked, nervous that he might slip up and show his hand.

'She moved into her own place in Glyfada, it must have been in the mid 80's. I seem to remember that we hadn't seen much of her the previous year.' She paused. 'In fact, she rarely visited us after you two met.'

'I wasn't aware of that,' he said awkwardly.

'I knew you were a great distraction for her,' she said, with a wide grin, 'her great passion. Occasionally she'd mention that you'd been together in Stoupa.'

'We met there a few times,' he admitted. 'They had a beautiful place overlooking the sea.'

'Everybody loved Bushra,' Chara continued. 'My older brother, Petros, adored her and would have died for her. My father used to get very angry. "She's far too good for you," he'd yell at Petros. I know Father loved her as a daughter. He was very protective of her.'

They were silent. He became aware of people moving about and talking in the foyer, their shared past seeming so remote from the present.

'Of course,' she said lightly, 'everybody knew of this crazy, talkative Englishman she was seeing. They knew you'd met in Libya in mysterious circumstances, which intrigued them. She told me later how it had happened. From the way she spoke of you the very first time, I knew she'd met her match.'

'Did she ever tell you about the country, what she did there?' he asked, hoping to draw attention away from himself.

'No, no she didn't,' she said. 'She came to see us. I remember it was around Christmas, sometime in the late '90s. We hadn't seen her for a few years.' She hesitated, as if trying to recall the visit. 'I remember she said she was going there much less frequently. Many of the people she'd been working with had either fled or disappeared. She said she had problems which had compromised her work.'

'Problems?'

'Libyan society was very conservative, it's probably worse today. Women could only play a small part. There is a Greek word for this type of society: *misogynḗs*. You say misogynistic. She was overlooked, abused, because she was a woman.'

'By anybody in particular?'

'There was one man, a leading Berber militant, an outspoken critic of the regime. I can't tell you how badly he treated her. Even today, it pains me to think about it.'

'Poor Bushra,' he said, horrified at the thought of her suffering, that he'd abandoned her, hadn't been there to support her.

'I think she would have killed him given time. She knew that if she'd continued with her work, she would have been driven to it.'

Chara excused herself and went to the reception to attend to a couple who were checking in for the night. He slumped back in the chair, unable to marshal his thoughts, overcome with shame. God, how he'd screwed up Bushra's life. How much better it might have been, he thought, if he'd behaved more responsibly, more courageously, more honestly all those years ago.

Chara returned minutes later.

'Her life wasn't all bad,' she said, as she poured him another glass of retsina.

'That's a relief to hear.'

'In the mid-'90s she went back to college and got a law degree. She also devoted herself to the charity work her mother, Elena, had started, helping women out of drugs, prostitution, you know, that sort of thing. She was always busy.'

'She'd have enjoyed working with Elena,' Jack said, realising that the rift between her and her parents after the twins were born must have healed eventually.

'Sadly, we drifted apart,' she continued, minutes later. 'I rarely saw her after that, maybe once or twice a year.'

'Did she ever marry?' he asked, immediately regretting he'd raised the issue.

'Marry?' exclaimed Chara, looking at him in astonishment. 'There were men in her life, yes, but marriage, never. There was only one person she was prepared to marry,' she hesitated, 'and he wasn't available.'

'I'm sorry, I shouldn't have asked, bloody stupid of me.'

'Don't be,' she insisted. She paused, glancing at him shyly. 'When you see her tomorrow, just enjoy being with her, thankful that you're together again, even if it's only for a few days.'

They talked and drank late into the evening. Occasionally she would attend to a guest at the reception desk, which doubled as the hotel bar. At other times, she'd disappear into the kitchen or drop into the restaurant to see how the diners were faring. He was impressed how she managed the place with a minimum of instruction. Later, at around ten, she called up the kitchen for some food, which staved off his impending hangover a little longer.

*

Chara woke him promptly at four the following morning. It was far too early, given the quantity of retsina they'd consumed. She'd prepared a substantial breakfast: yogurt and honey, fresh fruit, cold meat and boiled eggs, olives, bread and cheese and copious cups of black coffee.

She constantly reminded him that he had to be at the regional bus terminus off Kifissou Avenue by five-fifteen, to be assured of a seat on the Kalamata bus. Although he had already booked a ticket and reserved a seat, it invariably came down to first come, first served.

In the dry coolness of the dawn, she marched him off to Omonia Square to catch a local bus to Kifissou. The familiar concrete-tiled sidewalks, heavily stained with kerosene, food waste, urine and dog shit, were thronged. They weaved their way along Panepistimiou, passing crowded cafés, bakeries and groceries. He was surprised to see so many people up and about at this hour. As they hurried along, she told him that most people living in this district had long commutes, either on foot or on unreliable public transport.

'The metro is overcrowded twenty hours a day,' she lamented. 'The buses are few and far between, and never keep to a timetable. Jobs are so scarce that people are prepared to put up with any inconvenience to have money coming in.'

They got to the regional bus terminus at Kifissou just before five-fifteen. Jack felt depressed at the thought of the journey ahead; he knew he was getting too old for this.

The terminus was reminiscent of the Third World – dilapidated, filthy, crowded, noisy and a total mystery to an outsider unused to its *modus operandi*. Unperturbed, Chara guided him directly to the Kalamata bus, marooned in the middle of the parking area. Anticipating trouble, she climbed aboard with his ticket and immediately set about a young Russian conscript, who was sleeping in Jack's pre-booked seat. Wordlessly the soldier got to his feet and slumped into the seat across the aisle, instantly falling asleep again.

Jack squeezed his backpack into the overhead rack and sat down, whereupon Chara dropped a bag she had been carrying onto his lap.

'You'll find food and drink for the trip. Remember, it could be fourteen hours before you reach Kalamata, so don't finish everything at once,' she laughed. 'There are a few things there for Bushra as well. Tell her we miss her greatly. Tell her to visit us. There's always a room for her at the hotel.'

She leaned over and kissed him quickly on each cheek, as he tried clumsily to get to his feet to thank her. She turned to go, but not before he noticed that she was fighting back tears. At the door, just before she was swallowed up by more passengers clambering aboard, she turned to him and called out:

'Jack, look after her, don't leave her again, promise.'

'I promise,' he shouted, and she was gone.

*

At five-thirty the overcrowded bus inched its way out of the terminus, insinuating itself into almost stationary traffic. He realised that this was going to be a hell of a long day. He looked around at his expectant fellow travellers. Most were elderly Greek peasant farmers, judging by their rough clothes and weather-beaten features. Many were laden down with cheap household goods. At least a third, by his reckoning, were migrant families, ranging in age from newborn babies to the old and infirm. Five or six young Russian conscripts, dressed in shoddy, ill-fitting uniforms, made up the rest of the passengers.

As the bus crawled along the congested fume-filled street, an altercation broke out behind him. He twisted around in the rigid plastic seat but couldn't see what the commotion was because of the press of standing bodies. He noticed a young woman, possibly Syrian or Iraqi, with a baby tucked in her shawl, standing at his shoulder. He struggled to his feet to offer his seat.

'Sit down, please sit down,' he said repeatedly, pointing to the seat.

She flinched and tried to back away, clearly unused to such courtesies. Eventually, with some trepidation, she sat down.

Time passed. The heat and smell of unwashed clothes, sweating bodies, cheap tobacco and exotic herbs intensified. It was impossible to see where they were passing through. Most of the window blinds had been pulled down to cut out the sun. After a couple of hours lurching from one traffic hold-up to the next, with Jack wondering how much longer he'd have to stand, the bus shuddered to a stop.

A great surge from behind propelled him forward. Realising that this was a scheduled stop, he pressed to one side as people, mostly overloaded migrants, squeezed past. The young girl staggered to her feet, her terrified eyes briefly meeting his, and joined the file-past, the tiny baby crying pitifully at her breast. As the bus emptied, he slumped back into his seat. The tiny wizened old woman beside him, a small black bundle, remained asleep through the whole commotion. He looked across the aisle at the young conscript, now fully awake, who was eyeing him curiously.

'Fucking Arabs,' the man snarled in English, spitting into the void between them, as if to emphasise his disgust.

The suddenness of his grotesque outburst shocked Jack. Without waiting for a reaction, the conscript turned away and resumed his interrupted sleep. The bus pulled away.

Unable to see where they were going, he leaned stealthily across the old woman and gently raised the blind. They were passing through a limitless shanty town. To the horizon, all he could see was a chaotic jumble of cardboard shelters, timber shacks made from packing cases, corrugated iron hovels and tents of torn plastic sheeting and heavily oiled tarpaulins. All manner of primitive structure, made from every conceivable waste known to man, was crammed into every available nook and cranny. Dust hovered in the smoggy sunshine. Everything appeared distorted, shifting unsteadily in the shimmering heat.

He realised that this must be home to thousands upon thousands of refugees, who had fled war-torn lands beyond the Mediterranean. Now shut off and abandoned by their Russian overseers, their lives were as hopeless as the lives of those they had left behind in Damascus, Aleppo, Baghdad, Basra or wherever. In the mass exodus over a decade ago, he saw that they'd simply swapped one form of eternal misery for another. An analogy for the human condition perhaps, he reflected.

For a while he followed the unfurling landscape. Shanties gave way to treeless rocky scrub, occasionally punctuated by broken water windmills and naked pylons standing guard over abandoned and derelict farms, all this set against the backdrop of a distant dazzling silver sea. He assumed that they must be well beyond the old port of Piraeus, home to the Russian Mediterranean Fleet, on their way to Corinth and the gateway to the Peloponnese.

Without warning, a small claw-like hand emerged from the black shawl beside him and pulled the blind down. Too jaded to recover his e-reader from the backpack in the overhead rack, he wriggled himself into the least tortuous position the seat had to offer and dozed off. He slept sporadically, surfacing occasionally to ease his numbed limbs, before slipping into semi-consciousness again.

His thoughts hovered uneasily over the last few weeks. He and Emma had barely spoken since the traumatic evening when he had revealed much, but not everything, of his past with Bushra. They had spoken awkwardly just a couple of times, the last call from her to wish him a safe journey. He had tried phoning several times and on two occasions visited the cottage, but to no avail. He realised in hindsight that she had probably gone to stay with friends or even with Isabel in her London flat.

In one of the few conversations they'd had, Emma told him, somewhat formally, that she'd read the letters in the shoebox. He didn't press her on how she felt, and she gave no clue. At least, he appreciated at the time, she had acknowledged reading the letters. There was still so much he should have explained to her in person. The letters were full of anecdotes, details and references that she would not have understood. His cowardice in relying on them to tell his story consumed him.

By far the most significant revelation would have been Stavros. How could he not have told Emma about him when she was younger? He should have told her everything when she was a teenager, after he and Charlotte divorced. He had the opportunity then to make a fresh start with his daughter, to admit to her the events of his turbulent past; why her childhood had been so unhappy, their family life so dysfunctional. He should have sought her forgiveness years ago, so that together they could have moved on. But in the end, to his great shame, he had done nothing.

Stavros' story was buried in the past. It was already too late to say anything to Emma when he received Bushra's last letter in 2010, five years after the divorce. In a few terse words, Bushra had informed him that Stavros had been kidnapped and subsequently executed by the Green Brigade. It so happened that his death was the last time he and Bushra were in contact; until very recently, he never saw or heard anything of her again.

He knew Emma must feel betrayed; that he had hurt her deeply, and that there was no simple explanation as to why and how events had turned out so tragically all those years ago. No matter which way he tried to rationalise his behaviour and what he had concealed from her for so long, he realised that she would see things differently. Perhaps she would never be able to forgive him. The struggle to regain her trust, even her love for him, he recognised would be immense. He shuddered at the thought; salty tears slid down his weather-beaten cheeks.

He became aware of an increasing restlessness around him. People were coming to, shuffling in the shadowy dusty haze, rearranging clothes, retrieving bags and quietly talking. The bus slowed down and eventually stopped. Without warning, several people pounded its battered sides, yelling and cursing loudly. He looked about and caught the eye of the young conscript, who shouted at him in broken English.

'Internal border post, get out, inspection.' As an afterthought he pointed to Jack's backpack, shouting, 'Take bag.'

Jack stumbled out into searing heat, temporarily blinded by the sun. He was surprised to see that they'd pulled up in front of what looked like a well-fortified border post. It was set securely in a six-metre-high razor-sharp fence, which disappeared in each direction across an arid landscape as far as the eye could see. Zombie-like, he followed the other passengers towards a metal kiosk, not unlike the ones in the airport, and joined an orderly queue. Why the border? The whole thing made no sense to him.

He thought he recognised the countryside and guessed that they were close to the Corinth Canal, separating mainland Greece from the Peloponnese. He saw that all those in the line were Greek; clearly the migrants had disembarked at the first stop, disappearing into the vast shanty town west of Piraeus.

He went through the same passport rigmarole as before, placing it on a shelf above his head. This time, though, there was a different response. After a moment or two, a door at the side of the kiosk opened and an unshaven official emerged, a small cheroot clenched between his teeth. He indicated to Jack to follow. Fifty metres from the kiosk, he stopped in the glaring sunshine. He turned to Jack, waving the passport.

'Who are you, what are you doing here?' he snapped, in heavily accented English.

'Jack Meredith. I'm going to the Peloponnese for a holiday,' he replied steadily.

'No Peloponnese visa, entry not possible,' responded the official.

God, he thought, *I didn't know I needed an internal visa to visit Stoupa.* It had never occurred to him. Presumably Bushra and Chara had assumed he'd obtained one in London.

'I didn't know I needed one,' he admitted, lamely.

They stood looking at each other warily in the appalling heat. Each sized up the situation, buzzing flies their only distraction. Jack continued, trying not to plead. 'Can I obtain a visa here? Would you be kind enough to issue me one?'

'Is big problem, very expensive here, not cheap like in UK.'

Relieved, Jack realised there was a proposition being put to him. 'I would like to buy a visa now.'

'Three hundred US, cash,' the official said, before handing the passport back and wandering off to complete checking through the remaining passengers.

In London he had paid one hundred US dollars for his principal visa. Obviously, the market for visas issued here was very lucrative. Knowing the procedure but seeing that he was being watched by other passengers, he walked back to the shade of the bus. Out of sight, he slipped three bills into his passport. He joined the queue as if nothing unusual had happened. A few minutes later, his empty passport had been returned without a further word, complete with a local visa for the Peloponnese.

After ten minutes they were on their way again. Despite experiencing petty corruption in all its ingenious forms during his working life, the passport incident had unsettled him. The fact that the Russians had set up an internal border left him feeling imprisoned. He noticed that the young conscript had left the bus along with his colleagues. He suspected that they were all stationed there and had just returned from leave.

*

The weary passengers became more animated once they had crossed the Corinth Canal. He guessed that for them they were at last nearing home with no more borders to cross, no migrants to compete with and perhaps less intrusion from their Russian masters. It was mid-afternoon. They had been on the bus for nearly eleven hours and he was ravenous. He pulled out the bag that Chara had given him and ate a large cheese roll, after breaking off a piece for the old woman beside him. Wordlessly she'd grabbed it, noisily munching away with her toothless gums.

The journey across the Peloponnese to Kalamata was slow. The stops at the larger towns of Argos, Nafplio and Tripoli seemed to take forever, with people constantly embarking and disembarking. Towards dusk, as the bus ground its way up over the high mountain passes south of Tripoli, the blinds were raised. Jack had his first uninterrupted views of the countryside.

Looking north back over the plains surrounding the town, he saw several large solar farms glittering gold in the reddening sky. Maybe this traditionally poor region of Greece now under Russian occupation was becoming self-sufficient; how ironic, he reflected. He wondered whether they'd originally been funded by the EU or more recently by RFSS – an intriguing question.

As the bus freewheeled down through the near-vertiginous hairpins towards Kalamata, he began, like the few remaining passengers, to feel a sense of homecoming. Even after nearly forty years, he recognised the curve of the barren mountains rising imperiously overhead and the coastal plain far below. He spotted the occasional Orthodox church perched on a rock outcrop and small whitewashed farmsteads isolated haphazardly amongst the olive groves. All these long-forgotten images came flooding back.

By the time the bus finally reached the coast road leading into Kalamata, his anticipation at meeting Bushra was overwhelming. His mood swung wildly between fear and ecstasy, between feeling bone-weary old and carefree young. Would they recognise each other? he wondered. Finally, the bus inched its way into the crowded ill-lit terminus; the engine died with a shudder, its own unedifying death rattle.

As he got up from his seat the old crone beside him gripped his hand with surprising strength. She muttered a parting message incomprehensively in Greek. Her big toothless grin, as if divining his thoughts during their speechless hours together, seemed to give him courage for what he was about to face.

As he limped from the bus, trying to uncoil his aching back, he saw Bushra waiting under a dim light by the manager's office. In that moment, she saw him and rushed up, flinging her arms around his sweaty body in a long silent embrace.

After what seemed like an eternity, he gently unlocked himself, stood back and, holding her at arm's length, gazed into her eager, smiling face. Spontaneously they broke into uncontrollable laughter, tears of joy washing away the tension, their long time apart suddenly empty, meaningless.

'Bee…' he started to say, above the roar of a departing bus.

'Wait, Jack, not here,' she said putting a finger to his lips. She took his hand and led him out and across the bustling street, to her ancient battered Lada parked on the quay.

14

Fezzan, Early October 2031

Isabel awoke; only the dashboard lights cut through the darkness. She became aware that the storm was easing, the desert night lapsing into silence. She heard the faint snoring of the two men, sleep, she mused, reducing their differences to nought.

Fear returned to haunt her. Childlike, she squeezed her eyes shut, trying to rationalise her troubled thoughts. She failed. For the first time in months, old uncertainties returned. She started earnestly questioning what she had given up for this new life in North Africa, trying to reason why she was there, what she was doing. And in thinking about it again in the claustrophobic confines of the isolated truck, her fear increased.

*

She remembered with shame her behaviour towards her fiancé, Andrew. She saw that she had let him down terribly. She recalled with sadness how in their first year together at Edinburgh University, they had been intoxicated with each other, and as their relationship matured over the years, believed they were in love.

It was at the end of their final year that she realised she no longer cared for him, that he had started to bore her. She remembered how fearful she was of his lack of ambition, his concern for their material wellbeing, his dogged reasonableness and total lack of curiosity outside the confines of their studies, his family, and all things of the North.

Notwithstanding, she had to admit he'd deserved better from her. Instead of confronting him with the truth, she had fled overseas to North Africa, pushing him away, along with Emma and Jack. All this had been a desperate bid for freedom, a freedom from the simple conventions of family life, which she had come to despise. And then, in an act of what she now realised was abject cowardice, she severed her relationship with him, from the security of a frenetically busy life thousands of kilometres away.

A week after she'd arrived in Tripoli, she had written to him, ending their engagement. She told him that she believed it was the right decision, because of the way their lives were moving apart, which she admitted had saddened her. She falsely claimed being helpless in the face of events beyond her control. His reaction was predictable. He wrote saying he fully understood, he would wait, and she would change her mind and come back to him. Emma wrote to tell her how stupefied she and Jack were at this callous act.

Isabel had first slept with Philippe having known him for less than a month. It wasn't as if they were in love, they were not. They were physically attracted to each other and although she knew he had a reputation as a philanderer, she decided to let it happen.

This was a deliberate act, consciously undertaken to sever more thoroughly any links she might still have had with her past. She had succeeded in what she had set out to do, being alone, cut off, the price she assumed she had to pay to gain the independence she sought. Her attitude hardened. She became immersed in her work, losing herself to the outside world. She thought less and less of Andrew, Emma and Jack. Thoughts of home and all it represented receded.

Although she and Philippe saw each other infrequently because of where they lived and worked, their affair intensified. Their behaviour in public suggested otherwise. They were colleagues that enjoyed working together, no more, no less. However, four weeks ago and just days before his regular overseas leave, he'd let slip that he had a wife and young family living in Paris.

'We met in the Sorbonne. She was doing law and I was studying history and politics of the Middle East. She became pregnant, so we married. It was expected.'

You bastard, you bloody bastard, she remembered thinking at the time. She had suspected all along that he was probably estranged or maybe even divorced. Most of the expatriates, male and female, living in Tripoli were running away from their partners; she was no different. It was the curt way he'd consigned his wife to history in a few short sentences that upset her. She was too dumbfounded and ashamed to say anything to him at the time, and let the moment slip away.

The evening before he left on leave, he said, without warning:

'You know I never loved Louisa. She's a corporate lawyer earning millions. She has a live-in nanny bringing up our two spoilt kids. In her eyes, I'm just a feckless mercenary unable to shake off my *Pied-Noir* roots.'

Too true, thought Isabel; later it seemed churlish to raise the issue of his family again. Perhaps she was just too scared. In any case she admitted to herself that she had learned something, that he would discard her with the same ruthlessness when the time came. More importantly, she realised that she could never trust, never mind love this man. Knowing this, she had resolved to bring their affair to an end on her terms.

She recalled how, over the following weeks, she had come to realise that she was no different from Philippe, no better, no worse. She had metamorphosed into somebody who she, and certainly Emma and Jack, would never have recognised a year earlier.

But why should she care what they thought now? Her letters

to him had gone unanswered. Her mother had written only intermittently, showing little interest in her new life in North Africa, with virtually no news of Jack, except that he'd become withdrawn.

Initially the lack of communication had upset her; she just couldn't understand why they'd abandoned her so dramatically. After a couple of months, she'd reluctantly come to accept that, for whatever reason, this was the new norm in her family life; she just had to get over it. She wasn't yet prepared to accept that she was in any way to blame. She had never felt so alone, so isolated in her life.

*

Lying there in one of the remotest places on God's earth, pouring over in her mind her reckless behaviour, she experienced a sudden terrifying dizziness, an onrush of madness.

She sat upright, fully alert, her memories clearly etched in her seething brain. In that split second, she could feel the love she had denied, the treachery she had plotted, the pain she had caused, the deceit she had committed, every frazzled emotion she had experienced, overwhelming her in a torrent of anger and shame. In a living nightmare, she cried out, waking the others.

A hand slid behind her neck in the shadowy darkness and grasped her firmly.

'Isabel, Isabel, calm down, calm down,' whispered Philippe. 'What's the matter, why are you crying?'

'Oh God,' she said, sobbing, 'I've had the most dreadful nightmare.' She leaned forward, resting her head on his shoulder. 'We were being pursued through a sandstorm, losing ground,' she lied, in a hoarse whisper. 'One moment you were there, the next you were swallowed up. You simply disappeared.' Her whole body convulsed. 'I was terrified of losing you, of being left behind.'

Gradually his grasp relaxed. She sank back into her seat, her jagged nerves unravelling, cold sweat channelling down between her breasts into her groin. She felt feverish. In the minutes that followed, she slowly regained her composure, the madness draining like poison from her body. In the ensuing silence, she realised the Ghibli had blown through.

Philippe unlocked his door and stepped into the blackness, the night sky awash with stars and galaxies too numerous to contemplate. Still shaking, she and Omar followed, wordlessly gazing up into the heavens. She was profoundly moved by the enormity of what she saw. Time froze. A cluster of shooting stars arced down to the eastern horizon, breaking the spell.

'It's just after three,' whispered Philippe, unwilling to break the silence. '*There's nearly three hours till dawn, Omar.*'

They remained standing, rooted to the spot, for what seemed like hours. Omar was silent, head down. In the darkness, she watched him as he carefully moved away from the truck.

'What's he doing?' she asked, trembling in the desert coolness. '*Omar, what's up?*'

There was no response. Omar slowly retraced his steps to rejoin them. Even in the dark, she could make out his worried features. They were silent as he pointed to the ground where they were standing. She followed his gaze and froze, panic swiftly rising again through her wired body. She could just make out footprints, maybe three or four pairs, imprinted in the soft sand dusting the gravel floor of the desert. All the prints followed an anti-clockwise path around the truck.

'*Four Bedouin, not soldiers, were here, probably within the last two hours,*' Omar whispered. '*We're being watched, sir, do not move.*'

Sensing the seriousness of their situation, Isabel reached out to Philippe to steady herself. He absorbed her weight without moving. Minutes passed, three motionless statues swaying imperceptibly as fatigue set in.

'*They've gone, sir,*' whispered Omar, without warning.

'*How do you know?*'

'*They moved away, maybe two minutes ago.*'

'*I didn't hear anything.*'

'*I know, sir. They meant us no harm. If they were terrorists, we would not be having this conversation.*'

'What's he saying?' she asked, her Arabic failing her. Philippe translated, his voice suggesting disbelief.

'That's weird,' she muttered, shaking violently, cold feverish sweat clothing her body.

'*They walked across the border from the Russian side before going around the truck, sir,*' Omar continued. '*Then they retraced their steps, walking due east back across the border.*' And then, quietly, as if to emphasise the point, he added, '*The border must be open. They walked across unharmed.*'

'*There's no bloody way the border's open,*' Philippe whispered hoarsely. '*It would've closed automatically at the agreed time yesterday.*'

'*It should have been closed, sir, but it was open.*'

'*It couldn't have been.*'

'*If it was closed, they'd have been burnt alive. We'd have seen their charred remains,*' Omar muttered.

Philippe dropped the argument.

'*If Ramil's there on the other side, why didn't he try to stop the Bedouin? Like us, he'd have assumed that the border was closed.*'

'*With respect, sir, you didn't see or hear them. Ramil and his people would be no wiser, especially if they're some distance away, perhaps behind those low dunes.*' Omar continued, pointing across the border, '*You can see them, the ones 200, maybe 250 metres beyond the border. Maybe we'll see Ramil when it's light.*'

Philippe leaned resignedly against the truck, deep in thought.

'*Let's get some sleep,*' he said, after a lengthy pause. '*I'll try to contact HQ before dawn, find out what the hell's going on and reschedule the meeting.*'

He briefly explained to Isabel what Omar had told him and what he was planning to do. She climbed back into the truck, too terrified to speak, hoping for another couple of hours' sleep.

*

Just before sunrise, Philippe awoke and instinctively grabbed the radio. Omar had abandoned the truck, leaving a coarse crumpled blanket draped across the driver's seat like discarded reptile skin. The air was fetid, without oxygen, without hope.

Isabel could hear Philippe as he repeatedly called HQ. There was no response. After ten fruitless minutes, he slumped back in his seat.

'I can't get through to HQ. The system's still down.'

She could hear how weary he'd become over the last twenty-four hours.

'I heard,' she said from the back of the truck, feeling crushed and exhausted from lack of sleep. 'What will we do now?' she asked, barely awake.

'I'll try again shortly.'

A pre-dawn blush filled the eastern horizon beyond the invisible border. The dark silhouetted dunes softened as strengthening light filtered through low-lying desert haze. As he attempted to contact HQ again, she stepped outside and deeply inhaled the fresh desert air. This was the best time to be alive in the Fezzan, in the early morning before heat swamped any lingering night-time coolness.

Her eyes, becoming accustomed to the light, followed the footprints of their mysterious nocturnal visitors. She could clearly see now where they'd crossed and recrossed the border, circumnavigating their marooned truck. She was too exhausted, though, to summon up her recent fear. What really mattered was that the three of them had survived.

Who were these people, she wondered, how could they have crossed the border without being incinerated? She realised that if the border had been closed, as it should have been, their visitors would have triggered the warning system. She shuddered as she contemplated the consequences.

Fifty metres to the south of the truck, she noticed Omar. He was kneeling with his forehead on a prayer mat. Facing east towards Mecca and blind to the approaching dawn, he was enclosed in a world he shared only with his god. Save for his mumbled prayers, the silence was absolute, nothing stirred.

'No luck,' Philippe said quietly, as he joined her a few minutes later.

They stood together uneasily, staring across the border, unable to communicate or make sense of their predicament.

'*You slept OK?*' he asked, as Omar walked slowly towards them.

Omar raised his eyebrows fractionally as if to say, 'Why ask?', and threw his mat into the truck.

'*Sir, when it gets lighter, I'll follow the footprints across the border, see if I can contact Ramil,*' he said, as if his prayers had given him a fresh resolve, clearly not shared by the others.

'*How can you be so sure the border's still open, still safe to cross?*'

'*It was open several hours ago, nothing has changed.*'

'*I still can't contact HQ to check.*'

'*They'll change nothing until you get through and agree a new plan,*' he said with devastating logic.

Philippe explained Omar's thinking to Isabel.

'Seems OK to me,' she said, realising not for the first time in the last few hours that Omar appeared to have a much better grasp of what may have happened here. Whereas she and Philippe, both exhausted from lack of sleep, were incapable of thinking clearly, Omar had stayed calm and rational throughout, unbothered by any preconceptions. A characteristic of desert people, she thought.

'*Ramil's trucks are nowhere to be seen. I'll follow the Bedouins' footprints, check if his men are stationed beyond the dunes, it'll be quite safe,*' said Omar.

Philippe translated what they'd been discussing.

'I can't see anything near the dunes. There seems to be a depression between us and them, judging by the top of that thorn bush,' she said, trying to see the situation through Omar's eyes.

'Not deep enough to hide Ramil's trucks though.'

The three stood awkwardly together not knowing what to do next. She became fatalistic, resigning herself to the coming day.

'*OK, Omar, let's go with your plan,*' he said, after a few moments. '*We'll brew up some tea and eat something before you head off.*'

'Understood,' she said, relieved that he'd appeared to concede to Omar. 'I'll rustle up tea and something to eat. There's a bag of fresh dates I picked up in Ramlit that you two can get started on.'

They ate in silence in the truck, sitting where they had slept, each buried in their own thoughts.

15

Peloponnese, Greece, Early October 2031

I n the gathering dusk they stood on the quay, holding each other closely. Years of pain and separation slipped away. Through her loose cotton dress, her body felt firm and alive, just as he remembered her, all those years ago. It brought back one memory with extraordinary clarity: the hospital in Tolmeta, where she'd glided effortlessly like a dancer through the ward, between wraith-like patients and their downtrodden families.

Today, he saw the same generous face, lustrous blue-black eyes undimmed by age, her olive skin with barely a wrinkle. She was ageless. Her youthfulness astonished him.

'Jack, let's get going. We've several hours' driving before we're home,' she whispered. 'We'll stop in Kardamyli for something to eat. The old taverna down on the shore is still open. You'll remember it, the one with the rickety sundeck.'

He squeezed her gently, struggling to articulate his thoughts, unwilling to break his self-imposed silence.

'Yes,' he said, at last, standing back. 'Yes, let's go.' He gazed at her in the gloaming, lost in the reality of her presence and hesitated. 'I can't believe we're here, together again. It's incredible to see you looking so well, still so young.'

'Into the car then,' she laughed. 'Let's move before we're arrested for loitering.'

They sat in companionable silence as the old car climbed noisily up through scented pine forests away from Kalamata. The headlights swept the hairpin bends picking out swarms of insects and flitting bats. Soon they were freewheeling downhill at dizzying speeds, towards the inviting lights of Kardamyli far below.

He felt her hand gently squeeze his thigh.

'Just checking you're still there,' she laughed, as she flung the car expertly into another bend.

*

They parked next to the taverna under an old rotting palm tree on the water's edge. The night sky was moonless, a black velvety backdrop to silent galaxies. He heard lapping waves at their feet, punctuated by the rhythmic drumming of hidden cicadas. Plaintive singing and muted laughter drifted across the water. Memories surged back. They walked arm in arm up the steps and found an empty table out on the wooden deck overlooking the sea.

'Where to begin?' he asked, after a young girl had taken their orders.

'Where we left off,' she suggested, a huge grin on her face, 'all those years ago.'

'So much has happened,' he said quietly, 'so much of our lives spent apart, so much grief.'

'Yes, so much grief.'

'Seeing you here in this place tonight, the years seem to have vanished.'

They sat in silence, lost in the moment.

'How long will you stay, Jack?'

'I could only get a two-week visa, but in truth I want to be with you as long as it takes.'

'As long as what takes?'

His heart ached as he sensed her nervousness.

'To get to know you again, to try to make up for all the years we've been apart.' He reached out and gently wiped away a single tear from her cheek.

'It should be quicker to get a visa next time, assuming there is a next time,' she whispered, taking his hand. 'You could be back before the end of October.'

'There has to be a next time.'

'Tell me about our daughter,' she laughed, breaking the spell. 'Does she have her mother's pushy character?' she said, before adding impishly, 'And her famous good looks?'

He flinched imperceptibly, realising that whichever tack they took, whatever they chose to recall of the past, they would have painful tales to relate. Knowing Bushra as he did, he suspected that she was well prepared.

'Emma's a wonderful woman – warm, talented, my best friend. Somebody you'd be very proud of. She has a really gutsy daughter, Isabel.'

'We have a granddaughter?' asked Bushra, clearly taken aback.

'Isabel's just like you in so many ways.' He hesitated. 'She's working in Tripoli, has been since June.'

'Good God, Jack, Tripoli,' she exclaimed. 'How old is she?'

'Twenty. She qualified this summer as an anthropologist, got a job with EDA straight away and left for North Africa as soon as she could.'

'What is it about North Africa with your family?' she asked, grinning broadly.

A sudden chill clawed his soul; the last few months with Isabel before she left for Tripoli in June had been difficult. He'd become increasingly fearful that she was about to be consumed by the place, in the same way he had over forty years ago. He'd been in a state of paralysis, barely able to speak to her, unable to articulate his worries for fear of unlocking the past. Her unanswered letters were a testament to his state of mind.

'Our family,' he reminded her, suppressing his anxiety. 'With you as her grandmother, it's hardly surprising.'

'And her father, Emma's partner?'

'She's a single parent. She met Bill in university, but he left her as soon as he discovered she was pregnant.' He paused. 'Emma was a wild kid, very headstrong. You wouldn't recognise the woman she is today – an internationally acclaimed historian, well-known in academic circles in England.'

He told her about their daughter, recounting her life from the time she was grudgingly accepted by his ex-wife, Charlotte, into their London home.

'Up until recently, her main concern has been her daughter's job with EDA,' he said, unwilling for the moment to talk about the last few weeks.

'Isabel's got your genes, she'll survive.'

'Our genes,' he said, quietly.

'What's she doing there?'

'Working in a team liaising with the Russians on border issues; trying to manage nomadic Bedouin and UDPs; bringing an end to people trafficking, drug smuggling, that sort of thing,' he said, cursing himself for not having shown more interest in his granddaughter's work.

'God, she's got stuck in quickly, she'll be running the place soon,' Bushra laughed. 'It's very ambitious.'

'That's what I think,' he said, before he could prevent himself from adding, 'though nothing as dangerous as your efforts in opposing the dictatorship when you were her age.'

'Hardly. You knew what I was doing, we were together then, remember.'

'You were much more involved later on. Chara was…'

'Ah, that's Chara,' she interrupted, 'you don't want to believe everything she tells you. I was her hero when she was a kid. She thought I was some sort of freedom fighter back then.'

'One day you might tell me.'

'One day, one day.' She paused. 'All I'd say now was life for the ordinary citizen under that regime was a living hell. The outside world would never have known about this.'

'Me included?'

'You included, working as you did in the eastern desert, far from civilisation. Even in Benghazi, you were cut off from ordinary folk, everyday events.'

'I was hardly ever in Benghazi, spent most of my leave with you in Greece.'

'Don't I know it,' she grinned.

They talked on, recollecting the '80s and '90s, how those times had affected their lives. As parents, they studiously avoided the difficulties they'd both faced – for him, the fact that Emma had only recently discovered that Bushra was her mother. And how Charlotte, having no option but to accept Emma into their London home, had subsequently treated their daughter. He had no idea how Bushra would react to all this and hadn't the heart to discuss it now. And then of course there was Stavros; what could they possibly talk about, given that he was long dead?

The young waitress returned with their food: bread, olives and kleftiko, a steaming clay pot of oven-cooked lamb in potatoes, onions, garlic and spices, together with bottled water and a jug of local red wine. After lighting a well-used candle, she quietly retreated. Despite the heat, they were both ravenous.

'I've often wondered if we could have done things differently,' she said, after a while. 'I know we had very limited options at the time.'

'We did, although with the benefit of hindsight,' he hesitated, 'I should have.'

'Should have what?'

'Done things differently.'

'Don't go there, Jack,' she whispered, 'it takes two to tango.' She was silent for a moment. 'My parents were very angry, my mother more so with me than you.'

'To this day, I feel bad about them, especially your father after I got to know him when I stayed with you in Benghazi.'

'They were both fond of you, although I know they had no great expectations for our relationship,' she laughed, 'you know, marriage, that sort of thing. Remember I was the anarchist, wanting to bring down everything that the family had stood for, had cherished since the beginning of time.'

'You were hardly an anarchist.'

'In their view, I was. The best they could have hoped was for you to calm me down, distract me from the pernicious world of Greek politics, make me a slightly more rounded citizen.' She paused, and then said with a wide grin, 'Bedding an Englishman wasn't going to change their opinion of me, nor of you for that matter.'

He smiled to himself, remembering the spell she would cast over him with her feisty turn of phrase.

'The twins changed everything though.'

'The twins did change everything,' she repeated, quietly.

'My being married was the final straw for your poor parents,' he admitted, feeling his long-held guilt on the rise again.

'From the start, I knew you were engaged and would inevitably get married. You never pretended otherwise. We both understood the risks we were taking, at least we thought we did. We were both so bloody headstrong,' she said, grasping his hand across the candle-lit table. 'Falling in love, that's where we went wrong.'

'Perhaps,' he said, unconvincingly.

'Perhaps it wasn't love after all, just lust and reckless sex, fuelled by retsina and the aphrodisiac of Greek living.' Her laugh was tinged with sadness. 'We'll never know.'

'For me it was love,' he said, his voice breaking. 'From the very first days in the hospital in Tolmeta, I was besotted with you, still am.'

She squeezed his hand harder; he winced. 'I've always loved you,' she whispered.

She went on to tell him how Greece had been transformed by the occupation, suffering under a draconian austerity programme, which had impoverished the entire local population.

'And your brother, how is he?' he asked. 'Heavens, I can't even remember his name.'

'Alexis.' She hesitated. 'He's dead, Jack.'

'God, I'm sorry. I hardly knew him. I remember he was very protective of his little sister. What happened?'

He could see that she was struggling.

'Forget it, you can tell me another time.'

'No, I must tell you, but it's not good,' she hesitated. 'You remember my mother's family owned a shipping company? It wasn't big, but it was successful.'

'Yes.'

'Six, seven years ago, the fleet included three tankers, transporting crude from Ras Lanuf in Libya and Latakia in Syria to Elefsina refinery, just west of Athens.'

'I remember the refinery,' he said, 'going there on business in the early '90s. Afterwards I stayed with you in Stoupa for a few days.'

'The Russians commandeered the tankers in September '25, a couple of months after the occupation, claiming there was a national emergency. The family were promised compensation. They retained Alexis, although his job as managing director became impossible.'

'The poor man, what a terrible position to be in.'

'In May the following year, they revoked our shipping licence, effectively confiscating the business. My parents were forced to sell to a consortium of Russian businessmen for a tenth of its value. The day of the sale, Alexis disappeared.'

'God almighty,' he exclaimed.

'His body was found floating in Piraeus port a couple of days later. They said at the time that he'd drowned, that it was an accident. I didn't believe them, so I arranged to meet an old university friend working in the coroner's office down on the quays.'

He could see that she was fighting back tears.

'Don't go on.'

'I must,' she said, composing herself. 'My friend told me that Alexis had been struck on the back of the head before he hit the water. There was no water in his lungs. The bastards had murdered him.'

He was at a loss for words. She went on to tell him how all their other assets, except for property in Stoupa, had eventually been purloined, how the family had been made destitute, how her aged parents, then in their late eighties, had struggled to survive. They died within weeks of each other in '29.

He realised that in the last few years she'd lost everything – her parents, her brother and the family business – directly because of the occupation and yet, in recalling this distressing story, she had retained an unbelievable equanimity.

She amazed him.

*

The taverna grew quieter, laughter becoming more subdued as the night wore on. The noise of traffic in the town was sporadic, a solitary moped occasionally shattering the peace. He could hear an owl calling softly above in the pine woods. It was approaching midnight and the place was empty. It would not close, local hospitality dictating that they could stay as long as they wished.

A tall gaunt man of indeterminate age and smelling strongly of Turkish tobacco rambled out onto the deck and greeted Bushra profusely. She stood and, holding his hands, warmly returned his greetings. They talked quietly for several minutes before the man pointed to Jack; she nodded vigorously.

Turning to Jack, she said, 'This is Christos, fifth generation of the family to own the taverna. Our families have been friends since the '60s. We always stopped here on our way to Stoupa. He's just asked if you're the man I used to bring here in the '80s, the '90s, the one they knew as the "talkative Englishman".'

'Good God,' replied Jack, staggered not so much at being remembered, but at the intimacy of this tight-knit community, how he had been a small fleeting part of it, all those years ago.

He got to his feet and greeted Christos in the few broken words of Greek he had. Yes, he nodded, he was that man. She and Christos continued their animated discussion for several minutes before she turned to Jack again.

'Christos tells me there's a curfew at midnight. It's nearly that time already, we'd better be on our way.'

She handed over a bundle of roubles to him as he walked them back to the car, all the while regaling her with some long-forgotten tale which caused them great hilarity. He kissed her on both cheeks and shook Jack's hand in a bone-shattering grip, before shambling back to the deck, chuckling loudly.

*

'Are you worried about the curfew?' Jack asked, as they pulled out onto the deserted main street.

'No, the local military police know me well. They let me come and go as I please.' She hesitated. 'They all work for my tenant, Dorpadski.'

'Your tenant, you have a tenant? Who is he?'

'Ivan Dorpadski, regional governor of the Peloponnese. He lives in the villa with his family.'

'That's some tenant you've got,' he said, alarmed by what he'd heard. 'I thought you were living there.'

'No, I live in the old fisherman's cottage, the one on the foreshore. You remember the place. It's where we used to stay, hoping nobody would find us,' she laughed.

'How could I forget, but the villa, don't you miss it? The space, the comfort, those stunning views?'

'I can't afford to live there, Jack, I'm broke. It's not like the old days.'

He was silent for a moment, the reality of hard times she was living through seeping into his consciousness.

'This guy Dorpadski, presumably he pays you rent,' he said, before adding quickly, 'Sorry, that's none of my business.'

'No, no, don't worry. But the rent, well yes, he does sort of, but that's another story.'

'Who is he anyway?'

'Ex-army. Until two years ago he was the first military governor of UNMC, although to me, it's still Cyrenaica, eastern Libya, my father's homeland. After a four-year posting in Benghazi, he was transferred to Greece as governor of the Peloponnese.'

'He's pretty influential.'

'You might say,' she grimaced. 'He refused to move his family to Benghazi after FRSS occupied North Africa, preferring to keep them in Greece. They've been living in Stoupa in the villa for nearly six years.'

'Good God, how the hell did that happen?'

'It's complicated, Jack, I'll tell you another time.' She hesitated. 'What really sickened me, though, was that I found out later that he was one of the shareholders in the consortium that took over our shipping company.'

'Shit,' exclaimed Jack. 'I'm sorry, I shouldn't…'

'Don't be,' she interrupted, 'you're right, it's shit.'

He knew that their reunion was never going to be straightforward, but he hadn't anticipated so much dreadful news.

As if reading his mind, she continued, 'It's certainly not easy living in Stoupa. It never is with Dorpadski around. No doubt over the next few days, you'll get to know more about the man. All I need tell you is he's out of the country with his family at the moment, so we won't be bothered.'

Jack lapsed into silence, realising how little he knew of her life over the intervening years. During that time, he had rarely considered the impact the occupation of Greece and Libya was having on her family. He had simply taken it for granted that they were surviving and would be alright.

This former aristocratic family, who had moved in the upper echelons of society whether in Libya or Greece, had been virtually wiped out by the occupation, driven to their graves by loss of dignity, penury and, ultimately, murder.

Looking back, he reflected how his and Bushra's fortunes had diverged, his for the better, her life for the worse. Had he been more courageous, pushed back on social conventions and the competing aspirations of others, her life might have been so much happier, more fulfilling. In the darkness of her old rattling car, he felt deeply ashamed.

Soon they were climbing again up through pine trees, swaying in a freshening nocturnal wind. Leaving the forest behind, the road crested a high limestone ridge, outlined against the night sky. Far below, they could see the lights of fishing boats twinkling like fallen stars on the pitch-black sea. They didn't speak, each lost in distant memories of this very same road trip, many years earlier. The ancient Lada protested loudly as she put it through its paces on the twisting road.

'Dorpadski, what sort of person is he?' he asked, after a while. 'Chara was telling me how ruthless the FRSS administration is, especially towards migrants.'

'He's OK. He can be civilised when he wants to be. There are times when he and his wife can be refreshing company, cultured, intellectual. Generally, I find them unsettling – sometimes friendly and sophisticated, at other times boorish and threatening.'

'Considering what he's done to you and your family, you appear remarkably calm,' he said, hoping he wouldn't be misunderstood. 'I mean…'

'I have to be, Jack,' she said, brightly, 'otherwise I'd go insane. I'd kill the bastard, given half a chance.'

She caught him off guard, remembering what Chara had told him about Bushra wanting to kill somebody in Libya in the '90s. Maybe she really meant it this time.

'Don't worry, I'm not a killer,' she laughed.

The road had dropped down through numerous tight hairpin bends to the coast. They were driving south along low cliffs, looking out over the darkened sea, faintly dotted with small white horses, testament to the rising wind.

'How the hell does anybody survive in the Peloponnese?'

'In many ways, it's easier than the mainland. Senior Russian officials want to keep the Peloponnese for themselves, migrant free. The only other people are local Greeks or Greeks who have family connections living here. Unemployment is not too bad, if you can believe it. Locals are employed in agriculture, construction, on renewable energy projects.'

'It still must be difficult.'

'It is, especially for kids. Food and water are frequently scarce. Power is off for up to twelve hours a day, although solar now provides most of our basic needs. Unemployment stands officially at forty percent, but I think at best, only one in three has a job, better than the mainland though.'

'That's terrible, it could be the Third World.'

'You know, you're right, the bastards have pushed us back into the Third World,' she said bitterly, remaining silent for a few moments. 'The authorities have no answers, let alone the imagination to deal with such a growing crisis. Of course, we get the occasional adventurous tourist as well,' she laughed.

'Hence another reason for the internal border near Corinth.'

'God, I forgot to tell you,' she exclaimed. 'Did you get your local visa in the embassy?'

'Bought it at the border. Three hundred US in cash.'

'I'm really sorry, officially it's fifty.'

'I'll know the next time.'

'Oh, Jack, I hope you have to buy many more visas.'

They reached Stoupa shortly after one. At the entrance to the villa, a security guard saluted as they drove under the raised barrier. They continued slowly along the curved driveway between beautifully manicured lawns, past her family villa, partially hidden by dense shrubbery. The driveway gave way to a dirt track overshadowed by tall eucalyptus trees, which they followed down towards the rocky foreshore. The headlights picked out a small whitewashed cottage.

Memories came flooding back. He could make out the veranda on the south side, which looked out over the sweep of Stoupa bay. It must have been there where she'd been standing, when they spoke on the wallscreen weeks earlier.

Switching off the engine, she turned to him and, without warning, threw her arms around his neck, drawing him into a long and passionate kiss. He barely noticed the strong onshore wind buffeting the old car or the waves tearing into the rocks below.

*

Something had disturbed him. He sat up, temporarily disorientated in unfamiliar surroundings. As he adjusted to the dark, he saw her curled up beside him on the bed, her back to him. His eye traced the outline of her naked body, rising and falling in the gentle rhythm of a deep, satiated sleep. He stayed absolutely still, mesmerised, only vaguely aware of the wind, of rattling doors and windows throughout the cottage.

A banging noise brought him to his senses. One of the shutters had come loose. He eased himself carefully off the bed and closed it. He checked the time on his watch: three-forty. Standing over her, he felt a cooling draught eddying around his nakedness. He watched her. Even in her sleep she appeared to sense him. She stirred and rolled onto her back, her face still turned away. Legs slightly apart, she unnerved him. She shuddered; he remained still. Their lovemaking had left him physically and emotionally whipped, completely zoned out.

When they had first spoken on the wallscreen weeks earlier, a deep stomach-churning longing had surged through his weary soul, an ancient sensation he'd completely forgotten. What had she been hoping for from this reunion? Could their mutual passion ever be rekindled? She was five years younger and had, at least from what he'd seen of her on the wallscreen, retained her striking looks. The thought of wilting, literally, at some critical point during his visit had haunted him.

He hadn't slept with a woman for years. In the weeks before he came to Greece, the thought of sleeping with her again had terrified him. His irrepressible urge to make love, once a driving force in his life, had ebbed away. He knew that time had caught up with him, his ageing body losing its youthful tautness. With his greying hair and wrinkled skin, he'd assumed she would be appalled at the prospect of making love. From the moment he saw her at the bus station, his fear only increased.

She must have sensed his nervousness. She took control as she invariably did in the past. As they entered the cottage, she suggested that he take a shower to freshen up after the long sweaty bus ride.

'The one in the spare room on the right's better. You can use it while you're here,' she said, pointing to one of three doors off the kitchen-living room.

He went in, closed the door and stripped off, his shirt stiff with dry sweat. The shower was in a curtained-off corner of the small whitewashed room, which was simply furnished with a single bed, an upright chair for a bedside table and a low chest of drawers on which stood an assortment of books and candles.

The water pressure was good, and he soon scrubbed himself clean. Suddenly the curtain was pulled to one side and she stood there, naked.

'I forgot to mention that water is rationed here. I'm afraid you'll have to share your shower,' she laughed, handing him a bar of soap. 'Why don't you wash me?'

She stepped into the shower beside him.

'Come on,' she encouraged him gently, 'you used to be so good at this, remember,' as she steered his hand, the soap frothing her firm breasts, down the flatness of her stomach, between her splayed legs. She then eased the soap from his grip and slowly worked it around his chest, down his back, thighs and groin, slowly arousing him.

'Wow, Jack, you still look good,' she said, standing back and examining her handiwork. She knocked off the shower, led him out and gently pushed him back on the bed. Wordlessly she straddled him, their wet, naked bodies interlocking. As she gradually coaxed him, her hips slowly gyrating, he could feel his anxiety seeping away, his arching body becoming alive to hers, moving instinctively in harmony. She placed her hands on his shoulders, her dripping hair falling across her face, her opened thighs now pumping rhythmically until suddenly, tensing, she let out a short ecstatic cry and collapsed onto his chest.

Later, she led him to her room, where they flopped down on the oversized bed. Within minutes they were deeply asleep; that was nearly two hours ago. He was thirsty now and gingerly leaving the room found a jug of iced water in the cooler. Trying another door off the kitchen-living room, he stepped out onto the windswept veranda, hanging baskets swinging effortlessly around him.

He looked southwards over the inky blackness of Stoupa bay, the twinkling promenade lights flickering on the waves as they pounded the beach. He sank into the cushions of an old reclining seat, its coolness cosseting his heated body, and promptly fell asleep.

A shadow passed over his upturned face, forcing him awake. She was standing before him, her wet naked body glistening in the low early morning sun.

'Come on, lazy bones,' she said gaily, a broad grin on her face. 'It's time to stir yourself, have a swim. It's always refreshing at this time. Go as you are, nobody can see you down below the old pine tree. You know the place. Always a favourite of yours, diving off the rocks.'

He struggled to free himself from the cushions.

'I've been in already. Your towel's here,' she said, pointing to a small wicker table. 'I'll get breakfast.'

With that she disappeared inside. He hitched the towel around his waist and wandered around to the seaward side of the cottage, memories flooding back. He swam away from the rocks out to sea. Although the overnight wind had died away, there was still an onshore swell, which effortlessly supported his aching body.

Twenty minutes later and greatly rejuvenated, he retraced his steps to the veranda. She had set out fruit, yogurt, fresh croissants and jam and a large jug of coffee on an old camping table.

'You've been to the bakery already?'

'While you were asleep.'

'No wonder you look so well with all this fresh food, swimming every day. You don't look a day older than when we were last here,' he said, marvelling at her youthful body, now modestly clad in a bikini; she simply laughed.

They sat over breakfast as the shadows shortened and the heat steadily rose, reminiscing, gently probing each other's past, ever wary of destroying their common mythology, of facing unpleasant truths.

'There's something I need to tell you about the family, our family,' she said, turning her gaze to the sea. He noticed the sudden anxiety in her voice. 'It's about Stavros.'

'Stavros?' he said nervously.

'This will come as a shock, Jack. I'm truly sorry, but his story must be told.'

He sat up, bracing himself for whatever she was about to tell him.

'We've been apart for years,' she said quietly, 'neither of us could have been accountable to the other for so long.'

'Agreed.'

'There are many things I must tell you, things I should have done or said but didn't. I guess it's the same for you.'

'Yes,' he admitted, relieved at her candour, relieved that their past lives were about to be shared.

'Can you remember the last time you and I were in contact?'

'2010, but I can't remember the month. You wrote to me care of my old London address, advising of Stavros' death in Libya. I remember thinking at the time that he was far too young to die.'

He recalled the letter; it was brief and to the point. There was no date, no address; it was as if she hadn't expected a reply. The shocking news left him emotionally paralysed for weeks. In the end he couldn't bring himself to find out where she was living and offer his support; to his lasting shame he did nothing.

'Stavros is still alive.'

'God almighty, he's alive,' he exclaimed, falling back into the seat as if he'd been punched. He stared at her incredulously, unsure whether to laugh or cry. 'Stavros is alive,' he repeated. 'I can't believe it.'

He sat in silence, trying to absorb what she'd just told him. For the first time, he knew that he was about to hear the untold story of Emma's twin brother, whom he'd never set eyes on, even on the day he was born.

'After all these years thinking we'd lost him,' he said, his voice shaking. 'You must tell me everything.'

'I will, Jack, I will, but please don't get your hopes up,' she warned, meeting his gaze directly, pain etched on her face. He tried to calm down, preparing for the news, good or bad.

'I wrote to you in the October, after I'd heard from the family in Benghazi that he'd been killed by the Green Brigade.'

'I remember.'

'I'd been given no reason, no details, nothing. Didn't even know where it happened, where he was buried.'

'God, how bloody awful.'

'I never told you what happened next.' She hesitated. 'The following March, while living in Athens, I received a note from an old Libyan friend. He'd recently seen Stavros in the desert town of Sabha, apparently looking fit and well.'

'Why didn't you tell me?' he asked gently.

She sat in silence for a moment, tears welling up.

'I don't know,' she whispered.

'Was it your family? Were you under pressure not to say anything?'

'No. Nobody else knew of the note. I honestly can't remember.' She paused. 'I never got a reply to my October letter.' She hesitated. 'Perhaps I'd given up on you, I don't know.' Her voice faltered. 'We'd hardly seen or spoken to each other for years.'

He could see that she had been deeply hurt by his failure to keep in touch; she'd made her point.

'Did you manage to contact him?' he asked, now desperate to avoid a game of blame, counter-blame.

He could see that she was struggling.

'For maybe a year afterwards,' she continued quietly, 'I tried many times, but at each attempt I drew a blank. He'd simply disappeared again from my life.'

'Again?'

'He left the family home in Benghazi when he was fifteen, simply walked out. Nobody saw him again.' She paused. 'After so many years of silence, it was hard to believe that he'd ever existed.'

He was shocked and could think of nothing to say. He'd always believed that she and Stavros had stayed close throughout his short life.

'That is until four weeks ago,' she continued.

'And then what?' he asked, alarmed at more distressing news.

'Dorpadski dropped in one morning to suggest that I should join the family for supper.'

'Dorpadski?'

'This wasn't unusual. After we'd eaten, while the others were going about their business, he and I took our glasses and wandered off around the gardens. It was dark. Looking back, the whole thing seemed a bit weird.'

'Weird?'

'He was acting strangely. Without any warning, he started to tell me about worrying intelligence he'd received from his colleagues in the Desert Oblast, the term they fondly use for Cyrenaica.'

'About Stavros?'

'According to Dorpadski, he's one of several leaders of a growing anti-government movement that they've been monitoring closely for over a year.' Her voice wavered. 'They haven't thought them dangerous enough yet to be eliminated.'

He felt her pain as she recalled the scene.

'There's no knowing whether Dorpadski's telling the truth,' she continued. 'The whole thing could be a complete fabrication.'

'That's really bizarre. There's nothing of Stavros for twenty years and suddenly he resurfaces as a potential threat to the state. It's unbelievable,' he said.

'I don't believe it's a coincidence.'

'What do you mean?'

'Whether it's true or not, it's another way of putting me under pressure.'

'Why would Dorpadski do that?'

'He wants me out of his life, one way or another, so he can take this place, the few remaining valuables I have.'

'The bastard,' exclaimed Jack.

'He's like a chess player, plotting his next move,' she continued.

'He'll take advantage of your presence in Stoupa, someone to be used to further his ends.'

The idea of being a pawn in Dorpadski's game, designed to bring her down, sickened him.

'What else did he say about the movement?'

'It started life several years ago. It was political, non-violent. Recently it embarked on a series of spectacular attacks on the Russian military. The group's leaders have gone underground, disappeared off the radar,' she said.

Dumbstruck, he gazed out over the blinding light of the bay, unable to absorb the implications of what he'd just heard.

'I'm so sorry I never told you about Stavros,' she said, after a lengthy pause. She got up and went inside; he could see that she was crying.

*

Thirty minutes later, she returned with two iced beers and kissed him tenderly on his cheek.

'Are you OK?' she whispered.

'I'm fine.' Although her news was shattering, its rawness had ebbed away in the stultifying midday heat. 'I really don't know what to think, what to believe,' was all he could manage.

'I should have told you about our son years ago.'

'Don't blame yourself,' he said, quietly. 'Whatever has happened, we're equally responsible one way or another.' He took a long draught of beer. 'How did Dorpadski know about your connection with Stavros in the first place?'

'It's a long story, not a happy one.'

'It can wait.'

'No, Jack, it can't. We've let stuff wait for years and look where it's got us.'

'You're right.'

'Apparently, he'd started to research the family in the summer of '25, weeks before approaching us to see if he could rent the villa. He knew by then that my parents rarely used the place. In the process he learnt of your existence, of the twins. He knew that you'd taken Emma to England as a baby shortly after she was baptised an Anglican, that she's a UK citizen.'

'God, how spooky.'

'He also knew that my parents had prevented Stavros and me from joining you in England, that they'd insisted Stavros was taken to Benghazi and brought up by my aunt.' She paused. 'And how ultimately all this led to the break-up of our relationship.'

'The man's crazy. Why go to all that bother?'

'It was then that he found out about the family's shipping business, which led to the fleet being commandeered. Dorpadski uses information very effectively. Now he wants to be able to lean on me, blackmail me if you will, at any time in the future,' she replied, trying to steady her voice.

'Good God.'

'The more he knows, the more control he has, the more he can take advantage of me. Maybe there's something he wants now, something of value that I've still got,' she said resignedly. 'I'll find out soon enough.'

'What a miserable, scheming bastard.'

'Stavros' spectacular fall from grace is exactly the opportunity he's been looking for. He'll ratchet up the pressure. It won't be long before I, and probably you, will be implicated in this anti-government plot.'

'I don't know how you can live under this pressure, Bee, it seems relentless.'

'I have no choice.'

'I see that.'

'Our business relationship is a sham. We both know it. He's not my tenant at all, I'm simply his lodger,' she said quietly. 'Effectively, he owns the place. I've no legal redress to remove him as tenant or to change the status quo in any way whatsoever. Eventually, it will be assumed that the place has always been his. The paperwork may have been finalised already, who knows. I daren't protest and he knows it. His acquisition will go unpunished. He's above the law, acts with impunity.'

He heard in her voice a long-held acceptance of her situation; on her face, a brief look of resignation that he'd seen on countless faces of the downtrodden he'd come across during his working life. His heart went out to her, wondering at her quiet stoicism.

'Bloody state-administered theft,' was all that he could muster.

'No, this is personal theft. What he's doing is still technically illegal under the law here, but nobody's going to challenge a powerful regional governor of the Peloponnese, a war hero in North Africa.'

They were drifting off the subject of Stavros. Perhaps, he thought, she wanted to distract him, to give him space for his subconscious to work through the re-emergence of their son in his life.

'Does he really pay any rent?'

'Yes, but it's a pittance, a charade. It makes him look good in front of the local Greek community. It keeps envious government salary-men in Athens off his back. Basically, it's good PR.'

She appeared to hesitate, as if reluctant to continue. Absently, she put her empty beer bottle down, pushed her sunglasses up and gently massaged her eyeballs between thumb and forefinger. She shuddered, as if caught in a draught; suddenly she looked bone-weary.

'There's a large reward for anybody who brings Stavros in, dead or alive. Dorpadski's putting me on notice. It's as simple as that. He has no personal feelings in all this.'

'God almighty.'

'In any case, our son is as good as dead now and we both know it,' she whispered, her tearful voice trailing off. 'Twenty-one years ago, they said he'd been killed. Then six months later, I was told he was still alive. Now, not having heard from him for decades, I'm told he's a dead man walking. I'm devastated.'

They sat in silence for several minutes.

'Jack,' she whispered, 'whatever you've told Emma already about Stavros, I suggest you just leave it at that.'

'What do you mean?' he asked, suddenly terrified; images of the shoebox full of their letters squatting on Emma's floor briefly flashed through his head.

'That Stavros is dead, has been for years,' she said, tearfully. 'We can't trust a word that Dorpadski says. Let's leave it at that.'

Quietly sobbing, she leaned forward, covering her face with her hands. They sat lost to the world and each other, vainly trying to square the past with the present. The morning morphed into the afternoon, the glaring sun arcing to the west, the fierce heat easing.

16

Fezzan, Early October 2031

As the sun broke clear of the horizon, Omar left the truck. Philippe and Isabel, expecting the worst, got out and watched, immediately feeling the heat from the rising sun. With head bent low, Omar followed the footprints of their nocturnal Bedouin visitors across the border towards the depression, where he stopped. For what seemed like several minutes, he remained motionless. Then very slowly, he sank to his knees.

'What's wrong?' she asked anxiously, seeing the concern on Philippe's face. Her question galvanised him into action.

'There's something there that has him transfixed,' he said, quickly removing a small holdall from under his seat. 'You stay here while I see what's going on.'

'I'm coming with you. Remember, we're in this together.'

She could see him hesitate, before giving way. Following Omar's route, they walked warily along the well-trodden trail across the border, towards his kneeling body. Her legs felt weak, each step agonisingly heavy. She sensed that Philippe could hear her pounding heart. Her chest seemed constricted, she could barely breathe. Sweat, blinding her eyes, coursed down aching limbs.

She took little comfort that Philippe's training appeared to have kicked in. He moved agilely ahead of her, up the gentle incline towards the lip of the depression, to where Omar was kneeling. The moment she joined them, she glanced down and screamed. Omar, soiled tears channelling down through the dust and grime on his leathery cheeks, turned to them, speechless.

Badly shaken, she and Philippe knelt beside him. The three, one swaying bundle of humanity, stared at the carnage below them. Not twenty paces away, eleven corpses were laid out side by side in a line, flat on their backs, arms and legs bound with electrical cable. A single bullet hole marked the centre of each forehead, a ritual execution conducted with clinical efficiency.

She had never seen death before. A visceral dread swept over her. It was acutely different from her earlier panic in the suffocating darkness of the truck. Now her fear was born of a mortal threat – unknown, external, beyond her control. This was real, tangible.

She shuddered, remembering how Jack had once described his first contact with death, at the hands of the Green Brigade back in the '80s. He told her how he had escaped a similar execution, which had been meted out to two Libyan colleagues. She recalled his feelings of terror, guilt.

The features of each corpse could be clearly seen; all were dressed in Russian desert military fatigues.

'*Omar, do you recognise these men?*' Philippe asked quietly, after a lengthy pause.

Composing himself, Omar stood and scrutinised the scene below.

'*Ramil's guards, several I've seen before,*' he whispered. '*I can't see Ramil,*' he added, before pointing to the corpse of a very stout man at the centre of the row. '*That man you know, sir. Colonel Turgov, Ramil's boss. He's the one you played cards with the last time we met,*' he said, before adding, '*I don't see my brothers.*'

'*Your brothers?*'

The old man looked at them, anguish etched on his weather-beaten features.

'What's he saying?' Isabel asked, seeing his distress.

'He can't see his brothers, whoever the hell they are.' Philippe's voice was tinged with frustration.

'Ramil's driver, his standby driver, his mechanic,' she whispered. 'I remember he treated them as brothers.'

'Brothers?' he asked tersely.

'They're from his family village in the desert in the east, several hundred kilometres south of Benghazi.'

'That's crazy, the man's from Misrata in the west, EDA territory,' he retorted. 'His family can't possibly come from the east.'

'No, no, he's originally from the east,' she insisted quietly. 'I'll explain later.'

'OK,' he said, flatly.

She wondered, not for the first time, if he knew or even cared about the local people with whom he worked.

'*Is the place booby-trapped?*'

She saw Omar stiffen; his old Bedouin instincts reached out to the lifeless bodies below.

'*I don't think so, sir,*' he whispered hoarsely.

'*What can you tell me?*'

'*They were killed, probably between eight and ten hours ago, executed in this place during the sandstorm. I believe our Bedouin friends were here later, before visiting us in the night.*'

'What's he saying?' she asked, frustrated by her limited Arabic. He ignored her.

'*The Bedouin lived,*' continued Omar. '*There are no booby traps.*'

'*How can you be so sure of all this?*' he asked, irritably.

'*I can't, sir, but the bodies are covered in fine sand, haven't been exposed to the sun, haven't started to rot. They were killed here during the Ghibli.*'

'*But we'd have heard gunshots.*'

'*With respect, sir, we couldn't hear anything in the wind last night.*'

'*What else can you tell us?*'

'They weren't carried or dragged here, you'd see more marks on the ground.'

'Did our Bedouin visitors slaughter these men?'

'No, Bedouin use knives, cut throats. It's cheaper, quieter.' Omar hesitated. 'It's not the work of the militia either.'

'How can you be sure?'

'It's too clean, no decapitations, no burnt bodies.' He was silent for a moment. 'These men put up no resistance, didn't fight back. Perhaps they'd been drugged,' he suggested.

'Who in hell would have drugged them?'

'Possibly they were drugged then shot by people who knew them,' he said before adding, 'their own people.'

'Rubbish, man,' Philippe shouted, clearly exasperated. 'Rubbish, rubbish.'

She hadn't understood what had passed between the two but quickly sensed their mutual animosity. She suspected that Omar, although not understanding Philippe's rant, could see his anger, his disbelief in what he was hearing.

They clambered to their feet. She stared accusingly at Philippe, her face smudged with tears. She wondered why now, of all times, he had chosen to rebuke Omar, who was clearly distraught.

She was angry with Philippe, she knew not why. She felt strongly that they should all be working together; that they needed each other more than ever at this moment.

In the glare of the morning sun, Omar walked cautiously into the depression. He followed the footprints of their unknown visitors, slowly around the dead men. She shook uncontrollably at Philippe's side. He ignored her, apparently unaware of her terror.

'Please, Philippe, tell me what's happening.'

He told what had been discussed.

'Omar's got this all wrong. This has to be the work of UDP militias,' he said, with certainty. 'They slaughtered the Russians, let the Muslims go.'

'Militias aren't known for sparing Muslim lives,' she said. 'They'll slaughter anybody to survive, that's their philosophy.'

'Not in this case,' he said, sharply.

She held her tongue, knowing he was guessing. It dawned on her that Omar needed to draw a distinction between the corpses and the others, a distinction which eluded her. This was not the time to share her thoughts.

Omar stooped over the dead Colonel Turgov, gazing at his bound hands. He went methodically up and down the line, standing for a few seconds over each body. Finally, he returned to Turgov and bent down. Very gingerly, he lifted a filthy bloodstained plastic bag from the man's chest. He raised it to eye level and looked at it intently.

The suspense in his deliberate movements in the hot desert stillness was nerve-wracking. She suspected Omar was way ahead of them in his understanding of what may have happened here, of what he was seeing. She was determined that Philippe's arrogant insensitivity was not going to squash Omar's instincts. Finally, her morbid curiosity overcame speech-defying fear.

'What's he looking at?' she blurted out, turning to Philippe.

'*What have you got there?*'

'*Each man has had his left thumb cut off. They're all here in the bag,*' he said quietly, holding the bloodied bag aloft.

'*Good God, man, that's barbaric. And you say this was the work of the Russians? It has to be a UDP militia group.*'

'*As you think, sir.*'

Although not understanding what was said, she saw a look of contempt flicker across the older man's face.

Philippe turned back to her.

'Their left thumbs have been amputated. They're in that grotesque bag he's waving in the air.'

'God, that's vile.'

'He's still convinced these guys were killed by their own people.'

'And you don't believe him?'

She could feel tension between the two men, driven on by fear and frustration. Despite her limited Arabic, she had more empathy with Omar's apparent intuition.

Philippe's mind appeared closed to everything but the obvious, at least what was obvious to him. She felt he wanted to believe that this carnage had been the work of UDP militias, intent on furthering their anarchical cause in a bid to survive. She realised how quickly and simplistically he had evaluated what he had seen and heard in the last few minutes, how his ideas conformed to the established view.

Having lived in Tripoli for several months, she knew the unquestioning patter of her colleagues: 'FRSS is co-operating with us in North Africa' and 'FRSS is our ally against UDP militias'. This, and much more, was the daily mantra put out by Tripoli. It was simple, easy to digest and reflected UN-speak in the EDA administration.

Shrugging his shoulders, Omar looked up at them and then back towards the dunes.

'*I can see three Russian trucks about a hundred metres away. They've been hidden by a low-lying dune, which I hadn't seen before,*' he called over his shoulder. '*I'll check them out.*'

He turned back and casually lobbed the plastic bag which landed at Isabel's feet, before following the shallow prints of the four Bedouin, eastwards towards the dunes. Her gaze dropped briefly to the mess at her feet; her stomach turned.

Watching Omar tread carefully towards the trucks, she held her breath.

'A complete waste of time,' Philippe grunted, ignoring the bloodied bag. She felt his antipathy towards Omar steadily rising. 'He's just checking to see whether his so-called brothers can be found.'

Omar hadn't gone more than fifty paces when she noticed that he wasn't following the Bedouins' tracks, which appeared to veer to his right.

'He's not following the footprints.'

'He knows what he's doing,' snapped Philippe.

Suddenly Omar disappeared in a vertical column of sand and gravel rising tens of metres into clear air. In that instant, an ear-splitting explosion shattered the silence. The force of the blast knocked them to the ground, where they lay bleeding and gasping, in the ensuing silence.

'Are you OK?' whispered Philippe, shakily. After a brief pause, he repeated his question.

'I'm OK,' she sobbed, numb with shock.

'The poor bastard triggered a mine, could have killed us all,' he exclaimed. 'Bloody militia must've booby-trapped the area around the trucks.'

As the dust drifted away, he got to his knees. Taking a small pair of binoculars from his holdall, he scanned the area. Isabel lay on her side, silently crying, blood oozing into the fine sand from a deep gash in her head. Through her tears, she watched him closely. She was reminded of a hunted animal, motionless, alert, unseen senses straining for the rhythm of danger. After a minute or so, he looked down at her.

'Can you get up?' he asked quietly, his voice steadier now.

She struggled awkwardly to her knees, blood-soaked hair smeared across her face making it difficult to see, her head and shoulders throbbing with excruciating pain.

With renewed urgency, he whispered, 'Get up slowly and make your way back to the truck. Follow the Bedouin footprints closely. Don't take your eyes off the ground for a second.'

As he raised the binoculars again, she instinctively pulled the soggy bag lying at her side, into the fold of her torn jacket. Rising carefully and without a backward glance, she stumbled along the track, caked in bloodied dust and sweat, physically battered, emotionally broken. In the stillness, she heard what she realised he had been listening out for, a low groaning sound interspersed with incoherent mumblings, anguished prayers seeping through the death throes of a dying man.

As she collapsed by the truck, she heard two gunshots in quick succession before passing out.

*

Slowly she came to, totally disorientated, her mind blank. An unfamiliar pressure had settled over her eyes, she couldn't see a thing. She was lying on her back on what she soon recognised was the rear seat of the truck. She appeared to be tightly bound, her movements restricted as she struggled to throw off a filthy suffocating blanket. With agonising difficulty, she reached up and felt a coarse bandage around her head, her fingers probing its full extent.

She hovered on the cusp of consciousness, pain wracking her body, acutely, remorselessly. The truck was being driven at speed, the incessant rolling, bumping and banging accentuating her agony. Gradually reality receded as she slipped into a vortex of sleep.

Next time she woke, the violent motion had stopped. Philippe was lifting her purposefully into an upright position. The rancid smell of his sweaty body revived memories; images flooded back causing her to panic. Her feeble struggle soon slackened against his unyielding pressure. She had a biting headache. Although the earlier pain had eased, her body felt stiff, battered and raw. She was numb, as if she'd been sedated.

'Drink this,' he said, thrusting a cup of hot sweetened coffee between her trembling lips.

'Where are we?'

'About a hundred kilometres south-west of Ramlit. We'll be there before nightfall. Hopefully we'll see the others there.'

'And Omar, where is he?'

'He's dead. I left him where he fell,' he answered, flatly. 'It would have been too dangerous to reach his body. Desert dogs and vultures will pick it clean in a day or so.'

The shocking memory of Omar's dying moments and the abrupt sound of gunshots pierced her brain.

'You shot him,' she whispered, evenly.

'I managed to get through to HQ on the radio yesterday morning soon after you collapsed,' he drawled, blithely ignoring her accusation.

'Yesterday,' she exclaimed, weakly.

'They were relieved to hear from us, happy that we'd survived the storm.' He spoke rapidly. 'Everybody'd assumed the weather had disrupted communications in the area,' and then almost as an afterthought, he added, 'I told them of our misadventure.'

His off-hand tone bothered her. She remained silent.

'HQ agreed with our assessment that UDP militia had carried out the executions,' he continued confidently. 'Had probably abducted and killed Ramil and the others as well. We all know what the militias will do, it's just their style.'

She struggled with this emerging reality; Philippe's view was now officially 'our' assessment. Instinctively, she felt that he was wrong. Only Omar, a man whom she felt she could have trusted, might have had the answer to the riddle of the border incident. Throughout, he had appeared unaffected by Philippe's conventional thinking. *Now that he's dead, I may never get to the truth. How bloody depressing*, she thought.

In a few short days, her world had been turned upside-down. Philippe, somebody she'd once treated as a close friend and trusted colleague, had morphed into an insensitive, authoritarian, bigoted killer. She barely recognised the man.

'I'm in quite a mess judging by the bandage…' She trailed off, struggling to make sense of her predicament. 'What time is it?'

'It's midday. You've been out for hours.'

'Midday,' she repeated, aimlessly.

'After I'd fixed you up yesterday, I spoke to the boys in Ramlit. They were still waiting for the spares so couldn't get to us. We all agreed it would be safer if we stayed at the border overnight and started around dawn. We set off this morning, an hour before sunrise.'

He took out a large umbrella from behind her seat.

'I had to tie you in. You'd have rolled off the seat once we got going. You must get up, stretch your legs,' he continued, as he helped her onto her feet.

She gritted her teeth and forced her bruised and broken body to respond; she realised she barely had the strength to stand up, never mind walk.

'We won't go too far in this heat. At least we have a little shade,' he said, opening the umbrella.

An hour later, they started driving again into the shimmering afternoon sunshine, across a featureless stony moonscape. She was sitting upright, belted into the front passenger seat. She kept silent, trying to reconcile what she'd been through, too many unresolved issues floating around her aching head.

As she turned her back to him and the blinding flat shafts of sunlight, she was suddenly conscious of the plastic bag pressing against her ribcage, tucked firmly under her desert jacket. Amazingly, it was still where she'd hidden it the previous day. She hoped he hadn't noticed, as she positioned the bag more securely. Instinctively, she knew that she had to keep it from him at all costs.

'I still don't understand how we all crossed the border without getting pulverised,' she said at length, still facing away. 'It should have been closed.' He didn't respond. Maybe he hadn't heard her, so she turned to face him.

'Why weren't the Bedouin annihilated when they crossed over the other night?' she said, raising her voice above the noise of the engine.

'There wasn't a problem with our security system,' he replied, obliquely.

'There must have been.'

He remained silent, staring ahead, guiding the writhing truck into the sun.

'What was it?' she persisted. 'Come on, we agreed to share everything – information, responsibilities, risks.'

He stiffened, his left hand pushing dark glasses to the bridge of his nose, appearing to play for time.

'The gate was open all the time,' he said finally, as if this were normal practice, 'been open since our planned meeting the previous afternoon.'

'How come?' she asked, incredulously, knowing this simply wouldn't happen unless a revised border protocol had been agreed, impossible given the breakdown in communications.

He remained silent. It suddenly occurred to her that he was lying.

'How come?' she repeated, more forcefully.

'Ramil got there during the Ghibli, several hours before we did.'

'And then?'

'He contacted his people in Benghazi to tell them he'd arrived, told them of the appalling weather.'

'Really?' she said, remembering how Philippe had no radio contact with HQ at the time because of the weather.

'Benghazi then contacted our people in Tripoli,' he blustered. 'Our people confirmed that they still hadn't heard from us.'

'And?'

'With no word from us, the two parties finally agreed that the border should remain open for a further twenty-four hours.'

'When did they tell Ramil?'

'Sometime later,' he said, evasively.

'So, he was there the whole time we were.'

'I suppose so.'

'You suppose so?' she asked, barely concealing her frustration.

'They didn't hear from him again.'

'What?'

'It seems he's disappeared,' he said, as if this were an everyday occurrence.

Questions kept revolving around her head; there were too many inconsistencies.

Why was he so reluctant to admit to the border being open? How was it that Ramil got through to his people when at the same time, Philippe was unable to contact HQ? Were Benghazi and Tripoli really in contact with each other to agree a plan or was there an unknown third party who had control over the border? Could it have been Ramil, Philippe even? Assuming Ramil had been told of the revised protocol, why hadn't he been in touch as soon as the Ghibli had died away to reschedule their meeting? Nothing made sense.

Ramil always travelled with a security detail of twelve men, a number borne out by the three medium-sized vehicles that Omar had spotted near the dunes just before he was blown to pieces. So where were Ramil and Omar's so-called three brothers? She knew that they had all been issued with standard desert boots so it couldn't have been their footprints they'd seen beside Philippe's truck the other night, unless of course they'd discarded their boots. So whose footprints were they? Why the symmetry in the line of the corpses, the execution-style killings, the removal of their left thumbs?

The questions just kept coming.

Given that there were so many unexplained issues, she became increasingly bothered by Philippe's readiness to blame the militia.

And finally there was the question of trust. Would he have told her anything, if she hadn't pressed for an explanation? She knew the answer, acknowledging that the trust between them was slowly being eroded.

She turned her back to him again, huddling into the dirty blanket he had offered her as a headrest. The only vague conclusion she could draw from his convoluted story was that some mysterious third party, unknown to either administration, possibly had the ability to open and close the border at will. With this last thought scrolling through her head, she drifted once more into an uneasy dreamless sleep.

17

Peloponnese, Early October 2031

I n the cool of the evening after the sun had set, they walked the winding coastal path into Stoupa. Bushra led him to her favourite taverna at the far end of the seafront, greeting friends along the way. Occasionally she would introduce him to local villagers, a couple of whom he vaguely remembered from the past.

A walk that should have taken twenty minutes took forty. Not that he was bothered. They were both emotionally drained, their slow amble cathartic. He knew that he needed to calm down and adjust to her pace, if he were to survive the days ahead.

As the inevitability of Stavros' death sank in, their sorrow gave way to dumb resignation. Jack felt no emotion now towards his son, never having met him. Down through the years, he'd occasionally hear from her how Stavros was getting on in Benghazi, where he'd been taken as a baby. After hearing his son had been executed, any residual feelings that Jack had for him had been consigned to history.

Sitting at a table against the low beach wall, they ordered food. They avoided discussing Stavros, needing time to come to terms with their impending loss. Jack turned his attention to Bushra's parlous state, which greatly concerned him.

'I can't get over this theft-by-stealth business,' he said, over a flickering candle. 'How can you protect yourself from these corrupt officials?'

'We have a system that gives some protection to people in my situation,' she said, lowering her voice, 'an underground movement called "Delta". It operates via an app. Its purpose is to protect Greek-owned assets and punish criminals, potential or actual. Written in Greek street-slang, it's opaque even for many Greeks.'

'Does it work?'

'Yes. Threatened assets, the names of prospective thieves are anonymously registered. Activists respond via the app, offering support. It might include threatening, even killing someone.'

'Good God,' he exclaimed. 'A kangaroo court. Unaccountable and risky by the sound of it.'

'But extremely effective. Very difficult for the authorities to close down.'

'How would you use it?'

'If Dorpadski makes a move to acquire the villa, I'd register whatever details I have and put out a call for help. Activists would start putting pressure on him and on the authorities co-operating with him. If he persists, action would follow.'

'Such as?'

'They'd put him on notice that he's been watched.'

'Watched?'

'There are ways,' she grinned. 'Usually they daub a black delta sign in a conspicuous location, say near the front door, where he couldn't fail to spot it. Most people feel sufficiently nervous to back off at that point.'

'What happens if he threatens you directly?'

'I'd alert everybody of a more personal problem, activating a much quicker and wider response.'

'What then?'

'Delta's taken significant action since it was set up. It's resulted in damage to state property, cars being torched, kneecapping and the like, even the deaths of minor officials.'

'That's impressive.'

'It's something the authorities strenuously try to avoid. Over the last year or two, there's been a steady drop in illegal appropriations. It doesn't guarantee protection, but it's a big disincentive for the Russians.'

'It must be open to abuse.'

'Assets are invariably Greek-owned, the perpetrators almost always Russian,' she said. 'Anything out of the ordinary is treated with suspicion and not acted on. Delta's aim is to end the occupation with minimum loss.'

'I think it's a brilliant idea – summary justice for the people.'

'Its strength is the language. Greek is complex, almost impossible for non-Greeks to fully understand.'

'Don't I know it,' he laughed, greatly heartened by what he'd heard.

As evening slipped into another velvety night, they were lulled by the hypnotic sound of waves washing up the beach directly below them. Old waiters noisily stacked tables and chairs. An occasional drunk meandered along the deserted seafront. Having consumed several glasses of ouzo and a litre of local red wine, they summoned their energy and walked along the seafront, before threading their way home on the coastal path.

The unlit stony track clung to the northern perimeter of the bay. They reached a locked gate in a security fence, which had been installed by Dorpadski shortly after he'd taken up residence, isolating the headland, the villa and its beautiful gardens from the public. There was a small stone pier within the grounds, which for years Bushra's family had shared with a couple of fishing boats. The pier was now Dorpadski's private dock where he kept a launch to get to his yacht, *Kostroma*, which regularly anchored in the bay.

'I hate this bloody fence,' she muttered, punching in the security code. 'I'm a prisoner in my own home.'

They walked on in silence up through the garden to the cottage.

*

He woke before dawn, alone and disorientated. A fresh towel lay invitingly on the wicker table. He stripped and set off down the path. He could just see her, several hundred metres out to sea, swimming effortlessly towards the horizon.

He dived off the rocks and swam steadily in her direction, the sudden coolness taking his breath away. He had never been a stylish swimmer. Although he had plenty of stamina, she always out-swam him. After a few minutes, he noticed that she was heading back. Thirty metres away, she called out, looking for reassurance in the dim light. He waved, treading water to catch his breath. She glided up to him like a seal pup, barely throwing out a ripple.

'Oh, Jack,' she said, locking her nakedness around him, forcing him under. She laughed as he struggled to the surface, spluttering and coughing. 'Did I wake you?'

'No, I only came to a few minutes ago.'

'Let's swim back, I'm starving.'

'Slowly,' he pleaded, as they untangled themselves and headed for home.

'I've been thinking,' she said, some twenty minutes later, as she set down a breakfast tray on the wicker table. 'You ought to contact Emma, tell her you've arrived safely. We could call her on the wallscreen later.'

'You're right,' he said, the mention of Emma activating a nervous twitch in his left eye, forcing him to turn away for fear she'd notice. Absently, he took his mug of coffee, realising the time had come to tell Emma's story, vainly thinking how he might compress her childhood into a few brief sentences that would neither anger nor humiliate Bushra; time slipped by.

'What's on your mind, Jack?' she said at last.

'I don't know if this is the right time, but I need to tell you about Charlotte, Emma, our time together in London.' He paused.

'Your "Stavros moment",' she said quietly. 'Go on, I'm ready.'

Wrapped in a large dry towel, she sat opposite him motionless, her blue-black eyes watching him intently over the rim of her mug.

'When I brought Emma back to London in 1988, Charlotte was bloody furious, would have nothing to do with her, so we went to stay with my brother in Mayo, in the west of Ireland.'

'My God, the vicar. How long were you there?'

'Not long. I left Emma with Peter and his housekeeper for a few days and went back to London to confront Charlotte about Harry.'

'Tom's father.'

'She finally admitted to the affair, that Tom was Harry's son. Marriage to him had been out of the question because of his drug habit.'

He hesitated, marshalling his thoughts.

'Go on, Jack,' she said, quietly.

'The day I confronted her, Charlotte and I agreed to maintain the myth that she was Emma's mother. It was a trade-off,' he said, bluntly, 'Emma's mother and Tom's father, two self-cancelling deceits.'

'I see,' Bushra said quietly. 'What happened then?'

'I brought Emma back from Mayo and settled her into her new home.' He paused. 'Until very recently, Emma knew you only as an old friend of mine, somebody who, for some unexplained reason, Charlotte had always disapproved of.'

Bushra pulled her dark glasses down, to shade her eyes or conceal her tears, he couldn't say.

'You only told her after I called you,' she whispered, her eyeless gaze unnerving him.'

'Yes.'

He was at a loss for words; anything he said now would either be inadequate at best or misinterpreted at worst. The silence stretched out, each lost in a world of conjecture, unwilling to speak. Finally, she got up and, taking their mugs, went inside. He slumped back, his head pounding, and closed his eyes. Minutes passed, a shadow crossed his face; she was standing over him, holding out a mug.

'Here, take this, it's fresh,' she said gently, taking her seat opposite him again. 'We are where we are, Jack,' she said eventually. 'Neither of us can begin to explain what we did for our kids, why we did this or that. I know more will come out in the next few days.' She paused. 'Certainly my past with Stavros.'

The mention of their son's name set his nerves on edge again, constant anxiety never far below the surface.

Over breakfast, he told her about his loveless marriage, how Emma had been badly affected by their dysfunctional family life, by his divorce. It led to her wild university days, devastating affairs, one of which resulted in Isabel's birth, and her inability to find a steady partner. He recalled the poverty of her early writing career, her breakthrough to become an internationally renowned historian in the early '20s, and finally Isabel's university days leading to her job in North Africa.

The telling of his last few days with Emma was the most harrowing. He felt terrible, trying to explain how he had resorted to giving Emma their old letters, having just admitted that she was Emma's mother. From the letters, Emma would now know why he had taken her to England as a baby; why Stavros, her twin brother, and Bushra had been unable to join them. She would understand how this enforced separation eventually contributed to the break-up of his relationship with Bushra.

They finished breakfast in silence. He knew that she was struggling with the thought that Emma had only recently learnt that she was her mother.

'My behaviour has been inexcusable,' he said, quietly. 'I've been a miserable coward. I'm deeply ashamed and can only ask for your forgiveness.'

He could feel her anguish.

'This hasn't been all your fault,' she whispered, her voice faltering. 'We – my family and I – must share some of the blame.' She paused. 'Of course I forgive you.'

He got up as she started to clear away the breakfast things.

'Just stay here, Jack,' she said, gently. 'I'll be back.'

She returned an hour later, showered and refreshed. He stood and embraced her.

'I must…'

'No, Jack,' she interrupted, 'before we go any further, I want to say a few things about myself, about Stavros, how our lives turned out.'

The heat from the mid-morning sun was stifling, the air suffocating, the flat sea moving sluggishly like a mercury bath. While he struggled to keep focused, she seemed energised.

'You remember I'd managed to avoid seeing my parents for most of the time I was pregnant.'

'Yes.'

'When they eventually found out, it must have been in late November, early December, weeks before I was due. They were angry, very angry.'

'I think it was then that you told them that I was the child's father.'

'That's what pushed them over the edge,' she said, 'a feckless unmarried mother and a married man, a foreigner, with no commitment to their daughter or their grandchild. Some parents we would have made.'

'I remember thinking at the time it didn't look good.'

'I'm sure that's when they decided to take over, to arrange for the baby to be fostered by one of my father's aunts in Benghazi. I think their idea was that once the child got to school age, I would be old or perhaps responsible enough, to bring him or her up in Athens.' She paused. 'I'm afraid you weren't in the equation.'

'Everything's still clear in my mind – our endless discussions the day after I got to the hospital. You were very upset that they'd taken Stavros, that they'd be back for Emma as soon as the doctors were happy to release her.'

'I was horrified. I'd never been consulted, had no idea of their scheming until after Stavros was taken from the hospital.'

'It was then that we decided that I should take Emma back to England,' he said. 'What the hell were we thinking? We were crazy, utterly unprepared. I really don't know what we thought we'd achieve.'

'It was largely my fault. I was so bloody headstrong, believing we'd work something out when the time came.'

'I was no better,' he admitted.

'I was so ashamed of my parents, their attitude towards you, the twins,' she said, her voice tinged with anger, 'the way they rode roughshod over us.'

'We had our good times,' he reminded her, 'those precious years in the '80s, '90s when we'd meet secretly here, on my leave.'

'The best of times.' She hesitated. 'You'd regale me with stories of Emma; I'd tell you how I'd been in Benghazi with Stavros, how well he was getting on at school, how one day I hoped my family would relent, that the four of us could live together.'

'I remember,' he said, sensing trouble.

She was silent for a moment, clearly struggling to go on.

'What I told you wasn't true,' she said quietly.

'Wasn't true?'

'From the moment I took Stavros back to Benghazi, he was whisked off to my aunt, my father's youngest sister.' She paused again. 'I was never allowed to see him again.'

'Good God,' exclaimed Jack, 'how bloody cruel.'

'In the early '90s, when my parents moved permanently back to Greece,' she continued, 'he was left there, wasn't allowed to follow them.'

'You never saw him again,' he said, vainly trying to come to terms with what she'd said.

'At fifteen, as I told you, he ran away from home.'

'Did you know anything of his childhood, upbringing?'

'Of his early years, nothing. I'd always suspected that when he was a young teenager, he became involved in politics, you know, radicalised, fighting the regime. It didn't surprise me when I heard, much later, that he'd been executed by the Green Brigade.'

Her bluntness shocked him.

'I always dreamed,' he said, lamely, 'that one day we'd be reunited as a family.'

'No, Jack, it was never going to happen, not then, not ever.' She hesitated. 'I wanted you to think I spent most of the time in Benghazi with Stavros, when I wasn't with you. I kept up the pretence, thinking perhaps he was the reason you still wanted to spend time with me.'

'Rubbish, absolute rubbish,' he said emphatically. 'I've always loved you, loved you above all else.'

'Even the twins?'

'Even the twins,' he repeated, Emma's unseen presence tearing at his heart.

They sat in silence for a few minutes, each struggling with the other's story.

'I can't believe what they did to Stavros, it was inhumane,' he said at last. 'If you weren't with him, what were you doing all that time in Benghazi?'

'Much of what Chara told you the other day was true,' she admitted. 'I worked hard to support those suffering under the regime. It was dangerous and often humiliating work. When the Green Brigade started to assert itself in the early '90s, it became increasingly difficult to do anything constructive. I never went back after the summer of '94.'

This was not the time, he realised, to probe too deeply into those harrowing times, which Chara had alluded to.

'What did you do then?'

'Charity work, mostly in the slums of Athens. I worked with my mother. We were now on speaking terms again. I got a law degree. I was always busy, constantly in the public eye.' She paused. 'It became increasingly difficult to lead this double life, between my work and secretly here with you. Something had to give.'

'Things got a whole lot worse when I was transferred to Oman. It became almost impossible.'

'Yes, for the sake of my sanity, I had to finish with you,' she said quietly. 'It broke my heart writing that letter.'

'And mine.'

He stood up and gently pulled her to her feet, kissing her passionately. She led him to the cool darkness of her room where they flopped onto the unmade bed.

*

After breakfast the following morning, Bushra told Jack she was taking the car into town to do the weekly shopping.

'I'll come and help you,' he said. 'It's about time I got off my backside and did something useful.'

'There's no need,' she said, 'but you could walk to Dimitri's, the taverna down on the beach off the Kalamata Road, and pick up a couple of bottles of ouzo. His is the best stuff around here. We finished the last one yesterday.'

'I'd enjoy that.'

'I'll be an hour, there's no need to rush back.'

It took him less than twenty minutes to reach Dimitri's. Five or six ancient weather-beaten fishermen drinking ouzo were arguing garrulously under a tattered awning, which flapped listlessly in a dying breeze.

He ordered two bottles to take away, an ice-cold Mythos and a frappé, before settling down, as far away from the fishermen as possible, without leaving the shade. Even at this hour, the heat was torrid, the glassy sea sluggishly clawing at the pebbles on the beach. He ordered a second beer and a second frappé, hoping the combination of alcohol and caffeine would keep him from dozing off; they failed. He awoke with a start, when one of the empty beer bottles rolled off the table and hit the floor. He'd been away from the cottage for nearly two hours.

'You're adapting quickly to our Greek way of life,' Bushra laughed as he stumbled onto the veranda. When she removed her glasses, he could see the excitement in her eyes. 'You won't believe it, but Emma came on the wallscreen just after I got back, we only hung up ten minutes ago.'

'Good God,' he exclaimed, as he sat down. 'We were going to call her today. Was she OK? Upset?' Words tumbled out as the ramifications of the call sank in. 'Did she say why she was phoning?'

'Calm down, Jack, calm down, she's absolutely fine. From what I could see of her, she looks well. And no, she wasn't upset, just concerned for you, wanting to know whether you'd arrived safely.'

'Really?' he said, in disbelief.

'Come on, Jack,' she laughed. 'She's your daughter, she's naturally worried about you. She kept asking how you were, as if doubting me when I said you were fine.'

'What did you two talk about?'

'She told me she was nervous before she called, was sorry now that she hadn't come out with you.'

'I can't believe it,' he said, quietly.

Bushra leaned forward, elbows on knees, hands cupping her smiling face, eyes locking onto his.

'Jack, you must learn to trust us. We both love you, respect each other's hold on you. I may not have seen her since she was a baby, but between mother and daughter, there's always a bond. It's natural to talk as we did, it's instinctive.'

He rubbed his eyes, trying to hold himself together.

'What else?'

'She told me about the last time you were together, how confused and angry she was after you…'

'Angry?' he interrupted.

'Not just with you, but with her brother, Tom, with Charlotte, angry over her bewildering childhood, as she put it.'

'I can't blame her.'

'She said she went crazy when she learnt the real story of her early years.' She paused. 'Eventually things started to make sense, but not till much later. She admitted she was too emotional to talk to you before you left for Greece, cried for hours after you'd gone.'

'Oh God,' he cried.

Bushra paused, seeing his pain.

'Go on,' he whispered.

'It took her a week to read all the letters, to understand what you and she, in her own way, had been through. Her anger gave way to sadness, for you, for us, for herself and Stavros.'

'Stavros.' His heart raced uncontrollably.

'She mentioned him several times, imagining how they might have grown up together, what life must have been like for him as a child in Libya, what sort of man he was when he died. Her words just poured out.'

'God, this is unbelievable,' was all he managed to say.

'She mentioned Isabel, her new job in North Africa. It's clearly worrying her.'

His blood froze, remembering his granddaughter's unanswered letters.

'It's understandable,' he muttered.

'She'd assumed we'd spoken about it,' said Bushra. 'She wondered if I had up-to-date knowledge of the region's politics, you know, from a Russian perspective.'

'She's bound to ask your advice,' he said, the implications of their conversation rippling out in ever-widening circles.

'I didn't comment,' she said. 'You never know who might be listening.' She paused. 'How do you feel about her job?'

'My worries are different from her mother's. Hers are maternal, about Isabel's security, about her career prospects.'

'And yours?'

'That she's inherited the Meredith "self-destruct" gene. There are so many opportunities to come unstuck in North Africa. I think she's vulnerable,' he said before adding, 'I should know.'

'Perhaps her grandmother's genes will help her,' said Bushra, tongue in cheek.

'There's so much of you in Isabel. She's tough, a survivor, selfless and courageous, righting the world's wrongs…'

'Enough,' she laughed, 'enough of me.'

'Sorry,' he said, lamely.

For an hour or so they discussed every nuanced aspect of Emma's call.

'She wants you to know that she loves you,' Bushra said, finally, 'always has done, always will; that there's nothing she would wish to be different, nothing for you to forgive.'

He was about to say something when she put her finger to his lips and whispered, 'Leave it, Jack.'

She went indoors, returning moments later with two iced beers.

'Let's drop the past for now,' she laughed, passing him one. 'I want to spend time with you in the present, today, not imagining how things might have been, not wading through endless feelings of guilt, sadness, remorse.'

They sat across the wicker table from each other, lost in thought.

'Here's to the twins,' he said at last, raising his beer.

'Here's to us.'

18

Peloponnese, Greece,
Early October 2031

Despite their mutual desire to live in the moment, they spent their time together over the next few days endlessly dissecting the previous forty years, trying to make sense of their lives together, their lives apart. Long walks following the coast, daily swims and plenty of sleep gradually reduced their anxieties.

In the darkest hours of the night, she would draw him from the deepest of sleeps and gently arouse him. He found their lovemaking had a hypnotic, timeless quality, so different from the terrifying urgency of their youthful passion. Over the years, lust had given way to sensuality, gratification to inner peace. When he awoke several hours later, it was as if the whole episode had been a dream, a figment of his imagination.

*

It was just after sunrise on the fifth morning, as they swam back to the rocks, she noticed a figure standing next to the cottage.

'Damn it,' she exclaimed, with uncharacteristic vehemence, 'it's Dorpadski. He wasn't due back for several weeks.'

'Are you sure it's him?'

'His SUV is parked to the side of the villa. It wasn't there this morning.'

By the time they reached the shore, Dorpadski was nowhere to be seen. She was silent as they approached the cottage. Jack felt an invisible menace suddenly invading their space, intruding in their private world. She found a sealed envelope on the wicker table.

'He's invited us to dinner tonight,' she said, flatly.

'Us?'

'Yes, he writes, *Dearest Bushra, we would love you and Jack to join us for dinner this evening. See you both at seven. Your dear friend Ivan. PS please dress casually.* The bloody insolence of the man,' she snapped, tossing the letter onto the table.

'How the hell does he know that I'm here with you?'

'As governor, he controls everything, knows everything that goes on in the Peloponnese. A subordinate's job would be seriously at risk if he failed to report that you'd crossed the border the other day.'

'God, he's freaky.'

'Addressing the invitation to both of us is so typical. He's letting us know that he's aware that it's you, Stavros' father, who's with me. He's been away for weeks, turns up unannounced and wants to surprise us, catch us unprepared, the all-seeing bastard.'

'We could say we can't go, that we're expected for dinner with friends,' he suggested, unconvincingly.

'Dear Jack, this isn't any old invitation, it's a bloody order,' she said grimly. 'We refuse at our peril. We'll just have to turn up and go along with it.' She hesitated. 'It's his sudden appearance that's worrying.' She hesitated again. 'Maybe he has news of Stavros.'

The idea that they might have to discuss Stavros with Dorpadski left him cold.

'We must prepare for the worst,' he said, reaching out for her hand.

'If I'd had the money, I would've left Stoupa years ago, much as I love it here,' she said, as she turned to go indoors.

An exquisite dawn had spawned a tarnished day, leaving him dejected. Wrapping himself in a towel, he leaned on the rail and looked out to sea. His gaze followed the curving bay, tracing Stoupa's empty seafront around to the copse of eucalyptus trees towering above the villa. In the shadow of the building, he saw the SUV, a threatening beast ready to pounce.

She returned fifteen minutes later with the breakfast tray, her smiling face banishing his despondency.

'Dorpadski's not going to ruin our day,' she said, cheerfully. 'We'll worry about him later. I suggest we get away from here, go into the mountains,' she said, decisively.

The early heat was intense, hotter than the last few days. The sea had taken on a mercurial quality, flat and sluggish in the hazy sunshine. Not a whisper of a breeze stroked its shiny oily surface. He felt suffocated, becalmed.

'Great idea,' he said, somewhat relieved.

'There's a village an hour from here, high above Stoupa, rarely visited and almost inaccessible. I drove you there once.'

'I remember,' he laughed. 'An old church dominated the square. A very rotund priest, a friend of yours, showed us around. The whole place seemed medieval.'

'His people were friends of my mother's family, famous around Kalamata, part of the local resistance fighting the Germans in the war.'

'We walked up a rough track, very narrow and twisty, overlooking the village.'

'It's nearly 2000 metres at the top of the escarpment.' She hesitated. 'Have you a decent pair of walking shoes with you?'

'Yes.'

'It's a three-hour round walk. The views are incredible, although today's heat haze might be a problem. Are you up for it?'

'Absolutely.'

*

Twenty minutes later, they drove out past Dorpadski's security detail, three heavily armed men in military fatigues, wearing obscenely large sunshades.

'Well, there's no escaping the fact that he's in residence,' observed Jack wryly.

After fifteen minutes they drove off the motorway, which ran the length of the Mani Peninsula, onto a narrow, badly maintained road. No better than a farm track in places, it rose steeply through an endless series of tight hairpin bends, carved out of jagged limestone cliffs towering above them.

She pushed the old car to its limits, completely unfazed by the precipitous drop nudging the crumbling edge of the road. Without warning it levelled off, taking them through shady oak woods. They were driving into an enormous amphitheatre, a high valley surrounded on three sides by a towering limestone escarpment, and completely cut off from the coast nearly 1500 metres below. Eventually the woods gave way to rough pasture and orchards. He could make out a church tower dominating a village at the head of the valley.

'We're here,' she exclaimed, above the engine's woeful noise.

'Brilliant,' was all he could muster, as the car rattled into the square, scattering a flock of angry geese. She cut the engine, which spluttered and knocked in response before falling silent. Nothing stirred. Apart from chattering geese and humming insects, all they could hear was the mellifluous sound of running water, a cold clear mountain stream channelling through the village.

Suddenly the church bell started ringing, a rapid high-pitched clanging sound. It was ten o'clock, clearly a signal for people to bestir themselves. Several shutters were flung open. The taverna's metal security grill shot up; cajoling voices could be heard from within. The ringing stopped; a minute later an old priest slammed the church door behind him.

'We're right on time for the first frappé of the day,' she laughed, getting out of the car and stretching. 'This is a Russian-free zone, there's nothing to interest them here.'

They took their drinks out to a metal table under an enormous oak dominating the square.

'There's something bothering me,' he said, as they watched the locals effortlessly engaging in a new day. 'Do you ever check to see if the cottage is bugged, the car even?'

'You mean Dorpadski?'

'Yes.'

'Another Delta service,' she said, grinning. 'If they can hack into a ministry computer or blow up a government building, a bug check's chicken feed.'

He reached over and held her hand.

'You never cease to amaze me.'

'Don't get too sentimental,' she laughed. 'Perhaps I should tell you about Dorpadksi before you meet him this evening.'

'Let's get on our walk. It can wait.'

They were silent, absorbing village life unfolding around them. To Jack, the bucolic scene seemed surreal.

Thirty minutes later, having bought something to eat and drink from the local store, they set off, tramping up a steep shepherd's track, which rose steadily above the village. At last they came to a fork, the left-hand track dropping ahead of them away to the forest below.

'We'll go that way on our return,' she said over her shoulder, indicating the lower route. 'Circular walks were always our favourites. For now, we'll go up here to the right.'

He was reminded yet again how much she had retained of their past. It saddened him to think that they'd spent so little time together since they'd first met.

After climbing steadily on the track, which was carved into the cliff face on one side with a sheer drop of several hundred metres to the forest canopy on the other, she led him out onto a large flat rock, still in shadow.

'We're here,' she said gaily, turning to him, flushed from exertion. He was exhausted, his chest tightening, legs aching. He slumped down against a boulder to catch his breath.

'My God, you're fit,' he said hoarsely.

'You're OK for an old fellow,' she quipped. 'Live out here with me for a few months and you'll feel twenty again.'

From their rocky perch, they looked out over the forest below, cascading away to a narrow coastal strip. Stoupa appeared in the shimmering haze, only as a white blotch against an azure sea.

'So much for the view,' she said, before pointing out a stony path at the far end of the ledge, continuing upwards till it disappeared out of sight.

'The path from here is dangerously steep. It leads to pastures on the plateau above the escarpment. They're only accessible from the village on the track we've just come up. Farming is tough for these people.'

'Is it used much?'

'Resistance groups used it during the war. Occasionally local shepherds and others fighting the occupation use it today. We'll try it another time when you're feeling fitter,' she laughed.

'Oh God,' he moaned, 'I feel ill at the thought of it.'

Ignoring his protest, she settled down beside him.

'Hungry?'

'I could eat a horse.'

'Let's celebrate our first hike together,' she said, uncorking the wine.

*

The climb had emptied his head, blanking out his mind. They sat leaning against the rock and had their picnic, lost in the tranquillity of the mountains.

'Let me tell you about Dorpadski,' she said, after they'd finished.

'As you will,' he said.

'In the early '20s, he commanded the Russian invasion force in Syria, after they decided to put in ground troops.'

'General Ivan Dorpadski, of course,' he said, as the name came back to him. '"Ivan the Terrible". It was very apt, given his cruelty, his brutality.'

'He wasn't always like that,' she said. 'During the '70s, his father was attached to various Soviet embassies in the Middle East, including Damascus. He was a technical adviser, an agronomist and spoke Arabic fluently. Ivan, also fluent in Arabic, spent his early years working in the oil industry in the region before joining the army.'

'What went wrong?'

'We never found out. It wasn't for lack of trying.'

'War dehumanises people,' he said quietly, 'turns them into savages.'

'They say he got promoted too quickly, was manipulated by an older, corrupt clique around him.'

'Wouldn't be the first.'

'After success in Syria, he was given command in North Africa, more specifically, Libya and Egypt.' She paused. 'You remember their campaign in '24, the months they spent fighting their way along the coast west of Benghazi, how it didn't go to plan?'

'It would have been disastrous for the Maghreb.'

'That old Western fear, Russian domination from the Arctic to the Moroccan Atlantic coast, still exists today.'

'Thank God for UN intervention,' said Jack, Isabel never far from his thoughts.

'Dorpadski was responsible for the occupation of Cyrenaica. They desperately needed the eastern Libyan oilfields, the refineries at Brega and Ras Lanuf.'

'Was he involved in the UN negotiations?'

'No, he was never a diplomat, just an enforcer,' she said, 'although he was appointed the first military governor of Cyrenaica.'

'Soldier turned governor, how did he manage that?'

'Initially he relied on old, established Benghazi families to fill the vacuum in his administration,' she continued. 'He sought out those that had survived the dictatorship. He was interested in former politicians, tribal leaders, senior businessmen, anybody still with some influence and, of course, wealth.'

'Presumably that was when he targeted your family. No wonder he knew you so well.'

'Yes,' she said, her voice tinged with anger, 'and how he subsequently stripped us so thoroughly of everything we owned including, tragically, our dignity.'

Her voice had started to break, anguish constantly flaying her emotions. He put his arm around her, drawing her to himself.

After a few minutes she composed herself.

'In the turmoil before the UN mandate in '25,' she continued, 'my parents tried to transfer what they could of their remaining assets out of Benghazi before it was stolen. In the end, Dorpadski acquired almost everything, leaving them with virtually nothing.'

She pulled away, drawing her knees up under her chin, and stared out to sea, lost in the past. Eventually, she turned to him, tears welling up.

'The beautiful old townhouse where you stayed, other family homes, businesses, farms and livestock all disappeared over time,' she said quietly. 'Other than property, anything that couldn't be flogged or driven away was destroyed. Deeds of sale were illegally drawn up attesting to payments to the family that were never made. Dorpadski and his men had all the cover they needed, a carbon copy of what they then did in Greece when the bastards stole the family's tanker business.'

They sat on in silence for several minutes in the shade of an overhanging rock. Despite the altitude and a faint cooling breeze, he was hot.

'Where were we?' she asked, stirring herself.

'You don't have to go on.'

'I must, there's more to Dorpadski,' she insisted. 'I've forgotten what I was saying.'

'You'd just mentioned the family's tanker business.'

'Of course,' she said, pulling herself together. 'Conditions here were tolerable at first. There was a semblance of law and order. Athens was expanding rapidly, largely because of the huge inflow of refugees fleeing Syria. The city soon became lawless, ungovernable, a frightening place to live in.'

'As I see it today. It seems edgy, dangerous.'

'The Russian elite decided to turn the Peloponnese into a secure reserve for their sole use, away from migrants, and filthy, suffocating cities.'

'That's when Dorpadski must have caught up with your family again, hoping to rent the villa.'

'He and his security guys' threatening behaviour forced my parents to do a deal, eventually driving them out.'

'The same bunch that's there now?'

'There's ten, maybe twelve, all old army men who served under him in Syria, North Africa. They're based in the army barracks in Kalamata, operating a rota system in Stoupa,' she continued, 'generally three or four of them working at a time at the villa. The rest of their time, they're in Kalamata.'

'Doing what?'

'Guarding his yacht, *Kostroma*, docked in the harbour.'

'You mentioned her the other evening.'

'You missed *Kostroma* in the dark the day you arrived. She's a super motor-yacht, fifty-five, maybe sixty, metres long and tied up on the main quay, heavily guarded twenty-four seven.'

'That must keep them busy.'

'Not enough. Much of the time they're throwing their weight around town, terrorising the local people. Ask Christos, he hates them.'

'Christos, your friend who owns the taverna?'

'Yes.'

'God, how bloody awful,' he said, realising how just a few people can poison a whole community. 'Has Dorpadski still got interests in Benghazi?'

'That's the big question,' she said, getting to her feet. 'Some people think he has.'

'Are we going?' he asked, sensing her restlessness.

'I'm sorry I get so bloody miserable talking about the bastard,' she said. 'Let's go back down to the taverna and have a drink under the oak. We're not in a hurry to get home.'

'Great idea.'

Ninety minutes later and completely exhausted, they stumbled into the square. Right on cue, the taverna shutters rattled open, marking the end of siesta.

'Brilliant timing again,' she grinned, as they followed the landlord into the gloomy stuffy bar.

'God, I'm thirsty.'

'There's more about Dorpadksi, I'm afraid,' she said minutes later, as they sat with their drinks in the shade of the giant oak. 'We believe that he was transferred to the Peloponnese because he'd built up a successful international drug cartel, operating out of Benghazi.'

'I suppose the Russians were trying to clean the place up.'

'No, quite the opposite,' she said, grinning. 'Apparently his bosses wanted the business to thrive as it's critical to funding the administration in Cyrenaica. More importantly, though, they wanted to control it themselves, to enjoy the lifestyle it funds.'

'How bloody naive of me,' he laughed.

'From a Russian perspective Benghazi's very strategic. From there, using military contacts, the military governor controls the supply lines from Afghanistan and the east via routes through occupied Middle-Eastern countries. He also controls supply routes from west and central Africa through the Sahel.'

'So Dorpadski's no longer involved.'

'No, he is,' she said, 'they couldn't run the business without his experience. There's a rumour that he's still running the show but from Kalamata now, but to date we've no hard evidence.'

'Kalamata,' Jack exclaimed.

'We suspect he still has all the contacts, controls the supply routes. He must be indispensable to his boss, the new governor in Benghazi. There's a feeling that he's not bothered he's no longer top dog, he's made his millions. Probably reckons that working for more powerful people reduces his exposure.'

'And from Benghazi, where does the stuff go?'

'We think it's being shipped to Europe from a secret harbour location along the coast of Cyrenaica. It can't possibly be in EDA territory, so it's likely to be somewhere west of Benghazi, although there are few natural harbours. Nobody can be sure.'

Jack hesitated. 'You keep referring to "we".'

She paused, perhaps not wanting to reveal her source nor implicate him by association.

'Christos,' she said, eventually.

'Christos?'

'He's been around a long time, known Libya for years, still does. Back in the '80s, he left the family taverna business to work there,' she continued, 'worked with Greek contractors in oilfield construction for over fifteen years.'

'We must have overlapped, been there together,' exclaimed Jack.

'He was based in Brega, finally coming back when his old man died. He can still speak Arabic and has friends there, mostly in the east, quite a few in Benghazi, some known to my family.'

'Hence the connection.'

'Years ago, my father and he were friends, had a lot in common, much to do with the resistance. I never knew the full story.'

Although Jack trusted her with his life, he suspected that she did in fact know the 'full story' and was maybe even part of it. He realised that her apparent unwillingness to divulge anything significant was probably to protect Christos.

'We're close friends,' she said, evenly. 'We trust each other completely. Ironically, I've learnt more from him, here in Greece over the years, than from friends and family in Benghazi – what it was like under Dorpadski, what it's like there today.'

'You don't have to tell me any of this.'

'Jack,' she said, quietly, 'Christos and I, we are witnesses. You must also become a witness, a witness to the regime's crimes whether it's here in Greece or across the Mediterranean in Cyrenaica. We have to listen, to learn. This is how we survive.'

He was at a loss; he couldn't decide if this was a call to arms or whether she was simply warning him of things to come. For several minutes, they didn't speak; her words kept rolling around inside his head.

People started to drift into the square, to gossip, to smoke, to drink. He felt he was a guest at a large family gathering, where everybody knew, and had to be seen by, everybody else. Despite an underlying unease because of what she'd just told him, the atmosphere in the square had a calming effect.

'Jack,' she said abruptly, 'I've come to accept that we'll never see Stavros again, whether there's any truth in Dorpadski's story or not. If our son isn't dead already, they'll kill him as soon as they find him.'

Her directness startled him.

'Acceptance,' she continued, 'not in an emotional or philosophical sense, but as in a fact. He's as good as dead, has ceased to exist, that's all.' She paused. 'I refuse to be terrorised by Dorpadski, to have him torture me, especially with you, Stavros' father, there at his table this evening.'

'I won't be terrorised either,' said Jack defiantly, 'although what I've learnt these last few days hasn't really changed anything. To me, Stavros has been dead for years, my days of grieving long gone.'

'My time to mourn is still to come, but you will be there for me,' she said before adding, vehemently, 'I will not let the bastard denigrate our son.'

She amazed him; one minute she was so emotionally vulnerable, the next cold, angry.

'And we must protect Emma, say nothing of Isabel,' she continued. 'If Dorpadski finds out that our granddaughter is working in Tripoli, the consequences could be catastrophic.'

'God forbid,' he said, acknowledging that this had indeed crossed his mind.

Gradually the heat of the day waned, a cooling breeze shifting dust and dead leaves around the square. Just before they got up to leave, she reached across and took his hands in hers.

'Jack, I want you to know how much you mean to me, how much I love you,' she whispered. 'I'll always remember our time here today, this village, the peace we shared on the mountain and here under the oak.'

'I will too,' he said.

'We will come back again, keep coming back,' she said, adding enigmatically, 'till it's the last place we visit together.'

Her words unsettled him, seemingly prophetic, but before he had time to question her, she was on her feet. Within minutes they were on the road again. She drove the car recklessly down the mountain, constantly fighting the wheel.

'God, you're a terrifying driver,' he shouted, as the old car straightened up and made a dash for the next hairpin.

'I know,' she said, her face radiant with excitement.

*

They hadn't been back in the cottage two minutes, when he saw the red light on the wallscreen. They sat in silence, reading Emma's message.

Dad, Bushra, I received the following message from Tripoli at ten this morning and have been frantically trying to get hold of Isabel's point of contact at HQ ever since but to no avail.

Urgent Message from Security & Border Division, EDA Military Command, Tripoli, UNMTF to Emma Meredith (next of kin) on behalf of Isabel Meredith.

Isabel was involved in an incident in East Fezzan, (blank) kilometres, bearing (blank) degrees from Sabha, EDA Desert Garrison at (blank) hours on (blank) date.

She is currently being treated in Sabha Military District Hospital, where her condition is not deemed to be life-threatening.

You will receive an update, (blank) hours from receipt of this message.

Signed (blank), on behalf of SBD

I am beside myself with worry, please call me when you get this.

Love Emma.

19

Sabha, Early October 2031

n '25, EDA established Sabha, the largest settlement in the Fezzan, as a garrison town. Historically important, it was the ideal base from which to destroy the remaining UDP warlords, who had been terrorising the country, and turn back the rising tide of migrants making their way northwards to the coast. With its fertile oasis and plentiful supply of fresh water, the town had, for centuries, been a crucial staging post for desert nomads travelling between the Sahel and Mediterranean.

Philippe told Isabel that he had been instructed to take her to the hospital as soon as they arrived back in town. It was late when he deposited her and her few belongings at the reception, where she was met by a junior doctor on night duty. After an awkward farewell, Philippe drove off at speed into the dark.

The gash on her head was still raw. The doctor, initially concerned that she might have picked up an infection, assured her that after four or five days in hospital, she would return to full health. *Four or five days*, she thought, *that's insane. I should be well enough to leave in three*. She let it pass. She had more pressing concerns. It wasn't her weakened physical condition, rather her growing distrust of Philippe, which bothered her. Whatever had happened over the last few days, it had had a profound effect on her and especially on their relationship.

For the first time since they'd started working together, she found herself questioning his judgement. The savage events they'd both witnessed would, she knew instinctively, translate into two distinct narratives: his reported with total certainty would be believed; her speculative version would not. Immobilised in bed in the cool sterility of her private room, she realised that, within hours, his would be the official account. She sensed that military administrations, especially one like theirs, wanted unambiguous witness statements of such atrocities, so that they could act promptly and with impunity. Action, it appeared, invariably took priority over thoughtful reflection.

Just before she fell asleep, she remembered that the flask where she'd hidden the stinking bag of bloody thumbs was still in her backpack. To preserve them, she filled the flask with ice from the ice-maker outside her room, although guessing that this was probably futile. She wrapped it in dirty underwear at the bottom of her pack, hoping that even the most inquisitive hands would baulk at rummaging there. The smell of rotting limbs was pervasive; she prayed that the air-conditioner would purge the air before anybody noticed. Satisfied that she had done her best to support her version of events, she fell asleep.

She awoke late the next morning feeling totally gutted and surrendered to the ministrations of the hospital staff. Every muscle and joint in her body ached remorselessly. The duty doctor advised her that she was experiencing some form of post-traumatic stress. Apparently this was how her body chose to deal with it.

Oddly enough, she kept wondering how her mother and Jack would have reacted, if they'd been there. She knew Emma would have been worried, urging staff to provide her with ever more care.

She wasn't so sure about Jack. She knew that the vicarious role she played in his life would influence his reaction. Of course, he would have been concerned, but she suspected that other emotions, pride perhaps, would have been triggered. He would have seen her abject condition as a learning experience, necessary to survive the life she'd chosen to lead. He would have gauged her humour as an indicator of resilience. To this end, she hoped she wouldn't have let him down.

Gradually, over the next twenty-four hours, she began to feel stronger, less in pain and more in tune with the outside world. Initially she hadn't given any thought to the fact that nobody from her unit, least of all Philippe, had visited her or even left a message, enquiring after her recovery.

On the morning of the third day, a Sunday, she asked the nurse if there were any messages for her. Isabel was surprised to note her evasiveness. That same evening the duty doctor, not somebody she'd seen before, dropped in to see how she was progressing.

'I hear you asked Sam if there were any messages for you,' he said casually, after enquiring how she was feeling.

'I'm surprised I've had no visitors. I haven't heard from anybody since I got here. It's three days now. It's almost as if I've been forgotten.'

He hesitated.

'There were explicit instructions from the hospital manager.'

'Which were exactly?' she asked bluntly.

'That you were not to have any visitors or take calls for at least four days.'

'No matter how I was doing?'

'No matter how you were doing.'

'That's strange. Who's the manager anyway?'

'Mandy Lefarge,' he hesitated. 'She was a close friend of your boss, Philippe, until six months ago.'

'He's not my boss,' she snapped irritably, unable to contain her frustration. 'I'm sorry, I'm just a bit on edge.'

'It's understandable, don't worry about it. It's just that Lefarge told us you were his assistant, that he'd keep everybody informed

– everybody, that is, who needed to know of your whereabouts, of your recovery.'

'Bullshit.'

She was taken aback by her own forthright outburst; the doctor merely grinned. She was beginning to suspect that she was being manipulated. A moment or two passed in silence, except for the reassuring hum of the air-conditioning, which calmed her ragged nerves.

'Greg, Greg Hamilton and you're Isabel, I believe,' he said finally.

She heard a slight Scottish accent, which for her was a rare sound in Sabha; most in the military were either French or Dutch.

'Isabel Meredith, glad to meet you.'

'Let's see how you're doing,' he said, as he gently removed a swathe of bandages from around her head. As soon as she had arrived in the hospital, they'd shaved a patch above her left ear to reveal an angry but relatively superficial wound.

'Fortunately, you haven't picked up any infection. It's healing quite quickly. We'll have the bandages off in the next twenty-four hours. The wound will eventually disappear. Are the painkillers working?'

'Yes, although the nurses seem keen to keep me sedated,' she replied. 'What is it, morphine?'

'Yes, I'll check the dosages though,' he said. 'Have you any other aches or pains?'

'No, I think I'm on the mend. I'm told the bruising on my left shoulder and knee will take time to heal, but yes, generally I feel better. I shouldn't really be taking up a hospital bed,' she added.

'No, you must rest. You're not as strong as you think. Make the most of your stay here.' He paused, as if unsure what to say. 'We see a lot of Philippe. He's been a frequent visitor here for as long as I can remember.'

'He's always been in good health,' she said, surprised at what she'd heard, 'at least since I started working with him.'

'Indeed, he's very fit.'

'Why would he come here then?'

'The hospital has the highest concentration of expat women in town,' he said bluntly, avoiding eye contact.

Colour rose instantly in her cheeks, as she fought to suppress her embarrassment.

'I'm sorry,' he said, 'I shouldn't have said that.'

'Don't be.'

She struggled to sit up, after regaining her composure. Hugging raised knees under the bed sheet and not wishing to talk about Philippe, she asked Greg how long he'd been working there.

'Five years now. You wouldn't credit it, speaking to the other medics,' he laughed, generously.

She hesitated, unsure if she should confide in him.

'I need your help,' she said, realising she had little choice. 'I must contact my boss in Tripoli as soon as possible. For some reason my mobile's jammed. Is there an outside line that I can use?'

'There's one opposite the nurses' station down the corridor, but it's monitored around the clock. All hell would break loose if you were caught using it without the manager's permission.' He hesitated. 'You could try your chances in the wee small hours. The women behind the desk are invariably asleep.'

'Lefarge doesn't sound very efficient if her staff sleep the night away,' she said, warming to this curious Scotsman.

'She's very efficient as it happens.'

'How come?' she asked, wondering at the subtle workings of the hospital.

He hesitated again. 'All the young women working here, mostly Eritrean and Ethiopian, have two jobs, which are both controlled by the manager.'

'Two jobs?'

'They work alternative shifts at the Crocodile Club. It's on a side street off Revolution Square,' he said, as if this were normal hospital practice.

'I thought the place was a hookers' joint.'

He lowered his voice.

'These girls are high-class prostitutes, a role they were primarily brought here for. They've been trafficked and are virtual prisoners. Most end their lives here, either because of drugs, serious sexual assault or suicide.'

'Good God, that's awful,' she blurted out, wondering at his frankness. 'So Lefarge's a brothel keeper as well. How in hell's name does she get away with it?' she asked, her frustration rising again. She braced herself for more unpleasant truths, which she suspected he would reveal.

Greg was silent, as if gauging whether he should confide much more in her.

'She's part of a tight-knit group involved in people trafficking, and drugs and arms smuggling,' he said at last. 'Critically, she has protection.'

'Good God,' she exclaimed. 'Who protects her?'

'Philippe.'

'Philippe,' she repeated dully, realising she wasn't totally surprised.

'As head of border security,' he continued, evenly, 'nobody dares challenge him.'

Why was this Scotsman confiding in her, trusting her not to report him, she wondered. He clearly disliked Philippe, who she now saw more and more in an entirely different light. No longer her sometime lover and reliable work colleague whom she once respected, he appeared to be a ruthless and manipulative crook.

'Why are you telling me all this?' she asked, her curiosity getting the better of her.

'What I'm telling you is pretty common knowledge amongst the civilian population here in town. Senior folk in Tripoli must know, they just turn a blind eye, pretend it's not happening. Why do you ask?' he asked, turning the tables on her.

'I don't really know.' She hesitated. 'My trust in Philippe, and what he represents, has been seriously challenged in the desert this past week. And now this. My belief in our so-called mission is rapidly fading,' she said quietly. 'And the drugs, arms smuggling, people trafficking – is he involved as well?'

'Some of us think he may be the facilitator, you know the muscle, but we have no evidence. He's probably not the main guy behind the rackets, but he does have exclusive access to the border, as you yourself can testify. That's his domain. He's a wily fox, always just below the radar.'

'What use is that, the border's impregnable anyway. It's actually lethal if crossed illegally.'

'There's a feeling among the civilians, those of us who've been here the longest, that the border isn't as secure as it ought to be.'

Something in what Greg had just said resonated with what she'd suspected from her fractured conversation with Philippe on the way back from the border incident.

'What the hell do you think happened then over the last few days?'

'The official line is that your Russian counterparts were slaughtered by a rogue UDP warlord, apparently still intent on destabilising the region,' he said, evenly. 'We find it strange that these warlords have managed to avoid being caught, despite both sides of the border being officially free of UDP infiltration for nearly two years.'

'Doesn't make sense.'

'No, it doesn't. I never believe the military's version of events,' he said, bluntly. 'They've invested a lot of effort and the blood of innocent people to maintain this charade.'

'Charade?'

'It appears the military, both ours and the Russians', keep chasing and liquidating wholly imaginary UDP groups, apparently popping up on either side of the border. A few local Bedouin are sacrificed from time to time to maintain the illusion. Philippe and company report back to Tripoli that the threat has been eliminated, that the area is secure again. Everybody's happy.'

She wondered why he had willingly divulged so much in their first encounter; she was hopeful she'd find out.

'That's incredible,' she exclaimed. 'But why?'

'For most long-serving civilians here, it's not credible. For the administration back in Tripoli, it's entirely credible,' he continued. 'They never visit and have no reason to believe otherwise. If a little licence is taken by the military down here, it's a small price to pay for maintaining overall security. Unwittingly, they're supporting these spurious operations, which are probably designed to disguise what's really going on.'

Unclasping her arms, she slumped back onto the pillow. She felt suffocated by so much dissembling, deceit and corruption. She kept quiet, sensing that he'd revealed more than he wanted to.

Greg wandered over to the window and looked out over the well-groomed oasis gardens. He appeared unsure what to say or do next.

'I'll see that you're not disturbed,' he said, turning from the window, 'if you choose to use the phone outside the reception, say between two and three tomorrow morning.'

She roused herself, searching his face, doubting his offer.

'I appreciate your help but won't have you getting into trouble. It's probably a worthless gesture anyway, getting out before being let out.'

'I mean it. Most women who work nights are on drugs, prescribed or otherwise, combating fatigue, blocking out the horrors of the Crocodile Club,' he said, quietly. 'Their lives are hellish.'

'God, that's awful.'

'I guarantee nobody will be around.'

'Thank you,' was all she managed.

He turned to go, then hesitated. 'I presume you're embedded, no pun intended,' he grinned, 'with the military, probably confined to barracks.'

'Yes,' she muttered.

'If you've an opportunity to escape, we civilians meet at the tennis club, to the east of town. All the licensed taxi drivers know the place. I go there most evenings when not on nights, which I usually do on Fridays and Saturdays. I'd be happy to sign you in. You'll find a refreshingly sympathetic bunch of people. Just turn up when you can.'

And with that, he abruptly left the room.

She set her alarm and fell asleep.

*

Isabel woke before dawn to the sounds of shouting. In a furtive reconnoitre along the corridor, she heard Philippe arguing strenuously with the night-duty staff at reception. She gathered that her night-time call to Tripoli had caused problems for the unfortunate semi-conscious woman at the nurse's station.

After breakfast and having had her bandages removed, she was unceremoniously picked up and driven to the military compound, where she was billeted. An hour later, she reported to Philippe's office to be told that he was out until after lunch. She was advised that she was required to attend a formal debriefing on the border incident later in the day. *To what end?* she thought. *What a bloody joke.*

With little to do other than to ensure that the flask was well hidden from prying eyes, she showered and went to the canteen for an early lunch. As usual she joined Philippe's team, his security detail that had been held up in Ramlit al Wigh. They were pleased to see her, immediately making space for her at the table. She sensed that, whatever had befallen her in the last few days, these men had clearly played no part. As far as they were concerned, she had suffered minor injuries in a terrorist incident; a short stay in hospital was entirely appropriate.

'How are you feeling, Isabel?'

'I see you're on the mend, the wound must be healing.'

'We were shocked to hear of the attack.'

'Philippe told us how brave you were.'

Speaking in English for her benefit, they unburdened themselves, drawing her back into their close-knit group. She knew that in her own way, she was a member of this elite force, a modern French Foreign Legion. For their comradeship alone, she was both proud and grateful.

She felt sure that these men, fresh recruits out from France, were not implicated in whatever clandestine operation Philippe was involved. He had 500 men under his command in Sabha. A hardcore of about thirty, many of whom came from a similar *Pied-Noir* background, had been there since the start of the campaign; these, she suspected, were the stormtroopers he relied on.

But she no longer deluded herself. Unbeknown to these innocent foot soldiers, she now believed that senior staff in the Sabha military establishment were secretly manipulating the system, feeding a hedonistic life of drugs, prostitution and corrupted wealth.

'Their team was gunned down. So much for our game,' laughed André, the group's mechanic.

'The game,' she repeated lamely, thinking back to the football match that never happened, the bodies lying in the searing morning heat.

Did they really believe these eleven men constituted the football team they should have played on that fateful day?

'Imagine shooting the whole team, all eleven players, all ready to thrash us on the pitch.'

'But their captain wasn't among the bodies,' Isabel said, trying to follow their logic.

'Their captain?'

'Ramil, the non-playing captain. He told us he'd manage the team, not play.'

'He's dead now for sure, playing or non-playing captain,' said André, 'killed by the bloody terrorists.'

'We'd have been slaughtered too, had we turned up.'

'Lucky the old truck broke down in Ramlit.'

As she listened to their well-intentioned chatter, her thoughts drifted back to that fateful morning when they'd surveyed the corpses in the depression. She recalled the row between Philippe and Omar; how Philippe had insisted that the mass slaughter was the work of UDP terrorists, whereas Omar thought otherwise; how Omar believed that the dead men knew their killer or killers, whereas Philippe did not.

Philippe was also certain that Ramil had been killed because, like the others, he was Russian. But to Omar, she now realised, Ramil was a Muslim first and foremost, a Tartar Muslim, and for that reason he and the drivers may have been spared. Given the antipathy she'd sensed between Ramil and the Russian military, it suddenly crossed her mind that Ramil might have been involved in the killings. She shuddered involuntarily.

'Are you OK, Isabel?' asked André, pointedly. 'You were drifting off.'

Her head cleared instantaneously, seeing the concerned looks of her colleagues.

'I'm fine thanks. I still feel drugged from the stuff they gave me at the hospital. Maybe I'll go to my room for an hour or so. Tell Philippe that's where I am.'

Two handwritten messages had been pushed under the door when she got back. The first, delivered at twelve-thirty, stated briefly that the afternoon meeting had been cancelled, no explanation given. The second, delivered fifteen minutes later, advised that she was being recalled to Tripoli immediately; she would be picked up at five the following morning, to catch the early shuttle flight.

She knew now that Philippe was avoiding her, wanting her off his patch as soon as possible. Her plans started to unravel. How could she smuggle her flask with its precious contents onto the plane without being caught? She had planned to return to Tripoli by jeep, a two-day desert drive, which she always enjoyed. This time she'd been hoping to stop off for a few hours and visit the massive solar farm under construction south of Jebel Nefusa. She would need to get the decomposing thumbs secretly analysed as soon as possible, if she had any hope of challenging the official version of events at the border.

It occurred to her that Greg, whom she barely knew, was her only hope. She only had a few hours left to arrange everything. Her biggest worry was whether she could trust him and even if she could, would he agree to extract the DNA data and get it to her?

*

After resting in her room for a couple of hours, she managed to get, contrary to expectation, a pass to go into town for the evening. At dusk she caught a taxi to the tennis club. The drive took her through the old historic centre of Sabha. They passed the ornate mosque which dominated Revolution Square and the souk with its narrow sinewy lanes disappearing tunnel-like to the north and south of Fezzan Street, the commercial heart of the old town. The air was suffocating, the heat unbearable.

As the taxi crawled along the thronged street, she was astonished at the diversity of its people, of every colour and creed. She saw tall stringy desert nomads, stocky mountain men from the north and squat figures from distant tropical forests to the south. She became totally absorbed, trying to identify each ethnic group, stretching her limited knowledge.

She recognised local Bedouin from Fezzan, Berbers from Jebel Nefusa to the south and west of Tripoli and turbaned Tuaregs, travellers of the great Saharan sand seas. She saw tribesmen from sub-Sahel Africa, from Chad, from Ghana, from Liberia. Many came from Nigeria, including the Fulani and lean ferocious-looking Hausa from the north, fine-featured Ibo from the east and the face-scarred Yoruba from the coast. There wasn't a European to be seen.

She felt calm, fatalistic, her anxiety of the last few days easing. She knew that she had one chance to get at the truth, to challenge the status quo. Failing that, her relatively uncomplicated expatriate existence would continue. Another questionable border episode would be whitewashed into history. She was resigned to the fact that, one way or another, there was nothing more she could do.

It occurred to her that she'd never been downtown before. She'd never been out of Philippe's company nor out of sight of his many minions. Nobody had trusted her to spend time on her own away from the military compound. She realised how little she'd seen and experienced on previous trips to Sabha. She'd always been cocooned in the tight embrace of the military. Her every move, every field trip, every border meeting and her entire social life had been carefully choreographed.

On her regular trips to Sabha, she'd convinced herself that she was experiencing some form of adventure, away from the constraints of Tripoli. Nothing, she realised, was further from the truth. She wondered why she'd been kept on such a tight leash. Perhaps one day she'd find out.

A powerful urge came over her to stop the taxi, step out into the hot crowded street and simply vanish; disappear from colleagues, friends, even family. How exciting it would be, she thought, to reinvent oneself here, deep in the Sahara.

She saw the evening as a turning point. All her life she had conformed to the demands of the establishment, whether at home, in school or university. She had started to break with this conformity when she decided to work in North Africa; tonight would be another step along that road.

As the taxi freed itself from the clutches of Fezzan Street, she asked herself what Jack would have done in these circumstances. In his long and hazardous career challenging the establishment of the day, had he crossed the line in the interests of the truth? Sadly, she realised, it was unlikely they'd ever have that conversation, given his recent behaviour towards her.

And Greg, was he a man who would seek the facts, risking censure and the possibility of losing his job? She fervently prayed he was.

20

Peloponnese, Greece,
Early October 2031

mma's earlier message had left them feeling unsettled, on edge. Having tried several times to call her without success, they decided to abandon their efforts until later that evening. However, fifteen minutes before they were due at the villa, the wallscreen came to life with a second message.

> *Managed to get through to I's point of contact who said they had no record of EDA communication! Got pretty angry saying this was no way to treat next of kin. Woman was apologetic, said she'd contact the military at HQ and get back immediately... that was an hour ago! Am very worried about I, not certain now what to think. Emma*

At seven, as the heat of the day ebbed away, they walked up through the gardens for their appointment with Dorpadski. With Emma's concern for Isabel still filling their heads, they were ill-prepared to face him. Jack felt vulnerable, desperately trying to persuade himself that there was no connection between what had happened in the Fezzan and what might unfold during the evening, despite having no possible evidence to the contrary.

The front door opened mysteriously before they reached it. He did not recognise Hera, a local woman whose family had worked for the Benamers for decades; she was a young girl when he'd first visited Stoupa, back in the '80s. She glanced shyly at Bushra and beckoned them to follow.

Everything looked markedly different from the place Jack recalled visiting as a young man. In those days the villa, a haven of tranquillity, had been simply but tastefully furnished. In the main living room, which overlooked manicured lawns and the sea beyond, beautiful carpets had been scattered around, carpets woven from goats' wool by shepherds living in the Jebel Akhdar, south of Benghazi, their muted colours contrasting with local ochre-coloured floor tiles. Several Impressionist watercolours of immense value had discreetly adorned the white walls – no ostentation, no clutter.

Hera led them into the same room, randomly laid out with expensive modern furnishings: enormous black leather settees, a large glass-topped table, freaky metal sculptures, overbearing and vaguely pornographic murals and a fully stocked cocktail bar, jammed unsympathetically into one corner.

Although she had visited Dorpadski on many occasions and knew what to expect, Jack saw Bushra flinch as they entered. The place reeked of expensive colognes and Turkish tobacco. Three couples, with their backs to the room, were standing at the open patio doors looking out over the garden. They were speaking loudly in Russian.

Jack's heart sank. He had a sudden urge to turn and run; Bushra, sensing his hesitation, squeezed his hand.

'Ivan,' she said, clearly, 'this is my old friend Jack, Jack Meredith.'

On cue, all six turned. Dorpadski and his wife stepped forward to greet them. Slim with close-cropped grey hair, he stood out from the others, all of whom were younger.

'Ah my dear friend, Bushra,' he said, formally kissing her on both cheeks, 'and Jack, I've heard so much about you,' he said, taking his hand in a vice-like grip.

Jack briefly wondered how this could possibly be. He was surprised by his host, expecting Dorpadski to be more physically threatening. Instead he faced a man of medium height, clean-cut with the aura of a City banker. It was the eyes, though, that caught his attention – icy blue, almost transparent.

'Bushra, you know my wife, Lena, of course,' Dorpadski continued, nodding to the blond, waspish woman at his side, perhaps ten years his junior.

He introduced them to the two couples; nobody spoke, or at least admitted to speaking, English. As Bushra and the others followed Lena out onto the patio, Jack was astonished to hear her conversing fluently in Russian, again catching him off guard. Speaking in English, she asked for a vodka, which Hera went off to get.

'Whisky?'

'Irish if you've got it,' Jack replied.

'I'm afraid we don't stock Irish. The Russian palate is more accustomed to Scotch, certain Highland malts,' Dorpadski said, from the bar.

Dorpadski poured a generous measure in a beautiful cut-glass tumbler before handing it to Jack. As they walked out to join the others, he took a discrete sip; it tasted of diesel, like no other malt he'd ever had.

'So how do you find Stoupa?' Dorpadski asked. 'You haven't been here for years.'

'It hasn't changed much, not as much as I would have expected.'

'It must be forty years.'

'Yes.'

'I gather you two often stayed here.'

'Yes, back in the '80s, '90s,' said Jack, anxious to keep the conversation as banal as possible. 'We love to swim, the bay is so sheltered. I often thought it would be a great place to keep a small boat,' he continued, having no idea what they might have in common.

'I prefer larger boats, motor-yachts, they're faster, more comfortable,' he laughed icily, 'and you keep dry.'

Jack was about to ask him about *Kostroma*, berthed in Kalamata, but an inner voice urged caution against it.

Over the next few minutes, they talked of this and that, Jack giving away as little as possible. He found the atmosphere thoroughly disorientating. Coming here this evening, he knew would be like walking through a minefield. One slip of his tongue, one ill-considered statement, and the whole pretence might blow up in his face, doing untold damage to Bushra's precarious lifestyle.

He felt Dorpadski was playing with him, waiting patiently for his inevitable undoing. He caught Bushra's eye as he and Dorpadski joined the others, her wink briefly raising his spirits.

Just as dinner was announced, Jack excused himself and went to the washroom. He was struggling with the sour-tasting malt and poured much of it into the basin. He wasn't going to let the drink blunt his concentration. On his way back, Dorpadski passed him in the corridor, a wry grin on his face.

'There's no need to waste it,' he said, quietly. 'We've plenty of soft drinks for those who don't enjoy too much alcohol.'

Jack's blood froze.

Dinner was sumptuous and the conversation noisy, fuelled by the very best French wines and Russian vodka. Jack sat between Lena and one of the younger Russian women. The latter, who succumbed to drink early on, talked volubly to him incomprehensibly in Russian, completely unfazed that he had nothing to say.

On the other hand, Lena, in faultless English, surprised him with her knowledge of London, a city she clearly enjoyed. She recalled galleries she'd visited, operas she'd attended, her preferred playwrights, her favourite restaurants. She quizzed him on the latest fashions, which hotels he would recommend. He found himself discussing with her the relative merits of French and Russian Impressionists, a subject in which she clearly had a keen interest. He had underestimated this woman, who was turning out to be a surprisingly interesting hostess.

She told Jack how she travelled extensively, sometimes with her husband, at other times alone. They would stay in the finest hotels around the world, enjoying the best that cities such as Moscow, London and New York had to offer.

Jack knew that, over the years, Bushra had spent evenings with Lena when Dorpadski was away on business. She'd once admitted to him that these get-togethers had reduced her sense of isolation from a world of sophistication and culture that she and her family had once shared and enjoyed before their downfall. Sometimes she would convince herself that Lena felt guilty about her husband's appropriation of the family's wealth, that she was trying in a small way to compensate her for the loss. At other times, she believed Lena was simply baiting her, demoralising her, perhaps at her husband's insistence, for his own ends.

Despite his dubious reputation, Jack had learnt from Bushra that Dorpadski was well regarded in diplomatic circles as the man who had finally quashed religious fundamentalism in Syria and North Africa. International diplomats, suppressing their unease, would seek his advice in areas of the world where this still played a destructive role in the lives of ordinary people. His wife, well versed in literature and art, played a vital role at these awkward meetings.

Towards the end of the meal, Jack began to feel a little woozy; too much wine on top of the whisky, he thought. He became aware that Bushra, sitting opposite, was trying to catch his attention. Without warning, a hand gripped his shoulder; turning, he came face to face with his host. His heart missed a beat.

'My wife has been hogging your company all evening, Jack,' he said, bowing slightly towards her. 'I have Bushra's permission to show you around her family home. You might be interested in the changes we've made since you were here last.'

From the other side of the table he saw alarm briefly flicker across her face. It was his turn to wink, which he did as he stood to follow Dorpadski.

*

Wordlessly, he followed Dorpadski from the dining room to a door at the end of a long corridor. They entered a darkened room, which Jack vaguely remembered as being old Ali's study. It suddenly dawned on him that his host never had any intention of showing him around the villa; this, for whatever reason, was as far as they were going. Even when his eyes became accustomed to the dark, he could hardly make anything out, giving him the weird sensation that he was in police custody. Visceral fear clamped his chest, his breathing shortened, his heart rate soared.

There was nothing in the room: no papers, no books, no bookcase; just a single painting above an office desk, a couple of stainless-steel chairs and filing cabinet, and a large video screen in one corner. He remembered the room as it used to be: priceless paintings on the wall, books and papers everywhere, on shelves, tables and scattered on the floor, even a small Eastern sculpture on the desk – a haven of learning, of culture. *The bloody Russian's a philistine*, he thought.

Dorpadski indicated a chair directly in front of the screen; not a word was spoken. As he sat down, Jack suddenly noticed two bulky figures dressed in black, standing motionless to one side of the shuttered window; his heart missed a beat.

'You are here to listen,' Dorpadski said roughly, any pretence of hospitality instantly abandoned, 'just listen and perhaps learn. On no account interrupt. Understand?'

The atmosphere in the stuffy room was edgy, menacing. Jack nodded, too terrified to say anything.

'I've always hated Cyrenaica,' he spat out, abruptly. 'From the day I arrived, I despised everything about the goddamn place: the country, its people, their way of life, their culture, traditions,' he ranted. 'The people are filthy, poverty-stricken, feckless, dishonest. I found a country broken, ungovernable, beyond redemption.'

Jack was physically shocked, completely taken aback by this venomous outpouring.

For the next ten minutes, Dorpadski lectured him on the rottenness of life in Cyrenaica; what he'd experienced when he was sent there 'to civilise the place', six years earlier. He went on to complain bitterly that, despite his best efforts, he couldn't bring together local people, people of sufficient intelligence, integrity and strength, as he put it, to form a ruling class.

So much for Bushra's family, Jack thought, and people like them – old, respected, educated families, who even the regime had valued. Then, as if reading his thoughts, Dorpadksi launched into a scathing attack on her family, calling her father totally incompetent, an inveterate liar.

'But of course, they were just chicken shit,' snarled Dorpadski, veering off. 'The really evil player in this pitiful family is your bastard son, Stavros.'

So, Jack realised in horror, *this is what this whole tirade has been leading up to: Stavros.*

Dorpadksi ranted on about how Stavros had betrayed his country, his own people, how he and his fellow terrorists were secretly planning to overturn the mandate, return the country to its previous chaos, to its primitive origins. He said Stavros' lot were in complete denial of the enormous progress that he, Dorpadski as governor, had achieved. *Progress?* thought Jack in disgust. *What the hell does he mean by progress? The man's talking bullshit.*

Dorpadski started speaking in Russian. One of the men switched the video on. Then, turning to Jack, Dorpadski continued in English, 'This will not be pleasant, but you're about to see how we dealt with your treacherous son. It's very instructive.'

To Jack, the whole charade suddenly started to make sense.

The film was grainy, poor quality. He could just make out four or five armed soldiers milling around an enclosed courtyard, perhaps twice the size of a tennis court. The place was bare, featureless. The sun blazed down on the baked earth floor. High walls threw long dark shadows across the dirt, suggesting morning or evening. What appeared to be a heavy steel door set in the wall opened; three men dressed in rags were unceremoniously pushed out of the shadows. One appeared to be limping, dragging his left foot.

They had the look of condemned men, he thought.

Two of the three were pulled to one side. Without any warning, two soldiers stepped forward and shot them at point blank range between the eyes. The men simply crumpled and fell where they stood.

The sudden brutality of what he'd just witnessed stunned Jack.

'Stavros' accomplices,' Dorpadski growled, clearly angry now.

The camera then focused on the third individual, the one with the limp.

Jack looked intently at the man. Here he was, confronting his son, albeit an image, never having set eyes on him – a mythical somebody whom he had consigned to history years earlier. He felt no emotion as a father, just sorry for the man's plight. He braced himself for more barbarity.

One of the soldiers, an officer perhaps, started screaming in Arabic in the man's face. As soon as the officer finished, Dorpadski barked an order. The video promptly froze in mid-frame. One of the two men in the darkened room stepped forward into the dim light and translated for Jack what had been said.

That's bloody odd, thought Jack, *Dorpadski speaks Arabic, why the translator?* Perhaps coming from a third party made the speech authentic.

The gist of what the officer had said was that Stavros was a traitor. In short, he was accused of denying his fellow countrymen the civilising benefits of living peaceably under a benign and rational government. The translator rambled on in the same vein for a minute or so.

Do they really think I believe this bullshit, this propaganda? Jack thought. *Perhaps, like all dictators, Dorpadski is a fantasist, promoting 'truth' when all around is fiction, lies. Which then begs the question: am I looking at Stavros or some poor petty criminal? If Dorpadski knows that I suspect the latter, what is the purpose of this ghastly charade?*

Then a strange thing happened: apparently, the officer had condemned Stavros for 'being the bastard son of an American father and an Arab whore'. When Dorpadski heard the English translation, he went ballistic, shouting angrily at the translator in Russian, who then corrected what he'd just said. The man apologised, saying he should have said, 'being the bastard son of an English father and Greek mother', before adding offhandedly that Stavros would be punished according to the 'medieval practices of his people'.

The video continued. At this point, Stavros appeared to interrupt the officer, shouting at him. Then without warning, Stavros was struck from behind and fell to the ground, at which point the video froze again. When it resumed moments later, Stavros appeared to be staked out, face up, his body spread-eagled. Another man, a Bedouin judging by his dress, emerged from the shadows. He was carrying an axe with a shaft, about a metre long. Again the video faltered, then froze.

'This is how we deal with people who oppose the government,' snarled Dorpadski, as the footage restarted.

Without warning the Bedouin raised his axe and severed Stavros' left hand; within seconds, the right hand. His screams were terrifying as blood spurted from the wounds. Jack felt queasy, the sour whisky taste filling his mouth.

The officer then knelt and shouted into Stavros' face before turning back to the Bedouin. The man lifted his axe and with two swift blows, severed both of Stavros' feet. The officer kept haranguing him, as he lay screaming and writhing in the dust, his blood flowing freely, his body an island in a sea of black pitch. Jack stared in abject horror at the screen, bile rising in his throat, forcing himself not to throw up. The video froze again.

Moments later the video restarted. The courtyard was in near total darkness, lit only by a couple of low-watt bulbs. Jack squinted at the image when suddenly, without warning, his body convulsed. A dozen or so large rats were tearing the flesh from a headless body, now barely visible in the poor light. The video flickered again; it was daylight. The severed hands and feet were being nailed to a rough timber board. Something caught Jack's eye: the left foot was badly deformed, perhaps a clubfoot, he thought.

The video was turned off. He couldn't hold back any longer and threw up all over himself, the desk, the floor; the stink was appalling. Dorpadksi left the room, returning a few minutes later with Hera, armed with a bowl and towels. Jack kept retching until there was nothing left, his eyes streaming, his nostrils blocked with vomit. By now he was barely aware of his surroundings. Hera was followed by Bushra who instantly took control, insisting Dorpadski and his two flunkies leave the room. At that point, Jack slumped to the floor, losing consciousness.

*

Jack woke to the sound of waves, of wind sighing in the trees. It was dark. He was sprawled out in one of Bushra's easy chairs on the veranda, a cover thrown over his shivering body.

'Jack, are you awake?' he could hear her whisper. He opened his eyes, his throbbing headache intensifying. She was in shadow, sitting across from him, watching him intently. 'Do you want a drink?'

He nodded. He drank deeply, the cool water like nectar, cleansing the woolly staleness in his mouth.

'Was it the whisky?'

Whisky? He had no recollection why he felt as he did, how he got there; he had no idea of time. His mind was blank.

'Was it the whisky?' she repeated, quietly.

An image crossed his mind's eye: a man with a limp, dragging his deformed foot as he walked. Then in a technicolour rush, bloody images flooded his brain unlocking his memory. He sat bolt upright and shouted out, fearful for his life.

Bushra rushed to his side. She wiped the sweat from his face with a damp towel and pushed him gently back into the cushions. Slowly he regained his composure, processing every minute detail in his head, from the moment he and Dorpadski entered old Ali's study.

'Was Stavros born with a club foot?' he asked, suddenly.

Bushra looked at him in alarm, wondering if he was hallucinating.

'No, why do you ask?'

He was silent, gazing blindly into her face, his mind racing. *Dorpadski, the scheming, dissembling bastard*, he realised. What lengths the man would go to, to discredit her, linking her – both of them – to the principal existential threat to the Russian mandate. *Why, in God's name?* he wondered.

'It wasn't the whisky,' he said, at length, 'although it was spiked. This was all about Stavros.'

'Tell me, tell me everything,' she whispered, settling down on a cushion, at his feet. 'I'm ready.'

21

Sabha, Early October 2031

The Sabha Tennis and Social Club was located in the grounds of the former Fort Elena complex, which had been a military facility under the dictatorship. Isabel had read how French-led EDA forces had occupied and fortified the town six years earlier, but had been reluctant to locate EDA's Desert HQ in the old French colonial fort. Originally named Fortezza Margherita, it had been built in 1912 by the Italians on a rock outcrop above the surrounding desert, during their occupation of the Fezzan.

Towards the end of World War II, the Free French, having ousted the Italians from the region, managed to stay on, hoping to extend the French presence in Algeria throughout the Maghreb. They finally left when the Fezzan, as part of the United Kingdom of Libya, achieved independence in '51.

Seventy-four years later, and wanting to disassociate itself from the country's European colonial past, EDA built an entirely new fortified facility to the south-east of the town. Isabel thought it ironic that EDA forces currently stationed in Sabha were mostly French paratrooper units.

*

Her taxi pulled up outside the club. She walked into the reception area, bristling with security guards, just as a muezzin called the faithful to evening prayer from the minaret of a local mosque. As she signed the register, the familiarity of this ancient ritual steadied her nerves. A young boy was despatched by the clerk to find Greg.

'It's great that you could get here. I hope you haven't been waiting long,' he said, bounding energetically into the marble-floored hallway moments later, apparently impervious to the stifling heat.

He grasped her hand in a vigorous handshake. Standing beside him, she saw that he wasn't much taller than her. Beneath his confident façade, she sensed wariness.

'Not long. I knew from the register you were here, that you'd turn up,' she replied lightly, trying to stay calm. 'It's good to see people coming and going, everybody looking so relaxed. I'm just glad nobody's in uniform.'

'Are you coping OK with the heat? It's unusually hot for October, very unpleasant if you're not used to it.'

'I've never experienced anything like it. I think it was nearly fifty the couple of days we were at the border. I thought I'd die,' she laughed. 'I really dropped by to thank you for your help the other night. As you can imagine, all hell broke out the next day.'

'Everybody blamed everybody else for not keeping a closer eye on you. I heard there were lots of raised voices, Philippe's being the loudest.'

'I seem to have caused a load of problems. Anyway, I've been recalled to Tripoli, won't have a chance now to complete my field work.'

'I'm sorry, what a bloody shame. When are you leaving?'

'First flight tomorrow morning. It's at six-thirty. I'm being picked up at five.'

'They haven't given you much time.'

She noticed the rapidly gathering darkness beyond the front door.

'Let me show you round,' he said, cheerfully. 'Then perhaps we'll have a drink. Have you eaten yet?'

'No.'

'Would you care to have supper? It's simple cooking but the food's good.'

'I'd enjoy that,' she replied. Her spirits soared, realising she'd been given a chance to seek his help. 'It'll be a welcome change from the military canteen. I'm signed out until eleven, no questions asked.'

'For whatever reason they kept you in hospital, it's passed,' he said, lowering his voice, beckoning her to follow. 'Apparently Philippe's reported your unpleasant experience at the border. Tripoli's approved an appropriate response, without asking too many awkward questions.'

So much for their joint debriefing, she thought.

'I wonder what they mean by an "appropriate response"?'

'Working with the Russians to find and exterminate those responsible for the multiple killings,' he said, bluntly, taking her by surprise.

'An eye for an eye,' was all she could think to say.

'That's how the military operate. I've heard they're happy now, being in control again.'

'In control again.' She wasn't aware they'd lost control.

'They certainly don't want a civilian witness hanging around asking awkward questions,' he said. 'I'm sure that's why they're getting you out of here as quickly as possible. A harmless night out before you leave might temper your frame of mind,' he said, before adding, 'help you forget the incident.'

'Hardly.'

'Anyway, you're history now, I'm afraid,' he said, without any malice.

He dropped the subject as they left the building.

'I see you've a backpack, a tennis kit perhaps. I never asked if you'd like a game. Do you play?'

'It's not kit. I haven't played for months. Mountaineering is, or was, my thing. I'd enjoy a game sometime, though I suspect I'd be rubbish,' she laughed. 'I imagine it's like playing in a sauna.'

Her nervousness subsided. Still flagging in the blast-furnace heat, she followed him out into a large palm-fringed courtyard; towering above them on a rock outcrop were the floodlit walls of the original Italian fort. The area was bound on all four sides by two-storey whitewashed buildings. They looked as if they were once stables or workshops that had recently been converted into club rooms.

They passed a block of six floodlit hard tennis courts, three of which were in use. Beyond the courts to her left, she could see a good-sized swimming pool sparkling in subdued poolside lighting, surrounded by deck chairs and sunshades. She could make out groups of men and women sitting and standing around behind the pool, silhouetted by the lights of an outside bar.

Punctuating the comforting sound of distant laughter and thudding tennis balls, she could hear the shrill cacophony of cicadas hidden in well-tended flowerbeds. The brittle noisy restlessness of the surrounding streets faded into the velvety blackness of the night. The scene was surreal, the atmosphere soporific, something she hadn't experienced in Sabha before.

As they made their way to the bar area, Greg described the old fort's role in Sabha's recent bloody existence. It was far removed from the clubby atmosphere she was witnessing around her. To her surprise she heard a piano and recognised a Chopin *Nocturne*; how bizarre.

'Part of the dictatorship's elite desert combat force was based in this courtyard. We think this was where the vehicle maintenance workshops were. There was evidence of a prison block, even an execution chamber, over there,' he said, pointing to an area beyond the tennis courts. 'Later the cells were used by UDP warlords when they rampaged throughout the Fezzan, mainly in the three or four years up to '25. It was a derelict site, grim and foreboding, when we first got here.'

He sounded so matter of fact. Not for the first time, it dawned on her how she'd become so immune to the horrors associated with the country's bedevilled history. Initially the stories had unnerved her, but not anymore. Now she just felt overwhelmed, powerless to effect even the smallest change for the better in its fortunes. Her recent experience at the border compounded her feelings of worthlessness. She realised she wasn't even a reliable witness.

'I'm sorry for waffling on,' he said, turning around. 'You must be sick to death of hearing this sort of thing.'

'No, don't apologise. I was just thinking how hardened I've become,' she said, quietly. 'It worries me sometimes.'

He stopped and faced her.

'It happens to us all eventually,' he said, a generous smile softening his penetrating gaze. She noticed how his almond eyes reflected the healthy tan of an open, freckled face, his short cropped brown hair fringed with ageing grey. He was slim with the toned body of an obsessive distance runner. She guessed that he was in his early thirties and admitted to herself that she'd missed him after he'd left her room so abruptly the other night. Seeing his smile, she now saw what it was that had attracted her.

'What will you have?' he said, guiding her between noisy talkative drinkers crowding around the bar. He was clearly popular – nodding to one, shouting at another, tapping a third on her back, joking, cajoling and laughing his way to the bar.

She caught sight of several people she'd briefly met in Tripoli, when they'd been in town on local leave. She remembered the stooped, craggy Dutchman, an agronomist who was working on a controversial GM maize research programme based at the vast newly constructed irrigation project. She recognised the plump hearty Irish nurse who managed an inoculation programme from one of the outlying oasis clinics. She caught sight of a strikingly attractive Syrian woman, whom she understood ran the training centre in town. They acknowledged her uncertainly, never having seen her in the club before.

'A cold beer,' she mouthed.

He casually introduced her to several people as they made their way to a table near the pool. She was surprised to see that everybody around her was behaving entirely normally. The place might have been a busy West End bar back in London on a Friday evening. It certainly didn't feel like an exotic expatriate community living in one of the hottest places on God's earth. To her great relief, she realised she was no longer an object of curiosity or lust, her usual experience when staying in Sabha's military compound.

*

'You OK here?' he asked, as they settled into old cane chairs.

'I'm fine. It's a pleasure to be away from the military.'

'I'm sure.'

'The older guys who've been here since the start, they're always putting me down, reminding me that I'm only a civilian. I'd forgotten what ordinary socialising is like.'

'Most people here know something about the border incident and Philippe's official report. Nobody's taking it too seriously,' he said with a grin. 'They're aware that you got caught up in it. They didn't hear, however, that you were injured, in hospital. It's all about Philippe, I'm afraid.'

'Doesn't surprise me,' she admitted. 'Anyway my involvement doesn't matter one way or another. The truth of what really happened there does though.'

'Sadly, we'll never know.'

'Perhaps,' she said, so quietly he didn't hear.

'I see you recognised a few people,' he said, changing the subject.

'Several,' she said, recalling where they'd met and what she knew about them. Discretely, she pointed out a few faces.

'So old Maggie told you she was inoculating local tribesmen,' he laughed. 'Did she say against what?'

'I can't remember.'

'She'd be reluctant to tell an outsider,' he said, quickly correcting himself. 'I mean, somebody outside the Sabha community.'

'So what does she do?'

'She's dealing with the biggest problem these people face.'

'Which is?'

'Overbreeding. She runs a sterilisation programme for men and women,' he said, flatly. 'All women with two or more children are automatically dealt with, for men it's voluntary. Most, I'm ashamed to admit, don't fully understand what she's doing.'

'God, that's awful. I mean, not knowing,' she added, hurriedly.

She was suddenly aware how removed she was from the reality of what EDA faced on a daily basis.

'Pragmatism is one of our fundamental principles,' he said, as if reading her mind.

'That's understandable.'

'Maggie's work has dramatically reduced the birthrate since we got here. With falling numbers, the health of the local people has improved, especially the women.'

'You mean Bedouin?'

'Not just Bedouin, everybody who ends up here, whether they're part of the settled community or in surrounding transit camps.'

'Migrants they plan to repatriate?' she asked, incredulously.

'Yes,' he paused. 'Don't be too judgemental about what you hear going on here.'

'Just need to get my head around it, that's all,' she admitted. 'I mean, the work that all these people do, you yourself do,' she continued, glancing around, 'the work must be worthwhile, beneficial.' She paused. 'But why such a large military presence? It seems to me the troops are redundant.'

'There's no need for them to be here now, though nobody in Tripoli wants to withdraw them, you know, "just in case".'

'Presumably the numbers were necessary at the beginning.'

'Six years ago, yes. When French paratroopers first managed to fight their way here, this was a terrifying place,' he said. 'They faced injury and death every day, from landmines, mortar fire and drone-launched rockets, from snipers hidden in the dunes outside the town. There were many casualties, terrible injuries, agonising deaths. The tented hospital operated like a MASH unit. Ultimately the military prevailed, bringing peace, establishing normality.'

'It must have been very frightening. Were you here from the start?'

'I was the first civilian doctor, came a year later when the regional hospital opened at the end of '26. It was still incredibly dangerous. In my innocence, I thought I'd mostly be treating Bedouins, you know, caught up in minor skirmishes between retreating UDP warlords and our forces. It turned out to be a bloody four-year war against the warlords, the poor Bedouin caught up in the middle. How naïve was I?' he laughed.

'I don't believe it. How were you to know what it was going to be like,' she said, quietly.

'When I qualified from Newcastle, I thought I was sorted,' he laughed. 'As an innocent twenty-two-year-old, I headed for London with a view to specialising in trauma medicine.'

'You were young when you qualified. What then?'

'After five years as a junior houseman rotating through various London teaching hospitals, I got my first job with EDA.'

'A big leap, from London to Sabha.'

'It was tough. We civilians were very inexperienced. Likewise the military, especially when it came to fighting terrorists who blended so effectively into the desert.' He paused. She sensed his unease. 'Our troops were quick to learn, though, butchering the enemy with great enthusiasm. UDP forces were completely broken, in full retreat. By late '29, the Fezzan, as far south as the Chad border, had been cleared.' She saw he was uncomfortable. 'A remarkable achievement but inhuman and shameful as well.'

She was anxious to move away from the ignominy of the past and talk about the present.

'It seems things have changed for the better. You're in good company here, appear to enjoy your work,' she said, groping inadequately for the positives, trying to understand a reality from which she had been so safely insulated in Tripoli.

'Good company, yes, but as for enjoying the work, I'm not so sure now. In the first couple of years it was great, exactly what I'd trained for.' She could hear the excitement in his voice. 'I did my elective in Soweto. In many ways it mirrored what I was faced with here, although this was the first place I'd had to deal with landmine and shrapnel wounds. But with the enemy essentially beaten, our caseload changed.'

'In what way?'

'It's mostly drug related now – alcoholism, cocaine addiction, HIV, the odd stab wound. I think you'd call it First World medicine. Changing times.'

He fell silent, appearing to have run out of words. She saw a principled man tracing an inevitable downward spiral in his working life, a trend he appeared unable, or perhaps unwilling, to change.

'Whatever, I guess it must be satisfying, professionally speaking,' she said trying to remain upbeat.

'Used to be.'

'How come?'

'There's too much internal bullying, violence, too much collateral damage. Corruption is endemic. We always saw ourselves as a simple, altruistic society. Not anymore.' He paused. 'I think the establishment's rotten here,' he said, abruptly.

Not for the first time since they met, she was startled by what he had to say. He seemed embarrassed as he finished his beer. Wanting to draw him out of his introspection, she began to talk about her work. She told him about her life as an anthropologist; how she found working with the various ethnic groups rewarding.

'I never knew we needed an anthropologist down here,' he admitted.

Their roles were reversed; he probed, she explained.

'I came here to study Berber and Bedouin tribesmen, how they might learn to live together,' she went on. 'Tripoli wants to introduce a policy of integration to promote social cohesion. Initially my work was largely confined to the north, where I spent several weeks living in the Jebel Nefusa, Berber country.'

'And you know something about these people?'

He sounded surprised.

'I studied them as part of my degree course. I'm a specialist on the subject,' she said, uncomfortably. 'The powers-that-be soon decided it would be worthwhile including the multi-ethnic peoples of the Fezzan, extending the work in co-operation with the Russians along the border.'

'Hence your trip there.'

She was relieved that he appeared to be taking her seriously.

'I think working down here, especially in the border area, is infinitely more complex, but that's only my opinion,' she added, hastily.

'It would be a lot easier if you weren't embedded in the military, especially away from the border.'

'Really?'

'You'd be better off working in a civilian team.'

'Can't see them letting that happen.'

'You'd have more support, much more comprehensive data. Whose idea was it to have you embedded in the military?'

'I haven't a clue,' she said, realising that she'd never thought about this till now.

'They don't have the knowledge of the local tribes that civilians have.' He paused. 'And most of the time, you don't need that level of protection.'

He was silent, watching her closely.

'Maybe somebody was hoping your observations would be internally rather than externally focused,' he suggested, obliquely.

'Internally focused? I don't get it.'

She was confused now.

'Perhaps somebody was hoping you'd unearth something, you know, something abnormal in the establishment.'

What the hell is he suggesting?

'Establishment?' she asked, now really worried where the conversation was going. 'I mean, you and I are part of it, aren't we?'

He was silent for a few moments, perhaps weighing her up.

'Establishment everywhere is determined by those who have power and wealth,' he continued, quietly, 'the few who control everyday aspects of people's lives, usually to the detriment of society at large.'

'Where do we fit in then?' she asked, her curiosity growing uneasily.

'Most in this place – medics, agronomists, scientists, whoever – form part of society at large. Your military colleagues are the establishment.'

Why 'my' military colleagues? she wondered. *What was he implying?* The heat pressed down on her, suddenly draining her energy, her ability to think clearly. He waved to the barman, ordering another round.

This was rapidly turning into an evening very different from the one she'd envisaged when she set out earlier. In the dim light, she observed him closely, slouched yet alert, in the low cane chair. Beneath his charm, she sensed he was carefully analysing her response to his every word. In contrast she felt flat, sweat enveloping her entire body, her nerves tingling. She couldn't make out if he saw her as friend or foe.

He pushed her fresh beer across the table and, without a word, got up and wandered off as if looking for a menu. She found his behaviour puzzling. Her gaze followed him round the bar. He seemed predatory, holding back a barely controlled energy. His behaviour unnerved her, yet in a strange way she felt secure in his presence.

*

Struggling to cut through the miasma in her head, she was aware that she had to make a decision quickly. Could she trust him with her plan? Although she couldn't rationalise her thoughts, she felt instinctively that he would be sympathetic, even if he couldn't help.

'The kitchen closes at eight-thirty, in fifteen minutes. What do you fancy?' he asked, handing her a menu. After they'd decided, he caught the eye of a passing waiter and gave their orders.

'Do you think you'll be coming back?' he asked, offhandedly.

'It depends on many things,' she said; then with nothing to lose, she decided to bite the bullet. 'Actually, it might well depend on you.'

'Why me?' he asked, clearly surprised.

She had regained the initiative; her confidence grew.

'I need your help, now, tonight,' she said, lowering her voice conspiratorially.

He stood abruptly and beckoned her to follow. *Oh God*, she thought, *I've blown it. He's not what he appears to be, he is establishment*. He pointed to an empty table in the dining room, located unobtrusively near the kitchen door. They both sat down. He appeared to be as anxious as she was.

Suddenly he grinned.

'There's so much racket here, it's difficult for eavesdroppers. So how can I help you?' he asked, getting straight to the point.

Relief surged through her; this was her one chance and she had to take it. She chose her words carefully.

'I think there may be an entirely different interpretation of the events that happened at the border. I can't be sure though,' she said, wondering if he'd believe her story.

'Why does it matter if there is? It won't change anything. It certainly won't stop our beloved military and their dubious activities.'

She could hear his scepticism, but recognised that he was the first of many that would have to be convinced, if she was to have any chance of uncovering the truth.

'Even if I could establish the real motive behind the murders, I've no idea whether it would make any difference,' she admitted.

'Why don't you just tell me your version of events?'

Over the next fifteen minutes, she told him everything she'd remembered, including how access across the so-called impenetrable border had been compromised by persons unknown. She gave him as much detail as she could, except the fact that she'd managed to bring the bag of bloodied thumbs back to Sabha.

The arrival of their food broke the flow of her story. She began to wonder how she might go on from here. Fortunately, he was taking her seriously and had been listening.

'I can see from what you said that there might be another interpretation. Crucially, though, you need evidence,' he said, bluntly. 'Nobody would believe you, especially if you're challenging the word of a respected local commander.'

'I haven't told you everything,' she whispered, leaning forward. 'I have the bag of thumbs in a flask, here in my backpack.'

For the first time since they met, he appeared at a loss. He looked at her, faintly alarmed.

'What do you propose to do with them?'

'Get a thorough DNA analysis of each thumb. These eleven men were bound together in death. I believe they were bound together in life as well.' She rushed on with increasing confidence. 'Knowledge of their background might shed more light on the Russian security forces we're dealing with. It might possibly explain why Ramil and the others simply disappeared.'

'You may have a point,' he said, unconvincingly.

She continued, speaking rapidly for fear of losing her precarious logic.

'The information may highlight different, possibly competing, ethnic groups within their forces, their local communities. We might be witnessing internal schisms, previously not seen from the sanctuary of Tripoli HQ,' she ventured.

She paused, marshalling her thoughts as best she could.

'The whole football thing as well – slaughtering eleven men, possibly the team we were supposed to be playing that afternoon. Was this some form of coded message and if so, from whom?'

'It's far-fetched,' he paused, 'but you may be onto something.'

She had no idea whether this was making any sense to him, his smiling face revealing nothing. She had no choice but to carry on until she had unburdened her theory, inchoate as it was.

'And then there's Ramil,' she continued. 'He's a conundrum.'

'A conundrum?'

'He's Muslim from a Tartar background, a race that's been subjugated and persecuted by the Russian Slavs for centuries. At our one-on-one meetings, his interests ranged well beyond the conversational norms of formal security briefings. I remember that he once pointedly encouraged me to study forensic anthropology in St Petersburg. It would be very useful in my current job, he said. I've been thinking back over our conversations ever since he went missing.'

'Your whole hypothesis depends on the DNA results,' said Greg, after what seemed like an eternity. 'I think you were hoping somehow to get the work done in Tripoli.'

'I was hoping to, yes.'

He paused; she saw him in the dim candlelight, silently weaving a logical seam through her story.

'I assume, as part of your work in the Fezzan, you'd planned to drive back to Tripoli, the way you got here. Now unexpectedly, you're flying back at short notice and you risk the flask being confiscated at the airport. You'd have no evidence and,' he added, 'very probably, have a lot of explaining to do when you got back.'

'Yes,' she said, relieved at least that she had made herself understood. But would he be sympathetic, would he be prepared to risk helping her?

'And you want me to arrange the analysis.'

'Yes,' she said, blushing like a child caught lying.

He eyed her silently for a moment; she froze.

'After I left the hospital I was hoping, but not expecting, to see you again,' he grinned, 'but now, meeting you here this evening, I couldn't have asked for more stimulating company.'

She looked at him doubtfully, not knowing what to say or do next.

'Of course I'll help you,' he said, evenly. 'I'm as interested as you are in getting to the bottom of this.'

Her spirits soared, tension flowing from her weary body. She wanted desperately to reach out across the spluttering candle and touch his face, to acknowledge his support, wishing to share with him the complexities of this wretched country. She saw that he was having difficulty concealing his interest in her, struggling to cope with their sudden intimacy.

'What's next then?' she asked, quietly.

'I need the flask. The toilets are communal,' he said, business-like. 'Leave it in the last cubicle on the left. As soon as you're back, I'll go and retrieve it.'

Five minutes later, the transfer was complete.

'That's the easy bit,' he said, pushing an unsolicited fresh beer across the table.

'Have you anybody in mind that you could trust to do the analysis?'

'Yes, although I've got to get the evidence to Amsterdam.' He paused. 'I think I may have a secure way to do that. The problem's going to be getting the results back to you, undetected. We'd load them and any photographic evidence on a memory stick, which I'd have to give to you personally one way or another. All physical evidence would be destroyed, the digital data wiped, leaving no trace of the work.'

She thought about her plans for the next couple of months.

'I was due back in Sabha in a few weeks but given what's just happened, I may well be assigned to HQ for a time. Perhaps we could meet in Tripoli or even overseas. I've got ten days' leave from the middle of November.'

'That might work out. I'm away on the fourteenth for a week, seeing my daughter in Amsterdam.'

'You have a family?' she blustered, trying to hide her embarrassment.

'Josie's three,' he laughed. 'She lives with my ex-wife and her husband in a former merchant's house on one of the canals – well beyond my means.'

'I could fly home via Amsterdam.'

'No, that's too risky if you and I were suspected of being in collusion. It's too traceable.' He thought for a moment. 'We could meet in some easily accessible neutral place, say in France, Calais perhaps.'

'Calais, that's a great idea. What date do you suggest?'

'Say the 16th. It would be a simple day trip, lunch, a stroll on the beach and then back home on our separate ways. How does that sound?'

'I'm sure that'll be fine,' she said, trying to recall memories of a trip she made to the town, years earlier. 'I remember there was a hypermarket out in the suburbs on the Paris road. It had a pink mini airship permanently advertising its whereabouts, quite a landmark. I'm certain it's still there. It's a favourite for the English to buy wine. You might know it.'

'No, but I'll find it. I'll be standing near customer enquiries at ten in the morning on the 16th. Please be punctual, my leave is precious,' he emphasised. She nodded, aware of the risk he was taking, of his generosity.

'Thank you,' was all she managed.

'Here are my contact details,' he said, passing her a business card. 'Just phone if you can't make it.'

It was getting late and suddenly she was anxious to get away before her good fortune turned.

'Perhaps you should go now,' he said, seeing her unease.

'There's no need for a taxi, my driver will take you back. You'll be there by ten-thirty,' he said before adding, 'nobody will be the least bit interested where you've been this evening.'

In fluent Arabic, he called up his driver.

'His name's Asif, he speaks little English. He'll be at reception in a few minutes. He drives a purple Toyota jeep with tinted windows. Don't be alarmed. I won't come with you, the less gossip, the better,' he said, an enigmatic grin briefly lighting up his face. He leant across the table and squeezed her hand. 'Be brave, have faith in yourself,' he whispered.

He stood up abruptly. 'See you on the 16th, have a safe journey,' and with that he strode off into the heat, kitbag swinging from his shoulder, in search of friends at the bar.

22

Southern England,
Mid-October 2031

The flight back from Athens was turbulent. A prolonged high-pressure system over central Europe, which had pushed daily temperatures into the high thirties, not unusual for October these days, was rapidly collapsing. The atmosphere was unstable; storms raged over the Alps; massive anvil-shaped clouds lit up from within by lightning filled the sky. The recent dry spell, which had led to droughts in parts of France and Germany, was about to give way to days of torrential rain. Authorities along the Rhine, Danube and other major rivers were now warning of yet more extensive and potentially catastrophic flooding, the third since May.

Jack felt ill, disorientated. He was relieved when the aircraft touched down, thankful that he wouldn't have to face Emma at the airport. In an earlier phone call, she had suggested that on the day he got back, she would drop over to his apartment in the early evening; perhaps later, they'd walk down into town for supper.

It was an awkward conversation, neither of them able or willing to articulate their true feelings. He had taken more comfort when he and Bushra had spoken to her on a number of occasions from Stoupa. Although barely known to each other, the two had conversed as only mother and daughter can. He knew that the situation would be very different without Bushra at his side.

He recognised Emma's need to avoid her cottage, where they'd last met. He guessed the vivid memories of that fateful night, where for the first time for years she was angry with him, were still clearly etched in her mind.

He caught the Estuary Airport Southern Express, an elevated high-speed train that swung southwards out over the Thames Estuary from the massive offshore airport east of Canvey Island, into Kent and beyond. He gazed out at hundreds of wind turbines arrayed across the sunlit estuary, their profusion making it impossible to make out the east-west shipping lanes. Within a minute, the train was passing over East Stoke, a sprawling new settler town on the Isle of Grain. Built from scratch on marshland over the last eight years, this place, like all English settler towns, was specifically designed to absorb immigrants, after England was eventually forced to accept its share fleeing to Europe.

The aerial train swept overhead, as if passing over dangerous alien territory which, Jack was ashamed to admit, in a sense it was. The Estuary Airport Southern Express was never intended to service settler towns like East Stoke. The inhabitants living there were chained to the place, stateless citizens living in perpetual limbo. The town, cut off in every way from the community at large, was supposed to be self-sufficient with adequate housing, employment, healthcare, education and recreational facilities for its teeming multi-ethnic population.

Everybody living there had been through a rigorous screening process before being admitted. One of the most horrifying yet unspoken characteristics of this isolated community was that every person over the age of twelve had been sterilised, ensuring that without new intakes, the population would eventually die out.

Essentially, East Stoke was a large open prison, fenced off and closely guarded, a place which few managed to leave. For those lucky enough to get work outside, they had to go through a second vetting process before being issued with the necessary permits, enabling them to come and go on a daily basis. For many, East Stoke and the other dozen or so settler towns throughout England were an uneasy reminder of South African Bantustans of the last century.

He never ceased to be amazed how his homeland had changed so dramatically over the last ten years. He had witnessed the rapid growth of a relatively wealthy, sophisticated, technology-driven society, which now pocketed largely unseen no-go areas of extreme poverty and deprivation – prison states within the state. As the train raced on over the featureless factory farms of north Kent, he realised that his shame and frustration at this woeful state of affairs had been somewhat mollified by what he'd seen in Greece.

A personal buzzer alerted him to the train's arrival at his station. He stepped out under a blazing midday sun set in a cloudless sky; the storms he'd encountered over Europe hadn't reached here yet. At thirty degrees, it felt cooler and fresher than the heat and torpidity of Stoupa. He caught a taxi for the short drive to his apartment above the town, the early departure from Athens leaving him exhausted.

*

He had been away less than two weeks, but it seemed a lifetime. Meeting Bushra again, briefly sharing her life after so many years, had re-energised him.

His apartment had an unfamiliar feeling about it – stuffy and unlived in. His most precious asset, his bolthole, his personal space where he could read, write, philosophise and dream in complete equanimity, now seemed superfluous to his needs. He realised he had a lot to learn, having seen how Bushra lived, how she'd effectively been thrown out of her own home, how she managed with so few possessions.

A couple of messages were waiting for him on the wallscreen. In the first, Emma had sent him a reminder of their supper date. Within the last hour, Bushra had sent a brief message asking him to contact her when he got back, setting his pulse racing.

'Are you OK?' he asked, as soon as he could make her out.

'I'm fine, I'm just missing you. I wanted to talk to you the moment you got back.'

'Your message worried me.'

'Oh, Jack, it's so bloody lonely here without you. I wish I was with you, far away from here.'

He sensed that she had more to say. During their last evening together, they had agreed that they would exercise caution over the airwaves between England and Greece. They devised a simple code, fearing that Dorpadski, for whatever reason, might have managed to hack her system.

'How was your swim?'

'I had the sea to myself,' she laughed, meaning 'Dorpadski hasn't been around'.

'The best way to enjoy it. So what are your plans?'

'Tomorrow I'm going to pick up a few books in the library in Kalamata,' she replied, cheerfully. 'I've more time to read now that you're not here to distract me.'

Any mention of Kalamata was a reference to Christos, her link to the past, somebody who would come to her rescue if she ever had to cut loose and disappear.

'I hope they're light-hearted, not too serious.'

'No, I've chosen well. There's one on the Algerian resistance against French colonial rule. We talked about it recently,' she said, referring to the resistance in Cyrenaica. 'I'll let you know if I learn any new stuff. What about you?'

'I'm meeting my partner this evening,' he said, the partner being Emma.

'I hope she hasn't put you out of business since you've been away.'

'No,' he laughed, 'I don't anticipate problems.'

And so they talked on, each unable to end the call, struggling to convey what they wanted to say without actually saying it. He found the whole episode unsettling given their recent intimacy, where they had tried so hard to ensure that what they said to each other was exactly what they'd meant to say.

'Let me know about your holiday plans for Ireland.'

Ireland meant Greece, to where he had every intention of returning as soon as possible. In the end he had no choice but to finish the call.

'I must go, Bee, I've a lot to do before the meeting.'

'Of course, goodbye, Jack, goodbye, I love you,' she said hurriedly, just as the picture faded.

He slumped back into the settee, brushing away salty tears of frustration and exhaustion. *God, how I miss her*, he thought.

He unpacked, showered and tried to rest but sleep stubbornly evaded him. He felt edgy, restless, worrying how much he should tell Emma later that evening, wondering if she had any more news of Isabel.

While in Stoupa, Bushra had suggested that Emma should be told everything about Stavros, except his role in the armed resistance in Cyrenaica, for which they only had Dorpadski's word. They also agreed that, for now, Isabel should not be told about Stavros, knowledge that one day might jeopardise her work in Tripoli.

Although Bushra knew of Dorpadski's mendacity, the problem she constantly faced was sorting out his half-truths from his outright lies; to date, the learning curve had been steep. Back in the sanctuary of his apartment, her tenuous situation seemed even more alarming to Jack. Slowly he was coming to terms with the implications of what she was faced with living in a police state; nothing was straightforward, truth was elusive and trust in short supply.

*

At exactly six-thirty the intercom buzzed; his heart missed a beat.

'Hi, Dad, should I come up or are we walking straight into town?'

'Come up, come up,' he replied, trying desperately to control his emotions, 'it's still early.'

Moments later, Emma came in, dressed in a white linen jacket and dark blue knee-length skirt. A sense of relief surged through his tired body as he threw his arms around his daughter, drawing her tightly to his chest, unable to say anything for fear of breaking down.

'Dad, you're hurting me,' she laughed, struggling to get free.

'I'm sorry, Em,' he said, standing back and taking her hands.

Although she looked radiant, he noticed the ghost of shadows under her eyes. It occurred to him that she'd been dreading their reunion as much as he had. His heart went out to her; he adored her and would do anything not to hurt her.

'You're looking well,' she said. 'You've really benefited from all that sun and sea air.'

'I've a bottle in the cooler. Let's have a drink on the terrace before we go out, it's still warm.'

Outside in the early evening dusk, he composed himself.

'I'm so sorry…' he started to say, before she gently put her hand over his mouth.

'It can wait, Dad. I'm just happy you're here, back home,' she whispered, before kissing him on his cheek. 'I love you.'

'And I love you.'

'To us, to absent friends,' she said, raising her glass, before sitting at the terrace table.

'To us,' he said, sitting across from her. He was desperate to establish a sense of normality, to move beyond their shared pain. 'I hear you were away with some friends.'

'A week in the Shetlands. It's an unbelievable place. We were so lucky with the weather. We stayed for a couple of nights in Lerwick then explored the islands.'

'It's a place I've always wanted to visit.'

'Our favourite haunt was a tiny hamlet called Sadness, the westernmost point of the main island. The cliff walks from there are staggering, the bird life amazing.'

'I can imagine.'

'We went whale watching from Scalloway and saw minke and a couple of orca, dolphins and basking sharks. It was brilliant.'

'I'm very envious,' he said.

And so they chatted of this and that; very soon he was telling her about his trip, about meeting Bushra. She listened enthusiastically, constantly questioning some detail or other. Amazingly, there was no hint of anger or bitterness in her voice. He realised that he had greatly misjudged his daughter, underestimating her ability to understand, to forgive and, importantly, to love him.

'I found several old photos with the letters, of her, of you both, some in black and white. She looked stunning as a young woman.'

'She still looks ten years younger than her age. Remember her father was Libyan, her mother Greek,' he said before adding with a grin, 'They tend to have beautiful children. You're a testament to that.'

'Come on, Dad,' she laughed, before hesitating, 'and Stavros, was he a good-looking baby?'

Although he'd prepared for this moment with Bushra many times, the shock of hearing her asking about her brother by name unnerved him. For a moment, he was speechless.

'Ah, your brother Stavros…' he said, his voice edged with emotion.

'Don't, Dad,' she said, interrupting him. 'I'm sorry, it's too early to talk about him. It can wait. It's not as if he's around anymore.'

He realised that in her mind Stavros was dead. He could sense Bushra's presence strengthening his resolve. He remembered her advice: 'Tell it exactly as it is, Jack, as I did.'

'Em, this can't wait, not anymore.' He paused, seeing her shift uneasily. 'You remember reading Bushra's last letter. She wrote about Stavros, about him being executed by the Green Brigade.'

'Yes, clearly,' she replied, quietly. 'It must have come as a terrible shock.'

'I was gutted, just turned in on myself for months. I'm ashamed to say I never replied, never wrote to offer my love, my support. I did nothing.' He hesitated. 'We'd been drifting apart for quite some time, too many obstacles being put in the way by our families. Circumstances, everything, conspired to end our relationship. I hadn't the energy to go on. I was emotionally shattered. I let it end.'

'Dad, the past is the past. I've read the letters,' she said, leaning across and squeezing his hand. 'I could see how things were between you.'

'Early the following year, Bushra got news from an old friend in Benghazi,' he continued, quietly. 'Apparently Stavros was alive and well.'

For a moment Emma sat back, too stunned to say anything.

'Alive,' she whispered, as the significance of what he'd just said dawned on her. She got up, rushed around and hugged him, holding him tightly. 'I can't believe it, I can't believe it,' she kept repeating. Eventually she returned to her seat, tears in her eyes. 'Why didn't she write and tell you?' she asked, after composing herself.

'I never contacted her after her last letter. She'd given up on me, didn't think I cared. I can't blame her.'

'Yes, but why?' she persisted.

'We agreed in Stoupa there'd be no post-mortems, no recriminations. Neither of us could be held accountable for the past, we were both equally to blame.'

'Sorry, Dad.'

'But you're right to ask. There's no easy answer. We'd behaved recklessly. Our relationship deeply hurt her parents, they felt betrayed and of course,' he continued, flatly, 'it ultimately led to my divorce.'

They lapsed into silence.

'Stavros was taken from the hospital without Bushra's consent,' he said, abruptly, 'just an hour before I got there.'

'Good God, Dad, that's shocking. Who took him?'

'Her parents and one of her father's sisters from Benghazi. They'd have taken you, only you were under observation in an incubator.'

'Why, for heaven's sake?'

'They were furious with us, had absolutely no faith in us as parents. I think the plan was that the aunt would foster you both in Benghazi until they felt Bushra was capable of motherhood.'

'God, how bizarre. Where did you fit into this plan?'

'I didn't.'

'So how did I end up back in London with you?'

'Bushra was adamant you were not going to be taken to Benghazi. We endlessly discussed our options and finally decided that I should take you home with me as soon as possible. We'd face the consequences when we got there. She was to follow with Stavros at the first opportunity.'

'You must've been mad,' she laughed uneasily, brushing away her tears.

'We were. Anyway, after I took you back to England, her parents prevented the two of them from joining us, didn't want her to have anything more to do with me. Their plan had been thwarted, they were very angry.'

'You never saw Stavros.'

'Neither did Bushra,' he admitted. 'As it turned out, she was never allowed to see him once the aunt took him in.'

'God almighty, that's inhumane.'

They sat in silence for several minutes; a chilly evening breeze pushed dead autumnal leaves around the terrace.

'And Charlotte, how did she react?' Emma asked. 'I mean, without any prior warning, you brought your child, a baby girl, home with you. How could that have possibly worked out?'

'It was complicated,' he said, quietly.

269

'There's no need to go into all this.'

He could hear Bushra urging him on: 'Tell her the truth, she'll understand. You owe it to her.'

'The letters don't tell the whole story.' He hesitated. 'Six months after I met Bushra, Charlotte wrote to tell me she was pregnant.'

'Tom,' she exclaimed. 'She was pregnant with Tom.'

'We weren't married at the time and although unofficially engaged, I was already having doubts.'

'What a bloody mess.'

'Charlotte was desperate to get married. I had no choice. I'd got her into this situation, so I thought. I proposed to her in a letter from Libya. We married in August, a few weeks before Tom was born.'

'What do you mean, Dad, "so I thought"?'

'I'm not Tom's father,' he said, bluntly. 'I was no more his father than she was your mother.'

'Good God,' she exclaimed, clearly shocked, slumping back in her seat.

'Charlotte had no choice, she had to make a home for you.'

And then word for word, he recounted everything that he'd told Bushra, a couple of weeks earlier.

'I can still hear those terrible rows when you were on leave, the vicious fights between you and Tom,' said Emma, after she'd taken in what he'd told her. 'I remember Charlotte's frequent absences from the house when you were away, her wild mood swings – suicidal one day, euphoric the next. I thought she was missing you. And then there was her constant reference to the "harlot and her bastard children" when you two fought.'

'Bushra, you and Stavros,' he said, before adding, 'I'm afraid Charlotte was some bitch.'

They sat in silence, adrift in their own worlds.

'Everything's starting to make sense,' she said eventually, as if coming out of a trance. 'I'm exhausted, Dad. I can't really take it all in.'

'We'll leave it. We've all the time in the world to talk this over.'

'Agreed, it's all too much.'

'I so sorry, Em…'

'Dad, stop, there's nothing to be sorry for,' she said, quietly, reaching out across the table for his hand. 'Anyway I'm ravenous,' she laughed, quietly. 'Let's go into town and get something to eat.'

*

Over supper, he spoke about Bushra, of everything he'd learnt of her life during those long intervening years, about Dorpadski and his threat to her survival. He sensed that, no matter how much he told Emma, she would still have more questions.

'Did she ever get married?'

'No.'

'Maybe she was hoping that one day you'd come back to her, that you'd be together again.'

'Perhaps,' he said, awkwardly.

'Come on, Dad,' she laughed, 'she loved you, still does, no doubt. You could get married.'

'And I love her,' he admitted. 'I'm not sure about marriage though. I'm afraid of making a commitment I can't live up to, of screwing her life up again. Does that make sense?'

'Yes.'

An uneasy silence was broken by the waitress who came to clear the table.

'Another drink?' he asked.

'A coffee would be fine, thanks.'

He ordered a couple of coffees.

'She must be tough.'

'Her capacity to survive is amazing. The moment I arrived in Athens, I could feel a nagging underlying fear that comes from living in a police state.'

'Did it bring back memories?'

'Yes, but not all bad either. It's funny,' he said, 'you become fatalistic living in such a country, facing dangerous, chaotic conditions daily. Life becomes more energised, intense, immediate. Everything – love, hatred, even colour – is exaggerated. You find yourself a bit-part actor in an ongoing drama with no intermission, no end. And yet you feel at the centre of the universe. It's a bizarre feeling.'

'You shared this sort of life with her all those years ago. I find it weird.'

'Until very recently, that period of my life had been consigned to history, something to mull over occasionally in the middle of the night. Suddenly, I find myself being dragged back forty years or more.'

'It's always been unsettling for her, never knowing the stability, the security that you've had.'

'If I'd behaved differently, had had more courage, hadn't succumbed to conventional morality,' he said, candidly, 'we'd have stayed together.'

'You can't blame yourself. There were no guarantees that a life together would have run smoothly.'

He found her honesty so refreshing; his heart went out to her.

'I nearly blew it with you though…'

'Dad, stop,' she interrupted, 'you didn't. You've been the best father a daughter could ask for. That's the end of it.'

He looked away, his eyes welling up.

'And Stavros, your brother,' he said, turning back, 'you can't say that about him.'

'Not having a father around would have had a big influence on the way he turned out.'

He silently acknowledged a truth that he'd avoided for years; with unerring accuracy, she had got straight to the heart of the matter. He saw the sudden mortification on her face.

'Dad, I shouldn't have said that,' she blurted out. 'It was totally uncalled for and…'

'No, Em, you're right,' he interrupted. 'You're the only one who can say what needs to be said.'

'I'm sorry, Dad, I just can't get him out of my mind, wondering what he's like, how he lives, if he has a family, what work he does,' she said, desperately wanting to know more about her twin.

'We'll never know,' he said, his agreement with Bushra about not disclosing her brother's situation ever present in his head.

'Someday, I'll have to tell Isabel about Stavros.'

He froze at the mention of Isabel, her accident far removed from his thoughts.

'God almighty, I'd completely forgotten,' he exclaimed. 'How is she? Have you spoken to her recently?'

'She's fine now, Dad, she's fully recovered. She sent a message saying she'll be coming home on leave in November, around the 14th.'

'That's great, I'll be back from Greece by then.'

'You're seeing Bushra again?'

'Yes, I promised I'd get back as soon as I could,' he said. 'The embassy will only issue one two-week visa at a time. I should get another one in the next five to seven days and be back out before the end of the month,' he hesitated, realising that it was too early to be talking about going back. 'Em, I'm really sorry, I should've discussed this with you before going ahead.'

'No, Dad, you must get on with your lives, too much time has passed already. Anyway you'll be back in time for Isabel. She's been away ages,' she said, her voice tinged with sadness, 'almost as if she's been avoiding us.'

'Is there a problem?'

'No,' she hesitated, 'it's just that she's never had any contact with you since she went away.'

'I know,' he said, dumbly. 'I know.'

'But why, Dad? She's always turned to you for guidance, for inspiration. She loves you.'

He'd been unable to communicate with his granddaughter since she'd left for Tripoli. Anger and frustration had consumed him; he'd watched helplessly as she followed, undeterred, in his footsteps into the maelstrom of North Africa. It suddenly seemed all so pointless, his fear for her future, as if it were inextricably linked to the horrors of his past.

'Not now, Em, not this evening,' he pleaded. 'In the next few days, I'll explain.'

'It's OK, Dad, it can wait.' She paused. 'Maybe this whole North African venture won't suit her,' she said, acknowledging his old anxieties. 'She'll come back after a year, get a good job at home, pick up with Andrew again.'

He knew in his heart that his daughter was deceiving herself.

'Some chance, I'm afraid,' he said. 'She'll get totally involved out there in some cause or other.'

'How can you be so sure?'

'Just a feeling.' He paused, marshalling his words. 'She's got all the necessary characteristics: restlessness, curiosity and intelligence. She's focused, obsessive.'

'Come on, Dad.'

'She won't be afraid to tackle the many problems there,' he said. 'And she has courage. Remember her crazy rock climbing exploits in Scotland? She's courageous to the point of being reckless.'

'Just like you then,' Emma laughed, uneasily.

He let it pass; his daughter was right.

'And the letters, have you told her about the letters yet?'

'No, I decided to wait till she's home, tell her face to face.'

'Good idea,' he said. 'And when you do see her, I wouldn't tell her about Stavros for the time being.'

'You think so?'

'Having an uncle living in the Russian mandate, in Cyrenaica, might not sit comfortably with her bosses in Tripoli. Knowledge of his existence might jeopardise her work.'

'You're right.'

He noticed the restaurant was nearly empty. It was well past eleven; he could sense that she was anxious to leave.

'You must be exhausted.'

'My head hurts, Dad,' she said, yawning. 'I'd like to go now.'

'I'm sorry, Em. I'll get the bill,' he said, catching a waiter's eye. 'Will you stay over? The bed's made up.'

He could see her hesitate.

'Yes, that would be lovely,' she said, reaching out across the table for his hand. 'I'm meeting my publisher in Islington at three, and I've nothing in the morning.'

23

Calais, France, Mid-November 2031

The autumn had been unusually stormy in northern Europe. On the morning of the 16th, the weather in southern England appeared to have changed for the better; it was mild and calm. It suited Isabel, who was glad to be away from the pressing heat of North Africa. This was her first home leave since starting in Tripoli, although she was conscious that it might be her last.

Everything depended on the DNA results. If the results were inconclusive, she would return to her job in Tripoli, the border incident forgotten. If the results indicated something unusual, anything could happen. She even envisaged a scenario where her contract would be terminated.

Emma had dropped her at the station around seven in the morning to catch the through-train from Edinburgh to Nice. The swift non-stop journey to the tunnel entrance in Kent reminded Isabel of the progressive destruction of rural England, which she was having to witness even in her short lifetime.

In the minutes before sunrise, the train carved noiselessly through a featureless landscape, devoid of hedges and trees, flattened and engineered by the demands of industrial cereal production. It swept on over busy motorways and through joyless towns, bypassing an occasional isolated medieval village, cutting great swathes out of the chalk Downs, before disappearing headlong into the gaping jaws of the Channel Tunnel.

Her thoughts drifted back to her recent homecoming, two days before she was due to meet Greg in Calais. The idea of being reunited with her mother and Jack had been troubling her for weeks, given the strained atmosphere at home before she'd left for North Africa. Jack had clearly been so upset with her, that he'd never replied to her newsy letters during the time she'd been away, something she'd found unsettling, given how close they'd always been.

She had asked her mother if she could stay with her while on leave; to her relief, she was lovingly welcomed home. It was like old times, the two women falling gratefully into each other's arms, happy at being together again. This had been Isabel's longest time away from home. From her earliest memories, Emma and Jack had always been around, enfolding her with their love and protection.

On her first day, Isabel was startled to see how they'd changed in the months she'd been away. Although slight, the changes were nevertheless noticeable. Emma, lost in her writing and the lives of her historical protagonists, had become a little more detached. Jack, only just back from holiday, seemed less sure of himself, succumbing to a kind of fatalism, which Isabel had found disconcerting.

She appreciated their interest in her work and in the excitement and satisfaction she derived from it. She carefully avoided talking about Philippe, about the border incident and about her increasing disillusion with the veracity of EDA's mission in Tripoli. Jack in turn said little about his recent past and nothing about his holiday.

She mentioned Greg but only in the context of a work colleague, who had introduced her to the tennis club in Sabha.

Without mentioning that she was meeting him, she explained that her brief trip to France was a business trip, which in a sense it was.

*

The train shot out of the tunnel between razor wire security fences towering overhead on either side. As far as the horizon, all she could see was a world of linear steel: tracks, gantries, overhead power lines, gates, fences, watch towers, all glittering silver and polished grey in the early sunshine. The train ran on for several kilometres through a military/industrial complex, slowing as it approached Calais.

It was just after nine when she walked out of the main station into Calais' central business district. It had taken her thirty minutes to clear security after disembarking from the train. She had forgotten how the movement of people between European countries was so severely restricted. Anybody without a European passport or travel permit found it almost impossible to move around the Continent. Their options, once they left the country in which they were registered, were limited. Generally they were either forced to return to their country of registration or deported to their country of origin. Processing every passenger on this basis took time.

The whole experience heightened her anxiety. The meeting with Greg totally preoccupied her mind. She was beginning to doubt her ill-defined theory, which had driven her to get the thumbs analysed in the first place. She wondered if she had let her increasing distrust of Philippe cloud her judgement. What if the whole exercise turned out to be pointless, proving nothing? What would Greg think of her?

Up to fifteen years ago, Calais had been the clearing centre for hundreds of thousands of migrants. Initially the focal point for those seeking to get to England, the town was now surrounded by three secure satellites, home to second- and third-generation migrant families. The satellites, similar in many ways to the settler towns in England, were designed to be self-sufficient, providing all that body and soul would need between cradle and grave.

She had less than an hour to kill before she was due to meet Greg at the hypermarket on the edge of town, a fifteen-minute taxi ride away. She wandered along the central mall looking for some distraction to clear her muddled thoughts.

The town centre was eerily deserted. Almost everybody she saw was European. The place had a quiet complacency about it, exuding a sense of unearned wealth. She saw it in the upmarket fashion shops, boutique hotels, fancy restaurants and weird art galleries. Estate agency windows advertising fabulously priced properties, a preponderance of divorce lawyers and consultants pushing questionable investment opportunities in the satellites all confirmed the presence of unchallenged authority.

She couldn't remember when she was last in Calais, but what she saw around her didn't match her earlier memories. Unsettling images bothered her in a way she couldn't explain. Buying a couple of local newspapers, she drifted into a café and ordered coffee.

Despite her limited French, it was as she read the papers that she began to form an idea of what was upsetting her. From news articles, social and community bulletins and advertisements, from business briefings and reported sporting events, it dawned on her that she was seeing twenty-first-century apartheid in action. The local community was living off a cheap and captive labour market provided by the satellites. To her, the peaceful street scenes suddenly felt tarnished. She finished her coffee and wandered aimlessly back along the central mall, everything she saw reinforcing her initial perception.

Time passed, images and ideas swirled uncomfortably in her head. What she saw did not relate to much of England or other parts of France that she knew; this, however, did not improve her state of mind. In the central square, the town clock struck the three-quarter hour forcing her back to the present. *God*, she thought, *I've only got fifteen minutes to get to the hypermarket.* She was soon cocooned in a taxi hurtling along the ring road.

She saw Greg before he saw her taxi. He was standing, his back to her, in the shade of a vast entrance canopy, talking earnestly on his mobile. She paid off the driver and stood out of his line of sight, waiting for him to finish the call. Whoever was on the phone was clearly annoying him. He was speaking in Arabic, which took her by surprise. Her hovering shadow on the pavement must have caught his attention. Without warning he swung around and, seeing her, put his hand over the phone.

'Isabel, great to see you,' he whispered loudly, his face lighting up in a broad grin. 'One moment please,' he added, rather formally.

After another few heated exchanges, his call ended abruptly. They stood opposite each other, briefly embarrassed, unsure of what to say or do next. Without warning he leaned forward and kissed her on both cheeks. They laughed, the tension eased.

'That was my unmitigated bitch of a wife,' he said, cheerfully, 'as if she hasn't screwed enough out of me already.'

'She speaks Arabic,' Isabel said, immediately regretting it.

'Only when she's angry. She speaks perfect English when she's in a good mood. I rarely hear her English these days,' he laughed.

'Did you meet in Tripoli?' she asked, her curiosity getting the better of her.

'No, in Sabha. She's Tunisian, a medic. She was my assistant. We married and had Josie in the space of three years. Not a happy time for any of us towards the end. Anyway, that's enough of her,' he laughed, 'we need to find a quiet place to discuss a few things,' he said, indicating his jacket pocket.

'Where do you suggest?'

'I've heard that there are good cafés and bars out towards the west beach. We could take a cab, it's ten minutes.'

'Great,' she said, relieved that he was prepared to get straight down to business.

'How's your leave been?' he asked, as he hailed a passing cab.

'I've only been back a couple of days. So far it's better than expected.'

'Why?'

'I left home under a bit of a cloud when I went out to Tripoli. Just family differences really. It's amazing how time heals,' she said, not wishing to get drawn into the details.

They were in the back of the cab being driven at speed around the empty ring road. His suppressed energy filled the space between them like some powerful magnetic field. She recalled their first evening together at the tennis club. She remembered how she felt both unnerved and oddly protected by his presence.

'It's quite the reverse with Ameena, my ex-wife,' he said, clearly bothered by his recent phone call. 'Time seems to exacerbate our difficulties.'

Isabel remained silent, not wishing to show too much interest.

'I mean, having got what she wanted from me – a child, work experience and good references – she took off with one of the senior Dutch doctors as soon as she could,' he continued. 'He offered her a home and a European passport. She found what she was really looking for: security, wealth and status. And the bloody doctor, some conniving bastard he was, way outside my league,' he laughed.

'How sad for you,' she said, choosing her words carefully.

'It was at the time. But now I don't care one iota for her. I miss Josie though,' he said, not very convincingly.

'It must be difficult.'

'And to think Ameena means "faithful" in English,' he said, a great burst of laughter blowing his frustration away.

She remained buttoned up. Her thoughts were now exclusively focused on what she believed was in his jacket pocket: the DNA analysis report. She tried desperately to remain calm, telling herself that all would be revealed shortly.

A few minutes later the cab dropped them off on the seafront, devoid of life except for swooping gulls. As she stepped out into an unseasonably warm sea breeze, the plaintive cry of distant terns steadied her nerves.

'Let's walk, stretch our legs,' he suggested. 'It's still early. The day's glorious, as good as any English summer's day.'

'Good idea,' she said, hoping her voice hadn't betrayed jangling nerves.

They walked westwards along the boardwalk, past empty holiday apartments, cafés, bars, clubs – not a soul in sight.

'Everything's in the summary,' he said after several minutes, passing her a blank brown envelope, his voice giving nothing away.

It occurred to her that he'd probably read the report, which briefly bothered her. *Well, why shouldn't he?* she reasoned. *After all, it's the interpretation of the results that matters, not the results themselves.* As they walked, she pulled the report out and started to read it, her heart racing.

Not believing what she was seeing, she stopped and sat down absently on the polished timbers of the boardwalk.

> *… DNA samples taken from the eleven body parts show a remarkable similarity, suggesting a close ethnic, tribal, even familial relationship between…, … what is most interesting is the geographical correlation with similar DNA samples…, … linking this group to similar groups in the Crimea, parts of former Ukraine and…, … to samples taken from groups indicted in the Hague for war crimes in former Syria…, … all samples suggest that the limbs belonged to heavy cocaine users…, … traces of cocaine and other illegal narcotics were found in skin pores and under fingernails…*

Her attention was drawn to a footnote appended to the main report:

> *… this relatively new and deadly strain of cocaine, believed to be sourced in the remotest areas of eastern Afghanistan,*

was unknown in Europe until several years ago..., ...
European drug enforcement agencies believe that much of this
cocaine is entering mainland Europe through Greece from
North Africa, both areas under FRSS administration..., ...
worrying amounts have cropped up in German and French
industrial towns and cities..., ... a small pocket of users has
been identified in UNMTF...

Her whole body shook with relief. She wiped a tear from her cheek, barely able to grasp the full impact of what she was reading. After a moment or two, he sat down next to her and put his arm around her.

'You were quite right to be sceptical about Philippe's version of events,' he said, 'I'm as convinced as you are that there's something sinister going on here.'

She leaned against him, drawing on his energy, letting her thoughts freewheel.

'Let's keep walking,' he said, getting to his feet.

She stood up and clumsily threw her arms around him, holding him as tightly as she could.

'Thank you for believing in me,' was all she managed to say.

In silence, they continued along the boardwalk.

*

Around midday they found a small beachside café, empty except for a few wizened pensioners arguing volubly over local politics.

'We need a drink,' he said, pulling out an old aluminium seat at a table near the window. 'Beer?'

She nodded.

A couple of minutes later, the *patron* casually wiped the table and pushed two frosted beers into the centre, not a word said.

They'd hardly spoken since she'd read the summary, both content to let the sound of the sea and crying gulls fill the silence.

'A penny for your thoughts,' he said, raising his glass.

'I'm not sure where to start.' Competing theories in her head struggled to be heard. 'The results could mean so many things.'

'Forget the results for a moment, just try to recall what happened at the border that morning,' he suggested, quietly.

'What do you mean?'

'You've already told me your thoughts when we met at the club, but remind me how everybody reacted when you saw the corpses?'

'Philippe and Omar strongly disagreed with what had happened, who had carried out the killings. Philippe kept arguing that this was the work of UDP terrorists while Omar…'

'Well,' he interrupted, 'Philippe's theory, which is the official one, has already been discredited.'

'How come?' she asked, pulse racing.

'Shortly after you left Sabha, his men slaughtered a number of local tribesmen in the border area. He claimed, without any evidence as far as we know, that they were members of a UDP terrorist group that was directly implicated in the murders.'

'I hadn't heard this,' she said, feeling disorientated.

'Why would you? You'd left. The whole manhunt operation had been officially sanctioned. It only took a few days and then everything was forgotten.' He paused. 'However, it all turned out to be a bloody great lie. A civilian field team eventually identified the unfortunate men, verified their innocence. In fact, the murdered men had a proud history of resisting UDP terrorist groups on both sides of the border.'

'The official version was rubbish then,' she said, absently.

'Yes, but before the field team could alert Tripoli, the administration was congratulating Philippe and his men on another successful mission. As far as Tripoli was concerned, it was a case of "job well done, file closed",' he said, before adding, 'I can't count how many times over the past two years he's reported that terrorist groups have been finally driven out of the Fezzan.'

'You couldn't persuade anybody in Tripoli that he might be wrong?'

'Not a chance. They wouldn't listen anyway, it's not convenient for them to believe us civilians. They certainly wouldn't want to undermine Philippe, they're happy with the status quo.'

'I remember you said this at the club,' she said, sitting back and trying to make sense of it all.

'You told me that you found Omar's arguments more persuasive,' he continued. 'Remind me how he reacted.'

She was flattered to think that he'd remembered what she'd told him that night, intrigued to see what he had to say now.

'His main observation was that the men hadn't been killed by local terrorists because of the way they'd been ritually executed. He also saw evidence to suggest that the murdered men knew their killers.'

'I remember.'

'Omar was really upset that Ramil and the Bedouin drivers, whom I knew he treated as brothers, were nowhere to be seen. Philippe argued that they were spared by the terrorists because they were Muslim.'

'I think the DNA results bolster your original supposition.'

'How?' she asked.

'Let's suppose your hunch was right, that what you saw represented some kind of schism within Cyrenaica. On the one hand you have a close-knit military squad, who, judging by their DNA, were very probably experienced Russian stormtroopers, all ritualistically shot. Then you have Ramil and his fellow Muslims, who have all vanished. Natural enemies you might say. Right so far?'

'So far.'

'I remember you saying how Ramil emphasised his Tartar Muslim background. He intimated to you that he was not one of them, not part of the military. In fact, you inferred that his people hated the Russian military, a hatred that spanned centuries. You mentioned his behaviour. He stood apart from the others.'

'He painted a pretty clear picture.'

'Let's suppose for whatever reason,' continued Greg, 'Ramil and his three colleagues subdued the squad, not difficult if the soldiers had spent the day snorting coke, and then shot them all before disappearing.'

Isabel shuddered.

'It had crossed my mind, you know, that Ramil was still alive, that he might have been responsible for the carnage,' she said, her thoughts going back to the day she'd had lunch with Philippe's squad. 'I dismissed the idea. I just don't think he has a killer's temperament.'

'You and I, we don't have the training or experience to know the type of person capable of doing this.'

'Perhaps he hated these men so much that as soon as he had an opportunity, he shot them,' she said, trying to rationalise her thoughts.

'I don't think it's that straightforward. I think the whole thing may have been stage-managed, staged-managed just for you.'

'Just for me?' she repeated, incredulously.

'Continuing with my hypothesis, I believe his timing and methods were carefully planned. Even the fact that the meeting point, his choice, was as far south as you'd ever been. Apart from drip-feeding you with information, it was his idea to stage the football match between the two groups. The match was never going to happen, it was the analogy that was important.'

'Analogy?'

'You know, his squad as a team, whose members worked closely together, with him as their non-playing captain. He made it clear he wouldn't play with them, emphasising his status as an outsider.'

'Yes, I picked up on that.'

'And of course, it gave him the opportunity to leave critical evidence, the bloodied thumbs, which he hoped you'd find, hence his earlier suggestion that you should be more forensic in your work. It all conforms to a pattern.'

'What would have happened if Philippe had shown an interest in the bag?'

'I suspect, like everything else that didn't support his theory, Philippe would have got rid of it. Obviously Ramil had very few options to present his evidence, he just hoped that it was you and not Philippe that picked it up.'

'OK,' she said, still unconvinced, 'but what was Ramil trying to say? What does it all mean?'

'Ah, this is where it gets more speculative,' he grinned. 'The squad, as we now know, were all heavy drug users. I suggest they were actually trading in drugs. You know, most traders are addicts.'

'That's reasonable, but trading with whom?'

He paused, perhaps trying to gauge her reaction.

'Philippe.'

Suddenly, there seemed to be a logical thread linking everything that had happened to her since the border incident.

'Philippe, maybe, but where's the proof?'

For the next few minutes he told her about the rapid increase in drug usage in the Fezzan over the last couple of years. This was especially evident within the military community, as witnessed by staff working in Sabha's regional hospital.

He also revealed the rise in profligate spending by senior officers over the same period, seeing ever-increasing amounts of cash and expensive personal items being flashed about and a substantial increase in new cars and high-class hookers – expenditure way in excess of the men's earning capacity. He reminded her of Philippe's arrogance and his disdain for Sabha's civilian community, which he abused with impunity.

'It's not proof exactly, but it's strongly circumstantial,' he concluded.

'It's certainly plausible, although it still doesn't answer the question why Ramil should have involved me,' she said.

'I'm suggesting he wanted to give you a message, a message

that says, "We have a common enemy": drug smugglers operating on either side of the border, working together for mutual benefit.'

'OK, but why me?'

'Because you're the only person he could trust on our side.'

'It still doesn't make sense,' she persisted. 'By killing the squad, he's a wanted man operating outside the law in Cyrenaica, and yet you said, "we have a common enemy". Who the hell is he working for? I don't get it.'

He remained silent, finishing his beer.

'I've no idea, that's the problem. He's a complete enigma.'

'And he expects me to have worked all this out?'

'Hoping rather than expecting, but yes, I believe he may want your help, perhaps initiating action to stop it,' he added.

'This is far too speculative,' she laughed nervously.

'I've thought a lot about this whole business over the last few weeks.' He hesitated. 'But there's another thing I'd like you to consider, although I've no evidence. It's just a hunch, that's all.'

'Come on, Greg,' she laughed nervously, 'I can't keep up with your imagination.'

'Somebody, somewhere in Tripoli, not protecting or benefiting from Philippe, has suspected something all along,' he said, looking at her directly, 'and they've used you, an innocent newcomer, to fish for clues…'

'Absolute bullshit,' she interjected, now angry; she was certainly no patsy. She dumped her empty glass on the table and got up.

'Why were you embedded in the military? It never made sense and you know it,' he said, before adding, 'and completely by chance, the ploy's been spectacularly successful.'

She walked out purposely into the sunlight, trying to shut out what he'd just said and sat down on the boardwalk, emotionally drained, tears streaming down her face. He'd forced her to face reality, something he did with his staff and patients on a daily basis. More importantly, he seemed to be challenging her to question the status quo, even to raise the possibility of a cross-border drug trade. She felt bone-weary.

She began to reflect on the choices she faced. It didn't take her long to realise that in fact she had none. The die had been cast the moment she'd accepted the EDA post. It also occurred to her that all along, Jack had been subliminally preparing her for such a situation. After a few minutes her tears dried, her mood brightened, a deep-seated excitement slowly energising her. She stood up and called to Greg, who was waiting patiently for her.

'When's lunch? I'm starving.'

He smiled and, nodding to her to follow, set off along the promenade. A few hundred metres from the café they found a small restaurant and ordered the *plat du jour* and a carafe of local house wine.

'I'm sorry, I behaved like a…'

'Stop,' he interrupted. 'No more. This has been difficult for you, a new experience. You're doing well.' Pausing for a moment, he then said, 'I must tell you a few more things and then I promise, no more detective stories for now.'

'Go on, I'm ready.'

'After we heard that the slaughtered men were innocent, I had a hunch and decided to do a little investigation myself. I contacted an old friend in Security Ops who owed me a favour. Using GPS, they track all government vehicles, civilian and military, in case somebody goes missing in the desert. If there's a problem, a search and rescue mission is mobilised utilising the vehicle's latest GPS data.'

'Who oversees Security Ops?'

'Good question, I don't know. The military are supposed to scrub the data once a mission has been completed. However, we discovered that the civilian authorities in Sabha have been copied with the data for nearly two years now. These guys, for some reason, have kept their records, which she was able to access.'

'You're quite the detective,' laughed Isabel.

'I asked her for the vehicle GPS plots of the various routes taken by Philippe's squad over that period.'

'These would have covered the monthly trips I've made,' she said, stating the obvious.

He nodded.

'I also asked for the military escort details for each trip, you know, named personnel including drivers, support staff.'

'Omar, our driver, was he included?'

'Yes, he was a listed driver, but only on one trip each month and only since you started, suggesting that it was yours. It's the same for the rest of your crew.'

'That's amazing.'

'What's interesting is the correlation between all these bits of information. Of the three trips DPG make each month, there are two shorter ones, both patrolling the same section of border before stopping at exactly the same place each time. Philippe's drivers and military escort always comprise the same group of paratroopers, older men who I suspect have been with him for years.'

'And you think this is where the drugs may be coming into UNMTF?'

'The DNA report suggests that the cocaine is getting into Europe via Greece. It's possible the Russians have also developed another route through UNMTF with the support of a breakaway group here, which could well be Philippe's squad.'

'What happens then?'

'I've no idea,' he admitted, 'although interestingly Philippe's same three vehicles always return to Tripoli via the solar plant construction site.'

'We'd stop at a different location each time, the one suggested by Ramil for our meetings.'

'Exactly. Furthermore, I think it's the Russians that have worked out how to override the joint border security protocols. It has to be in their interest. Philippe's probably just a courier, although a very important one.'

'So it must have been Ramil who secretly kept the border open the day of the border incident.'

'I believe so.' He paused. 'One final point: somebody in Tripoli recently asked my friend for exactly the same information as I did.'

'And you think that somebody is the person who sent me on a so-called fishing expedition.'

'Yes, although unfortunately she wasn't able to identify who it was.'

'You're way ahead of me, I'm afraid,' she said, astonished at what she'd just heard.

'No, I've just been there too long. You made the breakthrough. I simply followed my instincts.'

*

After lunch they wandered further west just beyond the town before dropping down from the boardwalk onto a wide empty beach. Low dunes stretched westwards to a flat horizon, replacing the town's cosmopolitan waterfront. Considering the time of year, it was warm. The early sea breeze dropped to a listless whisper. The gulls had long gone, seeking fresh currents far out to sea.

Gradually the town receded; sea, sand and sky merged into a single amorphous silver-white landscape devoid of all forms of life.

'Fancy a swim?' Greg asked, taking her by surprise.

'It's November,' she exclaimed, 'the water will be cold.'

'Compared to Tripoli, yes, but it won't be much cooler than it was here in July,' he laughed.

Without waiting for her response, he stripped naked, shedding his clothes like skin, and rushed into the surf. She hesitated. His sudden nakedness shocked and excited her. Quickly, before she could change her mind, she dropped her small backpack on the sand, threw off her clothes and followed.

He was a strong swimmer, powering his way through the flat water. She waded out until the water caressed her breasts, unashamedly aroused. She felt reckless, wanting him to possess her, here, now. He swam straight to her.

She marvelled at his leanness as he stood up beside her and took her in his arms, crushing his erection between their wet bodies. His hand reached for her crotch, fingering her swollen clitoris. The small waves eased them inshore, exposing their nakedness. Then in one seamless movement, he raised her by her buttocks and slipped into her, nailing his body to hers. She wrapped her legs tightly around him, ecstatically riding his thrusting body. In a few short seconds they climaxed in a delirious frenzy, before he lost his balance, dumping them both unceremoniously in the shallow water. They came up uncoupled, panting and laughing hysterically.

Lying naked on their backs in the shelter of low dunes, they were too exhausted to speak. Minutes passed. The tide had started to recede, drawing the sea back from a widening beach. She awoke from a light sleep cool in the weak November sun. Rolling over onto her stomach she scanned the beach, ready to meet the disapproving looks of a passer-by. She saw nobody. He lay beside her, barely conscious, the faintest of smiles on his face, his body replete.

She reached out and with her forefinger gently traced his torso, working slowly down towards his crotch. Slowly she aroused him, his drowsy body inert save for a growing erection. She watched in wonder as it grew, her desire for him making her dizzy. She gently crouched over him before easing herself onto him, pushing him deep into her succulent body. He rolled her over onto her back and pumped her rhythmically; their lovemaking was intense, short-lived.

After another swim, they managed to dry themselves by running along the firm sand at the water's edge. The cooling sea breeze returned, bringing with it restless gulls filling the sky. Fully dressed, they retraced their steps as dusk turned to darkness. It was after six when they reached the promenade; they were both ravenous.

*

They went back to the place where they'd had lunch. The old proprietor smiled at them knowingly as he showed them to their table. Isabel had the strange yet not uncomfortable feeling that he'd been their companion all afternoon, watching with approval their frenetic fornicating.

They talked quietly over dinner, like a couple long used to each other's company.

'What is it about your work that drives you from one day to the next?' she asked, sensing that their intimacy had given her an opportunity to uncover this man, someone she was becoming increasingly attracted to.

'Why do you ask?' He sounded surprised.

'I don't know, it's a question I keep asking myself,' she replied, feeling a little awkward. 'I'd be interested to hear what you have to say.'

'There are several reasons, although I don't think about them much these days. I do know I'd sooner live out my life in North Africa than anywhere in Europe. Whether it's England, wherever, this part of the world holds no interest for me anymore, it hasn't done for years.'

'That's extraordinary,' she said in disbelief, trying to fathom what he'd said. 'But your daughter, you'd miss her.'

'Yes,' he said, hesitating, 'yes, you're right in a sense. But in truth, we're strangers. And sad to relate, I don't have any strong feelings for anyone in my family anymore. Sounds pretty heartless, doesn't it?'

'Not really. I can't imagine how you must have felt when your wife left you. It must have been heartbreaking.'

'People like us, you and I, can make a big difference in North Africa,' he said, changing the subject, clearly unable or unwilling to discuss his family. 'I look forward to the day when local people aren't compelled to emigrate, whether because of poverty, starvation, drought, disease, religious fanaticism, or whatever. I want them to be able to live normal lives there, not imprisoned in some godforsaken ghetto in Europe.'

'I'd never thought of it like that.'

She realised again how much she could learn from this man, his easy-going nature concealing a deeply thoughtful person, so much more stimulating than the hubristic military men she was used to.

'In Sabha, I felt my work, especially at the beginning, was important. Recently, it's become routine, more First World.'

'I remember you mentioned this at the club, something about shifting from working in a war zone to inner-city doctoring, from shrapnel wounds to drug overdoses.'

'That's neat,' he laughed, 'I'm hoping that if we can eradicate the drug epidemic in the Fezzan, my interest in medicine would be rekindled.'

'I never told you that Jack, my granddad, once believed he'd make a difference.'

'Where?'

'In Libya, in the '80s and '90s.'

'Really, doing what?'

She told him about Jack's years of prospecting in the desert, including finding one of the country's largest, most lucrative oil reserves.

'He loved the country, its people, despite having to live under a dictatorship. He was the first to raise the potential of solar energy with the government there, you know, as a means of protecting the country's revenues against the decline in its hydrocarbon reserves,' she said, proudly. 'He dreamed up all sorts of schemes to export solar energy across the Med to Europe.'

'He was ahead of his time,' he said, before adding, 'I'm sure you'll leave your mark there.'

They passed a pleasant few hours over supper. He told her that after his leave he was due to spend a couple of days in Tripoli, which she discovered coincided with her first few days back in town. They agreed to meet and discuss what they would do with the DNA report.

Back at the station, it was nearly midnight; the whole day had dramatically unwound in a way that she could never have anticipated. They wandered along the platform waiting for her train, which was due at twelve-thirty. He had a return ticket to Amsterdam; his train was due fifteen minutes after hers. To get home he would have to change in Lille at around two in the morning.

They sat down in silence on a backless metal bench, in the glare of station lights festooned with insects. Outwardly she looked as if she'd been on a twenty-kilometre hike, slightly flushed and a little dishevelled; inwardly she was at peace.

A few minutes before her train was due, he took a blank envelope from his pocket and gave it to her.

'Put this away carefully,' he said, quietly. 'There are two postcards here, both addressed to you in England. They've been stamped and franked as if they've been through the Dutch postal system. They're pictures of two famous, but rarely seen, Frans Hals portraits currently hanging in a well-known gallery in The Hague. A friend has sent them to you, urging you to visit her before the exhibition is over.'

'Is this a joke?' Isabel asked. 'You don't even know my address.'

'Everything except your name is made up. And that includes the suggestion, although another time I would be happy to take you around Amsterdam's famous art galleries.'

'I look forward to that,' she said, quick not to let his offer go unanswered, 'but what about these postcards?'

'Each stamp contains an encrypted nanochip on which the full DNA analyses and report are stored. Keep one safe in England, take the other back to Tripoli after your leave. The paper copy I gave you this morning must be destroyed. I have a similar postcard in a safety deposit box in Amsterdam.' He paused. 'I hope you're OK with this?'

'No problem,' she said, although she was struggling to cope with this sudden level of secrecy, behaving as if they were in the Secret Service.

'I'll arrange for the chipped data to be downloaded in Tripoli before we meet. We'll try to find out then who our man is.'

'Our man?' she asked, losing the thread again, as a feeling of helplessness overcame her.

'The person who secretly organised your fishing trip. In future we'll refer to him as "The Angler".'

'Fine,' she said, desperately trying to stay on-message.

All too soon her train's imminent arrival was announced. They stood and faced each other.

'Thanks for being such a good friend, for trusting me, giving me a purpose in Tripoli,' she said, before adding impishly, 'and being such a fantastic screw.'

'What a wonderfully refreshing woman you are,' he said, a huge grin on his face. 'I hope we remain good friends through all the crap that lies ahead.'

He took her in his arms as the Edinburgh-bound intercontinental express glided down the platform.

24

Tripoli, Late November 2031

I t was late afternoon when the aircraft started its descent, the sun's blinding image reflecting off the shimmering sea far below. An easterly breeze meant they had to fly in from the west along the coast. Isabel had a clear view of the heavily irrigated Jeffara Plain, stretching from the shoreline to the foot of the Jebel Nefusa, its craggy ridges shielding Tripoli from the northern Sahara.

Her thoughts returned to the last few days of her leave, when Emma had unexpectedly produced the shoebox and explained the significance of its contents. Isabel, who was astonished to hear of Jack's relationship with Bushra, was still grappling with the fact that her mother was part English, part Greek, part Libyan. This barely believable parentage induced in her a weird sense of entitlement when she surveyed the countryside below. And as for her long-dead Uncle Stavros, who had suffered so cruelly at the hands of the dictatorship, she was at a complete loss.

She emerged from the airport, sweaty and tired, longing for the coolness of her seafront apartment on Great West Road. It was dusk. The thronged highway into the city was hemmed in on either side by an endless line of decrepit buildings, all alike whether permanently under construction or being demolished. Gaudy hoardings and numerous temporary stalls were squeezed up against workshops and cafés, poorly lit by naked bulbs swaying in the evening breeze, all fronted by broken pavements awash with waste and rubbish spilling out onto the road; everything she saw induced in her a strong sense of homecoming. She felt alive, a palpable relief after the stifling emptiness of a cosseted Europe.

The top-floor apartment was stuffy. She pulled back the sliding door and stepped onto the balcony. In the darkness, she could just make out the rocky foreshore below. The sound of crashing waves drowned out the traffic on the other side of the building; she was at peace. The apartment block was home to over a hundred single professionals working for government. Although more salubrious, it reminded her of student accommodation during her university days.

The doorbell rang. It was her neighbour Kathy, a feisty Irish doctor in her mid-thirties, always up for the *craic*. It had only taken Isabel a couple of days after she'd first arrived to realise what the *craic* entailed: having a good time. Inevitably this involved booze and/or men and/or some unlikely adventure.

Kathy, a tough and experienced expatriate, had been in Tripoli for eight years. She was tremendously enthusiastic about her work, telling Isabel that it kept her sane in a society that she found brittle and unforgiving.

Isabel was very fond of Kathy, a striking auburn-haired woman with a broad freckled grin, which had seduced many of their male friends. She appreciated Kathy's free spirit, debunking government hubris and avoiding long-term relationships. In Kathy's opinion, most of the men she met were supreme egotists, coming and going in her life on a regular basis. After a few weeks of partying and casual sex, she would lose interest in her latest catch, walk away and stay celibate for several months.

She once confided in Isabel that marriage would imprison her and having children didn't hold any fascination; anyway, she felt too old for all that now. In the far south of Ireland, the Church and six children had wiped out her mother's life. In leaving Ireland, Kathy had escaped one trap; she was damned if she was going to fall into a second.

'Thank God you're back, Bel, it's been a real drag since you've been away,' she said as she rushed past her into the living room. 'God, you're always so bloody tidy. Can well believe you've no Irish blood in you,' she laughed, looking around.

'Have a beer while I sort myself out,' Isabel said, hoping her friend would dictate the course of the evening, 'you'll find a few cold ones in the fridge.'

Isabel unpacked, showered and dressed as Kathy polished off a couple of cans, while giving an unrelenting account of all that had happened since Isabel had gone on leave.

'And as for that freaky man of yours, Philippe, he's become an even bigger prick now.' She was never one to mince her words.

'He's history,' Isabel shouted, from her bedroom. 'Anyway, what's he supposed to have done?' she asked, coming into the living room, trying not to show too much interest.

'Apparently a few weeks ago, he and his soldier boy thugs killed a dangerous terrorist gang, apparently the one responsible for murdering those Russian soldiers just over the border.' Kathy rushed on, 'I assume that was the business you got caught up in before you went on leave.'

'Must be,' she said simply, not wishing to elaborate.

'The bloody military boys are cock-a-hoop now. They act like gods, thinking they can fuck us civilians around with impunity,' snapped Kathy.

'Let them bloody well try,' said Isabel, getting into her stride.

'Good girl, Bel, let's drink to that,' she laughed, lobbing Isabel a beer. 'I'm famished, do you fancy walking over to the club?'

It was Friday evening, the end of their weekend. The club bar was awash with friends and colleagues, whom they studiously avoided. There was a serious side to Kathy, which few saw but which Isabel appreciated. The two women had much in common. They confided in each other, sharing the same hopes for the local people, the same disgust at the ignorance of many of their colleagues, especially those in uniform.

Before she'd gone on leave, Isabel had told Kathy about the border incident, including her subsequent spell in hospital. Although she mentioned she disagreed with Philippe's official report, she didn't give any reason or explain her theory as to what she may have witnessed. She needed the DNA results before telling her side of the story.

Taking their beers, they found a quiet corner in the garden far from the madness of the bar.

'Calais bothered you,' said Kathy, matter-of-factly.

On the way to the club, Isabel had mentioned that she'd had a work-related meeting there with a colleague. She hadn't said anything about Greg; it was far too early. She did tell her, though, about the outlying satellite towns on which Calais preyed.

'The wretched satellites. I saw a twenty-first-century European version of apartheid,' she said. 'It sickened me, I found it really disturbing.'

'God, I'd never thought about them in that way. We've a couple in Ireland. They're small compared to the ones in England, across Europe.'

'Mum told me that Jack, her dad, was in Greece recently. The ghetto towns there are huge, totally beyond the regime's control. He described them as states within the state.'

'Bloody apartheid, you're right, the Bantustans were never a morally sustainable solution in South Africa,' said Kathy, 'they're even less so today.'

'Jack thinks these migrant towns will implode, ultimately threatening the very foundations of European democracy.'

'Is he right?'

'Absolutely, yes.'

'And the whole migrant business, what do you think?'

Recalling Greg's reasons for working in the mandate, she said, 'Make sure this country's worth living in, in every sense, so that the locals aren't forced to emigrate in the first place.'

'I'll drink to that, a bloody good philosophy,' Kathy said, forthright as ever. 'Same again?' she said as she headed to the bar, not waiting for an answer.

*

Isabel arrived at her desk early the following morning, somewhat the worse for wear. She was alarmed to see a note attached to her screen, asking her to report to the chief administration officer's secretary as soon as she got in. The CAO was the most senior civilian in the country, reporting directly to the military governor.

She had met Louis Vanmeer, a Dutch national, on a couple of brief occasions in the past. He had shown an interest in her work on the border, having read and commented on notes of her meetings with Ramil. Despite being an academic and an intensely precise man, she had not been intimidated by him. She'd often wondered, though, how such a character could cope with the many day-to-day problems of his office, although she remembered him as a man of eclectic interests, which she thought qualified him as a suitable CAO. She saw him as a positive force, somebody who worked tirelessly for the good of the country and its people.

'This is Isabel Meredith,' she said, over the phone, 'I'd like to speak to the CAO's private secretary.'

'Speaking,' replied a sonorous voice. 'I'm Ian Hamond. Thanks for getting back. The CAO would like you to attend a thirty-minute meeting in his office at twelve this morning. Can you make it?'

'Yes, I'll be there.'

The line went dead.

The morning passed quickly. As she worked through the paperwork that had piled up in her absence, she wondered anxiously why she was being summoned by someone so senior, so soon after her leave.

Vanmeer's office was on the top floor of a fifteen-storey building, the tallest in Tripoli, looking down on the old port. The views were stunning.

'Ah, Isabel,' he greeted her, as if they were old friends. 'Coffee?'

'Please,' she said, hoping to retain her composure for the next thirty minutes.

A moment later, Hamond arrived with two coffees.

'We're not to be disturbed 'til twelve-thirty,' Vanmeer instructed his retreating secretary. He turned to the floor-to-ceiling window and, waving his coffee mug absently, indicated the view below. 'I'm a complete obsessive with anything to do with the sea, the weather. I track weather patterns way out to sea, like a marine forecaster.'

Isabel was drawn to the window.

Standing at her shoulder, he continued, 'I know all the ships, naval vessels, ferries and trawlers that use the port. It's very nerdy, I'm afraid.'

'They say you're very knowledgeable on climate change issues,' she said, remembering hearing about one of his many obsessions, 'and are greatly interested in the solar farms in the desert.'

'Don't miss much, do you?' He smiled. 'Have you visited any of the sites yet?'

'No, but I plan to when I have some free time.'

'Remember, you'll need a pass from the local military commander.'

'I didn't know they were military projects,' she said, trying not to show her disappointment.

'Shouldn't be, but that's the way it is.'

She noticed a hint of frustration in his voice; perhaps he was resentful of the military's lead on what ought to be a civilian enterprise. She was tempted to tell him about Jack and his interest in the country's fledgling solar projects decades earlier; another time perhaps, she thought.

They sat down in easy chairs opposite each other, next to the window. She felt as if she were suspended out over the water.

'I understand you've just returned from ten days' leave.'

'Yes, sir.'

'Everything at home OK?' he asked, a little too casually for her liking. She started to feel uneasy.

'Absolutely.'

'It's just that this was your first leave since you started here. Quite a long absence from home,' he said.

'Yes,' she said simply, not wishing to divulge her personal life.

'And your work here, you're enjoying it?'

'Very much,' she replied, 'the whole experience is more than I could have wished for.'

'Good, good,' he said. He paused, his attention apparently diverted by something in the port below. 'I hear you got caught up in an incident on the border a few weeks ago.'

'Yes,' she said, realising the inevitable direction of their conversation.

'I was in Brussels at the time. I heard later that you'd had a bad time of it, were confined to hospital in Sabha for a few days.'

'Yes.'

He paused, as if distracted by the view again.

'You were sent back to Tripoli early.'

Another open-ended statement; he must have been a lawyer in a former life. She couldn't just let this one hang there.

'It was nothing, sir. I was fine after a couple of days and quite happy to stay on. I still had a field assignment to complete, which I was looking forward to. It was frustrating to have to come back,' and then without thinking, she added, 'others thought differently.'

'Others?'

'Yes,' she muttered, backing off hurriedly.

They were silent for a few moments; it was eerie.

'Can you be a bit more specific, Isabel?'

She hesitated.

'The Desert Patrol Group who accompany me to the border meetings.'

'Philippe and company?' he asked, casually.

'Yes.'

She felt she was talking herself into a trap. It would be so much easier if she knew where he was coming from. She shivered inwardly. Time stood still. Whatever she said in the next few minutes could make or break her fledgling career.

'You said "thought differently",' he said, continuing his interrogation.

'There was a difference of opinion.'

'Yours and Philippe's?'

'Yes,' she answered, feeling the net closing ever tighter around her – and around Greg, she thought in despair.

'You didn't think it was a terrorist attack, I gather,' he said, suddenly showing his hand. Clearly, he knew more than he was letting on, which, strangely, she found comforting.

'No, sir, I didn't.'

'Who was responsible then?'

She had come so far, there was no turning back. She realised she couldn't withhold anything anymore. Her biggest concern was to protect Greg's identity, his involvement. She took a moment, marshalling her thoughts. Every word was important now.

'I believe it was an internal problem.'

'Internal? You need to be more specific again, Isabel.'

'Within the UNMC military.'

'I can't see your logic here,' he said, sceptically.

God, she thought, *I feel like a defendant under cross-examination.* She chose her words carefully, desperate to sound credible.

'Sir, I think we witnessed a schism within their ranks; a fallout between their special border security force and the others – drivers, interpreters – all of whom had one thing in common.'

'Being what?'

'The others, Russian or otherwise, are Muslim.'

'Go on.'

She could see that she was telling him something new, detecting interest in his voice. She then proceeded to outline her theory about Ramil, the football match that never took place and the team that was slaughtered. He sat for several minutes absorbing what she'd told him. From his furrowed expression, she could see that he didn't buy it.

'This is all very hypothetical. Do you have any evidence?'

'We, I,' she said, quickly correcting herself, 'do have evidence, sir. It demonstrates a common bond between members of their special border security force, perhaps a common purpose.'

'In what way?' he asked tersely, unnerving her.

She suddenly realised that he might be 'The Angler'. If so, she was certain he hadn't thought through what she might discover, how complex it might be. She told him about the strong ethnic and tribal bonds between the soldiers and their links with other FRSS troops especially in Crimea and Syria, many of whom had been indicted for war crimes in The Hague.

'And what else?' he said, his impatience beginning to show.

'I believe they were all cocaine users, very possibly trading in drugs.'

He was silent, his gaze following an EDA naval vessel docking below them. She could see that he was having difficulty believing her story.

'How can you be so sure?' he said slowly. 'You'd need DNA samples, a lab analysis, before coming to this conclusion.'

From his tone, she sensed he thought she was winging it.

'I have,' she said, quietly.

He looked at her in astonishment before going to his desk and lifting the phone.

'Bring some fresh coffee.'

'Isabel, what's the greatest difficulty you've experienced working on assignment in Sabha?' he asked, throwing her off balance.

'Being embedded within the military,' she replied, without hesitation.

Hamond knocked and entered with fresh coffee and cups, picking up the used ones as he retreated. *It's not over*, she thought, *the worst is yet to come*. Vanmeer got up and poured their coffee, gazing out to sea before sitting down.

'That was my idea,' he said, flatly.

'Sir?' Her heart thumped loudly.

'I wanted you to work with them, be part of their team.'

Briefly, her optimism soared; if he were 'The Angler' setting her up as an internal spy, he must have seen her as an accomplice, someone he could trust. But she needed an explanation and none was forthcoming. It gradually dawned on her that, for whatever reason, she'd been used, just as Greg had intimated. *To hell with Vanmeer, I'll tell him as I see it.*

'My work would have been more productive if I'd been attached to a civilian group, sir.'

'Where's your evidence, your DNA analysis?' he asked, ignoring what she'd said.

Although she'd been anticipating this question for days, she still hadn't formulated a response. She certainly hadn't thought the interrogator would be the CAO.

'I haven't got the analysis, sir,' she said, evenly.

'You haven't got the analysis,' he repeated slowly, 'yet you've seen the results, clearly read the report.'

She could see he was struggling to contain his mounting frustration. Suddenly, without warning, he leaned across and shouted directly into her face.

'Isabel, stop fucking me about.'

She pulled back, startled by his obscene outburst. Silence followed. They were in new territory now, in a sense equals. She felt emboldened by his loss of composure; she held her nerve. Even if she were to lose her job over this, she was temporarily in control and wouldn't go down without a fight. She got up and stood behind her chair, shaking uncontrollably, convinced now that he was 'The Angler'.

'With respect, sir, I'm the one being fucked about,' she said, calmly, knowing she was taking a huge gamble with her career.

She was certain now that, without her knowledge or consent, he had sent her to spy, for whatever reason, on the Sabha military community. Instinctively, she knew that she had every right to say what she felt.

He appeared dumbfounded. Without a word he turned back to the window and stared out over the harbour. She remained behind her chair, not knowing what to do next.

'You have one week to come up with your evidence,' he said, without looking up. 'The meeting's over,' he said, dismissing her abruptly.

'Sir,' she said, as she walked resolutely to the door, hoping her terror wouldn't betray her. She walked straight past a wide-eyed Hamond, who had clearly heard his boss lose his temper, the faintest trace of a smile on his face.

25

Tripoli, Late November 2031

sabel had stayed back in the office, catching up on her work. It was Wednesday evening, four days after the acrimonious meeting with Vanmeer. The intervening time had been surreal. She had briefly mentioned the Vanmeer meeting to Kathy, simply saying that it hadn't gone well. Kathy was astute enough not to press her on the subject.

Isabel's anxiety levels had risen steadily over the previous few days. She hadn't heard from Greg, who she thought should have been back in Tripoli by now. Without him, there would be no DNA report, nothing on Vanmeer's desk on Saturday morning.

At least everything appeared normal in the office, her colleagues glad to see her back from leave. She had seen Ian Hamond drinking with his friends at the club. In the crowded bar, he had acknowledged her presence with a slight nod and vague enigmatic smile. She believed that whatever he'd heard during her fateful meeting with Vanmeer, he'd kept his counsel.

She had, though, a much more immediate and threatening worry. She had convinced herself that she was being followed. On several occasions, she was sure that she'd seen the same short, stocky man, casually dressed in Western clothes and usually on his phone, loitering outside her offices across the street on Great West Road. Another time, she thought she saw him outside the club. He seemed to be waiting, for what she had no idea. Nobody ever joined him; one minute he was there, the next he was gone.

She had discussed this with Kathy, whose initial reaction was that Isabel was suffering from paranoia. In the end Kathy had been persuaded, having seen the man for herself on Great West Road the previous day.

Meanwhile, and without good reason, Isabel had convinced herself that Philippe's military colleagues knew that she was still questioning his, and now the official, version of events. It hadn't taken long for her overworked imagination to conclude that Philippe feared she might formally challenge him, which could blow his carefully constructed story to pieces.

'What would Philippe actually achieve by following you around?' Kathy asked. 'I mean, the fact that you and he might disagree about what happened at the border shouldn't bother him.'

'I'm certain it does.'

'To the extent that he'd have you followed?'

'I think he's afraid I might question the official report.' She hesitated, unsure how much she should reveal. 'I think he's looking for an opportunity to silence me.'

'You've got to be joking, Bel,' laughed Kathy, incredulously. 'Is your opinion really that important? Are you really that important?'

'No, not at all, it's not about me. My life's insignificant in the great scheme of things.'

'Your life? Are you suggesting he'd try to kill you?'

Isabel paused for a moment.

'I was there when he blew a man's brains out on the pretext the man was suffering and was better dead.'

'Ye gods, Bel, what a bloody business you've got yourself involved in.'

That conversation had taken place late the previous evening. Back in her office, it was time to go. She had done what she had set out to do. She tidied her desk, packed her bags and took the lift to reception.

After her showdown with Vanmeer, she had decided to write a complete account of everything that had happened, in longhand, in a small notebook. She couldn't trust the security of the office IT system or even her own laptop, fearing that somebody could hack into it and destroy her private data. A handwritten account was her only option. The task had been completed that evening.

It was nearly eleven. Her office was located in the Central Administration District, an area normally quiet after the working day. She left the building, now empty except for cleaners and night watchmen, to catch the dedicated staff bus, which stopped directly across the street. The bus would deliver her safely and efficiently to her apartment complex further along Great West Road.

Tonight, traffic on the brightly lit main thoroughfare was sporadic. Across the road, the shadow of a man behind the glass bus shelter briefly caught her attention. He appeared to be on the phone. She hesitated, fearful, on edge. She wondered if he was the same man she'd kept seeing over the last few days. The shadow disappeared; her fear evaporated. She crossed the road and waited for her bus, the street empty of people.

A minute or so before the bus was due, she heard a muffled explosion. A vehicle, several hundred metres from where she was waiting, blocked the entire street and was burning ferociously. She froze, suddenly realising that her bus would be held up until the blaze was brought under control. Only one car, a battered jeep with darkened windows, managed to get past the blazing wreck.

She was thinking through her options when the jeep drew up alongside. Perhaps, she imagined fleetingly, she was being offered a lift. As it glided to a stop, the near doors swung open simultaneously and two men in balaclavas jumped out. Instinctively, she turned to run – a pointless gesture. In less than ten seconds she was roughly bundled into the back, her head forcibly pushed down between her knees, making breathing near impossible. It happened so quickly, she felt no fear, believing this was the end. The last thing she remembered before losing consciousness was a painful jab in her left thigh.

*

She awoke suddenly, as if from a nightmare. She couldn't see. She couldn't move. Her head seemed to be locked in a tourniquet, her whole body wracked in seamless pain. She was sitting bolt upright, tightly restrained, hands and feet bound. Gingerly, she pushed against the limits of her confinement, panic welling in her chest. The heat was stifling, the air nauseous. It was the silence, though, that terrified her.

She had absolutely no reference point to focus on, nothing to give her the slightest indication of where she was. She was acutely aware of her rapid breathing and the sweat coursing down her body. She was parched, her swollen tongue clamped to the roof of her mouth. Hunger gnawed at her stomach. Her memory was washed clean, as she drifted in and out of consciousness.

She had no idea how long she'd been there when she heard voices approaching, growing steadily louder. She recognised two, perhaps three, men speaking in Arabic. Cold fear instantly revived her, images tumbling through her head: the bus stop, an approaching jeep, men grabbing her, panic at being suffocated, the sharp excruciating pain in her thigh. It occurred to her that she was probably still in the jeep.

Car doors were opened with a flourish. She felt movement all about her, the pressure of bodies on either side. The voices continued unabated, her poor Arabic making them incomprehensible. She wondered briefly who the men were.

Suddenly, with absolute certainty, she knew that they were Philippe's thugs. Terror gripped her with such ferocity that she stopped breathing. A warm wet sensation spread between her thighs. *God, I've pissed myself*, she realised. She remembered suggesting to Kathy that Philippe wanted rid of her; how right she'd been.

The jeep took off with a lurch. The motion alternated between a rolling sensation like that of a boat riding waves on the sea and the repeated hammering caused by driving over hard, serrated sand. She was reminded of being huddled up in Philippe's truck as they'd hurtled back to Sabha after the border incident. Although weeks ago now, it seemed to her like a continuation of the same journey, the same protagonists, just that the stakes were higher.

She struggled, twisting and turning to relieve her aching, saturated body. The voices on either side turned in towards her, enveloping her in the sour and rancid smell of exotic diets. She jumped as the excruciating and now familiar pain stabbed at her thigh. By the count of five, she had lost consciousness.

26

Tripoli, Late November 2031

G reg got to his hotel overlooking Green Square in the centre of Tripoli, just after one on Thursday morning. He was exhausted. His departure from Paris had been delayed by over eight hours because of a threatened suicide attack in Charles de Gaulle Airport; it proved to be another hoax. It was too late to phone Isabel so he sent her a text suggesting they meet in the hotel bar at six that evening.

He had a meeting with the head of medical services in the Department of Health at seven-thirty in the morning. It was over lunch, several hours later, that he realised Isabel hadn't got back to him. He tried calling her number. A message advised him that her phone had been switched off. *Maybe she's at a meeting*, he thought, *I'll try later*. He phoned again at five and got the same message.

Now he was worried. He knew she worked at the Department of Social Affairs, which he rang immediately.

'Isabel hasn't been at work today,' answered the disembodied voice of one of her colleagues, moments later. 'Who can I say is calling?'

'Greg Hamilton. I'm a doctor working in Sabha Hospital. I'm in town for a meeting and have been trying her phone all day without any luck. I'd arranged to meet her in Funduq Kabir at six this evening.'

'I see,' said the voice.

'I wonder, would you mind telling me where I might find her.'

'Just a minute.'

After ten minutes, he was about to hang up when the voice returned. He guessed they'd been checking up on him, understandable in the circumstances.

'She lives in the government apartments on Great West Road. All the licensed taxi drivers know the place. The concierge will have her details,' said the voice, before ringing off.

Fifteen minutes later he was talking to the concierge, a rather grand title for a security guard.

'She's not answering her intercom,' said the woman, a tough no-nonsense East European of indeterminate age. 'Do you know any of her friends living here, anybody who could help you?' she asked.

'No, we met in Sabha where I work. This is the first time I've tried to contact her in Tripoli.'

'Ah, she often mentions going down to Sabha,' said the woman. 'Hang on a moment, I'll try her neighbour.' She retreated into her bulletproof glass box before re-emerging a minute later. 'Kathy will be down shortly.'

'Really appreciate your help.'

Twenty minutes later, Kathy signed him into the club. As they'd walked there, Greg told her briefly how he'd met Isabel in Sabha, how he'd just returned from leave and was hoping to see her that evening but hadn't been able to contact her. Kathy didn't seem unduly concerned, knowing Isabel would most probably be playing tennis with friends at the club.

'It seems odd, though, that she's been out all day,' Greg added.

Kathy just shrugged; she only seemed interested to hear more about how they'd met. He told her about Isabel's time in hospital after the border incident but nothing of her theory as to why it might have happened, of the DNA evidence and his own detective work. He said nothing of Calais.

'Wait here,' said Kathy, as soon as she signed him in. 'I'll go and get her, won't be more than a few minutes.'

Fifteen minutes later she returned; he could see she was anxious.

'I couldn't find her anywhere. I've tried her phone, checked with her friends, nobody's seen her this evening.'

'What shall we do?'

'Have a drink and wait. She's bound to turn up,' Kathy said, unconvincingly. 'There'll be a good reason she's not here, I'm sure of it.'

Armed with a couple of drinks, they fought their way through the raucous crowd to the garden. He realised that he had no choice but to go with Kathy's instinct and keep his emotions in check.

'What did she say happened at the border?' he asked, as they sat at an empty table.

Kathy recounted everything that Isabel had told her, from the day she'd arrived back from Sabha up until the evening she'd returned from leave.

'But you probably know all this. I don't know why I'm telling you.'

'Did she mention who might have murdered the Russians?'

'She said Philippe believed it was a terrorist group, although she seemed to have doubts,' she said, hesitating for a moment. 'Surprisingly, the CAO, Vanmeer, called her into his office, the day after she got back. Apparently during a fraught meeting, they'd had a disagreement about something. Bel seemed quite upset afterwards.'

'Vanmeer, no less,' Greg said, realising that the ramifications of what Isabel had witnessed were spreading in ever-widening circles. 'Poor girl. What a mess she's got herself into.'

It occurred to him that Kathy knew very little of Isabel's version of events at the border. Not knowing what was discussed at the meeting with Vanmeer, Greg was nevertheless worried that it had taken place before Isabel had the DNA report. Had the border issue been raised, the CAO would never have believed her story without any evidence.

'Isabel was convinced she was being followed,' Kathy continued. 'I didn't believe her at first, but then on Monday evening, she pointed out a man on the Great West Road.'

'Who did she think he was?'

'One of Philippe's thugs, she was really worried about him. She thought he might be trying to silence her, you know, because he knew she doubted the official report, might talk.'

'Silence her?'

'Kill her, she seemed to imply.'

'Good God, poor girl.'

They sat on in silence, Kathy's penetrating look making him increasingly uncomfortable.

'You don't think she's going to turn up, do you?'

'Give me a minute,' she said, rising to go. 'This is so unlike her.'

Ten minutes later, Kathy returned.

'Still no sign of her,' she said as she slumped into her chair. 'Her phone's dead. I'm really worried about her now.'

He was desperate to act, to do anything to find Isabel. He was fearful for her safety, suspecting something very unpleasant had befallen her. His head was awash with swirling emotions; he hadn't a clue where to start. Suddenly he had an idea.

'Did you see any holiday postcards in her room when she got back from leave?'

'Postcards?'

He could see that he'd lost her.

'There's one you might have noticed, an arty one of a famous painting.'

'No,' she replied, clearly exasperated. 'Is it relevant?'

'To Vanmeer, yes it would be.'

'Vanmeer,' she exclaimed. 'If I wasn't so worried about her, I'd just think you two were playing some bloody silly spy game,' she added, laughing bitterly.

He frowned.

'I'm sorry, Greg. I'm a simple woman. It's all too cryptic for mc,' she said, contritely.

'Don't apologise,' he said quietly, 'this is bloody complex, potentially dangerous.' He paused. 'There's a couple of things we could do. Can you help?'

'Of course.'

'We'll alert Internal Security immediately, tell them Isabel's missing and probably in danger. Then I need to find that postcard. Can you get into her room?'

'Yes, we each hold a key for the other in case of emergencies.'

'This is an emergency,' he said, getting to his feet.

They had no problem finding the postcard. However, it took them longer to convince the military police of her disappearance. By the time Greg got back to his hotel room, he was light-headed with exhaustion. Sleep evaded him as he worked through the endless possibilities of what may have happened to Isabel.

Something else struck him forcibly. It wasn't just that he was worried for a colleague's safety. He realised that he was under her spell and if he wasn't careful, might fall in love again. With that bittersweet thought, he spiralled into a deep sleep.

*

The following morning, he arrived for his meeting a few minutes after seven-thirty at the Department of Health, located in the Central Administration District, home to all government departments. The foyer was busy with self-important officials dashing in and out. In Tripoli, unlike other towns in the mandate, government offices were open seven days a week and did not adhere to a Middle-Eastern working week. He was late.

On the way, he had called into Isabel's office, which was on the same street, in the unlikely event that she would be at her desk. Security, having established his credentials, confirmed that she hadn't been in since Wednesday. Worryingly, nobody seemed too concerned, despite he and Kathy alerting the military police hours ago.

For now, he needed to focus on the morning's meeting. He was due to brief the chief medical officer on the changing nature of the hospital caseload in Sabha. He hoped his report would feed into the overall narrative of government's evolving role in this important desert crossroad town. Maybe, he hoped, somebody high up in the administration would recognise that security was no longer the priority down south, that health and social issues were more important.

A soberly dressed middle-aged European woman accosted him in the foyer, just as he was about to enter the lift.

'Dr Greg Hamilton?'

'Yes,' he replied, somewhat distractedly.

'I've been sent to ask you to attend a meeting at Admin HQ,' she said, brusquely.

'I'm sorry, I'm afraid it'll have to wait,' he said, turning to enter the lift.

The woman took his elbow and pulled him purposely to one side. The lift door closed.

'Damn it,' he snapped, trying to free himself, 'I'm late already. My meeting with the CMO was set up weeks ago. He's a busy man and can't be kept waiting.'

'The CAO is busier. I'm sure your boss would appreciate that.'

He shook himself free and looked at her closely. *The CAO, no less, how bloody bizarre*, he thought. He and Kathy had only been talking about him last night. He prayed that this was no coincidence; that perhaps Vanmeer was also concerned about Isabel's disappearance.

But he needed more proof before he'd agree to this irritating woman's demands.

'Who are you?'

'Assistant to the CAO's PPS.' He could see that her patience was wearing thin. 'We have to be there at eight sharp.'

'I'm not moving until you can prove to me who you are and more importantly, inform the CMO of the change in plans,' he said defiantly, unimpressed with her jargon.

She turned her back to him and briefly mumbled into her phone, which she then handed to him.

'Hi,' he said, neutrally.

'Greg, this is Ian Hamond, the CAO's PPS.'

'Hello,' he said, still waiting to be convinced.

'We got your message about Isabel during the night. We understand that you'd planned to meet her yesterday evening at your hotel.'

Poor Kathy, they must have questioned her before dawn and then waited for him to arrive for work at the ministry. Anyway, he reflected, at least they were on Isabel's case.

'What do you want?'

'The CAO wants to meet you in twenty minutes. Jan will bring you straight here. We've already spoken to the CMO. He's now expecting you at ten. See you shortly,' and with that the line went dead.

Pompous bastard, thought Greg, reminding him yet again how he despised these desk-bound officials.

'It appears I'm in your hands,' he said to the woman, returning her phone.

Her smugness was ill-concealed. A chauffeur-driven limo took them all of 300 metres down the street to the imposing Admin HQ building, all glittering glass and steel, a symbol of the wasteful mentality of those who occupied its inner sanctums. He was whisked into the CAO's private lift and in less than a minute was standing in his office. Vanmeer, back to the room, was gazing absently out to sea.

Greg remained silent. Reluctantly, so it appeared, Vanmeer turned, indicating that he should take a seat at the table near the panoramic window.

'Coffee, tea?'

Clearly, there was no need for introductions.

'Coffee.'

Hamond entered on cue; he must have been listening.

'After your call last night, we immediately checked up on Isabel,' Vanmeer said, getting straight to the point. 'She'd been working late on Wednesday evening, left her office about eleven. We've no idea of her whereabouts after that.' He paused. 'Did you speak to her earlier in the week?'

'No, I've been overseas and didn't get into town until very early yesterday morning. I sent her a text before I turned in, must have been about two. I thought it was too late to call her.'

'About the time she left work, a vehicle was blown up on Great West Road, very near her office.'

'Good God, I didn't hear about that. Do you think she was caught up in it?' he asked, his anxiety rising, thinking of all the possible calamities that might have befallen her.

'We don't know, although there was no sign of her when the area was cordoned off afterwards. We've CCTV footage of her crossing the road to the bus stop, seconds before all the cameras in the area went down, a minute or so before the explosion.'

'Do you think they're linked, you know, the explosion and the CCTV system going down?'

'The security guys are working on this, we might learn more later today.' Vanmeer paused. 'Have you any idea why she might have disappeared?'

'Not really, though she was convinced that she was being followed.'

'Followed? How do you know?'

'She'd discussed it with her friend Kathy, a neighbour on Great West Road,' he said, deciding that he'd share as much information as he could, given that Vanmeer was the person ultimately responsible for Isabel's safety.

'Who did she think was following her?'

'Somebody from the Desert Patrol Group.'

'For what reason?'

'Because of what happened at the border near Ramlit al Wigh several weeks ago.'

'I don't see the connection.'

'She has evidence which might be at odds with the official version of what happened there.'

'She discussed this with you?'

'Yes,' Greg replied. 'In her view, the murders were not the work of a terrorist group. The DPG commander is aware of her different viewpoint, which she thinks he might find threatening.'

'Threatening, that's interesting,' he said, with barely concealed scepticism. 'Does he know of the evidence she claims to have?'

'No.'

'You're sure?'

'Yes.'

Greg thought about Isabel's meeting with Vanmeer and realised how terrifying the whole experience must have been.

'And you've seen her evidence?'

'Yes, the lab report.'

He sensed that Vanmeer was in a hurry, believing that he'd already formed his own ideas and just needed them corroborated.

'We're talking about Philippe.'

'Yes.'

'It's important,' he said evenly, 'that we are absolutely frank with each other if we are to see Isabel again.'

'Yes,' said Greg, wondering if the man was capable of frankness, not the hallmark of a successful politician or diplomat. Still he had no option but to give him the benefit of the doubt. 'Agreed.'

'You can set it up now,' Vanmeer said, as he poured the coffee.

Instantly the light dimmed; the large glass windows darkened, turning opaque and snuffing out the brilliant Mediterranean sky. He found himself looking across Vanmeer's office at a large wallscreen. To his astonishment, he saw Isabel sitting in the same chair that he was in, quite still, as if in a portrait painting.

'I gather Isabel sustained minor injuries at the border. You subsequently visited her in hospital in Sabha.'

'Yes, she was briefly my patient,' mumbled Greg, not taking his eyes off the screen.

'Was that the last time you saw her?'

'No, we met recently in France while on leave.'

'Did she talk about the incident, what she thought happened?'

Before he could answer, Vanmeer continued.

'Perhaps it's better if you hear what she had to tell me last week. As you'll see, it wasn't an easy meeting for either of us,' said Vanmeer. 'OK, Hamond.'

For the next fifteen minutes, Greg sat spellbound watching and listening to Isabel and Vanmeer during their meeting. He was shocked as their early good-natured conversation descended into acrimony. At the close, he felt intensely proud of Isabel. She'd dealt with Vanmeer fearlessly and with great maturity; she was some woman, he reflected.

Like dawn arriving, blinding light from a seamless blue sky poured into the darkened room, bringing them back to the present.

'Does this mean anything to you?' asked Vanmeer quietly, as Hamond slipped deferentially from the room.

'Yes,' said Greg as he reached inside his jacket and withdrew the postcard, placing it squarely between them on the table. Vanmeer picked it up, pondered the Frans Hals painting and then read the back.

'What's the relevance of this?' he asked, bluntly.

'Her evidence.' He realised from seeing the video that Vanmeer was a literal man, not used to conundrums, so quickly added, 'Without wishing to prejudice ourselves and those who helped us, all I can tell you is that the data she wanted to give you is encrypted on the postage stamp.'

'Bullshit,' snapped Vanmeer. 'Don't you give me crap as well.'

'What I am telling you is true,' he said quietly. 'You'll have the data but I need twenty-four hours. You've got to trust me,' he said, trying not to sound as if he were pleading. 'You have to believe Isabel's story.'

'Why should I trust her or you for that matter?'

God, this man's difficult, he thought. Emboldened by Isabel's performance, he decided to raise the stakes to get through to him.

'Isabel had recently wondered why she'd been attached to the DPG rather than a civilian group when she was in the Fezzan. Her work would have been far more productive.'

'That was my idea,' admitted Vanmeer, tersely.

'I see that now.' Greg hesitated, wondering how far he should push. 'It was while we were in France that I convinced myself she'd been planted in the military to gather information, essentially to spy on them.'

'Go on.'

'Although she'd never been officially briefed, I had a gut feeling that somebody had sent her on a fishing trip, hoping perhaps to uncover something about the military.'

'And you still hold to this idea of yours?'

'Absolutely,' he replied, his heart pounding. 'I nicknamed the person who sent her "The Angler".'

'How appropriate,' Vanmeer laughed, grimly.

He sat back in his seat gazing absently at Greg, as if lost in thought. They sat in silence for several minutes, during which time Greg became increasingly uncomfortable.

'As "The Angler",' Vanmeer said, eventually, 'I'm ashamed to think what I've put the poor girl through. My behaviour here has been pretty damnable.' Greg was surprised at his sudden candour. 'The plan was so bloody amateurish. What a cock-up.' He paused.

'I appreciate your directness. Both of you have acted with great courage. I have nothing to show except my ineptitude.'

Hearing Vanmeer's admission was a huge relief.

'We're still no nearer to finding her,' Greg said, wanting to make the most of this brief opportunity. 'Is there anything I can do?'

'Get a copy of the analysis to me as soon as you can,' Vanmeer replied, suddenly all business-like. 'Go about your business with the CMO as if nothing is amiss. I'll arrange with him to have your stay in Tripoli extended by two days. And on no account go to the club or contact Isabel's friend Kathy. My PPS will give you a direct contact number when you leave here. Keep your phone with you at all times.'

Seeing the meeting was at an end, Greg got up to go.

'I just pray that we get her back unharmed,' Vanmeer added, before turning back to the view.

*

At nine the following evening, Greg called Vanmeer's direct number.

'Vanmeer.'

'It's Greg, I have the report you've been waiting for.'

'I'd be grateful if you'd bring it over immediately.'

Greg's contact had produced the document, which he'd received just before seven. Over dinner in the hotel, he reread and familiarised himself with the lab report and its conclusions. He also reread notes of his own investigation, which he had relayed to Isabel before they'd left Calais, which summarised Philippe's regular border patrols – dates, times, vehicle movements, border stop locations and personnel involved.

'I'll come straight over.'

'Don't leave the hotel. I'll send my driver. He'll meet you in the foyer in fifteen minutes.'

Half an hour later, Greg was sitting at the table beside the enormous plate glass window in Vanmeer's office. Early moonlight shimmered on the flat black sea, cutting a silvery path across the harbour. Several large container ships, lit up in their finery, rode at anchor. Three naval frigates, tightly docked within the seawalls, stood out from a flotilla of fishing vessels and rusty coasters. The scene, in the darkness, exuded order.

'Drink?' Vanmeer asked. 'Wine, whisky, a beer perhaps?'

'A beer would be great.'

Hamond miraculously appeared with a cold beer, an ice-filled cut-glass tumbler and a bottle of twenty-year-old malt.

'So, what have you got?'

Greg handed him an envelope containing the report. Absently pouring himself a generous measure of whisky, the CAO sat back and read it. The silence induced in Greg a sense of inner calm. He had done all he possibly could for Isabel; it was now up to Vanmeer to take responsibility for finding her, ensuring her safe return. Finally, Vanmeer placed the report on the table.

'It all tallies with her theory. Is there anything else you can add before we consider the next step?'

'I made a few enquiries of my own before I went on leave. The findings are summarised here,' replied Greg, pushing his notebook across the table.

Vanmeer quickly flicked through the pages, paying little attention to the details.

'You're very thorough,' he said, pausing. 'I've had my suspicions about Philippe and his squad for well over a year. I've had nothing concrete to work on until now.'

'Isabel's involvement has clearly paid off,' said Greg, immediately regretting opening his mouth.

'Cut it, we've been over this,' Vanmeer snapped. 'You know how I feel.'

'I'm sorry.'

Vanmeer refilled his glass.

'Another beer?' he asked, his brief anger spent.

Wordlessly, Hamond entered with a bottle.

'I've been looking at a lot of data recently, have seen some disturbing trends,' continued Vanmeer.

'Trends?'

'Yes, and there are many. I've read your recent reports on the changing nature of medical services in Sabha.'

'The ones I sent to the CMO?' asked Greg, incredulously. 'I thought they were routinely binned.'

'Not at all, they make interesting reading, the emphasis shifting from a field hospital environment treating war wounds to First World medicine, drugs and depression. But it's the rapid increase in drug-related illnesses that caught my attention.'

'They've completely distorted our caseload, there's so many.'

'I believe we have a cocaine epidemic in the Fezzan. Mostly officers, a couple of influential civilians, seem to be the most addicted. I think the military must have regular suppliers. They have the need and wherewithal.'

'Wherewithal I understand, but need?' asked Greg, attuning himself quickly to the other man's thinking.

'Bored, well-paid single men used to the excitement of battle, often acting with great autonomy. When the enemy's defeated, what do they turn to? Principally illegal money-making, sex and drugs. All possible in Sabha as I understand.'

'It's been getting worse for some time.'

'Which I'm aware of now,' he said, pausing. 'For me, though, the area's been off-limits, has been since I got here. Despite holding the most senior civilian post in the mandate,' he admitted, candidly, 'I've been prevented from imposing overall control in the Fezzan. I'm constantly being told that we're still in a state of war there, the frontline in our efforts to wipe out the terrorists.'

'With respect, that's rubbish.'

'As I've suspected for some time. Hence my need to get close to the military in the only way I could think of,' he hesitated, 'which, despite what has happened to poor Isabel, has yielded results.'

'Yes,' said Greg lamely, wrenching his thoughts back to the present, wondering where in God's name she was.

'Your notes,' Vanmeer said, changing the subject, 'I've the same data, probably acquired from the same source.'

As I suspected, Greg thought, having been advised by his friend that somebody in Tripoli had requested the same information.

'Really?' he said, feigning surprise.

'The thing I found strange was the fact they always returned via the solar energy plant at Brak, in northern Fezzan,' continued Vanmeer. 'Construction started there forty months ago, phase one came on stream last spring. I think the stopover's significant.'

'I'm afraid you've lost me.'

'The project is under the management of the Desert Construction Unit, ultimately the responsibility of the local military commander. Their remit covers all support services, including logistics and the importation of plant and equipment. Specialised containers bring the stuff in and are then returned empty to manufacturing plants across Europe, to be used again for the next batch of incoming equipment.'

He paused, letting his message sink in. *Good God*, thought Greg, seeing the extent of the problem.

'I think Philippe receives the consignments from his Russian counterparts at the border, which are then secretly containerised in Brak. The set-up provides them with a secure route to export significant quantities into the very heart of Europe,' continued Vanmeer, 'right under the noses of every law enforcement agency between here and the back streets of Berlin.'

'We learnt from Isabel,' Greg said, 'that it's probably the Russians who know how to override the joint border security protocols.'

'Exactly, it's in their interest. As a result they've got the market tied up.'

'If we had military-grade satellite imagery,' Greg continued, clutching at straws, 'we could check boot prints, tire markings and the like at the border with those of DPG.'

'They'll never release this imagery,' said Vanmeer. 'I tried using commercial imagery but it's not sufficiently accurate.'

'Is the military governor implicated?'

'No, I'm sure he isn't. The man running the show is the Fezzan regional military commander. He's the one responsible for driving out the desert terrorists over the last few years. A war hero, along with his frontline troops.'

'Including Philippe's squad.'

'They're untouchable,' said Vanmeer. 'We still have a significant problem though: despite all the evidence we've gathered, it's still circumstantial. I'm sure it wouldn't be enough to get the military governor involved.'

'I agree,' said Greg, 'but short of opening a container en route to the port, which would be very difficult to arrange for obvious reasons, we've nothing concrete.'

'I know it's a long shot, but if we could get corroborating evidence from the Russian side on the border transactions, we'd be in a much better position to move.'

'But we know nothing of their Russian suppliers.'

'Nothing,' said Vanmeer, 'except what Isabel has intimated. She's the only one who could unlock this puzzle.'

Greg shuddered involuntarily, realising what expectations she was raising, what a burden she was carrying. If only they knew where she was, that she was safe; that's all he asked.

27

Cyrenaica, Late November 2031

sabel regained consciousness. She found herself lying on a mattress in the centre of a small featureless room, staring up at a concrete ceiling. She sat up; the room was empty. Low sunlight poured through a high open window, striking the wall behind her. She felt no pain, just lethargic, as if she'd been drugged. The acrid body smell she quickly discovered was her own.

A rough wooden door set in one corner beckoned her. Pushing it open, she stumbled into an enclosed courtyard. From the shadows, a man dressed in military desert fatigues rose from a squatting position, startling her.

'*Come*,' he grunted, indicating a metal door set in the high courtyard wall.

She followed him, trudging zombie-like down a series of narrow empty alleyways between abandoned and crumbling mud buildings. The trapped heat was stultifying. Despite the fact that they were alone, she had a weird sensation that she was being closely, silently watched. It was unsettling. After several minutes the man, without warning, ducked through a doorway into a darkened room. Her eyes took a second or two to adjust to her new surroundings.

Standing directly in front of her was a second man, also in fatigues, whom she instantly recognised. She was completely taken aback; it was the last person she'd expected to meet.

'Ramil,' she exclaimed, temporarily swooning and slipping towards the floor.

He caught her, holding her until she found her footing. Nothing made sense in her addled mind, briefly imagining that Philippe and Ramil might be working together, partners in an illegal drugs business.

'So we meet again,' she managed to say.

'Indeed we do, Isabel.'

It was the voice she remembered – earnest, engaging. His lean, handsome features portrayed no anger, no hostility. It was as if he were conducting one of their regular co-ordination meetings at the border, normality itself. Except of course Philippe, who she expected to see at any moment, was not hovering in the background. The whole episode was surreal, unforeseen.

'You've had a rough few days,' he continued. 'I'm sorry…'

'Few days?'

'Yes, three to be exact. How do you feel?'

She sensed his concern.

'Three days, three whole days,' she mumbled, not believing what he'd said. 'Can I sit?'

'I'm sorry, yes of course,' he replied, indicating a battered table and several metal chairs to his right. 'Would you like tea?'

She nodded vaguely, so many troubling questions racing through her head.

'Where the hell's Philippe then?' she blurted out, desperate to understand her current predicament.

'How should I know?' he answered curtly; not the answer she was expecting. From the sound of his voice and the expression on his face, it dawned on her that he and Philippe were unlikely to be partners.

'Where in God's name are we?'

'It's not important,' he said, evasively.

'It is to me,' she retorted.

He hesitated.

'Let's just say we're in Cyrenaica, south-east of Benghazi…'

'The Russian mandate. We crossed the border and survived, weren't blown to shreds,' she exclaimed, astonished at her own admission. 'How the hell did that happen?'

'Later, Isabel, later.'

'I don't understand.'

'Don't worry, you're safe with us,' he said, trying to calm her.

'Why did you bring me here?'

'You'll find out shortly,' he replied ominously, before quickly adding, 'but please relax, nobody's going to harm you.'

She wasn't sure whether to laugh or cry; whether she was relieved or frightened. She rested her forehead on the cool metal table, dulled senses grappling with her situation. A mug of tea was unceremoniously set down at her side. As if reading her thoughts, Ramil continued.

'This is difficult for you, I understand. All I suggest for now is that you trust your instincts. They've served you well so far.'

'Trust my instincts,' she repeated uncertainly.

'Since we last met you've had a terrifying experience at the border. You would have assumed that it was going to be just one of our regular meetings.'

'I did.'

'And contrary to Philippe's judgement and the scepticism of others around you,' he spoke so quietly, she had difficulty hearing him, 'I suspect you've a very different opinion of what happened there.'

God in heaven, she thought, *what doesn't he know?*

'Yes,' she agreed warily, her forehead still on the table.

'I don't believe you really trusted Philippe,' he hesitated, 'especially after you slept…'

'Shut it,' she shouted, her anger instantly igniting. She sat up abruptly, knocking over the mug which shattered on the floor. Ignoring the damage, she stared at him directly.

'I'm sorry. That wasn't called for.' His apology sounded sincere. 'The fact is, after your driver discovered the bodies, I believe you had a hunch.' He waved to a shadowy figure who came forward to recover the smashed mug. 'Acting on instinct, you retrieved something, evidence maybe that might have helped you understand what you were looking at. My guess is you weren't sure.'

She remained silent, at a loss for words.

'You had to get it analysed,' he continued. 'It had to be done unofficially. That took guts, Isabel,' he said, admiration evident in his voice.

'How the hell can you say all this?' she snapped.

'I only know so much. I know you had help from Greg Hamilton, a doctor in Sabha. I know you gave him the bag of thumbs. I suspect he had it analysed overseas.'

'You're just guessing,' she said in exasperation. 'How could you possibly know I took anything from that slaughter pit?'

'I saw the bag was missing. It could only have been you or Philippe who took it. I suspected it was you.'

Her mind drifted back to that terrifying morning at the border. She could hear the explosion and see the column of sand and stones rising high overhead, Omar's inert body dropping, she and Philippe lying together, bloodied and bruised, all sequenced in silent slow motion. And from this recollection, a new and frightening truth emerged. Hidden from view, Ramil, very probably the author of this carnage, had been watching intently.

'You were there the whole time,' she said quietly, trying to control her fear. In an instant, she heard herself accusing him. 'You murdered those men.'

He remained silent, absolutely still, his eyes flickering for the briefest of moments.

'You laid the mine that killed Omar. Why, for God's sake? You could have killed us all.'

His silence was proof enough. A strange relief soothed her overstretched nerves. He was right; her instincts had served her well. For some time now, she'd suspected he might have been involved in the men's slaughter.

'I took a risk,' he answered, evenly. 'I guessed Philippe would take control having seen the bodies, ensuring you wouldn't move beyond where you were, where you'd walked.'

'And Greg and the analysis?' she said, frustration claiming her tired voice. 'Where's your proof for all this?'

'I know you two met in the hospital, that you visited him in the tennis club the evening before you left Sabha. I also know he had the bag in his room after you flew back to Tripoli. It wasn't there when he went on his leave.' He paused. 'I could only conclude that he took it with him.'

'You, one of you searched his goddamn room?' she said, shocked.

He leaned across the table and held her arms. She struggled briefly before slumping back. He went on, as if describing a normal everyday event.

'We've a few people, spies you might call them, in Sabha, in Tripoli, just to keep us informed of what your government is up to, what it's planning next.' He looked at her closely, smiling grimly. 'It took careful observation and a little intuition on our side. We got all the proof we needed.'

She pulled away roughly from him.

'Why did you murder those men?' Her anger was muted from exhaustion.

'You have the evidence,' he replied, calmly. 'You tell me.'

A sense of fatalism swept over her; she had no choice but to tell it as she saw. She hesitated, forcing herself to concentrate, retelling her story in all its detail. Unlike the previous occasions when she'd spoken tentatively, speculatively to her listeners, this time she knew she was talking to the author of that story, that the facts were correct.

'Well done, Isabel,' he said, after she'd finished. 'I realised shortly after we met that you were a smart, observant woman who…'

'Don't patronise me,' she snapped.

Ignoring her, he continued, '… who could help us expose the link between our two military organisations.'

'The link, what link?'

'You still don't get it,' he said gently, 'despite all your evidence.'

Indeed I do 'get it', she thought. At last they were getting somewhere; she sensed he was about to divulge the cross-border drugs trade.

'Philippe and his Desert Patrol Group have been willing drug traders with our people for years. We source the drugs, your people provide the markets. It's extremely lucrative for both parties.' He paused, before adding, 'Highly illegal, corrupting and morally indefensible.'

In the heat and fear of the moment, it gave her little comfort to realise that what Greg had suggested to her in Calais about Ramil was correct. Ramil's straightforward confirmation of what they'd discussed still came as a shock. What Ramil had done was not now the issue; the issue was why.

'Of course, the trade is only possible because our two military groups control their own areas either side of the border. This makes it difficult, almost impossible in fact, for anybody else on either side to scrutinise what the two groups are up to, over a great swathe of the desert.'

'But crossing the border illegally is deadly.'

'Not if you're capable of overriding the security protocols undetected,' he said quietly, 'and deactivating the system.'

'And Philippe, can he…'

'No,' he interrupted, 'only our people have learned how to do that, which they need to when delivering the drugs to him, his people.'

'So Philippe's known all along that your people can cross the border any time they like, a border he's supposed to be protecting,' she said, barely believing what she was saying.

'Yes.'

'And the night of the sandstorm, the day we were going to have our meeting, it was you, wasn't it?'

'Me?'

'You who walked across the border, around our truck,' she said, recalling her fear when Omar first pointed out the mysterious footprints in the sand.

'I just had to be sure it was you and Philippe.'

'But why kill your own men? Why not simply report your concerns to your boss, let him deal with them?'

'They're not, never were "my men", never,' he said angrily, spitting on the floor as if to emphasise his disgust. She could see that her relentless questioning was having an effect, his outburst unnerving.

'But why did Omar, an innocent man, have to die?'

'His death was unavoidable, collateral damage I think they call it. This I regret.' His words were detached, unemotional.

'Unavoidable, regret, collateral damage – don't hide behind bloody words, Ramil. Just tell me why,' she demanded.

'We had to mine the area. For obvious reasons I didn't want anybody approaching our trucks.'

So that's where he was hiding. By the grace of God, she and Philippe had only just survived becoming collateral damage themselves.

'Who the hell are you, Ramil?' she shouted, unable to contain her frustration.

He appeared startled at her directness, sitting back, as if unsure what to do next. Eventually he turned to his shadowy companion, mumbling incomprehensibly. *What now?* she thought, her barely suppressed panic on the rise again. The shadow stepped forward with another mug of tea. She drank the hot sweetened liquid in silence, regaining her composure.

'What would have happened if I hadn't taken the bag?' she asked at last.

'I had other plans,' he said, dismissively.

'Involving me?'

'It's irrelevant now. You took the bag, the rest we know.'

'But nothing's changed. I haven't shared the analysis with our people. Apart from Greg, nobody else knows. No action will be taken against Philippe.'

'Everything's changed,' he said, getting to his feet. 'Come, please come, Isabel.'

*

Before they left the darkened room, Ramil insisted that she cover herself in a coarse black abaya, which, together with a hijab, covered her body from head to toe. She felt suffocated in the unfamiliar garb, cut off from her surroundings, only her eyes and bare feet visible to passers-by. She stuck close to him as he led her through narrow alleyways before entering a thronged thoroughfare of dazzling colours and exotic smells.

She was briefly reminded of the souk and surrounding streets in the centre of old Sabha, the evening she first met Greg at the tennis club. *'Be careful what you wish for.'* She smiled bitterly to herself; this wasn't what she'd dreamt of while waiting in the stationary taxi.

After a few minutes, they entered a whitewashed courtyard through a heavy metal door off one of the quieter streets. Trellised bougainvillea in glorious reds and yellows shaded the entrance to a simple villa of perhaps half a dozen rooms. Nothing stirred; it appeared the place was empty.

From the way in which Ramil showed her around, it occurred to her that this quiet haven, breathless in the morning air, was to be her new home. A few things caught her attention. The place was spotlessly clean, simply furnished and had modern plumbing, air-conditioning and a well-equipped galley kitchen. What she really noticed, though, was the main living room, which was stuffed with books, on shelves, tables, on the floor, books on philosophy, politics and economics, on the environment and the arts in English, French, Russian, Greek and Arabic. *Who could possibly own this place?* she asked herself.

He explained that his servant Abdul, the 'shadow' who had followed them from the meeting place, would come three times a day with her meals, all precooked. He advised her to keep the outer metal door locked and on no account leave the place, for her own safety. With that he left, saying he would return in a few days. *'Three times a day', but for how many days?* she wondered with alarm.

She locked the heavy metal gate and went to explore the villa. Locking herself in, rather than being locked in, initially conferred on her a sense of independence. Like so much recently, this proved to be an illusion; even if she were to walk out, where in heaven's name would she go? Better to stay put and enjoy peace and comparative freedom, she reasoned.

She was pleasantly surprised to find a wardrobe full of freshly laundered clothes, in both Arab and European styles. Discarding her own filthy clothes, she took a long cool shower before sprawling naked on a vast unforgiving mattress and falling into a deep sleep.

For the next few days she found herself living in a surprisingly agreeable, although highly restricted environment. There was no apparent reason why she was being held, essentially as Ramil's prisoner. A numbing fatalism invaded her, as she learned to live for the moment, resigning herself with equanimity.

She soon developed a simple daily routine to keep her mind and body active. Awakened by the call to prayers before dawn, she devoted the early morning to exercises before showering and choosing fresh clothes from the wardrobe. As regular as the muezzin's earlier call to prayers, Abdul would arrive an hour after sunrise with her breakfast: dates, olives, cheese, yogurt, coarse bread and an aluminium jug of fresh goat's milk.

During the morning, she delved into the many books in her living room or studied an English-Arabic primer, hoping to improve her basic understanding of the language. Later she would sit on the roof terrace and absorb the sights and sounds of the town as it came alive in the coolness of the evening.

At any time of day or night, her thoughts would abruptly return to Greg, a man, she admitted to herself, she had fallen hopelessly in love with. She greatly missed his calming influence, memories of his wry sense of humour lifting her spirits from her depressing and threatening circumstances. *God, I wish he was here*, she thought, as tears flowed into her sodden pillow in the small hours of the night.

Although time passed uneventfully, she was never bored. Occasionally, though, panic would set in; who in Tripoli could possible know where she was? Had Greg alerted the authorities when she hadn't turned up at his hotel or at work the following day? What would happen if they couldn't trace her, forgot about her and gave up? Would she forever be hostage to Ramil and an Arab way of life? Then the heat would muzzle her overanxious brain or Abdul would arrive with food and her panic attack would subside.

On her fourth afternoon, Isabel had her first visitor. She unlocked the metal door to a tall woman dressed in a black abaya.

'So you're Isabel,' she said in a barely traceable East European accent. 'I'm Anna, Ramil's partner.'

She pulled the abaya over her head and threw it to one side. Isabel saw before her a tall big-boned bottle-blond woman, probably in her late forties, dressed in a thin white cotton dress. Dark rings encircled clear blue eyes set above high cheekbones, contrasting with her pale complexion. Perhaps Russian, maybe from one of the central Asian oblasts, Isabel guessed. Her initial thought was that the woman was ill.

'Isabel Meredith,' she said, visibly taken aback. Ramil had never mentioned his family, let alone a partner.

'Don't be embarrassed,' Anna said cheerfully, seeing Isabel's reaction. 'Men never talk about their women in these parts. It's considered unseemly. We're still men's chattels, no matter what others here want the outside world to believe.'

'Would you care for a drink, tea perhaps?' she asked, as Anna swept into the villa with a proprietary air.

'Please, iced tea.'

Minutes later, the two women settled outside in the shade of the trellis drinking tea.

'So how do you find our old home?' Anna asked, catching Isabel completely off guard.

'Heavens above, I didn't know this was your place,' she exclaimed, realising that she was probably wearing Anna's clothes; hence larger sizes than she would normally wear. 'And the wardrobe…'

'My old cast-offs, don't worry. A little on the big size, I see,' she laughed.

Anna went on to tell her how she and Ramil had met at university in St Petersburg where she had been studying commerce and Arabic. They had been together for over twenty years but had never married, he being Muslim, she Orthodox.

'It's never been a problem, although it is for my parents,' she admitted, 'they've spent all their lives in Omsk, an industrial city to the east of the Urals. North Africa is as remote to them as the moon,' she added with a grin. She talked of her life with Ramil in Benghazi and to the south of the Jebel Akhdar, where they'd lived for the last five years, a place which enabled him to lead his double life.

'Double life?' Isabel asked, alarmed.

'Well, yes,' Anna said, hesitating. 'I thought Ramil might have…'

'Ramil's told me nothing,' interrupted Isabel, her recent composure unravelling. 'I've no idea where I am, why I'm here.'

'Men, they're all the bloody same,' Anna laughed, as if he'd forgotten some trifling chore. 'No doubt, he'll reveal all to you shortly,' she said, before abruptly changing the subject. 'I see you're reading an Arabic primer, a thirty-year-old edition. I've brought you a much later one, which you'll find easier,' she continued, pulling a large volume from her linen shoulder bag. 'I'd be happy to spend a little time each day helping you master the language.'

'That would be great,' said Isabel, trying desperately to suppress her rising anxiety. 'My ability is pretty basic. I'd really benefit from talking to somebody equally competent in Arabic and English.'

However, it was company she craved, not a language teacher. They sat on talking of this and that for the next hour. She suspected that Anna was holding back, unwilling to divulge anything that might compromise Ramil and his plans for her.

'I must go,' Anna said, without warning, glancing at her watch. She rose promptly, pulled on her abaya and strode to the metal door. Just before she left, she turned to Isabel.

'Things might get difficult for you here but have faith in Ramil and his people. They mean well and will look after you as best they can,' and with that she was gone. Her parting shot, 'as best they can', left Isabel feeling slightly nauseous.

*

Late the following evening, Isabel was surprised to hear loud knocking on the outer door. At first she ignored it, but the knocking persisted.

'Who's there?' she called, nervously.

'It's Ramil.'

She recognised his voice and, pulling back the bolts, opened the door.

He ushered three men ahead of him into the courtyard, all of whom bowed slightly, acknowledging her.

'My apologies, Isabel, for disturbing you so late in the day,' he said, shaking her hand firmly. 'I would like you to meet my friends. They've heard so much about you.'

'You're welcome,' she said, her fear subsiding. 'Please come in.'

She quickly realised that this was no casual visit; that she would have to offer them refreshments. Once seated over tea in the main room, Ramil introduced the three. Anwar, perhaps in his early seventies and wearing a spotless white thobe, was a respected tribal leader from Benghazi; Daud, dressed in a white collarless shirt and grey trousers, was a well-known economist living in Tolmeta and the youngest of the three. Both spoke excellent English.

It was the third man, Fawzan, a tall bearded man perhaps in his mid-forties and dressed in a djellaba, that caught Isabel's attention. Ramil introduced him as head of their planning committee, whatever that was, she wondered. He had a noticeable scar running under his right eye; she guessed he'd recently been in the wars. He spoke softly but only in Arabic; she suspected he understood English, even if he couldn't speak it. Although her Arabic was still poor, she knew when he was talking about her, constantly referring to her as 'Isabella', despite being corrected several times by Ramil, who eventually gave up.

Ramil explained that they were interested to hear about her life in Tripoli and what her job entailed. She felt comfortable telling them what she did, as much of it involved working with Ramil, which she presumed they knew about. As the evening wore on and over many cups of tea, the conversation gradually shifted to other matters to do with how EDA administered the mandate. Initially she was reluctant to delve too much into the day-to-day workings of government.

'Isabel,' said Ramil, after she'd shied away from describing the importance of solar energy to the mandate's economy, 'you're amongst friends here. Don't be afraid to tell them everything you know,' and then as an after-thought, added, 'these men have more reasons to hate the Russians than you do.'

Isabel was completely thrown off balance. She wondered who they represented – perhaps some form of opposition, maybe a government-in-waiting. Sensing she had no choice but to trust Ramil and realising she had little to lose, she opened up to them.

They were unfailingly courteous, their curiosity never-ending, switching constantly between English and Arabic, presumably for Fawzan's benefit.

They left just after midnight, leaving Isabel exhausted but oddly exhilarated, as if she'd been talking to kindred spirits. Over the next three evenings, the four returned with ever more detailed questions. Frequently Fawzan, to whom the others always deferred, would ask a question through Daud or Ramil on how she would approach such and such a problem. Their questions were endless and wide-ranging, whether it was on Bedouin healthcare issues, managing coastal migrant camps or related to government functions in Tripoli.

She found Fawzan unsettling, inscrutable. Although polite, quietly spoken and somewhat professorial, there was a darkness about him; a threatening, dangerous, psychopathic otherness lurking just below the surface. Whatever he had to say, it was invariably directed at her, as if the others weren't in the room. Given that she had little idea what he was talking about, she found his attention disconcerting. Sometimes remote, sometimes familiar, she nevertheless was drawn to him. Surprisingly, she felt no fear in his presence.

During their time together, Isabel struggled to work out who they represented, what political philosophy they espoused and why they were so interested in EDA, down to the smallest and most banal detail. Throughout, she sensed no hostility or criticism towards her or the administration in Tripoli. They might have been academics, she mused, trying to understand the workings of a Western democracy.

Nobody had ever sought her opinion on such diverse subjects, many of which she was ill-equipped to answer. Even when she pleaded a lack of knowledge on a particular issue, they insisted on hearing her personal views. Being so enthusiastically valued made her feel good about herself, a feeling long-forgotten. How satisfying it would be, she thought, to work with these people, how much more rewarding than working for EDA, the very idea taking her completely by surprise.

Late on the final evening, although at the time she didn't know they wouldn't be coming back, Fawzan addressed her directly, which Ramil translated from time to time.

'*Our people are the dispossessed, those who have survived the carnage that was once Libya, people who have fled here from the tyranny of so many other places: from Ukraine, Crimea, from Aleppo and Damascus in Syria, from Beirut and Baghdad, from Palestine, from broken countries south of the Sahel, from Eritrea, Ethiopia and Sudan in East Africa. They desperately need to be woven into the fabric of a new society, a society without prejudice or fear, a society respecting the rights of every citizen. This is our challenge in Cyrenaica.*'

In the brief pause that followed, she wondered yet again who Fawzan represented, on whose authority he could speak with such certainty.

'*In the long-forgotten silence that will settle over our lands when the Russians have fled, our time will come. We'll rebuild our broken homes, hospitals and schools, repair shattered water wells, and replant date palms in villages of the oases and almond orchards and chammari forests in the Jebel Akhdar. We'll harness the energy of the sun and forge a new way of living drawing on the traditions that sustained our forefathers.*'

It was time to go. As she walked them through the courtyard, they were effusive in their thanks. At the gate, Fawzan turned to her once more.

'*But you, Isabella, you understand what has been said here,*' he said before adding enigmatically, '*and one day, God willing, you will play your part.*'

And with that, he bowed and led the others out onto the silent street.

She couldn't sleep that night as she struggled to make sense of Fawzan's parting words, which induced in her astonishment, terror and ironically, a deep-seated excitement.

The following evening, Isabel was surprised to open the door to Anna, who declined her invitation to come in for tea. Instead, she rummaged in her bag and withdrew an old manila folder held together with twine.

'Ramil asked me to give you these papers, which he wants you to read, homework I'm afraid,' she said, handing over the folder. 'He'll drop by later and go through the stuff.'

Isabel took the folder, went indoors, slumped down on the settee and opened it. It took several moments for her to appreciate what she was looking at: pencilled schedules, set out in columns of dates, locations, package details and names all neatly, almost childishly, handwritten in Arabic and English. It looked like a shipping manifest.

Gradually it dawned on her what these papers represented: a historical record of illegal cross-border drug shipments, the weight by drug type, the date and place of the transactions and critically the people involved, both suppliers and buyers. Philippe's name appeared in every single transaction, going back nearly two years.

28

Sabha, Mid-December 2031

It was late evening when Greg waved to his boisterous friends at the bar and stumbled uncertainly past the tennis courts to his waiting taxi outside the club. He had been back in Sabha for ten days following an extended stay in Tripoli, where he'd been frenetically shuttled back and forth between the Department of Health and Vanmeer's office.

The CMO was clearly intrigued as to why Greg had to attend so many unscheduled meetings in Admin HQ but was far too discrete to enquire about what was going on. He had known the young doctor since the latter's arrival in North Africa and greatly appreciated his demanding work. He was determined to make the most of their fractured time together.

Vanmeer and his Internal Security team had been unable to trace Isabel's movements from the moment she'd left work on the night she went missing. Despite their best efforts, nobody could link the CCTV's outage with the vehicle explosion on Great West Road, which together might have yielded clues of her disappearance. She had simply walked out onto the street and vanished.

Greg, driven to distraction and the seductive numbness of alcohol, had become increasingly anxious for Isabel's wellbeing. For some time now, he realised that he was completely smitten by her, something he hadn't experienced since he started going out with Ameena.

Isabel, twelve years his junior, an articulate, intelligent and good-looking woman, attracted him in many ways. For someone so young, she exuded the experience of somebody well beyond her age. She had about her a fearlessness that put curiosity and principles before security and self-interest. She had a feisty sense of humour and was constantly stimulating company, whether analysing potentially life-threatening situations or abandoning herself to reckless sex.

Vanmeer desperately needed to widen the search, which was proving almost impossible. Greg understood the quandary in which the CAO found himself; how could he seek the military's assistance to find Isabel when he suspected that they were responsible for her disappearance in the first place?

To buy more time, the two men had agreed that the official reason for her absence was that Isabel had had to return to England unexpectedly because of urgent family business. They also agreed not to inform her family back home until they had exhausted all lines of investigation. Greg had been instructed to tell Kathy, who needed no encouragement, to perpetuate this story.

Eventually, as a last resort, Vanmeer decided to inform the military governor, who the CAO believed was not implicated in any nefarious drug business. As it was, it took him some time to convince the governor, a German entirely focused on his impending retirement, of the seriousness of the problem. Greg realised that having convinced the governor, all Vanmeer had done was to shift the problem upstairs; the governor was in the same bind as the CAO.

*

The club car park was deserted except for Greg's driver, who was casually leaning against his old Toyota, partly hidden in the shadow of a sweeping acacia tree. A smiling, toothless Asif stubbed out his half-finished cigarette and opened the back door.

'*Good evening, sir.*'

'*Asif,*' grunted Greg good-naturedly, slumping onto his familiar seat, '*home, my good man, I'm afraid I'm a little pissed.*'

'*Sir.*'

Asif eased the car forward when suddenly an old man lurched out of the shadows into its path. Asif hit the brakes, barely missing him, as he stumbled on his way as if nothing had happened.

The far-side back door opened silently. A young Bedouin slipped in beside Greg just as Asif shouted '*Fucking camel*' at the departing figure. From beneath his loose white thobe, the Bedouin produced a handgun of uncertain vintage.

'*Please follow my instructions carefully,*' he said courteously, in a deep guttural voice. '*You will come to no harm provided I'm not obliged to use this,*' he continued, raising the gun carefully to Greg's chest, as Asif swung round in his seat.

'*Do as he says, Asif,*' Greg instructed, trying desperately to focus, remain calm. Asif nodded vigorously, too terrified to speak, which Greg took as a sign that he had no part in whatever was going on here.

'*Drive into town, to Revolution Square. Drive slowly, don't speak, either of you.*'

Asif drove carefully into town, not in his usual carefree accident-prone fashion. Greg, struggling to make sense of what was happening, never took his eyes off the gun, which the young Bedouin held resolutely to his chest. Was he one of Philippe's associates? His ancient weapon suggested otherwise. Although lethally armed, he lacked something which Greg couldn't pinpoint. Perhaps, he reasoned, it was the man's innate politeness that he found unsettling.

As they entered an empty Revolution Square, the Bedouin instructed Asif to drive on to a nearby entrance to the souk, where

Greg was told to get out. In the brief moment when the gun was no longer pointing at him, he managed to suppress an instinct to make a dash for it. It was just as well, as two older Bedouins moved seamlessly in on either side of him.

'*Go, leave now, this instant,*' the younger man shouted at Asif through the car window. '*And stay away, don't come back. You'll be in serious trouble if you do,*' this time, more threateningly. Asif needed no encouragement; he spun his old Toyota round and tore off across the square, trailing a plume of black smoke.

Greg's heart sank as the three men steered him away through a warren of narrow streets and passageways. It was late; people were homeward bound. Traders, oblivious to his plight, were closing shop, cramming unsold goods into tattered cardboard boxes; unhooking wares with long poles from overhead wires hanging high above their tiny crammed stores; carefully sweeping the day's detritus into uncollected piles; pulling down metal shutters, rattling shrilly in the gathering quietness.

Abruptly, the small posse turned into a darkened corridor and up a flight of rickety wooden stairs. Even at this midnight hour, it was hot. Greg, not helped by a belly-load of whisky, felt nauseous in the thick fetid air. Fear clawed at his stomach, his rapid breathing and pounding chest made him feel dizzy. At the top of the steps, the young Bedouin knocked on a metal door.

He was shown into a small windowless room. It was lit by a single bulb hanging so low from the ceiling that he could only just make out a thobe-clad torso standing beyond the circle of light. The metal door creaked briefly behind him; he was alone with the silent torso, which stepped forward and sank to the floor.

'Please sit,' a man's voice said, quietly.

Surprised at being addressed in English, he lowered himself gingerly onto a low stool that he could just make out to his left, desperately trying to clear his fuzzy head. As he adjusted to the gloom, he found himself facing the man sitting cross-legged on the floor. It was then that he noticed a woman sitting on a low seat to one side. She was wearing a black abaya and hijab, only her eyes and narrow feet visible.

'My name is Ramil,' said the man. 'I'm sorry to have inconvenienced you at this hour, Dr Hamilton.'

Good God, thought Greg, *what the hell's Ramil doing here?* And then in that split second he saw it, a small red butterfly neatly tattooed below the ankle bone of the woman's left foot, his mind racing back to the first time he'd seen it, that crazy afternoon on the beach in Calais, the shock temporarily cutting through the effects of the alcohol.

'And this is your good friend Isabel,' the man said, at which point he turned around and pulled back her hijab. They stared at each other in silence. He was shocked by her appearance; her eyes, usually so alive, now listless, said it all. Ramil stood up.

'I will leave you two together for a few minutes. Don't do anything rash, doctor. Just listen to Isabel. She has something important for you,' and with that he disappeared from the circle of light and out of the room.

'My dearest Isabel,' he said, clumsily reaching for her with outstretched arms. 'I've been so worried for you,' he said, his voice breaking. It was then that he saw that her hands were tightly bound to her feet by a short length of electric cable, making it impossible for her to straighten up.

'Oh, Greg, I've missed you,' she whispered, tearfully.

He knelt in front of her. She buried her head, now shorn of its beautiful hair, in his embrace. For several moments, he clung to her, her hot silent tears mingling with his sweat. Eventually she pulled away.

'Take this,' she said quietly, indicating a tattered folder at her feet. 'You'll find all the evidence Vanmeer needs to arrest Philippe and his gang. It corroborates everything we suspected.'

He gazed at the folder, realising what she'd achieved by her courage. His heart went out to her, seeing her brought so low, terrified at the thought of what she must have endured; he was at a loss for words.

'You must give it to him, you're the hero, uncovering this whole bloody business.'

'I can't,' she said, her voice barely audible, 'it's out of the question.'

'Why, for God's sake?'

'I have to go back with him.'

'Go back?' His voice trembled with anger and frustration. 'Where to, for God's sake?'

'I'm being held in an oasis town in Cyrenaica.'

'God almighty, you were kidnapped by Ramil, by the Russians, it makes no bloody sense.'

'Apparently they're not ready to release me.'

He could sense her helplessness.

'What in God's name can you still do for them, for Ramil?' he asked, fearing for her survival, his voice rising. 'They're bloody inhuman.'

'Greg, Greg,' she pleaded, the fear in her eyes shredding his emotions, 'keep your voice down.'

'How are they treating you?'

'The first few days were the worst,' she whispered. 'I was convinced I'd been abducted by Philippe's people. I was taken south of the Jebel Akhdar…'

'Jebel Akhdar,' he exclaimed.

She nodded; he sensed she was anxious to talk but was inhibited.

'The whole atmosphere's quite different there,' she whispered, after a brief pause. 'I'm living in Ramil's villa, am well catered for. I'm even brushing up on my Arabic,' she added, managing a wry smile.

'But you can't leave?'

'No, not even the compound. I'm their prisoner.'

Suddenly, he felt overwhelmed. 'I feel we're in some ghastly unending nightmare.'

'Greg…' she whispered urgently, her eyes beseeching him.

Suddenly she stiffened. He could see her terrified eyes focusing on something over his shoulder. The last thing he heard was the click of the metal door behind him; the last thing he felt, an excruciating pain in his right thigh.

29

Greece, Mid-December 2031

On a cool hazy morning, the battered taxi pulled up across the street from the St George. The driver testily insisted on US dollars, after refusing a large rouble-denominated note, a sure sign of the times. Jack extracted himself with his bags and, taking his life in his hands, ducked and weaved between filthy, fume-spewing lines of traffic, before struggling into the hotel lobby.

Dumping everything with a flourish, he quickly took in the familiar surroundings, relieved to be back; he had hoped to return at the beginning of the month, but this time he'd applied for a three-month visa, which had taken longer.

In November, on his second visit to Greece, he'd taken the bus straight through to Stoupa. This time Bushra had insisted they meet in Athens. He knew that life was difficult for her at home, the principal cause being Dorpadski's increasingly abusive and threatening behaviour. Thankfully the tyrant had been out of the country for most of the previous month.

Travelling by bus, Bushra had arrived at the St George three days earlier. It was only at the hotel that she felt it was safe to phone Jack in England. It was during the call that he discovered why she had to be in Athens.

Apparently at the beginning of the month, Lena, Dorpadski's wife, had returned from an extended visit to Moscow. She'd been to a number of the leading art galleries, the Bolshoi and several concerts. She invariably travelled alone, meeting up with wealthy friends as she went; this trip had been no different. Dorpadski had not the slightest interest in music or the arts and was happy for her to go on her own. It gave him an opportunity to indulge in his two passions: loose women and recreational drugs.

She told Jack that after Lena had got back to Stoupa, Dorpadski made an unexpected late-night visit to the cottage. When Bushra told him on the phone what had transpired, she'd broken down uncontrollably.

During a trip to one of the galleries, Lena had discovered that the one painting still hanging in the villa in Stoupa, which Jack had seen in the study that fateful evening in October, was extremely valuable. It was a portrait of an infamous Siberian count, the work of a well-known nineteenth-century Russian Impressionist. What really caught Lena's attention, though, was the fact that it was originally one of a set of three portraits of this notorious family; anybody who managed to acquire all three would be worth tens of millions of dollars.

With plenty of cash at her disposal, Lena had retained one of Moscow's top art experts to track down the whereabouts of the other two. Within a couple of days, he contacted her with some astonishing news: Bushra's father, a passionate and wealthy art collector, had at one time owned all three.

Bushra admitted to him that her father had indeed owned the three portraits, which she'd inherited, although at the time she hadn't appreciated their true value. She told him that, completely by chance, a year before Dorpadski arrived in Stoupa, she'd taken two of the paintings to an art restorer, an old friend of her father's, who worked in Athens. Unknown to everybody, the two restored paintings remained safely out of the way in his Athenian studio.

Where were the other two, Dorpadski had demanded that night, the clear implication being that Bushra had withheld what he rightly considered to be his. She knew that she was a marked woman in occupied Greece after Dorpadski had claimed, without credible evidence, that Stavros was leading the resistance against the government in UNMC. She had come to Athens to collect the two paintings, with the intention of giving them to Dorpadski, hoping against all the odds to buy some temporary goodwill. Jack guessed that in her heart she knew this to be a futile gesture. She had absolutely no bargaining power; it was only a matter of time before Dorpadski would dispense with her.

*

Chara rushed out from behind the reception desk to greet him.

'How good to see you, Jack,' she said standing back, holding his hands. 'Bushra will be so happy,' her laughter filling the lobby.

'You look well,' he said.

He remembered his first visit in October, when she'd chaperoned him for the twenty-four hours up to his dawn departure from the bus station. Seeing Chara again reminded him how thoroughly depressed he'd felt back then, having run away from a very angry and confused Emma; this time felt very different.

'Is Bushra around?'

'She had an early appointment at the hairdresser. I thought she'd be back by now. She's always preferred my local saloon,' said Chara, with a grin. 'They can't cut hair to her liking in Stoupa. Let's get your things up to the room,' she said, picking up his bags and dashing to the lift. 'You have time to freshen up before she gets back. How relieved she'll be to see you got here safely.'

He found himself in the same large room at the back of the hotel. The silence after the cacophony of the streets was total.

Bushra had taken full possession of the space. Every surface – bed, desk, chair and even the floor – was piled high with books, clothes and shopping bags. She'd been on a massive shopping spree, so unlike her. He cleared a small area by the window for his bags, stripped off and had a quick shower. By the time she arrived thirty minutes later, he was scrubbed clean and dressed.

She dropped everything at the door and ran to him, holding him in a silent embrace. He was shocked by her appearance. At the end of his visit in November, during which time Dorpadski had been away from Stoupa, she'd looked so happy, so well, her old vitality restored. Clearly his recent intervention in her life had been traumatic, visibly ageing her. She clung lifelessly to him, the sparkle gone from her stunning blue-black eyes, her face drawn, her natural gaiety seemingly drained away.

After sorting out their room to make it more habitable, they walked to Skoufa and then to the steep steps leading up to Lykavittos Hill, where she suggested they have lunch. Below the hill, the polluted air was suffocating, his eyes smarting, his breathing laboured. Traffic noise and the constant buffeting by an endless stream of pedestrians made conversation impossible. He followed closely as they climbed, aware that despite her strained appearance, she was still a remarkably fit woman.

It was an hour later, when he realised how wrong he'd been in thinking that Dorpadski had been the cause of her distress. Everything paled into insignificance, when she told him what they were both now facing.

*

Lykavittos Hill, bathed in winter sunshine, sat above the smog-hazed city. They sat outside a local bar huddled in winter jackets and ordered a couple of beers, taking in the view below. Bushra, dark glasses masking her anxiety, sat silently opposite him.

'It's lovely to be back with you,' he said, struggling to engage her attention, lift her out of despondency. 'The wait's been killing me.'

'Me too,' she said, placing her hands over his on the cool metal table.

'How long will we be staying in town?'

'Just another day.' She paused. 'Two weeks ago, I'd arranged to pick up the two paintings I told you about from the restorer, Andreas.'

He nodded.

'I'd hoped to collect them yesterday. However, he still has to finish packing them. I'll pick them up early tomorrow morning,' she said, quietly. 'Chara has kindly offered to drive me back to Stoupa with them. The bus trip would have been impossible.'

'And you still intend giving them to Dorpadski?'

'Dearest Jack, I have no choice.'

'The bastard,' he muttered under his breath. 'And for you, there's nothing, not a bloody cent?'

'Not really. I did hold out for several days, saying I wanted something in return.'

'And?'

'He's offered to increase his monthly rent, to double it in fact,' she said, dully. 'If he stays good to his word, I'll be getting about a quarter of the market rate, which should help with the bills.'

'Well, at least that's something tangible.'

Knowing her straitened circumstances, he had on several occasions offered her cash. She always refused, saying she was his friend and lover, not his whore. He admired her gutsy independence but bemoaned her pride. Two ice-cold beers were placed on the table; they drank in silence.

She seemed so low, as if all the fight had been knocked out of her.

'Jack, I've something important to share with you, something I've been dreading,' she whispered. She removed her glasses and rubbed her eyes; he waited, fearing the worst.

'Early yesterday morning, Christos arrived on the overnight bus from Kalamata and came straight to the St George. He knows I always stay there. He was very agitated.' He could see her eyes welling up. 'You remember I told you he has many old friends in Benghazi.'

'I do,' said Jack, wondering where this was leading.

'They still keep in regular contact, helping each other when they can, especially since both Greece and Cyrenaica fell into Russian hands.' She paused. 'One of his closest contacts came to see him the other day, warning him of the possible imminent collapse of the Russian mandate which could have serious consequences for us here.'

'I don't follow you.'

'You know we've always suspected how both administrations, here and in Cyrenaica, have come to rely heavily on an international drug trade to finance their operations.'

He nodded.

'Christos heard that they've been using two secure routes to their markets in Europe, the first through Tripoli while the second, unsurprisingly, is through Kalamata.'

'Good God, Tripoli, that doesn't sound possible. But Kalamata, we talked about it in the mountains back in October. Dorpadski has to be involved.'

'He is.'

'Apparently his yacht, *Kostroma*, is the control centre of the entire operation.'

Silence ensued as Dorpadski's spectre dominated their thoughts again.

'What did he have to say about Tripoli?' Jack asked, eventually.

'He mentioned that opposition to the regime in Benghazi had always been fractured, had achieved little,' Bushra said, her tongue loosening, 'but in the last twelve months, one dominant leader has emerged, bringing the various groups together, and they've had some notable successes.'

357

'Such as?'

'The most recent, and probably most significant one, is the temporary closure of the Tripoli route. Christos' friends suspect it has been operating as a joint enterprise between Russian officials close to the governor in Benghazi and corrupt army officers in EDA.'

'How the hell did they find out about this?'

'It's all a bit vague,' she said. 'Apparently they'd heard that in early October, a number of Russian troops were ritually killed, prior to a prearranged meeting with EDA officials at the border. The whole business provoked a significant reaction in Tripoli when it was discovered that the murdered men, all implicated in the drugs business, had had close connections with EDA's border forces.'

'What happened then?'

'According to Christos, an elite paratrooper group, including its French commanding officer, were detained indefinitely without charge in Tripoli, while the authorities there try to gather more evidence of collusion in the drugs trade. It's all been very low key, but it appears to have temporarily closed down the Tripoli route.' She paused. 'This, bizarrely, followed the abduction of a young female EDA employee from the streets of Tripoli to Cyrenaica.'

'God, this is convoluted,' said Jack. 'I just can't see the connection.' A thought suddenly struck him. 'Wasn't Isabel caught up in a border incident about that time?'

'You're thinking she's the one who's been abducted?' Bushra asked anxiously.

'No, I'm sure we'd have heard from Emma if something serious had happened to her,' said Jack. 'But Christos, why did he feel you ought to be aware of all this?'

Bushra went quiet again, withdrawing into herself.

'The new leader,' she said, eventually, 'has a nickname. They refer to him as the "Mad Greek".'

'Who he thinks is Stavros,' exclaimed Jack.

She nodded.

'So there was some truth in Dorpadski's bloody video show after all.'

'Yes,' she said, 'but the main reason Christos came to see me was to pass on this letter which one of his contacts had given him.'

She rummaged in her shoulder bag and pulled out a plain grubby envelope, which she pushed across the table. A message in Arabic was scribbled in pencil across the top of the envelope.

'What does this mean?' Jack asked, pointing to the writing, bracing himself for yet more unsettling news

'It says, *"For Bushra Benamer, but only to be opened in the presence of Jack Meredith"*. This is what I've been dreading.'

Gingerly, he took out several rough sheets of closely written Arabic text and stared at it. The writing was formless, no address, no salutation, no date and to him, completely meaningless.

'What the hell's this?' he asked wearily, passing the sheets back, his pre-dawn start and early morning flight from London suddenly catching up with him, his adrenaline seeping away.

For several minutes, she read and reread the scruffy text. He was alarmed to see how difficult this was proving to be, tears coursing down her ashen face.

'It's from Stavros, isn't it?' he guessed, his impatience getting the better of him.

'Yes,' she whispered. She finished her beer, placing the empty glass directly in front of him. 'Why don't you order another couple,' she said, flatly.

After catching the waiter's eye, he turned to her, waiting. For a while she just sat there, staring blankly into space, saying nothing.

'The note is too long, certainly too painful to read right through now,' she continued, tearfully.

'Painful?'

'He's addressed this to both of us in a classical Arabic greeting, invoking God, reminding us who we are, who he is,' she read, scanning the rumpled pages. 'He goes on to tell us that he's the leader of the most effective opposition group resisting Russian occupation in Cyrenaica, something that we and our forebears should be proud of.'

Fresh beers arrived. She took a long draught and continued.

'This is dreadful, Jack,' she sobbed. 'We are accused of disowning him as a baby, leaving him as a child to rot under a despotic dictatorship, denying him an education and the opportunities that we, his parents, took for granted when we were young. He writes how he could never understand why we showed such favouritism towards his twin sister, why they weren't treated equally.'

She stopped, now crying uncontrollably. Several people sitting nearby shifted uncomfortably in their seats. A couple got up, frappés in hand, and wandered away. Jack was speechless, unable to think of anything to say. He just stared at the offending note, drinking deeply.

Suddenly he had a flashback. It was something Emma had said after he'd returned from his first trip to Greece. They'd been discussing Stavros, when she said, 'Do you think he felt the same way about his childhood as I did about mine, the unfairness of it all?' My God, how prescient she'd been.

'It goes on for another full page. When he was older, he couldn't understand why I didn't visit him or even appear to care about him. His foster mother said I didn't want anything to do with him. Why did my aunt lie to him about me?' Bushra cried. 'Why wouldn't she allow me to take him back when he was older as we'd agreed? She poisoned him.'

'Don't torture yourself,' said Jack quietly, reaching out to her, 'you know you tried many times to see him, hoping to be allowed to bring him back to Athens.'

She sat for several minutes, before regaining her composure.

'On the third page, there's a change in tone,' she continued reading. 'He writes that his campaign against the Russians is under threat, undermined by corruption, drugs, deserters. Progress is slowing, even being reversed in some areas.'

She followed the text with her finger.

'Then without warning, he writes that he's known for some time that Isabel is our granddaughter, his niece.'

'Oh God,' he groaned, 'how could he have?'

'There's no explanation. He just says that she'd been present at an incident on the border, had seen murdered Russian soldiers.'

'EDA authorities had told Emma that she'd been involved in a minor accident, some bloody accident.'

'According to Stavros, Isabel has an important role in his campaign after she recently met his people in Cyrenaica.'

'Isabel must be the EDA woman they abducted,' Jack exclaimed. 'She's his niece for God's sake, the man must be insane,' he said, frustration rising in his voice.

'And we are his parents,' she whispered.

'Yes,' he admitted, 'we are his parents.'

'Why abduct her though?' he said, his voice rising, anger getting the better of him. 'The whole thing's crazy.'

'Jack, Jack, stop it,' she cried, bringing him to his senses.

'I'm sorry,' he said, chastened. 'I just can't believe what I'm hearing.'

'He writes that the military government in Benghazi relies heavily on a lucrative drugs trade with Europe.' Bushra continued, 'Moscow provides little funding for the territory, so the trade pays for most of the administration's costs. It also funds an extravagant lifestyle for all its senior officials.'

'Which we've known all along,' he said. 'So what's Stavros proposing to do?'

'He says he needs to wipe out the trade completely if he's ever going to overthrow the military and establish some form of independent state.'

'Bloody brilliant,' he snapped, his anger rising again. 'And where does poor Isabel fit into this great scheme of his?'

'Jack, Jack, just listen to yourself,' she said, softly. 'This is our son, our granddaughter we're talking about here. Much of what he writes about us is true and we know it. We've been in denial for years, stuck in our own past. We are as culpable as anybody in this mad situation.'

His reeling mind stalled. *God in heaven, she's right*, he thought, *they're our flesh and blood and all I can do is rant and rave.*

'I'm sorry, I'm really sorry,' he mumbled. 'I'm completely out of order.'

'He writes that Benghazi had developed two secure routes into Europe,' she continued reading. 'The first through Tripoli, which has just been closed down; the second one through Kalamata is still active.'

She continued reading in silence.

Unable to contain himself, Jack suddenly asked, 'Is he suggesting that Isabel can help end Dorpadski's operation in Kalamata?' shocked to think that Stavros might even consider her capable in such a situation.

Bushra looked out over the smoggy city, before turning back to him. 'Nothing, absolutely nothing's expected of her, Jack.' She paused. 'She just has to sit tight in Cyrenaica and wait.'

Then it hit him.

'That's our job. We've got to sort out Dorpadski.'

'Stavros uses the word "eliminate",' she said, her voice drained of all emotion. 'And when that's done, Isabel will be free to go home. At the end of the letter, he writes that once this has been achieved, you and I will be forgiven.'

*

The rest of the day and late into the night back at the hotel, they talked endlessly of the woeful predicament they found themselves in. At least they agreed on one thing: it was critical that she deliver the paintings as soon as possible to Dorpadski, who was getting more irritable by the day.

Neither of them had ever contemplated ending another person's life. Even if it meant freeing Isabel from a life of servitude in Cyrenaica and ridding the Peloponnese of a tyrant, they were unsure if they could overcome their abhorrence of murder and commit such a dreadful act. In any event, they would need time and considerable help if they were to fulfil Stavros' demands.

Bushra knew that she could rely on Christos, who had returned to Kalamata by bus at dawn. He and his many friends from the Peloponnese had personally experienced the terror of occupation on both sides of the Mediterranean. Jack knew that he and Bushra had absolutely no idea how they could satisfy Stavros' demands; Christos' help would be essential.

To avoid any problems entering the Peloponnese at the internal border, Chara had suggested that Jack should travel to Stoupa by bus, while she and Bushra would travel in Chara's car with the paintings. He saw her logic, realising that two Greek nationals would be waved through without any fuss.

Before dawn the following day, the two women collected the packages from Andreas, while Jack set off from the hotel. Chara reminded him exactly what he must do to catch the early bus to Kalamata, which left from the regional bus terminus at Kifissou. He had mixed feelings: unease at leaving the women to make the hazardous journey on their own, but relieved that he would have time to reflect on what lay ahead.

After an incident-free journey, he was surprised to see Christos, a cigarette hanging precariously from his lower lip, waiting for him at Kalamata bus station; there was no sign of the two women.

'Don't worry, Jack, everything's fine,' shouted Christos, barely audible in the clamour and chaos of the bus station. 'The women drove straight through to Stoupa this afternoon,' he added with a knowing twinkle in his eyes. 'Bushra will come early for you in the morning. You, my friend, will stay with us tonight. Perhaps we will enjoy a little ouzo together.'

*

Early the next morning, Bushra drove to Kardamyli to pick up a severely hung-over Jack from Christos' taverna and take him back to Stoupa.

'Dorpadski came to the cottage yesterday evening, a couple of hours after Chara and I got back,' Bushra shouted, above the roar of the straining engine, dragging the old Lada up the steep hill out of Kardamyli, on their way south. 'I'd arranged for Chara to stay with friends in Aghios Dimitrios. Fortunately, he arrived after she'd left and I'd hidden the paintings. I didn't want her getting mixed up with the bastard.'

Christos' late night hospitality came back to haunt him, a scrunching headache trying to close down his system, calling for an uninterrupted twelve hours' sleep. He knew it wasn't to be.

'What did he want?' Jack shouted.

'Asked when he could see the paintings, was very insistent, angry even. I don't think he realised I'd been away. My car had been outside the cottage all the time.'

'And then?'

'Told him I'd bring them over at six this evening, but I needed to be left alone during the day. I know he saw me leave this morning when I came for you. He may have thought I was going to collect them.'

The noises, both inside and outside his head, reached fever pitch. He stopped fighting his tiredness and slumped into his seat and dozed off. The next moment he found himself being violently thrust forward as the car slewed to a halt, Bushra shouting in his face.

'For God's sake, Jack, wake up, wake up.'

He opened his eyes. Directly in front of the car, he saw a man dressed in leathers getting off a powerful motorbike, quickly pulling off his helmet and goggles. How the hell she'd managed to stop the car without running the bike down was a mystery.

'It's OK,' she whispered, evidently relieved, 'it's only Christos, I'd forgotten he rode a bike,' as she wound down the window to greet him. Jack immediately saw the concern on his face; something was amiss.

Christos furtively looked up and down the empty road, before stooping down and talking rapidly in Greek; she simply nodded. Thirty seconds later, he kick-started the bike, wheeled it around and tore back in the direction of Kardamyli.

'What was that about?'

She was still, eyes staring blankly at the road ahead, hands clutching the wheel. She turned to him, eyes welling up, shaking as if in a fever. He put his arm around her, drawing her to his chest. It took her a moment to compose herself.

'He got an urgent call after we left his place this morning,' she said dully. 'His Benghazi contact suspects Dorpadski knows of Stavros' plan to close down the drugs trade here. Christos also thinks he's aware of Stavros' demands, our involvement. He believes Dorpadski will want to keep this information to himself, having convinced everybody that Stavros is dead.'

'God almighty, what the hell do we do now?'

Silence ensued; gradually he felt her body relax, her breathing becoming slow and measured.

'Jack, I suggest we do exactly what we'd planned,' she said, evenly. 'We'll turn up at the villa at six this evening with the paintings, which I will present to him. I'll ask him for a signed copy of our new rental agreement, his side of the bargain. We'll have a drink if we're offered one and leave as soon as good manners dictate.'

He looked at her smiling face in astonishment, then burst out laughing.

'You're absolutely bloody right. To hell with him, to hell with them all. Oh God, how lucky I've been, to have loved, been loved by you. You never cease to amaze me,' he said, hugging her tightly. 'And if he bumps us off tonight, at least we go together. If he doesn't, well who knows.'

'Who knows,' she repeated, starting the engine and driving on towards Stoupa.

30

Stoupa, Mid-December 2031

The morning was dry and sunny; the unseasonal mild weather blanketing Greece was coming to an end, with reports of imminent snow storms being driven by strong northerly winds straight from Siberia. Taking advantage of the warmth, Jack and Bushra swam far out to sea, which raised her spirits and cleared his head of Christos' hospitality.

They spent the afternoon in bed, their lovemaking intensified by an unspoken fear of the future. Later, they showered and dressed as if for an important occasion, reasoning that if they were going to die at the hands of Dorpadski that evening, they would face death with style.

They avoided discussing their predicament, except when Bushra raised the issue as to whether they should try to contact Emma. It only took a moment to agree that they shouldn't, knowing that if they lived through their ordeal, Emma would have suffered unnecessarily.

At six, on a cool moonlit evening, they left the cottage each carrying a package and walked up the path to the villa.

'Look,' said Jack, '*Kostroma* is moored in the mouth of the bay. God, I'd no idea how big she was. She seemed smaller in Kalamata.'

'She must have dropped anchor during the afternoon. She's beautiful in a vulgar sort of way, wouldn't have suited us though.'

'Wouldn't suit us,' he corrected her.

'Of course,' she laughed, uneasily. 'When all this is behind us, we'll buy a small boat, spend our days sailing around the islands.' She reached up and kissed him. 'I love you, Jack, always have and always will,' she said resolutely, placing her finger on his lips.

Before they turned the corner of the villa, she stopped.

'Just a minute,' she whispered, looking out over the beautifully tended garden, bathed in moonlight. 'I'll always remember this view of the cottage, our bolthole, and the sea beyond.'

Was this her farewell, he wondered, now that they were faced with the tragic inevitability of their situation. It wasn't so much their possible demise at the hands of Dorpadski that freaked him; it was the fact that, despite all the years they'd been lovers, their actual time together had been so short.

Dorpadski and Lena met them at the front door. Jack saw Dorpadski wince imperceptibly; it occurred to him that he wasn't expected. Notwithstanding, he and Bushra were welcomed as if they were old friends. Hera the maid took the packages and placed them reverently on a large smoked-glass table in the living room. In exchange, he and Bushra were offered two large glasses of champagne. In a strange way, it felt normal.

He shuddered at the memory of his last visit. The same four, who had been at that extremely unpleasant dinner party, were there. With backs to the room, they looked out over the moonlit sea, talking loudly in Russian. It was as if they'd never left.

'My friends,' boomed Dorpadski, 'our honoured guests have arrived,' at which point, the four turned in unison, like a well-trained dance troupe. 'I believe my dear friend Bushra has brought us a rare gift. Jack, if you would be so kind,' he continued, passing Jack a thin silver letter opener.

He carefully slit the packages open and gently lifted each painting; the first he handed to Dorpadski, the second to Lena. Barely glancing at the paintings, the couple turned and showed them to the group, who gave a collective gasp before breaking into applause.

'The long-suffering count will now be reunited with his wife and daughter,' said Dorpadski with a flourish, pointing to a third painting hanging on the wall, which Jack recognised as the one he'd seen in old Ali's study. As if on cue, two men dressed in blue overalls entered the room. Within a couple of minutes, they'd hung the two paintings, wife and daughter, either side of the count.

'To the count and his long-lost family,' roared Dorpadski, raising his glass to the trio; then turning to Bushra, 'and my dear friend who has looked after them so well.'

'I'm so glad they're together again,' said Lena, as she sidled up to Jack. 'I do so much admire our Russian Impressionists. You know their work is greatly undervalued in Europe and the States,' she continued, 'I really don't understand why.'

'Maybe it's simply a lack of familiarity. It must have been difficult in the past for them to exhibit outside Russia,' he said, trying to sound engaged.

'No, I think you people just don't appreciate them,' she said, brusquely.

As they stood in front of the paintings discussing their relative merits, Jack noticed Bushra being drawn to one side by Dorpadski. After several minutes of muted discussion, he handed her an envelope from which she withdrew a single sheet. Jack guessed that it must be the rental agreement she had mentioned earlier. He was relieved to see her smile and shake Dorpadski's hand. Evidently he had kept his side of this ludicrously unequal bargain.

Bushra, clutching her envelope, joined Jack and Lena, who continued lecturing him with a steady stream of facts and figures on the latest art auctions in London, Paris and Moscow – which painters were in fashion, which galleries were showing what. He tuned out, saying just the bare minimum to appear interested in her droning monologue. This evening, he found her dull and self-absorbed. After a moment or two, Bushra slipped away, indicating to him that she was going to the bathroom.

She returned and stopped briefly in front of the portraits, staring at them intently. Jack's heart went out to her, feeling her pain at losing the last works of her father's fabulous art collection. The noise level rose as the champagne flowed, with Bushra and Jack being forced to listen to Lena's monologue. After thirty minutes or so, Dorpadski banged his fist on the table, calling for everyone's attention.

'My friends, my dear friends, this evening we must celebrate the reunion of the count's family. You're all invited to dine with us on *Kostroma*,' he bellowed, indicating his yacht moored out in the bay. 'We'll walk down to the jetty where the launch is waiting.'

The others, now well lubricated, cheered and moved haphazardly out into the garden, bathed in a full moon. Jack and Bushra, glancing at each other, hesitated.

'Jack, Bushra, you must join us, I insist, absolutely insist,' he continued, taking her firmly by the elbow and following the others. Lena took Jack's hand in her jewel-encrusted grip, gazed at him disarmingly and pulled him firmly after her husband.

'I know you two love the sea,' she purred. 'You'll just adore *Kostroma*. He bought her from an old Greek shipping family, such interesting people.'

Another precious family asset purloined, thought Jack. He had difficulty keeping in step with this strident, passionless woman, stumbling down the path beside her as if he'd been drinking all day.

He caught Bushra's eye as he stepped into the rocking launch, a beautifully varnished wooden boat in keeping with *Kostroma*'s status as a super-yacht. Discreetly, she raised an eyebrow and pursed her lips as if to say, 'What can we do? We've no choice.' Barely suppressing his anxiety, he smiled grimly at her, realising that they were sleepwalking into a well-prepared trap. There seemed no chance of escape. The launch pulled away with a violent growl, throwing its well-oiled passengers off balance.

*

Kostroma lay at anchor head-to-wind in the mouth of Stoupa bay, about a kilometre from the jetty. The yacht, a streamlined black steel hull perhaps fifty metres long with an all-timber and glass two-level superstructure, looked awesome in the light of the moon.

Jack noticed that the breeze had picked up since they'd left the cottage over an hour earlier; it was much cooler. He moved easily with the surfing launch, feeling the wind on his face. He was in an emotional hell, his will broken. The thought that by this time tomorrow they might cease to exist tore at his heart. Their deaths would leave Stavros' demands unfulfilled, subjecting Isabel to a life of unremitting misery or worse, the idea of which only compounded his agony.

He could see Bushra standing in the bow, her back to them all, holding tightly to the guardrail. With head raised, she looked out to sea. He was relieved he wasn't in her line of sight; he couldn't have made eye contact, knowing that the anguish they shared would reduce him to a blubbering wreck. His powerlessness was complete; they were entirely in Dorpadski's hands.

The launch docked alongside a low landing platform extending from the cut-away stern. A young Russian crew member, immaculately dressed in white, helped the inebriated party aboard. They were led through steel and glass bulkhead doors, through the aft locker room and up a wooden companionway.

Jack noticed that the locker room was part boathouse, part armoury. Enclosed in a steel mesh cage on the port side, he could see at least a dozen stacked automatic rifles. On the starboard side, there was a workbench above open lockers. Amidships, a magnificent varnished wooden speedboat, about six metres in length, looked smugly over the platform out to sea. She sat in a cradle below an extendable gantry, ready to be launched at the push of a button – a faultless embryo in the womb of a beautiful woman.

A mahogany table had been set for dinner in the top-deck stateroom, aft of the bridge. In subdued light, everything gleamed. Polished brass and varnished wood exuded unexpected taste, which surprised Jack; such a contrast to the trashy feel of Bushra's old home. Before dinner, Dorpadski insisted that he show Jack and Bushra around *Kostroma*. They were obliged to inspect her in minute detail, from the bottommost bilges to the bridge. She was certainly a boat one would be very proud of, thought Jack.

It was a harrowing hour. He desperately wanted Bushra to himself, to be away from this maddening megalomaniac. Dorpadski seemed to be playing with her – a torturous game of cat and mouse. He would refer to her family's past, belittling their social status, achievements and modest wealth, in the tiniest of throw-away comments. *Why?* Jack kept asking himself. Maybe Dorpadski was assuaging his miserable conscience; killing low-lifers must be relatively easy.

The slightly sinister *Kostroma* was the perfect stage for Dorpadski's unfettered ego, prompting barely believable boasting about his life, past, present and future. There was no talk of their future. *Why should there be?* thought Jack, panic-stricken; they hadn't one. By the end of the tour, he had convinced himself that Dorpadski knew that they were aware that he'd uncovered Stavros' plot.

By the time the three returned to the stateroom, the wind had picked up, shrouding the moon in high hazy cloud, a sure sign of an impending storm, thought Jack. He noted the crazy amount of alcohol the others had consumed. They were still noisy, but no more so than they had been an hour earlier.

Dorpadski took his place at the head of the table, his back to the bridge, with Bushra sitting on his right. Lena sat at the other end, Jack on her right. Dinner was sumptuous: Baikal caviar, Norwegian lobster, Italian cheeses, French wines, impossible to source in this remote area of occupied Greece.

Lena talked to Jack incessantly on all things art. Driven to distraction, he tried to recall all he'd seen everywhere he'd been on *Kostroma*, trying to work out if escape were at all possible. At the same time, he was looking for the slightest change in their surroundings, something tiny and inconsequential that might signal their impending doom. Lena was so self-absorbed; she hadn't noticed his agitation.

*

As the evening wore on, the wind steadily rose, driving breaking waves around the headland into the bay. Despite *Kostroma*'s size, he could feel a distinct pitching motion as she strained against her anchor. At one stage, he noticed the darkened hull of a local fishing boat, completely devoid of navigation lights, surge astern of the yacht. Well after dinner was over, the skipper emerged from the bridge and spoke quietly to Dorpadski, who then called for everybody's attention.

'My skipper has informed me that the weather is deteriorating. He needs to find a safer anchorage. He suggests that if anybody wishes to go ashore before we weigh anchor, they should do so immediately. Lena and I will remain on board. You're all welcome to stay.'

The group of four noisily and unanimously opted to stay. Jack saw Bushra get to her feet.

'My dear Lena,' she called out clearly down the table, 'Jack and I have had a wonderful evening, but I think it's time we left. We've an early start tomorrow. We've planned to visit Epidavros. It'll be a long day.'

'Such a shame,' cried Lena. 'Hopefully we'll see you both again soon. Jack is so knowledgeable about art, so refreshing.'

Jack, his mind numb at this unexpected turn of events, fell in with Bushra's charade.

'She's been promising to take me there for ages,' he said to Lena as he rose, kissing her briefly on both cheeks before joining Bushra. Dorpadski nodded to his skipper, who retreated to the bridge, returning moments later with two bulky life jackets.

'Take the launch, Jack. You're both experienced seafarers, you can easily manage her on your own,' Dorpadski laughed, handing the jackets to him, 'but you'll need these, just in case.'

Jack and Bushra donned their jackets and, after lengthy farewells, the crew member who had helped them aboard took them down to the lower deck. As they entered the locker room, she stopped and cursed softly in Russian, gesticulating to the young man, pointing to the companionway. He nodded and ran back.

'Jack,' she whispered, fiercely, 'take the bloody jacket off. Be careful, very careful.' She gingerly swapped her jacket for one lying in the speedboat. Wordlessly, he did the same. *What the hell's wrong with them?* he thought, they seemed standard issue. 'Suicide jackets,' she whispered again.

'Good God,' he muttered, realising how vicious Dorpadksi was. The swap had taken less than thirty seconds.

The crew member returned a few moments later and spoke to Bushra, shaking his head. She laid a hand on his arm, speaking in Russian. He smiled and indicated that they should get into the launch. He knelt on the platform, switched on the launch's navigation lights and explained to her how to start the inboard engine and select the gears.

A moment later, Bushra, standing amidships, steered the launch away from *Kostroma* into the pitch-black night and oncoming waves, which crashed over the bow, drenching them in seconds. Above them on *Kostroma's* aft deck, a ragged cheer went up. Jack could see the Dorpadskis and their guests standing at the guardrail, glasses raised in a farewell salute. He and Bushra waved back as she pulled the boat around in a sweeping arc into the bay.

'Are you OK? Are we safe?' he shouted, above the noise of the engine.

'I haven't a clue,' she shouted back, laughter in her voice.

Two quick explosions shattered the darkness. Stunned, they turned to look at *Kostroma* as Bushra slowed the launch. The sight was electrifying. The locker room forward of the aft platform, which they'd left only moments earlier, was spewing flames.

Before they could draw breath, the ammunition store blew up in a series of minor explosions like a demonic firework display, spraying the area around the burning *Kostroma* with whistling ordinance. Columns of water erupted from the sea just metres from the launch.

'Let's go,' yelled Jack, 'this place is lethal.'

Within seconds, a fireball amidships rose fifty metres into the sky, temporarily blinding them, followed immediately by an ear-splitting thunderclap, which reverberated around the bay. The six Russians at the aft rail were instantly engulfed in flames, their black silhouettes dancing frantically, their screams clearly audible above the wind.

'The fuel tanks,' she shouted.

She pushed the throttle down hard and the launch jumped forward, surfing down the waves running on towards Stoupa beach. *Kostroma* was now totally consumed in flames. Jack knew nobody could have possibly survived the floating inferno.

He turned around just in time to see the rapidly approaching unlit bow of a fishing boat, barely visible in the boiling sea.

'Ahead,' he screamed.

In a split second, Bushra pulled the wheel violently to starboard but not before the launch sustained a glancing portside blow, which threw the launch wildly off course. As the stricken boat swerved away, she lost her footing and flipped backwards over the side, disappearing into a frothy void. Jack grabbed the wheel and instantly overcorrected the turn, at which point the launch rolled into a frenzied capsize. The last thing he remembered was a sharp crack to his head as he flew through the spray.

31

Stoupa, Mid-December 2031

It was early afternoon. Christos was in bed with a hangover, unable to sleep. He got up, grabbed his cigarettes and wandered down to the shuttered bar. The message he'd received from his old friend in Benghazi early that morning had greatly unsettled him. Having managed to warn Bushra of the danger she and Jack were in while they were driving back to Stoupa, he felt at the time that he had done all he could. As the day wore on, however, he realised this wasn't enough.

Although he had no plan, he knew he had to get to Stoupa; they would need his help. Instinctively, he called two old friends, one of whom had a jeep; they immediately agreed to join him.

At dusk, the three stopped at a roadside taverna, a traditional stone building high on a hill overlooking Stoupa bay. In the twilight, they could just make out the village, its sweeping seafront defined by promenade lights and the Benamers' villa on the northern headland. They were surprised to see *Kostroma*, normally docked alongside the quay in Kalamata, anchored in the mouth of the bay.

They couldn't decide what to do. It would be too risky to drive directly to Bushra's cottage; they'd never get past security at the main gate to the villa. Approaching from the sea might be possible in the dark, but they would need a boat with a knowledgeable skipper – impossible to arrange at short notice.

The strengthening breeze blew dust and litter along the road; the temperature dropped dramatically as night set in. All they could agree on was that they needed a bed for the night. Nikias, the taverna owner, was happy to oblige, having a few simple guest rooms above the bar.

They huddled over meze and a bottle of ouzo, trying to keep warm in the draughty bar. Nobody stirred, the drinking continued unabated; their sense of urgency faded as they got caught up in the local gossip.

About midnight, they heard muffled explosions. Everybody in the building ran out onto the road, just as a dramatic firework display rent the darkness above *Kostroma*'s aft deck. Within seconds a large fireball shot into the night sky above the super-yacht, immediately followed by an ear-shattering thunderclap. *Kostroma* was soon engulfed in flames. All were speechless, rooted to the spot, mesmerised by the unfolding drama. Eventually, as the flames died down, people found their voices.

Over the next hour or so, as the news spread, locals came down from the small whitewashed houses stacked haphazardly above on the hillside. They stood outside the taverna in the cold and buffeting wind, staring out into the darkness, a distant glow on the sea, the only indication of the earlier devastation.

Speculation was rife, theories abundant. People started to make the connection between the burning *Kostroma* and the reviled Dorpadski, praying that he and his wife might have been on the yacht, might have died in the explosions. Christos was agitated, constantly smoking and flicking his *komboloi* over the back of his hand, the beads clattering back and forth. It was nearly one in the morning before all the talk finally galvanised him into action.

'Let's go,' he whispered to his friends, not wishing to elaborate on his hastily conceived plan. Slightly inebriated, the three jumped into the jeep and tore off down the hill to Stoupa.

'Where to?' asked Petros, their headstrong driver.

'To the villa,' Christos said. 'We need to find out what's going on, who's still there, where Bushra and Jack are.'

Fifteen minutes later, they drew up in front of the main gate, surprisingly open and unmanned. Instinctively Petros switched off the headlights and drove slowly up to the villa.

'Petros, for God's sake, stop,' hissed Christos, after seeing several furtive figures, heavily laden, staggering from the shadows of the house towards a large black truck.

Petros ignored him.

'It's the fucking guards, they're looting the place,' Christos shouted. 'Look out, they'll be armed.'

Without warning Petros accelerated towards the group, headlights now ablaze.

'No,' yelled Christos. 'For God's sake, no, Petros.'

Like a man possessed, he drove furiously at the guards, who Christos could see were very drunk, now grouped around the tailboard of the truck. They turned and gazed vacantly at the racing jeep bearing down on them, frozen in their tracks. In a couple of seconds it was over, four bodies instantly crushed between the two vehicles.

'Shit, Petros,' Christos shouted, 'you've killed the bastards.'

'I know,' he laughed, as he cut the engine. 'I fucking know,' he said, his voice rising hysterically. 'I've wanted to do something like this for years, bloody years.'

'You're crazy, man, out of your tiny fucking mind,' Christos cried. He turned to the third man sitting in the back. 'Andreas, you OK?'

'Fine,' came the muted response.

The silence was complete, just the ticking of the cooling engine, as each man tried to come to terms with what had happened.

'What now?' asked Andreas after a minute or so, his voice shaking.

'Just back up, Petros,' said Christos, 'let's see what damage you've done.'

Petros reversed several metres. With the jeep's headlights focused on the back of the truck, Christos and Andreas approached the four men lying under the tailboard, while Petros inspected his jeep.

'She's a tough old bitch,' he laughed uneasily, seeing that its previously battered condition gave little hint of the impact.

Christos knelt beside the bodies, checking to see who was still conscious. The smell of alcohol was overpowering. The two older men showed no signs of life; the others, groaning as he turned them over, stirred. He recognised them, men who had terrorised the locals in Kalamata with impunity for years. Pent-up hatred swamped him, pushing him over the edge.

'Throw them into the truck,' he shouted angrily at the others, 'we'll torch it and get the hell out of here.'

'Two are still conscious,' cried Andreas.

'Just do it,' Christos screamed, 'now, this fucking minute.'

While Andreas and Petros hoisted the broken bodies over the tailboard, Christos siphoned fuel from the truck before pouring it liberally over everything. As Petros reversed the jeep back to the main road, Christos got out a canister of spray paint and daubed several large black delta signs on the security hut and around the front door; he knew nobody would go near the place now.

With everybody ready to leave, he retreated to the jeep from where he hurled a blazing Molotov cocktail at the truck, which instantly exploded in a ball of fire; screams of the dying men quickly faded.

'To the seafront and slowly, man,' Christos said, grimacing, 'we've done enough damage tonight.'

One thing was clear, he realised, as they headed into the village: the guards wouldn't have looted the place if nothing had befallen the Dorpadskis. The owner and his wife must have gone down with *Kostroma*.

*

They sat in the jeep in a small empty square several streets back from the seafront. Minutes seeped away, nobody spoke; they were in shock.

'We can't sit here all night, dwelling on what's happened,' Andreas said evenly. 'What's done is done.'

'We still don't know where Bushra and Jack are,' whispered Christos. 'We couldn't hang around once we'd killed those bastards.'

'Leave it,' Petros snapped, irritably. 'I'm sure we'll find them in town, maybe later back at the cottage.'

'Or washed up on the beach,' said Christos, quietly, 'but enough of this.'

Although he was furious with Petros for acting so recklessly, he was anxious to calm the underlying tension.

'What's our plan?' Andreas asked.

'Let's go to the beach, see what's happening, if anything's been washed up from the wreckage,' said Christos. 'Maybe somebody's seen them,' he added, more in hope than expectation.

In silence, they walked down the narrow street towards the sea. The freezing wind funnelling up from the beach blew sand in their faces. The place was deserted. Loose shutters rattled angrily, adding a sense of desolation to the night. As soon as they reached the promenade, they saw several large waterfront properties, which had long been commandeered by Dorpadski's stooges, on fire at the south end of the beach.

'It's a bloody war zone,' exclaimed Petros.

They crossed the promenade and looked down onto the beach. Christos could make out about twenty people strung along the water's edge, several wading in the shallows, while others gazed out into the darkness. The sea was wild; short steep waves dazzling white in the street lights repeatedly broke and ran up the flattened sand.

As his eyes became accustomed to the dark, he could see an overturned semi-submerged hull riding the waves, just beyond where they were breaking. One of the village fishing boats was trying to tow it back out to sea with little success.

Petros touched his arm, pointing to a pile of debris on the sand directly below the promenade wall. Christos could make out lengths of smashed timber, some with brass fittings still attached, piles of knotted rope and lengths of anchor chain, boat cushions, fenders.

'Looks like they've been collecting stuff from the overturned boat,' shouted Petros, above the wind, 'could have been *Kostroma*'s tender.'

They leant on the railings, speechless, still numb from their experience at the villa.

'Come on, Christos,' urged Andreas, 'there's nothing much we can do here. Let's go back, get some sleep.'

*

They arrived back at the taverna, dark and lifeless, just before two. A note pinned to the front door directed them to a small freezing room over the bar. While the others grabbed the two narrow beds and instantly fell asleep, Christos slumped in a wicker chair; sleep evaded him as he thought of the dead Russians. Much as he hated them, he couldn't justify killing four drunk and defenceless men. Although active in Delta, he never thought his involvement would go beyond co-ordinating underground activities or threatening potential troublemakers.

At dawn, he heard muted voices outside the front door. Curiosity got the better of him; he crept from the room, leaving the others asleep. Nikias was leaning into a car window talking earnestly to the driver. Not wishing to disturb him, Christos crossed the road and looked out over the bay. The storm had blown out in the night, although it was still bitterly cold. An early sun cast its golden net over Stoupa below, bathing whitewashed houses in pinks and reds. It caught the burnt-out upper decks of *Kostroma*, her once fine hull partly submerged in the mouth of the bay, her potency destroyed.

He was exhausted, his head in turmoil: guilt over the killings, anguish at not knowing of Bushra's whereabouts. Accepting he could do nothing about his guilt, he resolved to ignore it, praying that time and circumstances would absolve him. As for Bushra, they would devote all their efforts to finding her.

'Christos,' Nikias called, as the car drove off, heading south, 'coffee?'

Released from his reverie, he crossed the road, deciding to sit outside the front door despite the cold.

'You were late back,' Nikias said, returning with two cups minutes later. 'Did you go to the beach? I hear they pulled a couple from the sea.'

He and his two friends needn't have left the bar, Christos mused; Nikias was undoubtedly better informed than they were.

'Dead or alive?'

'I didn't hear.'

'We went down to see what was going on,' Christos said, drawing on his first cigarette of the day. 'There was an upturned hull floating off the beach, a lot of debris under the road.'

'Do you think the Dorpadskis were on the yacht? They usually stay on her when she anchors in the bay.'

'Nobody seemed to know,' he replied vaguely, not wishing to encourage Nikias.

'And the burning villas, I think they were owned by Dorpadski's mob,' Nikias said, knowingly.

'We saw the fires. Nobody made any effort to put them out. The fire engine was nowhere to be seen.'

'Stands to reason.'

They sat drinking coffee, absorbed in the peace of the early morning.

'Later there was a massive explosion near the headland, must've been the Benamers' old place,' Nikias muttered eventually, glancing furtively at his guest. 'I understood Dorpadski rented it.'

'So I'd heard,' said Christos, wondering if Nikias suspected their involvement.

They sat on in silence as the winter sun rose over the bay.

'The guy who's just driven off, an old friend from the south of the Peloponnese, has just returned from Corinth,' said Nikias at length. 'He told me he'd seen a significant number of large cars during the night, going north to the border.'

'Russians?'

'Had to be, we could never afford the like,' he laughed. 'It was chaotic. The road north of Kalamata was partially blocked by the snow. Quite a few had skidded off the road, were abandoned.'

'Rich pickings,' grinned Christos.

'My friend's convinced Dorpadski's dead. There's no other reason why so many would take flight so quickly.'

'I'm sure he's right.'

'Others have called with the same story: Russians racing north, appalling weather, treacherous conditions, wrecked cars. One guy in Corinth said they'd even abandoned the border post.'

'Good God,' said Christos, suddenly seeing the significance of what Nikias was saying. 'Perhaps it's the start of the end of the occupation, at least down here.'

'God willing.'

For the first time in hours, his guilt eased. Maybe, just maybe, their murderous act would be seen by future generations as just another skirmish on the day in which local Greeks drove their oppressors out. Let history, he prayed, not his conscience, determine the morality of their actions.

*

Thirty minutes later, the others joined Christos for breakfast.

'We'll head back to the villa, see if Bushra's there,' he said, after Nikias had left them. 'We'll get the local Delta guys to get rid of the burnt-out truck and secure the place.'

They checked out of the taverna at eight. Fifteen minutes later, Petros drove slowly through the security gate and up to the villa, giving the wreck a wide berth; everything appeared to be just as they'd left it.

'Close the gate,' Christos instructed Andreas. 'We don't want anybody snooping around while we're here.' He turned to Petros. 'Let's see if we can find a tarpaulin, something to throw over the truck.'

Petros took his knife and quickly forced the lock on the garage door. They found remnants of green plastic sheeting, lengths of which had been fixed to the boundary fence to screen the gardens. Within minutes they cut it up and camouflaged the truck; now out of sight and therefore out of mind, the three visibly relaxed.

Christos pushed the front door open. Everywhere they went they were faced with scenes of utter devastation. The villa had been ransacked in an orgy of destruction. Wine and spirit bottles had been smashed on the floors and against the walls, stained red like a madman's slaughterhouse; chairs and tables reduced to splinters of wood and shards of glass; beautiful woven carpets sodden; beds upended and linen shredded; cupboards emptied of their contents now scattered to the four corners; and everywhere a pungent smell – a cocktail of cigars, alcohol and stale urine. They stepped gingerly over the broken glass and around the debris, working from room to room.

'Quiet, everybody, quiet,' Petros whispered. 'Can you hear it?'

'Hear what?'

'I don't know, a faint whimper, like a puppy,' he paused. 'There, there it is again.'

'It's coming from that room,' said Andreas, pointing to a door at the end of the corridor.

Very slowly, Christos pushed it open and peered in; the room was in darkness. Behind him, Petros felt along the wall and found the light switch. The light revealed somebody sitting in an office chair, their back to the door. Christos swivelled the chair around.

A middle-aged woman, with tape over her mouth and eyes, was tightly bound with electrical cable to the chair. She was wearing a knee-length linen skirt and open-necked top, both of which were badly torn. Dressed in white, her clothes were smeared in what appeared to be blood. Christos laid a hand gently on her arm; she jumped as if she'd been electrocuted, struggled briefly and then slumped back. Petros cut her hands and feet free, while Andreas carefully removed the tape from her eyes and mouth. She was speechless, her terrified eyes staring, unfocused.

'Who are you?' Christos whispered. There was no response. 'Andreas, get some water, she's dehydrated.' Turning to the woman again, he said softly, 'You're with friends, we mean you no harm.'

Andreas returned with a glass of water and offered it to her; she remained motionless. She shivered as if in a fever. Suddenly without warning, she opened her mouth and screamed like a banshee. The three men froze, locked in a conspiracy of silence, afraid to say anything that might induce another outburst. After a few moments she muttered something, repeating it several times. Christos bent low to catch what she was saying.

'I think she said "Hera", her name's Hera,' he said. He pointed to his chest, 'Hera, I'm Christos; this is Andreas, Petros,' indicating the others. 'We're from Kalamata, we're your friends.'

'Christos, Andreas, Petros from Kalamata,' she repeated slowly, a glimmer of recognition in her eyes.

'She must've thought we're Russian,' said Andreas, seeing the tension draining from her face.

'I'm Hera, I'm Hera,' she kept repeating, more clearly as her confidence grew.

'Do you live here, Hera?' Christos asked.

'I work here,' she said shortly. 'Always have. Work for Dorpadskis now, work for them now.'

'And before the Dorpadskis?'

'Benamers, good people, the Benamers,' she whispered. 'Dorpadskis are terrible people, hateful, cruel people.'

Over the next twenty minutes, her fear gradually dissipated. She drank several glasses of water and ate some bread which Andreas had found in the kitchen.

'What happened here last night?' Christos asked, eventually.

'The Dorpadskis were celebrating with their friends, drinking heavily. They all left for their yacht. It had anchored earlier in the bay.'

'Including Bushra?'

'Yes and her friend.'

His heart sank; Bushra and Jack had been on *Kostroma*, just as he'd suspected. The question now was, were they still on the yacht when she'd exploded and sunk? He looked at the others. Petros shrugged his shoulders as if to say, 'It was inevitable.'

'What were they celebrating?'

'I think it was the paintings.'

'The paintings?'

'Bushra and her friend brought two paintings to the house around six. They gave them to Dorpadski. He made a speech and they all got drunk.'

'After they left, what did you do?'

Christos felt uncomfortable bombarding her with questions like a police detective, but he had no choice if they were to find out where Bushra was, dead or alive.

'I cleared everything away, tidied up and prepared something for myself in the kitchen. I knew they wouldn't be back till this morning, so I went to my room.'

'Your room?'

'I have a small room off the kitchen where I stay if I'm not going home. It's safe from the guards. They wouldn't normally come near the place.'

'But last night?'

'Last night was no different at first. They start to drink when they know the boss is out for the evening,' she paused. 'Dorpadski knows they drink his booze, doesn't seem to care as long as they stay reasonably sober. I locked my door as usual and went to sleep. It was about ten-thirty.'

'What happened then?'

'About midnight, I was woken by gunfire, loud explosions. My room lit up. It was like a summer storm. Shortly afterwards, I heard the guards. The racket was terrible – shouting, cursing, laughing, smashing glass. It got louder and louder. The next thing, somebody started banging on the door.'

She stopped and drank some water. Christos could see she was having difficulty telling her story.

'You don't have to go into the details,' he said, gently.

She nodded.

'They tied me up here, they wanted me out of the way. I suspected they were taking stuff out to the front, looting the place, God knows why.'

'Do you know where the explosions came from?' he asked, realising that she probably didn't know of *Kostroma*'s fate and that of her owners.

'It must have been in the village, they were that close. Later there was another explosion, much nearer this time. I thought the villa was going to burn down. I was terrified, stuck here as I was. After that everything went quiet.'

'And the guards?'

'I don't know, they probably left. And this morning, the Dorpadskis didn't appear either. It's weird, as I was expecting them. Nothing makes sense.' She closed her eyes, the effort of the last few minutes draining her energy. 'I must walk,' she said at last, raising her arms to Christos, who helped her to her feet.

She must have been an attractive woman once, he thought, her wasted figure now ravaged by years of hardship. He led her back to the living room. She gasped as they entered.

'The place is destroyed,' she cried. She stood motionless, gazing at the wreckage. 'I never liked the way they kept it,' she whispered, 'no taste, not like the Benamers, but this is terrible.' She walked slowly to the centre of the room, leaning heavily on Christos for support.

'You're in pain, did they beat you?' he asked. 'The blood on your clothes, did they…' He stopped short, not knowing how to say it, fearing the truth.

She looked at him steadily.

'They didn't rape me if that's what you're thinking.' She hesitated. 'Although a young one tried. Fortunately, he was too drunk, couldn't undo his trousers,' she said, a faint smile tracing her gaunt face. 'It's red wine, not blood,' she added, looking down at her torn clothes.

'I'm sorry, Hera,' Christos said, 'shouldn't have asked.'

'You didn't.' She turned slowly, staring at the wall. 'Thank God the paintings weren't touched.'

They followed her gaze.

'Those three paintings were old Benamer's greatest love.'

She went to the patio doors and stopped, staring out to sea.

'The explosion last night, it was *Kostroma*, wasn't it?' she whispered, raising her hand to her mouth.

The others nodded.

'The Dorpadskis, Bushra and her friend, did they survive?'

'We don't know yet,' said Christos. 'They probably all died when *Kostroma* blew up.'

He caught her as she slipped and fainted. He and Andreas laid her out gently on one of the leather settees.

'Stay with her,' he said to Andreas. 'Petros, come, we'll check out the fisherman's cottage down on the shore.'

As they walked through the gardens, he looked across at *Kostroma*. Only her broken upper deck was visible above the water.

Yesterday a classic super-yacht, a plaything of the rich; today she was a blackened hulk, the graveyard of many Russians, once feared and hated.

Petros quickly forced the lock on the patio door.

'There's nothing here,' said Christos, a couple of minutes later. 'There's no food in the place, the fridge's empty. The only evidence that anybody's been here recently is the state of the bedroom.'

Petros looked at him knowingly.

'Let's go,' said Christos. 'We'll drive to the village, try to find out who was pulled out of the sea last night.'

Hera was sitting up talking to Andreas when they got back.

'She's not there,' she said listlessly, pained resignation on her face.

'There's still a slim chance she came ashore alive.'

They secured the villa and, taking Hera with them, set off to the village for one final search for Bushra and Jack.

32

Tripoli, Late December 2031

sabel woke, desperately cold and hungry, and found herself in the back of an ancient jeep parked in a dimly lit street. She was disorientated, as if she'd been drugged. Voices, some shouting, dragged her back to the waking world. She struggled to sit up, restrained by her crumpled abaya. The voices became faces staring in at the windows. She felt uncomfortable, threatened. Somebody opened the door and pulled her roughly out onto the road.

'Stop,' she screamed, fighting back, throwing off her hijab, 'stop, don't touch me.'

Her English caught her assailant by surprise and he immediately released her. The small crowd that had gathered stepped back, silenced. She had no idea who these people were, where she was.

'*Does anybody speak English?*' she asked, in faltering Arabic. '*English, does anybody speak English?*' she repeated.

A young man dressed in jeans and a cast-off military jacket pushed his way to the front.

'My name is Abdu,' he said, quietly, 'can I help?'

'I'm Isabel Meredith,' she said, realising she had no choice but to tell him who she was. 'I work for the government in Tripoli.'

To her great relief, she found herself in an outer suburb of the city, surrounded by sympathetic local people. It took her several moments to appreciate the fact that she'd finally been released, that she was home at last.

Before sunrise she was safely deposited by Abdu on the street outside her office on Great West Road. He drove off in the jeep; adequate compensation she felt, for getting her back safely.

As usual, security in the ministry building was tight; she was asked to stand to one side while they phoned through to her boss, who apparently was still at home. Government workers, many of whom she knew, including a couple with whom she worked, had started turning up early for work. She pulled the hijab over her head not wishing to be recognised and stood waiting, away from the front desk.

Thirty minutes later, a large black sedan escorted by several motorbikes swept up to the front of the building. She was startled to see Vanmeer jumping out before the car had come to a complete stop.

'Isabel, Isabel,' he shouted as he rushed into the foyer, all the dignity of his position laid bare. His voice betrayed unusual emotion, which she could see surprised several of the early morning staff. 'How glad I am to see you,' he said, firmly taking hold of her shoulders, as if afraid she'd disappear again.

They drove straight to his office just down the road, where his ubiquitous secretary, Hamond, was waiting for them in the foyer. Within minutes, she was sitting in the very same chair overlooking the harbour that she had first occupied several weeks earlier. Now dressed in her black abaya, she felt completely disorientated.

Although evidently pleased to see her, Vanmeer was clearly preoccupied.

'How are you feeling? Did they mistreat you?' His questions, which kept coming, remained unanswered. 'Are you hungry? Would you like something to eat, drink? Would you like something more comfortable to wear?'

Her mind was blank, unable to focus on anything he was saying.

'I'm sorry,' he said, at last, 'too many damn questions, I'm sorry, Isabel.'

'A coffee would be great,' she mumbled, shifting uncomfortably in the abaya, her aching body crying out with fatigue. The low December sunshine reflecting off the sea to the east hurt her sore eyes.

Hamond arrived shortly with a large pot before wordlessly retreating to his outer office. Vanmeer watched her in silence for several minutes as she consumed several cups of black coffee.

'I've no idea what to say to you,' he said, quietly. 'The only thing I know for certain is that I owe you a huge apology.'

'Apology?'

'Because of my gross stupidity, my misplaced confidence in my own ability, I've let you down very badly.' He paused. 'And for this I am truly sorry.'

'I survived,' she said, a weak smile tracing her tired features. 'Things can only get better.' She pulled Ramil's battered file from beneath her abaya and placed it on his desk. 'A present from Cyrenaica,' she muttered.

Vanmeer was about to open it then hesitated.

'Isabel, there's something you must know before we can move on.'

She nodded, immune to being told anything, good or bad.

'Several days ago, we heard from our agents in Athens that the governor of the Peloponnese, a man by the name of Dorpadski, had died.'

'Doesn't mean anything to me,' she said, struggling to understand the relevance of what he was saying.

'He, his wife and close associates were killed on his private yacht, which blew up in Stoupa bay.'

'Stoupa,' she said, forcing herself back to the present, 'I think that's where Bushra, my grandmother, lives.'

391

'Your grandparents were on the boat. They managed to escape before it blew up.'

'Good heavens,' she exclaimed, 'why would they mix with Russians?'

'I'm terribly sorry to have to tell you,' he continued, dropping his voice, 'that your grandfather, Jack, drowned as they…'

'Jack,' she cried, as his words hit her, 'Jack's dead…'

She slumped forward, smashing the coffee cup against the vast window, and, falling to the floor, passed out.

33

England, Late December 2031

Guthrie, the aptly named first storm in December, struck the south of England with unusual ferocity. Just north of Paris, the London-bound flight from Tripoli started its descent from a cruising altitude of 15,000 metres. The pilot came over the intercom and warned his passengers to expect severe turbulence during the final thirty minutes into London's Estuary Airport.

Hunched in her window seat, Isabel vividly recalled the day of her release nearly a week ago now, a week that had changed her life forever. Her thoughts drifted back to the harrowing time she'd spent in Vanmeer's office, recalling minute details, now indelibly etched in her memory.

After she had regained consciousness, Vanmeer told her what he knew of Jack's death, of the sinking of *Kostroma* and of Dorpadski. She subsequently learnt that this horrifying event was the catalyst that led to the sudden demise of the occupation of Greece. Dorpadski's death appeared to have unnerved the Russian elite living in the Peloponnese, who fled northwards in their thousands over the course of the following days.

He went on to tell her how, lemming-like, other outlying Russian communities throughout the country had followed, fleeing to Athens, seeking the security and solidarity of their fellow countrymen. Within days, the area under direct occupation in Greece had shrunk to the metropolitan area around the capital. In vast swathes of the country, the rule of law had reverted to the people, now released from the tyranny and fear of subjugation.

Although in shock after hearing about Jack, she had been astounded by Vanmeer's news.

After the meeting, she was sent to the only private hospital in town, where she spent several days under observation, recuperating. Jack's death had initially left her stupefied, in complete denial, too exhausted to react. With time to reflect, denial had given way to sorrow and finally to anger at her impotence, loss.

Cocooned now in the belly of the huge aircraft, her grief came back to haunt her. *Why, why, why?* she kept repeating mindlessly. *Why was he not there for her now? Why had he abandoned her at this critical juncture in her life?* She needed him now more than ever. She knew how absurd and unreasonable she was being, behaving like a spoilt child, something for which he would never have forgiven her.

She could see far below, an infinite carpet of swirling cloud forms like whipped cream, tinted gold in the low winter sun. How she would have loved to have flown on into the deep blue tranquillity of space, back to a time when his love and experience had protected her. She closed her eyes as the aircraft shuddered violently, a foretaste of the turbulence to come.

Jack would not be at home to welcome her, listen to her stories, understand her worries, allay her fears and, most importantly, encourage her to embrace an uncertain future, more uncertain now than at any other time in her life. She knew that he would have had the intuition and courage to know what to do, had he been in her situation.

Another violent shudder forced her back to the present. In a couple of minutes, the aircraft was swallowed up by dense cloud, which got darker and more sinister as it descended. Visibility was so restricted she couldn't see the upturned end of the wing. Suddenly she felt the massive airframe lift, as if surfing on the crest of a wave, and then the turbulence hit. Although she had braced herself, the violent jolts, followed by sudden drops of hundreds of metres, completely unnerved her. Several people around her screamed; a stale smell of vomit permeated the air.

The aircraft ploughed on purposefully through the buffeting storm for the next twenty minutes, before dropping clear of the clouds. Through streaming rain, she could just make out the grimy River Thames spewing from the city away to the west. The wing dropped as the plane pivoted into its final approach to Estuary Airport.

*

Isabel, who was now on extended leave over Christmas and the New Year, had not spoken to Emma since she was home in November. She saw her mother as soon as she came through customs.

'Mum,' she shouted, running over and throwing her arms around her. They clung to each, laughing and crying, relief at being together again.

She pulled back and gently wiped her mother's tears away, realising how exhausted she looked. Seeing her pain at their loss, Isabel realised how selfish she'd been, never thinking beyond herself, how her mother had had to cope with her daughter's abduction, the sudden and unexpected loss of her father.

'Oh, Bel, I've been so worried about you, not hearing from you for weeks, people telling me that you were on a secret mission in the south, then suddenly being told that you were back in Tripoli after being abducted,' she said hurriedly. 'I was beside myself with worry and without Jack…'

'Mum, Mum,' she whispered, 'not here, not now.'

'You're right,' Emma said, pulling herself together eventually.

'Let's get home, everything can wait.'

'If we're quick, we could catch a train at twelve, be home for lunch.'

The train rose swiftly and noiselessly up over the Thames Estuary before swooping south into the storm-tossed Kent countryside.

'I've moved into Dad's apartment,' Emma said, apropos of nothing, several minutes later.

The news surprised Isabel, not so much that she'd moved, but realising that from now on, things would be different at home.

'It's a beautiful place,' was all that Isabel could think to say. Although knowing that Jack would have approved; it was far too early to invoke his name.

They sat on in silence, Isabel's emotions running riot. Discretely, she glanced at her mother, staring impassively at the passing countryside. She found Emma's stillness, in complete contrast to her own overwrought feelings, unsettling. Conversation was spasmodic, neither ready to talk about Jack and the awful void he'd left in their lives.

*

It was strange walking into Jack's old apartment again. She found it surreal, briefly convincing herself that he'd suddenly appear from his bedroom, a huge smile on his face, delighted to see her. She knew it wasn't to be.

'I haven't made any changes to the place,' said Emma. 'Dad's furniture, everything here, is so much more usable, more comfortable than my old stuff.'

Isabel couldn't deny that her mother was right, yet it was sad that she'd chosen not to bring anything from the cottage, apart from a few watercolours.

Jack's absence hung oppressively in the air. She wondered anxiously how long it would be before her mother's reserve broke, before she herself couldn't suppress her ragged emotions any longer. She owed it to Emma to stay strong, willing her mother to be the first to broach life without Jack.

She wandered over to the glass wall and gazed out on the windswept terrace, barely visible in the murky winter light.

'I see you've been planting. I always felt he could have done more, you know, grown something with a bit of colour. It always looked so bleak.'

'I've read a lot recently about inner-city roof gardens. It'll look a picture come the spring.'

Isabel's mind went blank; she was at a complete loss as to what to say or do next.

'Maybe you'd like to freshen up after the flight,' Emma suggested, reading her daughter's thoughts. 'Why don't you have a shower? The spare room's all yours. I'll get lunch. You must be starving.'

She hugged her mother by way of response and hurried to her room, unable to contain herself any longer. She slumped onto the bed, her tears soaking the pillow, and succumbed to her pent-up sorrow.

Emma was suddenly by her side, lifting her into her arms.

'Bel, Bel, I'm so sorry, I know this is hard for you,' she whispered. 'We'll miss him dreadfully. It seems so unfair, so wrong that he's not here with us, not here to welcome you home.'

They clung to each other in mourning. Slowly she set her daughter down on the bed, where they sat entwined in each other's arms. Isabel struggled to think clearly, to speak, overwhelmed by grief.

'I'm sorry, Mum, I just couldn't…'

'Don't, Bel, don't,' she said gently. 'There's no need to say anything.' After several moments, she continued, 'Jack meant so much to both of us. He was our love, our strength, our inspiration and now he's left us. Our time has come. We must be strong, look out for each other. That's what he would have wanted, what he would have expected.'

Gradually the storm in Isabel's head eased, her mother's warmth seeping through her weary body. She was a child again, enfolded in love, shielded from the terrors of life. Slowly the world around her reasserted itself.

Emma, brushing the tears from her cheeks, kissed her.

'I'll be in the kitchen,' she said, pulling away.

'I love you, Mum.'

'I love you too, Bel,' she replied softly, turning back at the door.

I must pull myself together, Isabel said to herself as she got undressed. The hot shower soon revived her and although she felt emotionally drained, she was ready to face her mother.

She saw that Emma had been busy preparing lunch. With the table laid and the local classical radio station just audible, a fragile normality pervaded the room, calming her nerves.

'Bushra's greatly looking forward to seeing us all at Jack's memorial service,' Emma said quietly, as they sat at the table to eat. 'I spoke to her yesterday. She was telling me the weather's been appalling. They've had up to thirty centimetres of snow on the mountain passes in the Peloponnese.'

'Do you think we'll have trouble getting through?' Isabel asked; anything was better than talking directly about Jack, of their mutual anguish, she thought.

'She's expecting milder weather next week, reckons most of the snow will have melted by the New Year. We must take winter jackets though. I don't imagine Stoupa will be too warm.'

'Is the memorial service being held in the town?'

'No, it's in a remote village, above in the mountains. The place seems to have had a special significance for the two of them. She wants Jack's ashes to be buried in the graveyard in the grounds of the Orthodox church.'

'Strange, given neither of them was a church goer,' said Isabel.

'Father Anthony, the local priest, was only too happy to oblige Bushra's wishes. He was the one who suggested the date, thought it most appropriate.'

'Why the fifth?'

'It's the Eve of Epiphany. Epiphany is a very important day in the Orthodox calendar, perhaps even more so than Christmas.'

'I wonder what Jack would have thought of all this.'

'I'm sure he'd have been happy with the arrangements,' Emma said. 'I've found that few people ever reveal their inner beliefs. He was no different. Anyway, Bushra's hoping the ceremony will be simple, that not many will turn up.'

Isabel tried to imagine what Bushra must have been through since the day Jack died; how she was coping in her bereavement. So much had changed in her personal life, in Greece as a whole.

'How's Bushra been managing?'

'Surprisingly well,' said her mother. 'I've spoken to her several times. She's very philosophical about Jack, their time together. Perhaps fatalistic would be a better description.'

'She's very strong.'

'She said that the gods had offered her a Faustian choice,' continued Emma. 'Jack's love or Greece free of the Russians, but not both. In the end fate decided, taking Jack and freeing Greece.'

'She'd have forgone that freedom to have Jack still,' said Isabel.

'You're right. Aside from the devastation of his death, I think what really saddened her was that they'd never been together, you know, in what you might call normal times.'

'I hadn't really thought of them like that.'

'The early years were traumatic enough. And then to meet again during the occupation after so many years apart, it seemed so cruel. I think they dreamed of a time when they'd be free, to live the life that had eluded them all those years ago.'

'God, how awful. To think it might have been so different if he'd survived.'

'Such was their fate,' said Emma wistfully.

'It's so sad you couldn't get to the funeral.'

'The Greek Embassy in London was adamant. There was no way they were going to give me a visa.'

Emma got up and switched off the radio, which suddenly seemed to trouble her.

'You heard of course about the circumstances surrounding Jack's death,' she said, returning to her seat, 'how Bushra was the only survivor after Dorpadski's yacht, *Kostroma*, blew up and sank.'

'Yes, Vanmeer filled me in on the facts, basically what his agents had told him.'

Isabel could see that her mother was agitated.

'It's just that the embassy people were really unpleasant when I told them I wanted to go to Jack's funeral. I realised later that they might have associated me with the whole Dorpadski business.' Emma hesitated. 'Maybe there's more to this than we realise.'

'Mum, I'm sure there is but there's no way we'll ever find out.'

'Even from Bushra?'

'Especially from Bushra.'

34

England, Early January 2032

Standing on a freezing platform just before midnight, the thought of Greg's imminent arrival left Isabel feeling nervous. She smiled to herself recalling the last time she'd waited for a train; it was in November in Calais, the end of a crazy day in which he'd presented her with the infamous DNA results; the day they'd made reckless love on the beach. So much had happened in the ensuing weeks; lust had given way to love, pointing her to an exciting but uncertain future.

The train was running late. She wasn't bothered. Emma had told her that she wouldn't wait up, that she'd be in bed when they got back to the apartment. She suspected that her mother wanted her to have time on her own with Greg, knowing there would be much to talk about.

At twelve-thirty, the train glided silently into the empty station. She was the only person waiting, he the only passenger alighting. She ran up to him, arms outstretched. Dropping his bags, he threw his arms around her and whisked her off her feet.

'God, am I glad to see you, Bel,' he laughed, kissing her fervently before putting her down.

Her recent anxiety gave way to unalloyed happiness at seeing him again.

'It's cold and wet. We could get a taxi, or perhaps you'd prefer to walk,' she said, as they left the station. 'It's not far, maybe fifteen minutes.'

'Let's walk, I need to stretch my legs. I've spent too much time sitting on planes and trains, hanging around lawyers' offices.'

The bitter weather had driven people indoors; the streets were deserted.

'Did everything go OK?'

'Better than I could have hoped for.'

'And the alimony payments, are they sorted?'

'She waived them. There's nothing more to do now, thank God.'

'That's fantastic. What a huge relief for you.'

'Maybe her guilty conscience caught up with her in the end,' he laughed. 'She knew she'd behaved badly. It wasn't as if she needed the money.'

'Are you OK to come with us then?'

'Yes. I managed to get a seven-day visa from the embassy in Amsterdam just yesterday morning,' said Greg. 'While in town, I also booked a seat on tomorrow's flight from Estuary to Athens, the same one as yours.'

'Brilliant,' said Isabel, 'I'm really glad you can make it. I know Mum will be pleased.'

As soon as they got to the apartment, he went off to have a hot shower. She left one of Jack's old dressing gowns on the bed, knowing he would have offered it to Greg had he been around; it seemed entirely natural. Ten minutes later, he joined her in the living room.

'God, this is some place,' he said. 'Jack had great taste, I'm very impressed. Even his clothes…' He trailed off, indicating the dressing gown.

'Would you like a drink?'

'I'd love a whisky, ice, no water.'

'They're mostly Irish blends, the place is awash with them,' she laughed. 'I'll join you.'

They settled down on the settee.

'How's your mother?' he asked. 'It must've been difficult for you both, you know, meeting here without him.'

'It wasn't easy. She was very pent up on the train from the airport, almost speechless, which was difficult. Things started to change after we got home. We said little at first, just cried a good deal. It was an amazing relief for the two of us.'

'It must have been tough for you both.'

'Time spent together over Christmas and the New Year was very cathartic. Mum was brilliant.'

'Did she ask about the abduction, your time in Cyrenaica?'

'Later, much later, after we'd got over the initial shock of Jack's absence.'

'I suspect you're similar, both very strong.'

'I don't know. She's had a very difficult life, copes with situations much better than I do. I still feel a kid around her.'

'You're no kid,' he laughed, 'especially after what you've been through recently.' He paused. 'I had to meet Vanmeer before I left.'

'Vanmeer?' Her heart missed a beat.

'He insisted I come to his office.'

'What was so important that it couldn't wait?'

'There were a couple of things he said you ought to know.'

'I wonder why he didn't tell me himself.'

'He said you'd been through enough already, didn't want to burden you while you came to terms with your loss, recovered from your ordeal.'

'Go on,' she said, her heart racing in anticipation.

'Philippe and his thugs, along with the military commander in the Fezzan and his associates, about forty military personnel in total, were detained indefinitely without charge, a couple of days after you were abducted.'

'Good heavens, did you know about this?'

'Not a clue,' he said. 'As far as I was concerned, finding you was Vanmeer's top priority. He told me he had his suspicions about the military for some time but despite all your detective work…'

'Our detective work,' she interjected.

'He said he'd needed corroborating evidence from the Russian side before he could press charges. After a lot of hassle, he managed to convince the military governor to detain the group, pending further investigation.'

'Ramil's file was all he needed.'

'Exactly,' Greg said. 'Charges were pressed while you were in hospital.'

'God, that's great news,' she exclaimed. 'What'll happen to them?'

'At the moment they're being held in the maximum-security prison in Sirte, east of Tripoli. Apparently, the senior guys, including Philippe, are facing charges of treason, murder and a whole range of drug-related offences.'

'Where will they be tried?'

'Probably The Hague. They could get up to thirty years. Vanmeer reckons they'll never be released.'

'That's unbelievable.'

'He said it was all down to you. He's immensely proud of what you achieved, appears to have great plans for you when you get back.'

'We'll see,' she said, her recent scepticism holding her in check.

'The fact that your courage, your conviction led to the collapse of the cross-border drugs trade, without any government support whatsoever, really impressed him.'

'I had all the help I needed.'

'Help?'

'You,' she laughed. 'Just you, that was enough.'

'Hardly, anyway, you've done a huge service to those seeking a better life on both sides of the border.'

'Enough,' she said, feeling uncomfortable. 'And what was the other thing you were to tell me?'

'Earlier this week, Vanmeer learnt from his agents in Athens that they had evidence,' he hesitated, 'evidence that Jack and Bushra were involved in blowing up *Kostroma*, killing Dorpadski.'

'Good God, I don't believe it,' she exclaimed, stunned at the revelation.

'Apparently the evidence is irrefutable.'

'Jack and Bushra killers,' she cried, completely baffled. 'They couldn't have done it, they wouldn't harm a fly. Or sink a super-yacht. It's just not possible.'

'They've become national heroes in the Peloponnese.'

She was speechless; the whole idea was bizarre, grotesque even. Her head was spinning with half-formed plots, intrigues and conspiracy theories involving her grandparents.

'Why would they have done it? And why kill Dorpadski, evil as he was?'

'Vanmeer described the man as an international drug dealer, the despotic governor of the Peloponnese, who still had close links with Benghazi. Apparently, he'd been a constant threat to Bushra. She hated him, everything he represented.'

'Was that really a sufficient reason to kill him?' She glanced at Greg, waiting for an answer; he said nothing. 'I really don't think so,' she said, bluntly. 'It just doesn't make sense.'

'Vanmeer told me they'd been specifically instructed to kill Dorpadski,' he said. 'The other deaths were just collateral damage.'

'Who was supposed to have instructed them?' she asked, alarmed at the thought.

He finished his whisky while she got up and walked over to the glass wall, trying to clear her head. It had started to rain again; the rising wind was tearing at the wintry trees, spidery silhouettes thrashing in the dark. The view without increased her sense of isolation within, cut off from the physical world beyond the glass as surely as she was from the events of that fateful day when *Kostroma* was destroyed in Stoupa.

She turned to Greg.

'Who the hell would have instructed them?'

'Emma's brother, your Uncle Stavros.'

For a split second, she lost the thread of their conversation and then it hit her: Stavros, her mother's twin brother, somebody whose existence she'd only recently heard about, had instructed his parents to commit murder.

'Stavros, that's crazy,' she said, emphatically. 'Why on earth would he have done that? I can't see the connection.'

She wandered back and slumped onto the settee, speechless.

'Vanmeer's agents believe Stavros is leading the resistance against the Russians in Cyrenaica, but they can't be sure.'

'Leading the resistance,' she repeated. 'Come on, Greg, do you believe this bullshit?'

'Bel, Bel, what I think is of no consequence. I'm just telling you what I've been told.'

'I'm sorry. You're right, this isn't about you, us,' she said, quietly. 'But those two killing Dorpadski, it makes no sense. What else did he have to say?'

'He could only talk of Dorpadski. Apparently up until the day he died, he was the puppet master pulling the strings of the Russian administration in Benghazi. Although living in Greece, he was still effectively the military governor of UNMC.'

'So, Stavros used my grandparents to get rid of him,' she said, disbelief in her voice. 'Why them, for God's sake, why them?'

'Dorpadski controlled the drugs trade in Cyrenaica. Kalamata, near where he lived in Stoupa, was one of two links between the Russians and their markets in Europe,' he said, quietly, trying to reason with her. '*Kostroma*, based in Kalamata, was the control centre of his entire operation.' He paused. 'I'm afraid they were just convenient foot soldiers in Stavros' struggle against the occupation.'

'It can't be that simple,' said Isabel. 'I'm sorry, Greg, I just don't buy it.' Absently, she topped up their glasses; time passed, only the wind breaking the silence. 'Of course, the second link was Philippe's route through Tripoli, which is no more,' she said, picking up on his earlier remark.

'Exactly.'

'Just supposing for a moment Vanmeer was right about Stavros, you know, leading the resistance in Cyrenaica,' she continued, after a lengthy pause, 'there'd have to have been a connection between what happened in Stoupa and what happened at the border,' before adding, 'in fact, what happened to me.'

'I've been thinking about that ever since I left Vanmeer.'

'That's weird, you know, linking the two,' she said.

'God, it's suddenly hit me,' he exclaimed. 'Do you remember the night we met in Tripoli, when you were Ramil's prisoner?'

Isabel nodded.

'You told me you had to go back with him, he wouldn't release you,' he said excitedly. 'I suspect you were being held hostage until Dorpadski was dead.'

'That's possible,' she said, barely believing what he was saying.

'You were released a day or two after *Kostroma* sank and Dorpadski was killed,' said Greg. 'They had to be linked.'

'Good heavens.'

Greg was silent for a moment. 'But for that to work,' he continued, 'there must be a connection between Stavros and Ramil.'

'I did tell Ramil, who could well have been working for Stavros, about Jack at one of our earlier meetings,' she admitted. 'I'm guessing it wouldn't have taken Stavros long then to work out the family connections,' she said. 'Coming up with a plan to blackmail my grandparents was pretty straightforward,' she said, before adding, 'It's all pretty plausible, but why, for God's sake, why?'

'Stavros must have had a very good reason to do what he did, involving his family in such a dangerous and convoluted exercise.'

'It's baffling, just baffling.'

'The hold over your grandparents must have been overwhelming for them to do what they did,' Greg said.

'Kidnapping their granddaughter was pretty extreme,' Isabel said. 'Only Bushra would know the full story.'

She slumped back, trying desperately to make sense of everything he'd just told her. They sat on in silence; minutes passed.

'Being held hostage by my uncle, it's unbelievable. I'll never discuss any of this with Mum, with Bushra, never,' she added emphatically.

'Good idea.'

'Greg, I'm shattered, you must be too. Let's leave it for now, we'll have plenty of time over the next couple of days to unravel all this.'

He stood and gently pulled her to her feet, before embracing her.

'Hell, I'd completely forgotten,' he said, standing back. 'Vanmeer gave me an envelope, addressed to you, delivered anonymously to HQ several days before our meeting. I have it here,' he said, taking a crumpled envelope from his jacket pocket.

'It can wait,' she said, drawing him in again.

*

She lay beside his satiated body, her mind on edge, going over everything she'd learnt that evening; nothing seemed to make sense.

She needed to get up, move about. She crept out of bed and into the living room, now bathed in moonlight; the storm had passed, all was calm. It was then that she saw the unopened envelope, where he'd dropped it. Switching on a low light, she flopped onto the settee and opened it, pulling out several sheets, each covered in a dense Arabic scrawl. She tried in vain to read the text. Finally she gave up, realising she'd have to wait for Greg.

She reached for an old rug, pulled it over herself and quickly fell asleep.

She awoke with a start. He was gently rocking her.

'Isabel,' he whispered, anxiously. 'Are you OK?'

'I'm fine,' she said, drowsily. 'I couldn't sleep.'

She sat up, dislodging the handwritten sheets, which fell to the floor.

'Your letter,' he said, picking up the papers. 'Couldn't you read it?'

'I can just about converse in everyday Arabic,' she muttered, 'but as for reading, I'm hopeless.'

He sat beside her and started to read.

'God in heaven, this is astonishing,' he said, after a few moments. 'It's been written to you by Ramil on behalf of a person called Fawzan and, I quote here, his "planning committee".'

'Fawzan. I met him with a couple of his people a few times in Cyrenaica.'

'Apparently you so impressed them all when you were their guest...'

'Guest,' she interjected. 'Some bloody cheek.'

'Impressed them,' he continued reading, 'with your knowledge of how EDA operates, with your suggestions about what could be done in Benghazi to improve welfare, agriculture, tribal integration, etcetera, etcetera. It goes on and on, in quite formal Arabic, praising your ideas, extolling your virtues.'

'So, what do they want?' she asked, barely believing what she was hearing.

'They want you to work with them in Cyrenaica after the Russians have been thrown out, to rebuild their society from "ground zero" as he puts it.'

'Working in Cyrenaica,' she exclaimed, 'they can't be serious.'

'From the language, the prose, I think they are.'

'He goes on to say how much they appreciated your enthusiasm, saying there is so much to be done there, you would never be short of interesting work.' With a broad grin, he continued reading. 'I can't believe it, in the last paragraph, he invites you "to ask your friend Dr Hamilton to join you. We know he is a like-minded person and an experienced doctor and his help would be invaluable in reorganising our health system".'

'This is insane. I need a drink,' she said, struggling to her feet.

After pouring two generous measures of whisky, she told him about her meetings, while in captivity, with Fawzan and the others. They reread the letter several times, unsure what to make of it.

'Just before he left at the end of our last meeting, Fawzan spoke about his people and the challenges they faced, what needed to be done when the Russians had gone.'

'Who's "they"?'

'I've no idea, but I suspected at the time that they were some sort of government-in-waiting, but I've no evidence.'

'How strange they should turn to you, to us.'

'The whole time we were together, I couldn't make out on whose authority Fawzan was speaking,' said Isabel. 'He, his people, they were very rational, hardly fundamentalists or even nationalists, neither were they socialists or communists as we might label them.'

'Maybe they're still forming their ideas.'

'I think the nearest explanation came from Fawzan himself. It was right at the end of their last visit. He talked about "our" people, calling them the dispossessed, people who had to be woven into the fabric of a new society, something about a society without prejudice or fear, one respecting the rights of every citizen.'

'Weaving the dispossessed,' Greg laughed, 'that's neat.'

'Oddly just before they left – it must have been way past midnight – he turned to me and said in effect that I understood exactly what they'd been discussing and, I quote, that, "God willing, I will play my part".'

'There you have it,' he exclaimed, 'their offer foretold.'

They talked for another hour, one minute agreeing that this might be a chance in a lifetime that would never come their way again; the next, that to take up the offer, they would have to give up well-paid, secure jobs – a suicidal career move.

Reality finally hit them: Fawzan had to be part of a regime that was complicit in Jack's death. They could never contemplate moving to Cyrenaica because the two issues were irreconcilable. Having made the decision, they went back to bed.

35

Stoupa, Early January 2032

She woke with a start. The rising sun sliced through the shutters, bathing the walls in pale orange stripes. Greg had his back to her, soundless, inert, a rough blanket pulled up over his head, covering him like a corpse. She was freezing. She wondered vaguely how Bushra survived the bitterly cold winters in this place, the new norm for the Peloponnese.

She slid out of bed and pulled on her chinos and the heavy fleece she'd travelled in the previous day. The smell of freshly ground coffee drew her to the kitchen, where she found Hera busy preparing breakfast.

'Good morning.'

'Isabel,' Hera replied, with a broad smile, 'I hope you slept well, though I'm afraid you must have found it cold.' She poured coffee from a copper jug sitting on the hob into a mug and handed it to her.

'Thanks,' said Isabel, grateful for its warmth.

Hera was at the villa to meet them when they arrived at midnight on a cool clear night. Although Jack had never lived in the place, Isabel felt his unseen presence as soon as she got there, unnerving her, making her restless.

'What time will Christos be here?'

He'd met Emma, Isabel and Greg at Athens airport early the previous morning, driving them directly to his taverna in Kardamyli, where they'd stopped for an evening meal before coming on to Stoupa; it had been a long day.

'Around ten-thirty. You've plenty of time for breakfast, to get ready,' said Hera, bustling round the kitchen. 'I'm coming with you. It'll be a bit cramped for us all in his old car,' she laughed.

Isabel had been surprised to find that Bushra was not at the villa to meet them. Apparently, the previous afternoon, she'd gone up to the mountain village where Jack's memorial ceremony was to take place. She'd planned an overnight vigil in the old church. She'd told Hera that she wanted to spend her last night alone with Jack, before his ashes were interred in the graveyard.

On the drive from Athens, Isabel had wondered whether Jack would have approved of this whole memorial business, of the posthumous commotion that was being made by so many on his behalf. While she knew he was a philosophical and thoughtful man, he had no faith and despised institutions that fostered religion. How ironic, she thought, that Bushra had arranged for his remains to be buried in sacred ground; better by far, thought Isabel, that they were scattered over the side of an old boat sailing around Stoupa bay.

'How long will it take to get there? I thought the ceremony didn't start till one.'

'On a good day, it shouldn't take longer than forty-five, fifty minutes,' Hera replied. 'Christos is worried that the road up will be busy. It's little more than a mountain track in places and quite steep. It can get blocked quickly if anybody breaks down or there's an accident.'

'He's expecting a large crowd?'

'You know your grandparents are heroes, not just here in Stoupa, but in the Peloponnese, the whole of Greece.' Isabel could sense Hera's excitement, reminding her of the significance of what they'd done. 'Their courage led to the beginning of the end of the occupation,' Hera said, emphatically. 'Today, you won't see a Russian outside Athens.'

'Of course,' said Isabel, turning away, asking herself for the umpteenth time how Jack and Bushra managed to blow up *Kostroma*; she had no doubt that they were brave and honourable, it's just that she doubted their ability to kill.

'There could be hundreds then.'

'Yes, hundreds,' Hera said, cheerfully.

Yesterday in the car, Isabel had listened to Emma and Christos discuss his relationship with Bushra, his long association with Libya and the events surrounding the sinking of *Kostroma*. It became clear that their two families had been close friends for decades.

Nothing that he'd said or even implied could shed any light on the one thing that consumed Isabel; if he was aware of Stavros and his involvement in the sinking of *Kostroma*, did he know what hold Stavros had over her grandparents that drove them to kill Dorpadski?

Sitting now in the bright sunny kitchen, Isabel accepted that she'd never know what had transpired between Stavros and his parents; as a result, she and Greg could never work in Benghazi for Fawzan and his committee to rebuild Cyrenaica.

She also learnt of Christos' active involvement in the resistance in the Peloponnese, in which he appeared to have played a leading part. She was fascinated to learn how precipitously the occupation had collapsed after Dorpadski had been killed.

She'd always had the impression that the Russians held Greece in a vice-like grip, from which there was no escape. Christos' narrative shed an entirely different light on the occupation. He told them that the Russians didn't have the military, financial or administrative capacity to hold down the occupation much longer, because they were fighting on so many fronts throughout the Balkans, Caucuses, Middle East and North Africa. For the Russians, Greece had little strategic value and no natural resources; in short, the occupation had become a liability and was bound to fail.

'And your family, friends, people from the town,' Isabel asked Hera, 'are many going?'

'I know of at least twenty, maybe more.' Hera paused. 'We have a duty to honour your family. Local people suffered greatly at Dorpadski's hands. He and his people caused misery for so many around here. They were responsible for many thefts, suicides, even deaths over the years.'

'And you…' said Isabel, instantly regretting what she'd said.

'I was simply his servant,' Hera said brusquely, clearly not wishing to discuss the matter further.

'I'm sorry, Hera, I shouldn't have…'

'Don't be, it's in the past, today we celebrate,' she said, her cheeriness quickly reasserting itself.

Just at that moment Emma, wrapped in one of Bushra's dressing gowns, wandered into the kitchen. Isabel was relieved to see her mother looking rested; the dark shadows under her eyes that were so noticeable in the airport had magically vanished.

'The smell of coffee, I couldn't stay in bed any longer,' she said, hugging her daughter before turning to Hera. 'Is there any in the pot?'

'Of course,' she said, filling another mug.

'How are you, Mum? Did you sleep alright?'

'I did, but not brilliantly. I was cold. Greece for me has always been about warmth, hot balmy days on the beach. This is more like an English winter morning.'

'With that sunshine,' laughed Isabel, 'hardly. Just look at the clear blue sky, it's magical.'

'No more wind and snow,' said Hera. 'From today for the next week, it will be fine, probably windy but mild.'

'I hope you're right,' Emma said.

'If it snows again, we're all in trouble,' said Hera. 'There won't be enough food and beds in the village for everybody if the road's cut off,' she laughed, 'and as for the stocks of ouzo…' Seeing the other two frown, she added quickly, 'Don't worry, Christos will look after us if there's a problem.'

'I'm amazed everybody's gone to all this trouble,' said Emma. 'And I still don't understand how Bushra arranged to have Jack's memorial service in an Orthodox church, given that he was an agnostic.'

Isabel noticed a quizzical look on Hera's face.

'I thought Bushra was a practising Muslim,' Emma continued, 'had been since her childhood days in Benghazi.'

'You're right,' said Hera, quietly, 'the family were devout Muslims. However, the week after Jack died, she and I drove up to the village, which they'd visited a couple of times over the years. I think being there brought her closer to Jack, brought her inner peace, especially in the old church. And Father Anthony was happy to help her.'

'Will she convert?' asked Emma.

'No, no,' laughed Hera.

'And the service, will it be formal?'

'I doubt it,' she replied. 'You know Jack was cremated. It's still frowned upon by our church. I imagine this doesn't worry Father Anthony. They say he'll perform a short simple service just for the family, close friends in the church.'

'And what about the hundreds of people you're expecting?' asked Isabel.

'They'll probably wait outside. Maybe a local monk, a cantor will sing a lament, which they'll amplify around the village square,' continued Hera. 'It'll be interesting to see what Father Anthony has arranged. Whatever happens, I'm sure he'll say a few prayers and bless the crowd afterwards.'

'It all seems very appropriate,' Emma said, evidently relieved.

'It'll be good for Bushra and those wanting a proper memorial for Jack,' Hera said, 'without offending local people, older worshippers, in the area.'

Isabel fervently hoped that today's ceremony would lead to some sort of family catharsis, enabling all of them to move on.

*

The steep road, not much more than a track in places and twisting like a snake, cut into the face of the mountain. It was busy, mostly older cars throwing out black smoke at each gear change, crawling up ahead. Finally, turning into an elevated valley, the road levelled off through dense oak woods, giving way to a landscape of rough goat pastures and small olive groves.

Christos pointed out the village at the end of the road, still in the partial shade of a towering cliff face. The queue ahead slowed to walking pace. Eventually they were stopped by two older men, clearly known to Christos, who asked him to pull over. He got out and greeted the two, kissing them formally on each cheek. There was much hilarity; it took a minute or two before his friends allowed them to get on their way.

They left the car in a long line of parked vehicles and walked about a kilometre to the village. The air was bracing, cool in the shade, the sun warm on their faces. Along the road, they passed isolated ancient pine trees, sighing in the bitter easterly wind, which scattered twigs and leaves through the air. Isabel felt energised, feeling their excitement building as they walked.

The church bell rang out as they made their way into the main square, dominated by the church. In the centre of the square stood a large holm oak bathed in bright winter sunshine. It was midday. A large crowd had gathered. People of all ages – stooped old women dressed in mourning black, older men in woven jackets, younger men, many in army fatigues, young women in colourful skirts and shawls as if it were high summer, children running wild beneath their feet – all gave the place a surreal carnival atmosphere. Somebody at the foot of the church steps was playing a bouzouki; several voices sang in harmony.

Many people stopped to talk to Christos, who appeared to be a man of some authority in the community, reinforcing Isabel's earlier view that he'd played a significant role in the resistance in these parts. Occasionally he would introduce somebody to Emma, explaining the person's relationship to Bushra and her family. One woman whom Christos was clearly surprised to see was Chara, who had arrived from Athens in the early hours on the overnight bus to Kalamata.

'People have come from far and wide to be here today,' he said, seeing Emma's astonishment at the size of the crowd. 'They've come to pay tribute to Bushra, to remember Jack; their courageous act, the turning point in our struggle against the occupation. We've never looked back since the day *Kostroma* sank,' he said, smiling broadly.

'I understand.'

'I'm surprised by many who are here, people I haven't set eyes on for years.' He looked around. 'See there, under the tree,' he said pointing to the oak, 'those two old guys in city clothes drinking ouzo. They were apprenticed to your grandfather, old Ali Benamer, when he ran the shipping company. Good men, they stayed with the family to the bitter end.'

'I still don't fully appreciate the significance of Dorpadski's death,' said Emma, 'the impact of what my parents did.'

No, thought Isabel, *and thankfully none of us will ever know the motive that drove your twin brother to use your parents in the way he did.* She fervently prayed that the spectre of Stavros would fade away, and what he meant to them as individuals would soon be consigned to history; that family links between Greece and North Africa would finally be erased. Today, she believed, would be the start of that process.

'Have you noticed anything unusual about some of Christos' friends, mostly the men, although there was one woman as well?' Greg asked her discretely, as they squeezed their way into the square.

'No.'

'Many of them, including Christos, have a small triangle of black ribbon sewn onto the sleeves of their jackets. One man had a similar-shaped tattoo on the back of his hand.'

'I'll ask Hera when I get a chance.'

'It's odd,' Greg continued, 'it doesn't feel we've come to hear an old priest commit Jack's remains to eternity. It's more like a public holiday.'

'In a sense it is, at least that's what he would have wanted.'

'Then that's how we should treat it,' Greg laughed, turning to the others. 'Would anybody like something to eat, a drink perhaps? We've got plenty of time.'

'Why don't you all stay here?' suggested Christos. 'I'll look for Bushra, find out what Father Anthony has organised. I'll meet you under the tree in twenty minutes.'

The taverna was doing a roaring trade; tantalising smells of grilled lamb, fresh herbs and local tobacco wafted from its cavernous interior. Families and friends squeezed around rickety metal tables under the huge oak, eating, drinking and talking with an earnestness common to all village folk in the Peloponnese.

'Nothing to eat, thanks,' said Emma, 'but a large Metaxa wouldn't go amiss.'

'The same for me,' said Isabel.

'Hera?'

'I'm fine, thank you.'

Greg returned with three large brandies, several minutes later.

'To Jack,' he said, raising his glass.

'To my parents,' Emma said. 'To all their friends who managed to get here today.'

The noise level kept rising steadily, as more and more people thronged into the square, their excitement palatable. Isabel drew Greg to one side.

'The ribbon, the delta sign, is the symbol of the resistance movement,' she said, quietly. 'It's a classical underground organisation, built on a tight-knit cell structure. Hera said it was very effective in the south of the Peloponnese, thanks largely to Christos.'

'That explains a lot.'

'Apparently, they've all been ordered not to bring their weapons today,' she whispered. 'Christos was afraid the whole thing might turn into a victory party, you know, with everybody shooting randomly into the air.'

'Could've been lethal,' he laughed.

'Nobody would have openly admitted to being a member when the Russians were here. Membership meant certain death. Now they've gone, people are starting to wear it, proud to have been involved.'

'Thinking about it, somebody had painted a black delta on the wall of the villa. I just thought it was some mindless graffiti.'

'According to Hera, that would have been a warning to the Russians that the place, those living there, were under the movement's protection.'

'They wouldn't have had a hope against this lot in the long run,' Greg said, grinning.

A few minutes later Christos returned, pushing his way through the crowd.

'How's Bushra?' Emma asked, anxiously. 'When will we see her?'

Isabel knew that her mother was very nervous at the thought of her first face-to-face meeting with Bushra, ever since the day she'd discovered that Bushra was her mother. Although Emma had rarely spoken of the significance of the meeting, she'd kept alluding to this day in numerous throwaway remarks, alerting Isabel to her mother's mounting anxiety.

'She's well, in good spirits, despite her overnight vigil in the freezing church,' said Christos. 'She's looking forward to seeing you.'

'What's the plan, Christos?' Isabel asked.

'Twenty of us have been invited into the church. Everybody else will hear the service through speakers. There's one hanging from the oak there,' he said, pointing to a branch. 'Afterwards, Father Anthony will give a short address and a blessing from the front steps. The whole business will be over in thirty minutes.' He turned to the women. 'Remember to wear your headscarves.'

*

Shafts of sunlight poured through stained-glass windows, throwing a myriad of rainbow colours over the flagstones. Dust particles, caught in the light, drifted in the still air. The church, smelling strongly of wax and incense, was bitterly cold. It took Isabel a moment to adjust to the gloom.

Suddenly she saw Bushra, her back to them and wrapped in a shawl, sitting on a simple bench directly in front of the oak-panelled iconostasis, the screen separating the nave from the sanctuary.

Hearing their footsteps shuffling up the aisle, Bushra stood to welcome the three. Christos and Hera hung back. Even in the poor light, Isabel could make out Bushra's radiant face, belying her age. She came to them, arms outstretched.

'Emma, Isabel, how wonderful to see you,' she said, embracing the two women. 'So, we meet at last,' she said, standing back, taking their hands and looking at each in turn. 'Emma, my daughter, my granddaughter Isabel,' she whispered at length, fighting back tears. 'Jack was right,' she smiled, 'we have two beautiful girls. No wonder he was so proud.'

Isabel dared not look at her mother, who she knew would be struggling to rein in her emotions. For her part, Isabel simply leaned forward and kissed her grandmother on the cheek, unable to utter a single word. Her mother did likewise, tears now flowing unchecked.

'We mustn't keep Father Anthony waiting,' Bushra said lightly, breaking the spell, before turning to Greg. 'You must be Greg, I've heard all about you,' she laughed, kissing him on both cheeks.

'Nothing too outrageous, I hope.'

'Nothing that would have alarmed Jack.'

In that brief reference to Jack, Isabel could feel their unspoken anxiety slip away. She glanced at her mother, now falling under Bushra's spell; Emma hadn't looked so happy for a long time.

Bushra peered down to the back of the church.

'Is that you, Christos, Hera? Come, come and join us,' she called. They came forward through the shafts of light, each to be greeted. 'Father Anthony tells me that there are many hundreds of people in the square, says it's like a festival day, and so it should be,' she added.

'I've recognised many faces, friends of yours and the family, young and old,' Christos said, 'many from the distant past, people I'd completely forgotten existed. You'll be truly surprised.'

Isabel saw the delight on Bushra's face and the easy intimacy between these two old friends, as he reverted to Greek. He could have been her younger brother, the two of them discussing a family wedding.

'In a minute or two, we'll congregate by the main door which will remain closed,' said Bushra, turning to the others. 'Father Anthony will conduct a short service, while the cantor sings a traditional Greek lament. I think there'll be a microphone so that everybody in the square can listen, join in. After the service, we'll all go out onto the front steps where he'll give his blessing to the people.'

She then turned and indicated a small box made of polished oak on the bench, which Isabel hadn't noticed before.

'Later, Father Anthony will take us round to the graveyard behind the church where Jack's ashes will be buried.'

'Are you expecting anybody else?' Christos asked, speaking in English.

Bushra nodded.

On cue the church door opened noiselessly, flooding the nave in bright sunlight. A group of perhaps fifteen people filed in, their dark silhouettes making it impossible to make out who they were. The last person, a large portly shadow, who Isabel guessed was Father Anthony, closed the door returning the nave to darkness. Soon everybody was holding a candle, the flames throwing grotesque flickering images on the walls. Without warning, the church bell started to ring in a rapid repetitive monotone.

'Come, let us join the others,' said Bushra, her head covered, as she led them down the aisle.

They all stood with heads bowed in a circle around the priest, who held the oak box and faced the iconostasis at the far end of the nave. Standing between Greg and Emma, Isabel focused on a roughly carved cross in the flagstone between her feet. The sound of prayer, the people's responses and the high-pitched repetitive clanging of the bell overhead induced in her a kind of hypnosis. Finally the bell stopped.

The cantor's lone voice filled the void as he started to sing the lament. The sad sound echoed around the square as the small congregation made its way out to the top of the church steps. Isabel was surprised to see the large crowd before them, young and old, standing respectfully in near total silence.

A low-slung rope had been tied between two small pine trees to keep everybody back from the front of the church. Suddenly, in the corner of her eye, Isabel saw a tall clean-shaven man, wearing dark glasses and military fatigues, stepping over the rope. She stared in disbelief, as he slowly raised a handgun above his head. For what seemed like an eternity, nothing happened, nobody appeared to notice, nobody reacted. A single gunshot rent the air. The cantor's voice faltered and stopped, the bell ceased ringing and the crowd hushed; an uneasy atmosphere filled the square. Three more gunshots followed in quick succession.

The numbed crowd suddenly came to life; people started shouting, crying, pulling back from the rope in terror. Isabel glanced at the others, paralysed at the top of the church steps, unable to comprehend what was happening. Only Christos had the presence of mind to act. He grabbed the microphone from Father Anthony and shouted to the crowd above the noise, imploring everybody to remain calm.

The man dropped his gun to the ground and, stepping forward, stood below them at the bottom of the steps. The crowd fell silent, baffled by his presence; nobody moved, nobody spoke.

'*My name is Stavros,*' he said clearly in Arabic.

Isabel was transfixed, reeling at the name 'Stavros', his name turning over and over in her head. Her emotions ran the full gamut: anger, fear, curiosity, even love. Yet there was something about the man that troubled her.

'*I have come from across the sea, from the mountains and deserts of North Africa to honour my father, a man whose spirit and courage brought freedom to your country. I have come here today to celebrate his life with you.*'

He then moved in front of Bushra and removed his glasses. She appeared to be in a trance, speechless, mesmerised by her son, whom she hadn't seen since the day he was born.

'*But my main reason for being here,*' he said, addressing her, his voice carrying out over the square, '*is to beg for the forgiveness of my mother. She has been cruelly robbed of the only man worthy of her love, of the only man she ever truly loved.*' He paused. '*Before God, before you all as my witnesses and from the depth of my soul, I beg for your eternal forgiveness.*'

He bowed his head and opened his arms in supplication.

So here was the legendary Stavros, the cause of her grandfather's death, standing before them and seeking his mother's forgiveness. Isabel, completely spellbound, gazed at Bushra with Emma, standing at her mother's side totally unaware of what had been said.

In the ensuing silence, it suddenly struck Isabel that whatever had driven him to do what he had done, Stavros had clearly never intended this outcome, the death of his father. She knew that his very public confession would only have been understood by a handful of the people. Yet despite this, she sensed that many in the crowd felt the tension arising from his short speech, everybody waiting for they knew not what.

Finally Bushra, with tears streaming down her face, took Emma's hand and slowly descended the steps to confront her son. Without hesitating, she stepped forward and threw her arms around Stavros, who swept Emma into their embrace. The relief was palpable, the crowd shouting and cheering.

The three stood huddled together in front of the ecstatic crowd for several minutes. Eventually Isabel saw Stavros turn and point to where she and Greg were standing at the top of the church steps. He stepped away from the two women.

'Isabella,' he called out clearly in English, above the singing and shouting. 'Isabella, come down, come and join us.'

Isabel's blood froze. It had to be the man she knew as Fawzan, the man who had insisted on calling her Isabella during her imprisonment in Cyrenaica. It was only then that she saw the fine scar running beneath his right eye and realised that he'd shaved off his beard.

In that moment of unsurpassed happiness, she could feel Jack's presence, heard his voice, full of love and laughter: 'Embrace the future, dear Bel. Your goodwill, your courage, your instincts will take you far.' Suddenly, on this halcyon day, everything seemed possible.

She took Greg's hand and went down the steps.